The Man with No Borders

Center Point
Large Print

**This Large Print Book carries the
Seal of Approval of N.A.V.H.**

The Man with No Borders

RICHARD C. MORAIS

CENTER POINT LARGE PRINT
THORNDIKE, MAINE

This Center Point Large Print edition
is published in the year 2020 by arrangement with
Amazon Publishing, www.apub.com.

Originally published in the United States
by Amazon Publishing, 2019.

This is a work of fiction. Names, characters,
organizations, places, events, and incidents are either
products of the author's imagination or are used
fictitiously. Any resemblance to actual persons, living or
dead, or actual events is purely coincidental.

The text of this Large Print edition is unabridged.
In other aspects, this book may vary
from the original edition.
Printed in the United States of America
on permanent paper.
Set in 16-point Times New Roman type.

ISBN: 978-1-64358-522-2

The Library of Congress has cataloged this record
under Library of Congress Control Number: 2019954766

FOR SUSAN

PROLOGUE

My mind drifts back to those days when I was young and full of vigor and just starting my career as a private banker. It is the nature of old age, I am discovering, to remember the *entire* panorama of the past, everything from those difficult memories we spend a lifetime trying to suppress, to those inconsequential moments that seemed so trivial at the time, but now, with hindsight, take on added meaning and weight.

In particular, I remember a day from that summer of the late 1960s, shortly after Lisa and I had moved to Zürich so I could learn my trade at Swiss Federal Credit Bank, the universal bank with headquarters on the Bahnhofstrasse.

An elderly Swedish couple came to the bank in the late afternoon to make changes to their will and estate. They were valued and respected clients of the bank, so my supervisor, Herr Albiez, ushered this remarkably spry and distinguished-looking couple into the grand conference room overlooking Paradeplatz, and ordered them coffee and sugar biscuits.

I was his assistant at the time and came shuffling into the conference room with the accordion of documents we had prepared for their visit. The couple sat opposite, white-haired and leather skinned, looking like tanned beef hides after a decade living under the Riviera sun. They lived in a harborside penthouse in Monaco for most of the year, to avoid confiscatory Scandinavian taxes, and had come to Zürich for one purpose that day—to cut their children out of their will.

I pushed forward the last document, the amended trust.

"Please sign here. And here."

The elderly couple signed.

"It is over," the man said.

The finality of the signing touched something inside of them, and their emotions spilled out from their normally carefully enforced Swedish borders, as if we could somehow absolve them of their decision. Their daughter was a heroin addict, they told us, and had gone missing with her baby somewhere in India. Their son lived in Tangier. He was fond of entertaining rough sailors and was constantly getting robbed and asking his parents for more money.

The couple could barely spit out the words, they were so full of disgust. They seemed to both loathe their children—who, they said, did nothing but break their hearts and disappoint them—while at the same time they were racked with guilt for washing their hands of their own flesh and blood.

"Yes, it is over and good riddance," the wife

said. "Now I can finally sleep. If Josephina over-doses now, at least it won't be our money in her veins."

When the couple stood again, they were old and stooped, as if their robust Riviera life had been stripped away by this act of family betrayal. I was shocked by their transformation, and, unsettled by the entire meeting, I suspect I conveyed a certain amount of cold contempt. Herr Albiez, without saying anything specific, managed in contrast to convey great empathy, and he thanked the Swedes for their visit and wished them a safe journey back to Monaco, as we escorted them to the elevators.

Herr Albiez and I turned heel, when the elevator doors shut, and began to walk down the bank's long corridors to our offices.

"Your performance with the client today was not what I was hoping for."

My supervisor was blue-eyed and silver-haired and said little, but when he spoke, his comments carried weight. I glanced nervously in his direction.

"In what way?"

"You must think more like a priest in a confessional and less like a banker on the Bahnhofstrasse."

"I've never thought about our work in that way."

"You will hear lots of stories from the clients. Some of them will be unpleasant, some even distasteful. Reserve judgment. Families and their issues are complicated. Remember, you are not really in the business of managing money. You are in the business of keeping family secrets."

I absorbed his comments as we turned down the next hall, the echo of our footsteps reverberating through the corridor.

When I finally spoke, I did so with far more vehemence than I intended.

"I can keep family secrets."

Part I

2019

ZÜRICH, SWITZERLAND

ONE

I've asked Herr Heinrich to prune the pear orchard a little earlier this year," my wife says, pausing just long enough for an intake of breath. "He tells me we should expect about twenty kilos of honey from the beehives and that he will dispose of any surplus we don't want . . ."

The truth is the silence that hangs like tombs between the words.

"The price for honey is up this year—it's the bees, they're all disappearing—but I want to make sure our friends all get a jar for Christmas. Not like last year. So, I'm not entirely sure there will be a surplus . . ."

A nurse steps through the door and everyone in the waiting room lifts their head at the same moment, like gazelles at a watering hole as a leopard slinks through the tall grass. The nurse looks up from the clipboard and says "José María Álvarez de Oviedo" with that Swiss singsong inflection.

Lisa squeezes my hand, finally silenced. The others in the waiting room drop their heads back to their magazines, and I stand up, alone, my loden raincoat draped over my arm. That phrase—it's vaguely familiar, but I can't precisely remember where it comes from—keeps pushing its way into my head.

The truth is the silence that hangs like tombs between the words.

Dr. Sutter's offices are at the University of Zürich, and after his staff puts me through the MRI machine and takes blood, Lisa is escorted back to the oncologist's office, just as I arrive as well. We smile wanly at each other, the shorthand of old couples, and step through the door.

The doctor stands and greets us from behind his desk, offering us hibiscus and rose-petal tea of his own making, which Lisa and I both decline. We've had his home brew before and it is awful.

We wait for the MRI images. Dr. Sutter's office looks down over the gray-stone university; two red construction cranes are visible in the corner of the window. He has on his desk a silver-framed picture of his wife and three young children, sailing on the Lake of Zürich. It is the only personal object in his otherwise impersonal office.

We make some small talk about our children. Dr. Sutter's salt-and-pepper hair is swept back, and he is handsome and fit in that natural Swiss way. I imagine him taking his children out on weekends to run the Vita Parcours, the military-like obstacle course in the woods around every Swiss village, his entire family engaged in chin-ups and jogging and stomach crunches. The thought of it makes me weary.

We are rescued, finally, by the pictures popping

up on Dr. Sutter's backlit computer screen, red and green and blue blotches that look like abstract art and seem to have little to do with me.

For a few minutes, Dr. Sutter sucks the end of his eyeglass stems as he silently flips back and forth between the screen shots. He turns in our direction then, and speaks in a dispassionate, factual way. After showing pictures of my lower abdomen, and the tumors sitting like clumps of underground truffles, he switches to a new series of images. "The cancer has returned in a pattern similar to what we saw last time, but for one important difference. The cancer has spread to the brain. See this picture?"

Dr. Sutter points his ballpoint pen at the center of the illuminated screen, where a red-and-green blot sits glowing. "This is a tumor. Here. I think it is unlikely you will experience hyperalgesia, which is intense pain everywhere in your body. No, no. The pain you experience will most likely be intermittent, sometimes intense and sometimes not at all, because this tumor is now pressing on the brain's cortex. This is the center of the pain communication system, what we call the neuromatrix. This tumor is, in effect, suppressing and interrupting your ability to experience pain. It is consistent with what you have described, Herr Álvarez. No pain—and then a sudden attack."

Lisa says in a small voice, "That's a blessing of sorts."

"Yes, it is. This is very good news."

"I see. What will happen next?" I ask.

"It is entirely possible," he says, turning back to the screen and again tapping the red blotch with his pen, "that you will periodically experience extreme disorientation, a kind of dementia, and the deterioration will not happen in a straight line, I would say, but is likely to look like a string of ever-smaller islands of lucidity sitting in a growing sea of darkness and confusion. Intense hallucinations also cannot be ruled out."

Neither Lisa nor I say anything for a few moments. When I am able to find my voice, I say, "*Finalmente*? The end. How will it come?"

"*Ach.* That is the great mystery. We won't know what cancer will first eat what vital organ—until it has happened. It could be the liver or *die Nieren* . . . the kidneys. The pancreas. *Die Lunge.* It could very well be the brain itself or, most likely, everything at the same time. We will watch and see what happens. It's very unpredictable, the path the cancers take. There is much for us yet to learn. The main thing is to keep you comfortable throughout the process."

Comfortable.

I keep turning that word of his around and around in my head.

Lisa and I return to our Niederdorf pied-à-terre, a small penthouse atop a seventeenth-century guild house on Hechtplatz, and collapse on our beds. We are so exhausted by the doctor's visit that we fall into a deep sleep. But there is much more to be done, and, in the afternoon, after our nap, we take the elevator down from our apartment.

Hand in hand, we cross the Rathaus Bridge spanning the Limmat River, threading our way through the city's cobblestone backstreets, until we slip through a horse-wide lane onto the Bahnhofstrasse.

The private bank I founded for the family decades ago—Privatbank Álvarez GmbH—is located in an unassuming office building, directly opposite the massive limestone offices of Zürich Union Bank Wealth Management. Plaques outside identify a few tenants—Bank Arabia AG, Banque Jacques Rothschild et Fils GmbH, Park Wong Family Offices (Europe)—and I am visited by an unexpected flood of pleasure, when I see, once again, the Privatbank Álvarez name next to the prime top floors of the office building that is part of our property portfolio.

Hans-Peter Grieder, my protégé who took over as the bank's managing director when I retired, is waiting for us upstairs, as the elevator doors ping open. He shakes my hand and kisses Lisa's cheeks, left-right-left, as is the Swiss custom. Hans-Peter sports the black-rimmed eyeglasses and porcupine haircut of a rather dull provincial Swiss military officer, which is entirely misleading, since he is a sophisticated and INSEAD-educated international banker with a brilliant mind.

He guides us to the client conference room in the back of the office, down the corridor walls lined with Man Ray and Cartier-Bresson prints from the 1920s. A few secretaries and client managers come out to greet me when they see me hobbling down the hall, and I have to stop and ask each small questions, about their boyfriends and babies and holidays. But not long afterward, Hans-Peter has Lisa and me sitting around the conference table, ready to work.

He is everything I could wish for, solicitous and efficient in helping us get our affairs in order. The trust lawyer, a young woman who graduated with honors from the University of St. Gallen, is called in. We agree the grantor-retained annuity trust, which I long ago set up for Lisa and the boys, needs to be updated, decanted into a new trust with terms reflecting the boys' maturity and my coming end. The trust only has ten million Swiss francs at this stage, and needs more of my wealth transferred into it, so we can avoid estate taxes. Papers are signed and a small portion of the investment portfolio liquidated and prepared for disbursement. There is only a slight pause of the pen, a rapid eyeblink, when we come to discussing how the estate, in its entirety, will be divided after my death.

"Lisa will get the farm in Ägeri, the apartments in Zürich and New York, plus the forty-six million Swiss francs sitting in the money-market accounts. The private equity investments should get paid out directly to her, over time, as they mature and liquidate. But I want you to manage the real estate properties for her. Furthermore, she can't . . ."

"Seriously, José?" Lisa is staring at me. "You're going to control everyone and everything from beyond the grave? Seriously?"

I stop. Take a deep breath.

"Lisa can do with the properties what she likes," I say. "Sell them. Live in them. I don't give a damn. It's her choice."

My wife doesn't say another word, but Hans-Peter is studying her out of the corner of his eye. "This is very difficult for you, Lisa. Part of the anxiety comes from not knowing how things will change after your husband has passed. It is entirely understandable. But, in my experience, I have seen, again and again, how it all becomes clear, in time, as to what must be done. And when it does, I hope you will not be shy about calling on me—in any capacity where I might be of assistance."

The kindness in my old partner's voice sets off a wave of emotion, and Lisa lowers her head and fishes inside her purse for a tissue. "Thank you, Hans-Peter," she finally says. "You have always been a good friend—to the entire family."

Hans-Peter, giving her some space so she can gather herself again, turns his attention back to me. "And the rest of the estate? We haven't sent you your statement yet, but we just did the calculations, and the fiscal year-end valuation of the Privatbank Álvarez shares was one point two billion Swiss francs. We will be recommending to the board, after such a profitable year, that a special thirty-four-million Swiss franc dividend be paid the shareholders. Are the bank's shares to be divided equally among your three sons?"

"No."

Lisa gasps. "José!"

I hold up my hand, a warning to remain silent. "I haven't decided yet how much will go to the boys. I will let you know what I have decided, when I have decided."

They hear the resolution in my voice, and no one could say, at that moment, I am not compos mentis and in full control of my faculties.

"As you wish," Hans-Peter says, "but with such a disease, at such an advanced stage, I trust you will let an old colleague remind you that it is unwise to postpone your decision for long. There might come a day, unexpected, when you are incapable of making a decision; or, *um Gottes willen nicht*, you make a decision that your sons can challenge in the courts, due to your mental condition at the time you gave me your instructions. There are practical matters to consider here."

20

"I am aware of that. You will have my decision soon."

"It is very difficult to give away what we have accumulated in our lifetime. It feels like we are giving away our inner reserves. But that is what is required at this stage of life. We must all, at one point, do a proper accounting and empty the gold we have accumulated in our vault."

"Yes," I counter dryly. "But preferably in a way that firmly marks your time while on this earth. I will ponder all this—and get back to you."

There are some other small matters to attend to, and then the meeting ends on another round of firm Swiss handshakes. Lisa leaves the room before me, and I hesitate briefly in the conference room's doorway, looking down the bank's corridor. Hardworking staff is coming and going from their offices, folders in hand, and the air is filled with the sound of printers churning out documents. Light is streaming in through the west windows, as my wife, in a blue dress, disappears down the corridor's funnel.

I have built the Álvarez family's private bank. It has been my life for so long, but now it is passing on without me, no other Álvarez interested in its future well-being.

So be it.

I turn and shake my colleague's hand.

"Thank you, Hans. Thank you for everything."

"I owe you much, José. It is the least I can do. You are in my thoughts and prayers."

Lisa is waiting for me down on the Bahnhofstrasse. "Are the tumors already pressing against your brain?" she snaps. "What were you thinking in there? There is nothing to debate here. The boys should get your estate."

We start walking. She is furious.

I stop in my tracks. "Do you think I love my sons?"

Lisa looks down at the sidewalk. "Yes. Of course I do." But when she looks up again, her eyes are sparkling with defiance, a look that is particular to independent American women. "But do the boys know that? It will kill me if you die without making peace with your sons."

"*Mujer.* I need space. I have to work this out my way. In the time I have remaining."

"I am so sick of this. It just sucks—sucks shit."

"Lisa! This is no way for a woman to talk!"

"Well, it does. And will you please stop being so patronizing? Honestly. It's so annoying. What's getting into you? It's like you are reverting to some autocratic, old-fashioned *cabeza de familia* Spaniard by the minute."

So, we stand there, unable to move forward or backward, each of us adrift in a riptide of overwhelming emotions. But across the street a glass door suddenly slides open, and in that moment we both know how to move on. We cross the Bahnhofstrasse, dodging the vicious trams determined to run us over, and climb the steps to the café above the chocolatier, Sprüngli.

I am panting at the top of the steps and have to hold on tight to the banister while I catch my breath. For a few moments we hover at the dining-room entrance, eyeing the tables, alongside the other shoppers awaiting a table. In good Swiss tradition, we are all ready to elbow the other out of the way at the first sign someone is paying their bill. Lisa, always good to have on your team for such things, almost flattens a ninety-year-old grande dame in her dash to secure the suddenly free table in the corner, before our less agile competition.

A dour waitress in a black apron and white blouse takes our order. Even Lisa, in the gloom of the moment, abandons her perennial diet and has a mille-feuille pastry alongside her usual sugarless mint tea. I have a plate of *Luxemburgerli*, an almond macaroon that is the house specialty, and a double espresso, with, *naturalmente*, a shot of Williamine.

We pick at our sweets in silence. The room is filled with the smell of roasting coffee and melted Gruyère, and the clattering din of silver scraping china and the singsong of Swiss gossip. After a few minutes, Lisa leans over and says, fiercely, "I won't wind up like that. I won't."

I follow her gaze to a table, where an elderly

Swiss woman sits primly erect in a Chanel suit and pearls, her hair coiffed into a spun-sugar pile atop her head. She sits catlike before a monstrous Coupe Dänemark, the house-made vanilla ice cream topped with freshly whipped cream and served in a fluted glass goblet with a silver urn of melted chocolate by its side. The stiff and formal woman pours the chocolate over the dessert, and begins eating it, slowly, her eyes suddenly glistening like a drunk's. It is so obvious this afternoon *boul de glace* is the highlight of her lonely existence, a widow's dairy highball in midafternoon.

"That decides it. I am moving back to New York when you die," Lisa says, slapping her linen napkin down on the table. "I won't stay another moment in this goddamn country and wind up like that. I am going home. After fifty years here, because of you, I am going home."

So that is that. It is all ending, the life we built together. We are slowly preparing to go our separate paths. I am so full of sadness and ache, I can barely move, and I think of that fateful evening in New York, from sixty years ago, when our journey together began: It was our third or fourth date, at a French restaurant in the West Village, and I had opened up a little about my family and background, and, uncharacteristically for me, let Lisa know that my mother had been an alcoholic. Lisa was quiet for a moment and then stuttered she understood what I was talking about. Her father was also an alcoholic—and physically abusive to boot.

That evening, when our fingers interlaced and we walked back through the leafy and lit streets of the West Village, to the hotel room I had booked for our first night together, we somehow knew we had just struck a pact with each other: *Let us do everything in our might,* rose our mutual but unspoken prayers, *to raise a wholesome family far from the madness of our own childhoods.*

Here we are now—at the other end of that journey.

Lisa pays our Sprüngli bill, stands, and I follow suit. This time we take the elevator downstairs. Two chattering Swiss teenagers in faded jeans, their shirts half unbuttoned to reveal gold necklaces and firm cleavage, push their way into the elevator, just as we are trying to depart.

One of them bumps Lisa, doesn't apologize, and a sudden heat comes over me. I wait for the right moment, lift a cheek, and let out a loud fart in their direction, just before exiting the elevator. It's highly satisfying to see their utter disbelief and hear them gagging, right before the doors close and trap them inside with my gases.

Lisa is waiting for me on the street, a look of alarm and revulsion on her face. "You didn't. Tell me you didn't do what I think you just did."

"I can't help it," I say. "It's the tumor."

On our final day of errands in Zürich, we visit St. Agatha's Hand of Mercy, a convent up on the Zürichberg, to take care of the last item on our checklist. It is so lovely up on the mountain. Cypress trees protectively encircle the cream-colored convent, like a mother might cradle a baby in her arms, while a faint late-summer breeze rustles their branches. Below us, the industrious city is spread out, from the curved bottom of the Lake of Zürich, down the Limmat River.

"Even I have to admit, it's a beautiful city," Lisa says.

We turn and enter the eighteenth-century courtyard door, have a word with the nun at the desk, and then climb the convent's gloomy staircase to the hospice director's office.

The smell of the hallway's beeswax polish is laced with acrid medicinal fumes and the sickly sweet odor of rotting flesh, strange smells seeping out from under the closed pine doors. And the silence—it screams. It would make heaven sound like a Friday night on Las Ramblas in Barcelona, and my spirits, as we walk these corridors of death, plummet to a new low. But that's also when I understand how it has to end, and when we sit down in the director's neat office, I instantly blurt out, "I don't want to die here. I want to die at home."

"It's a very common wish," says the abbess. "And where is home?"

Lisa and I stare back at the nun, stumped by the question. We must think for a few moments. "We live in Ägeri. In Canton Zug."

"Aaah, such a lovely part of the country, Central Switzerland. That will not be a problem. Some of our Sisters drive."

The requests, they pour out of me. I want a bed set up in the middle of my downstairs study and Alfredo's bed next to mine. "He's my dog," I say. "And that is where I will die." As I make each pronouncement, Lisa slowly lowers her head a bit farther, like I am walloping her with my fist. She fishes inside her purse for another tissue.

I put a hand on her thigh and give it a squeeze. The Mother Superior discreetly looks away, but turns her attention back when I take out my checkbook and write a large check in my shaky hand. She takes the proffered green slip, scrutinizes the sum, and takes off her glasses.

"We will arrange everything, Herr Álvarez. We wish to be of service."

On our way back to our apartment, Lisa and I take the No. 6 tram down toward Zentral. I sit by the window. Lisa sits by my side, purse on lap, staring out into space, lost in anxious thoughts about the future.

As the tram whooshes down Hirschengraben, clanging its bell, the yellow-stone tower of the

Liebfrauenkirche to the right catches my eye. The Catholic church is up on a raked hill, and requires, from the penitent, he climb a set of steep stone steps, through a thicket of rhododendron bushes. The tram turns and lurches into Zentral. We exit. "Lisa, you go ahead. I have a few errands I still need to run."

She nods, kisses me, and crosses the street, relieved, I suspect, at having a little time to herself. I don't blame her. Dying, it turns out, is a rather tiresome affair. I stand for a moment, watching her disappear down Limmatquai, imagining she's off to have a restorative bath with the perfumed oils and unctures that do nothing for me but seem to provide my wife with great comfort.

I am a sweating and gasping mess by the time I reach the oak doors of the Liebfrauenkirche. I have to stand panting for a few minutes on the top step, holding the balustrade, wiping my brow with the linen handkerchief from my jacket pocket.

A young man with long hair comes up the stairs, two by two, and, without a glance, sidesteps me and slips inside the heavy doors. My impression, I don't know why, is that he is a waiter who has just dashed up from the corner pizzeria. He leaves a trace of lavender perfume in the air.

I know that smell.

It is Suavecito, a blue-bottled Spanish pomade

that we all wore, back in time. Faint memories, from long ago, float up, and I am filled with an ache that radiates from the center of my being, like the pressing of a tumor.

The church inside is cool and airy, enveloped in a black hush. The waiter is already on his knees in a pew up near the nave, his hands clasped in prayer and his head bowed. I am suddenly unsure of myself. I stand in the gloom, not sure why I am there and what I should do next.

My eyes adjust slowly to the twilight. The church is late nineteenth century, a mash-up of Renaissance murals and Byzantine architecture. I slip into a pew, and for some time sit like one of those black-dressed crones from my childhood in San Sebastián, staring at the emaciated and bleeding Christ on the crucifix. The last time I was in church, I was a teenager, kneeling next to my black-shrouded mother, the perennial martyr and penitent in our family. I see her in profile— the aristocratic nose, the brow furrowed in guilt, repenting her many sins.

I look down at the leather pocket hanging from the bench before me, and see a stack of bibles and some white pamphlets. I pull one out, and, under the heading "Jesus Calls Four Fishermen to Follow Him," find a printed excerpt from Matthew:

And passing along the Sea of Galilee, he saw two brethren, Simon who is called Peter, and

Andrew his brother, casting a net in the sea, for they were fishers. And Jesus saith unto them, "Come ye after me, and I will make you to become fishers of men."

There is a crack and creak from somewhere behind the altar. A priest with a speckled-silver head emerges, wearing the purple sash of confession around his neck. He goes down the right side of the church, enters the confessional, and waits for penitents. It is 4:00 p.m.

I know, then, why I am here, and stand, shakily, to make my way to the cubicle. The confessional is dark and enclosed like a wooden coffin, smelling of dust and sweat, a semen-like whiff of spilled sin. The panel between us slides open, and through the reed grille I can just make out the priest's profile, as he faces forward, never looking at me.

He asks, in Swiss German, when was the last time I took confession. I immediately detect the accent.

"Hablas español?"

"Sí, mi hijo."

I think then that perhaps God has guided me here, on this particular day, to sit opposite a Spanish priest. For I know it would have been impossible to unburden myself in Swiss, or even English, the language of my household for the last fifty-two years. I must return to the language of my childhood and my mother and of the mother Church, to do what I have to do. So, I hold up my head and proudly announce, in Spanish, "It has been sixty years since my last confession."

"God is listening, my son."

And so I confess, confess to all the bad things I have done in my life, the cruelty and indifferences, the hurts and slights and neglect, all the pain I have inflicted or enabled to happen over the course of time. I recall how I despised my mother and hated my father. How I drove my uncle away and abandoned my wife; how I ruthlessly cast my friend Miguel aside and taught my own boys to be duplicitous and economical with the truth. And I save, to the last, the worst of all my sins—the role I played in my brother's end.

But I meticulously lay it all out, in a dry and unwavering voice, and write the church a check for one hundred thousand Swiss francs, which I hand over, with a list of names—starting with my wife and sons, of course, but also including my brother and parents and uncle, and Miguel and the names of my friends and worst enemies—all the figures alive and dead who haunt my sleep.

"On the first day of the month, for ten years, I want you to pray for everyone on that list."

The priest eyes the check resting on the divider before us, and I can sense his animal-like excitement and greed through the grille. "It shall be done," he says, before delicately reaching out

31

to take the check, like my dog, Alfredo, might cautiously pull a piece of beef from my hand, worried his master might suddenly snatch it back. The priest places the check in his bible, like a bookmark.

Our business transaction conducted, he prays for my forgiveness, dispenses my penance, an arbitrary but long list of Lord's Prayers and Hail Marys that is nonsense, of course.

I am both sweating and chilled but rather pleased I have successfully achieved my purpose. I wipe my brow with my handkerchief, and head to the pew to say the required penance of prayers and complete my pact with God. But as I move to a pew at the front, the young waiter in the second row gets off his knees, makes the sign of the cross, turns heel, and heads my way.

As we pass each other, he presses a piece of paper into my hand, like we are spies conducting a clandestine exchange of secrets. I instinctively grasp the note before I know what's happening. When I do register what has just occurred, the young man is already down the length of the church and out the main door, trailing that smell of Suavecito.

I look down at the note. It, too, is in Spanish. "You don't fool anyone. You and I both know that was not a proper penance."

The priest emerges from the confessional and heads back to the nave.

"Who was that young man?"

The priest turns, smiling unsurely, as if I am going to make another bizarre demand of him. "I am sorry. What young man are you referring to?"

I stretch out my hand, to hand him the note, but nothing is there.

TWO

I do not tell Lisa about what happened at the church, or in fact that I went to the basilica at all, and we later return to our farmhouse in Ägeri. Before we go to bed, I look over at my wife, in the quiet of our chalet living room, as she drinks her evening rooibos tea. Her face, so droopy and lined by worry, makes me recall a long-forgotten phrase that my father frequently repeated about my mother: *That woman is sad, sad to her marrow.* But Lisa is a great intuitive, and, perhaps sensing she is the subject of my thoughts, she looks at me over the rim of her teacup and says, "I can't stand this. It's unconscionable."

She is sitting in the armchair, I am on the couch, and between us the room is darkening, as the embers in the grate collapse and die. But I can see in her face how she is struggling with my choice not to fight the latest spread of cancer. She simply doesn't understand I want to manage the end my way, to face its reality and not cling to some delusional cure for what is clearly a death sentence.

I suddenly remember a time from when we were still young and courting. Lisa and I were walking in the woods just behind the village of Milford, Pennsylvania, when I heard anguished peeping coming from a logger's woodpile. I pushed a fern out of the way. A young mourning dove was squashed between two logs, a gray-blue clump of downy feathers, one wing laid out flat. Its wing, at an odd angle, was clearly broken and I knew it would never fly. When the exhausted bird stopped chirping and lowered its head, I stepped forward and put my hands on it, like a healer might, and then, with one quick motion, broke its neck.

"Oh, no! You didn't! How could you!"

Lisa burst into tears, turned back the way we came, and ran. I was left dumbfounded by the log pile. I eventually found her sipping black tea on the porch of Hotel Fauchere, the inn where we were staying. I sat down beside her. She explained how mourning doves were special to her, how they constantly showed up in her own poetry, because when she was growing up and sad, she used to wander behind her family's home on the Mainline outside Philadelphia. She'd walk under the fir trees and see a mourning dove nest filled with gently cooing parents, and would watch them tenderly feed the chirping chicks with the gaping beaks.

This vision of family life as it should be, it filled her with peace and awe and hope—that she, too, would have a happy family life one day. I in turn told her of my upbringing, of the quail hunts with Papá and Uncle Augustin, and how it was a point of manly honor, of kindness, to step forward and instantly put a suffering animal out of its misery. I apologized that I did not think about how she might react at seeing such a thing, but killing a suffering animal, quickly and confidently, it was second nature to me, and the way a young Spanish gentleman is bred. And then we sat for some time, both of us sipping afternoon tea, silently wondering if we could marry if we were so different.

This memory from long ago calms me down and allows me to be patient with Lisa. We have, I realize, disagreed on so many subjects over the years, and I remain calm even though she is challenging my right to decide how I end my life.

"This is my last journey," I say softly. "You must let me plan my final trip."

"You're selfish, José María. Always have been. How can you leave me like this?" She holds the saucer under her teacup in such a way I think it might snap. "And what about your boys?"

"Do you think I want to leave them? To leave you? This is how it is, Lisa. My time is up."

The tears come, then. She puts her cup down on the coffee table, blows into a tissue, and comes around the couch, to curl up next to me, her head in my lap. I stroke her hair. Her chest is heaving, and from it rises that faint and familiar scent of Bal à Versailles perfume, heading heavenward with her heat. But, finally, there is a profound sigh of surrender, a moan that seems to emanate from her gut.

"It's your life, José. Do what you need to do. I forgive you."

I am so moved, I cannot speak, so we sit like that in the fading light.

"But please tell the boys you are dying," she finally says. "I beg you. They have a right to know what's going on. They'll be so hurt that you have frozen them out—once again."

I look out the window. The night sky is clear and a silver moon is shining bright through the branches of the pear tree outside our living-room window. A few more leaves have fallen. A shadow moves and I discover we have a new neighbor, which I now see for the first time. It comforts me. A long-eared owl has moved into the ancient horse chestnut outside our house. He emerges from his lair, ruffles his feathers. His ears are tufted and pointy, and he rivets his head intensely to some sound down below, ready to take off and hunt the night.

"I cannot tell the boys. Not yet. But soon. When I am ready."

Dying is so boring. No one ever warns you about that.

Lisa is doing the dishes. I am watching her.

She stops scrubbing the roasting pan, lowers her head, and weeps.

"I think you need a vacation," I say dryly.

She can't resist laughing. No matter how bad things got between us, we could always make each other laugh. Lisa lifts her apron to her face and wipes away her tears.

"I don't think a vacation would do it. Maybe heroin."

I put my arms around her from behind, and whisper in her ear that I am serious. She needs a break from all this. I insist she take some time off for herself. She should go to the opera in Zürich, spend the night at our Niederdorf flat, and get drunk with her strange English friend, the ugly-looking Jungian analyst who makes her laugh. I don't stop until she agrees and goes upstairs to pack an overnight bag.

I stand in the frame of the farmhouse's front door and wave, as she backs out of the flagstone courtyard in the Mercedes and drives off to Zürich. I turn and head back up to the kitchen. A weight has lifted. Not only is Lisa's perennial dark look a constant reminder of my approaching death, I realize, but she also watches my diet like one of those beady-eyed nuns of my childhood, which is, as my sons might say, a drag.

So I embrace this momentary liberation from the tyranny of her diets, and head directly into the kitchen with a light step, feeling remarkably free. I pour myself a glass of white wine, hum a Basque song about independence, and make *my* kind of dinner: chorizo simmered in hard cider, and a blood pudding and cabbage dish as sharp and regal as the Spain from where I come. I feel like celebrating *life*—the life I lived, my way, regrets and all—and I open a fantastic Romeo "Contador" Rioja 2005, a gift from John, our restaurateur son living in New York.

Then, toward the end of the meal, I cut myself a wedge of Asturian sheep's cheese, which I smear over walnut bread and generously dribble with the honey we make on the farm. The salty-sweet flavors dissolve on my tongue, and I close my eyes, travel back to my long-ago childhood, where the Picos de Europa mountain range meets the Bay of Biscay in Northern Spain. I hear the Sella River gurgling at my feet and my uncle's deep-throated roar as a salmon takes his fly and the reel screams. I can smell the rising sap of the scrubby spruce behind me, and the crackling skin of the suckling pig our cook, Conchata, is spit roasting over an open fire down on the riverbank.

The memories, they are heaven.

I rinse and put away the dishes in the Bosch dishwasher. After the kitchen is cleaned up and wiped down, and the machine is humming, I heat some Armagnac in a crystal snifter held over an open flame. I enjoy its warmth in the palm of my hand, as I sit back on the living room's leather couch and watch the late-night news on Swiss TV.

I go to bed utterly content and at peace.

• • •

The cracks of gastrointestinal thunder under the duvet make my limbs violently jerk and scrabble about. I fall out of bed three times during the worst attacks, crawl moaning back onto the mattress. The pain, it is like the devil himself has plunged his pitchfork into my intestines. I sweat through my pajamas. On my knees by the side of the bed, I clutch my stomach and swear in Spanish—"Shit on the milk! *Coño!*"

It is 4:15 a.m. I cannot stand this any longer. I use my knuckles to feel my way in the dark around the bed, cry out, "Lisa! Lisa!" even while knowing full well she isn't here and won't respond. But I can't help it. The longing for my wife is so powerful that I actually see Lisa before me, that familiar and reassuring bedtime lump under the luminous duvet, just a few cockatoo-like tuffs of her bleached-blond hair poking out over the linen-white edges.

Enough of this mierda.

Rigid with pain, but determined, I manage to pull on some pants in the dark and pass from the bedroom. In the hall with the leaded windows, I sit down on the cool ceramic bench, over the oven that in winter is fed wood coal from the kitchen side of the chalet. I pull on a pair of battered boots and am again hit by a wave of pain.

It passes and I carefully descend the wooden central staircase and let myself out the front door. The September night is still pitch-black, but clear, and filled with stars. I wipe the film of sweat from my forehead and look up at the bedroom where my wife and I have slept for the last half century, rump to rump, behind the top left shutters and window of our 287-year-old Swiss farmhouse.

It is over, the life I had. Finalmente.

The courtyard sensors under the chalet's eaves are tripped, and harsh light suddenly filters eerily through the geraniums in the window boxes above my head. Alfredo, his Italian Spinone ears alert, hears and smells my presence, gets up and whines in his pen in the back of the house, urging me to let him out. It hurts greatly to do so—I want his warm comfort almost as much as I ache for my wife—but I ignore him. A man, in the end, must make this journey alone.

My determination renewed, I cross the courtyard and enter the barn we converted into a three-car garage. There is a faint smell of Williamine in the air, as a few ripe pears have fallen from the trees standing at the farmhouse's entrance. The fallen pears are squashed into the Volvo station wagon's tire treads, as I slowly back the car out through the courtyard and into the lane. My arthritic hand has trouble getting the gear out of reverse, but I finally get the stick shift into first after a few grinding tries unleash another torrent of Spanish curses. I turn the car down the country road, toward the town of Ägeri.

I cross the Rimmenfluss Bridge, bookended by sylvan copses of ash and birch. This is the stream where my young sons caught their first brook trout, and I suddenly see my three boys marching along the riverbank in parka coats and rubber boots and in descending order of height, each carrying a casting rod and a perforated tin box filled with worms.

Tears blur my vision, but I peer intently through the windshield at the road ahead and where I have yet to go. A light mist hangs over the pastures and chapels like a curtain separating this world from the next.

A few lights glow down in the town of Ägeri, nestled at the end of the lake between the Zugerberg and Morgartenberg mountain ranges. Bäckerei Müller, the bakery just over the village's stone bridge, is warmly lit up in the dark. I park behind the baker's delivery van and haul myself up out of the front seat. Another sharp pain roars up from my pelvis, and for a few moments I think I might faint, but all that comes out in the end is a gasp, a slight exhale of breath into the night.

I abandon the car and take the path along the town's stream, under the covered passageway that connects the local inn, Das Goldene Kreuz, with its dining room overlooking the river. The smell of an already simmering veal stock deep inside the kitchen passes out into the breaking day.

The stream runs into the town canal. Wooden boathouses emerge before me in the morning's mist like miniature Swiss chalets. They are nineteenth-century follies with slate roofs and neatly painted trimmings, and a small wooden door facing the canal's path. My arthritic hands are stiff with morning cold and so it takes me some time to unlock the door of my boathouse.

Inside its wooden gloom, adjusting to the dark, I smell gasoline and river grass, hear the water gently lapping against the boat launch. I think of those long-ago February nights, when my boys were young and the boathouses were festively strung with lights on that one night of the year when the Swiss villagers drop their normal reserve and set up tables against the snowbanks opposite the boathouses. On such occasions, all the town's fishermen, professional and amateur, gather together in the snow to grill bratwurst over wood fires and toast next year's fishing with shots of kirschwasser, before solemnly engaging in the torchlit procession down to the lake and the ritual of pushing a paper boat filled with fish bones into the black water, all blessed by the local Protestant and Catholic clergymen, a pagan-Christian offering to God for good fishing in the year to come. How my sons—Rob, my youngest, in particular—loved that ritual, so utterly unique to our small mountain village.

My boat is hoisted on chains, hanging just

under the darkened pitched roof. I turn on the light and throw the big switch mounted on the post. An electric motor begins to whirr, chains grind, as the wooden craft overhead is lowered to the water. I have, then, a pang of earthly regret, for the boat is so sweetly handsome, with its white trim, bottle-green sides, and shellacked hull.

I wish I was a Viking. I want to be buried with my boat.

Two casting rods and a large net are sitting inside it. From the tidy rack on the wall, I take down the spare anchor, and, grunting with effort, drop it with a clang into the bottom of the vessel, alongside the one already resting in the bow. I gingerly step in and the boat rocks, as I make my way back to the engine. I push off, through the boathouse opening, and ease into the canal. A touch of the starter and the twenty-five-horsepower Evinrude engine begins coughing into the dawn.

I pull at the tiller, give a little gas. I want to remain anonymous, in the undercover of night, but dawn is coming fast as the boat crawls up the canal, past the village's low-rise apartment buildings and the town's football pitch.

I turn at the bend. Ägeri's fishmonger, Walter Iten, is putt-putting back down the opposite side of the canal, after having just checked his nets in the predawn.

This is not what I want. Normally, Iten and I will cut our engines and drift alongside each other, exchanging a few words before we continue on our journeys. It is during such times that I ask Walter what his nets have yielded, and he usually sighs and makes a small speech about how the *Felchen*—a bony Swiss lake fish that looks like carp but is in fact distantly related to the trout and very good eating—aren't as plentiful as they once were. But he always finishes by offering a valuable tip on where I might fish the lake that day.

This morning, however, I keep my boat hugging the right bank, bow pointed to the mouth of the canal, my hand held up in acknowledgment as I increase the throttle, indicating I'm not stopping today. Walter nods and respectfully holds up his hand in return—and so we pass.

A Jugendstil villa, with stained-glass windows and its own boathouse, marks the canal's entrance to the lake. The grand house passes to my right, the canal opens out, and I open the engine full throttle.

The mist hovers in ephemeral wisps atop the water, hesitant, like the air itself is somehow conscious its time on earth is limited. The bow of the boat lifts slightly, and we surge through the mist and flat water, not even a ripple of wind evident across its platinum-gray matte.

I am full of pain, and though I can't tell at

the moment whether this internal searing is physical or mental, I do know something must be done—this state of affairs simply cannot continue. So I point the bow toward the stone gates at the far end of the lake, a memorial to the fourteenth-century battle of Morgarten, the pass where fifteen hundred fierce Swiss mountain men fought for their independence against the Austrians and gave birth to this tiny country. But as the mist lifts in the dawn, I see that a handful of fishing boats are already clustered at that end of the lake, and, wanting solitude, I abruptly turn the engine handle to the right, sending the boat careening left toward the old tuberculosis sanatorium sitting up on the mountain.

The lake here, I know, is green-black deep, as the mountainside drops almost straight down into the water. I cut the engine two hundred meters from the shore, just under the watchful gaze of the nineteenth-century sanatorium, now an incubator for technology start-ups coming out of universities across the country. The boat glides for a few moments, until the utterly still lake slowly drags the wooden skiff down, and it comes to a lapping, lulling rest in the glassy reflection of mountain and sanatorium.

I sit for a few moments. The morning is very still and quiet, but for the cry of ravens in the yellow-leafed chestnut trees along the shore.

As I bend down, another wave of pain shoots

up from my pelvis, but this time it is lighter and passes quickly. I move onto the seat at the bow, and, with wheezing effort, tie the blue nylon anchor rope tightly around my right ankle. I tug at it, make sure it is secure. On my left ankle, I wrap the chain of the reserve anchor, and push shut the lock. It bites the flesh.

I swing my legs over the boat, both anchors held tightly in my swollen fists. The anchors and me—we are balanced precariously on the wooden rim. I stare into the green water, and a rippling bald head and set of arthritic hands grimly gripping anchors stare back at me. The man I once knew, with a shock of long black hair slicked back with pomade—he is entirely gone.

I close my eyes and say a silent prayer for Lisa and the boys, my brother, and—this surprises me—Miguel. Then, slowly, I gather my courage, for the final drop into the dark below.

But something, I'm not sure what, makes me open my eyes. The sun is visible over the ice-capped Alps at the other end of the lake, and it sends beams of light skittering across the water. I look down.

A silver shadow is spiraling slowly up to the water's surface.

It is a massive brown trout, rising from the deepest recesses of the lake, coming to rest just a meter from the boat. I hold my breath. Walter Iten once showed me pictures of one such prehistoric-looking fish caught in his net two decades earlier. It weighed nine kilos and was black with age. But such massive lake trout are very rare, and never in my five decades fishing the Lake of Ägeri have I witnessed one of these near-mythic fish.

But here one is. It has risen slowly and majestically up from the depths, settling into a slow-finning stillness near my feet.

I sit clutching the anchors, afraid to move while the fish hovers just below the surface, a mere meter away from me. It is ancient as time and scarred, its black back the length of my leg and raked with wounds, the old markings of eagle attacks or the narrow miss of a net.

The trout is so close now that through the water I can make out the golden and red-rimmed spots flecking its fleshy flanks, like blotches from a Miro painting, its pale underbelly glowing luminously silver through the dark water. I can't take my eyes from the fish's many wounds, the net markings and fish eagle scrapes, the scars of its life, and it is like I am looking at an underworld reflection of myself, at all the things I have deep within me but have never fully examined or looked at. There they suddenly are, up from the deep.

Before I can ponder this strange notion further, however, a nymph, almost impossible to see with the human eye, comes floating down the undercurrent. The great beast darts forward a few centimeters, sucks the nymph into its gaping mouth, and then languidly drifts back into its exact former position, hovering in the invisible crosscurrents of underwater life.

My chest is swollen to bursting. To see this rare and mysterious creature rise from the darkest part of the lake, at this particular moment, it is almost too much for me to bear, and a voice, from deep inside me, similarly rises to the surface, slowly repeating, again and again, the same lines. *You have unfinished business. Unfinished business. That was not a true penance.*

My mother appears in the lake ether before me. She is dressed all in black, her hair in a tight bun in the back of her head, her skin the color of turbot. She is sitting in her favorite armchair in the San Sebastián living room, near the gray light of the bay window, her head bent over her embroidery.

"No good will come of this ending," my mother tells me in a clear voice. "Trust me. I know of what I talk. No good. You must take the entire journey, properly, to make it all worthwhile."

The fish and I sit there for what seems like an eternity, my head bowed like a penitent in a church pew, awed before God by a powerful mixture of shame and strange elation. There we are, together: I, gripping the anchors that still rest on the boat's lip and are meant to drag me to my

49

death; and the great trout, hovering just below the water's surface, hearing my confession.

I am not sure how long we sit like this, but eventually a Fiat Spider with racing stripes roars down the Seestrasse, its radio blaring Swiss hip-hop. This silly noise rolls across the water, makes me turn my head in irritation, and the swiveling upper torso must rattle the chain on my ankle, sending movement reverberating through the water, because the trout darts forward, like a powerful submarine, and forever disappears into the deep.

I swing my legs back over the edge, resting the anchors on the bottom of the boat. I am panting from the exertion, and it takes me several minutes to untie the rope and unlock the chain from my ankles. I am shaking and a little feverish.

But I know it's the right thing to do.

Lisa comes home, shortly after noon. I am quietly waiting for her in the light of the chalet's living-room window, sitting in the red *Chinoise* armchair, staring out the window. I am listening to El Caracol, the great flamenco *cantaor*, his cry of the soul coming from the speakers of the iPhone docking station behind me.

Lisa is wearing a tan raincoat, belted, her hair glittering after a visit to her Zürich hairdresser. I lean over and turn down the music's volume. Lisa bends down to kiss the top of my baldpate.

I am overwhelmed by her familiar smell, but I hide my emotion, just pat her hand and look up.

"*Hola, mujer.* Was the opera any good?"

"Avant-garde. You would have hated it. Haven't decided yet what I think."

She takes off her coat and talks about the world premiere she has just seen at the Zürich Opera House. The work is called *Déracinée*—a French word meaning "uprooted"—and the performance involved lots of cymbal-crashing atonal music and a rather large Welsh tenor, and an even larger Bulgarian soprano, both in great anguish. The opera is about Russian exiles living in London, she tells me, residents who are never really citizens of their adopted country, but isolated and lonely foreigners floating rootless through their British life, pining for their Russian homeland that no longer exists.

My wife leaves the room briefly to hang up her coat in the hall closet. I took a painkiller, as instructed by Dr. Sutter, and am floating on its effects.

"How was your night? Did you eat the kale I left you?"

"No. I made my own dinner."

Lisa stiffens with irritation, is about to say something, but then lets it pass. She goes to the kitchen table and flips through the mail. "Did you see this? There's a postcard here from Sam. What a strange-looking card. Who are these people holding up knives? Where is this?"

"Greenland. They're Inughuits."

"That boy can't sit still. He is so like you."

"God, I hope not."

"What should we do for lunch? I'm not really hungry."

She stops in her tracks and looks intently at me. She has a sixth sense.

"What is it?"

I look back at her, blink. The doorbell rings. There is so much I intend to say, but when the moment comes, the words fail me, and a few moments later Kamila, the Czech maid, comes to tell me my guests are waiting in the office.

François Kreuz, the chairman of Médecins Sans Frontières, and his German assistant are up from Geneva. They are sitting on the couch facing the French doors. The rose garden outside is bathed in morning light. Kamila has brought them a tray—a white porcelain pot of coffee, matching cream-and-sugar holders—and the young German assistant is leaning forward, handing his superior a saucer and cup, just as I enter the room.

"Good afternoon, Monsieur Kreuz," I say. "Please don't get up." We shake hands all around. I can't remember the aide's name. "Hello, young man. Good to see you again. Your team, FC Bayern, is doing well."

He laughs, delighted I should remember our last conversation. "They are top of the league!"

I take my seat opposite. Kreuz stirs his coffee with a silver spoon, and a delicate tinkle fills the room as his spoon grates against the porcelain walls of the cup. "Thank you for seeing us, Herr Álvarez," he says. "Let me say, on behalf of the entire board at Médecins Sans Frontières, we wish you all the best in your battle with the cancer. We were all very upset to hear the news."

"News travels fast."

"Switzerland, you know, it is really just a small village. Your neighbors know your business—before you do."

His assistant and I laugh. "How true," I say.

"Dr. Sutter is excellent," he continues. "The best in Switzerland. But if you want a second opinion, in New York or London, the doctors in our organization are entirely at your disposal. Just give us the word and we will make calls and find you the best specialists in the world and get you in for an appointment."

"That's very kind. Thank you. But I am quite happy with Dr. Sutter and my treatment. It is what it is. In the end, we must all die of something."

"True."

"Now, Monsieur Kreuz. Thank you for your concern but you requested this meeting for a reason. How can I help?"

Kreuz pauses for a moment, looks out the

French doors, and then turns his head back in my direction. "You have, over the years, been a wonderful patron and advocate of our work. We are extremely grateful for your support."

I brush some fluff off my knee. "Doctors Without Borders is a wonderful organization. I like to think that is also how I have lived my own life—without borders. I am proud to support and be associated with your fine organization. There's no need for us to say more."

"Thank you. We are equally proud to be associated with you and the Álvarez bank."

We stare at each other, Monsieur Kreuz and I, and then he says, "It's very difficult for me to bring this up. But it's my job."

"You are among friends. You can speak plainly."

"Every year it seems the wars are growing in number and ferocity, all across the globe. We can't keep up. Médecins Sans Frontières is stretched dangerously thin. We need more capital, to increase our capacity and respond to the urgent needs around the world."

"Yes, I just saw your letter. I see you will report a deficit this year. The first in the organization's history."

"Which is why I am here. Not to put too fine a point on it, we would be very grateful if you would remember Médecins Sans Frontières in your estate. Is this too bold of me to ask?"

"Not at all. I am a realist and value straight talk. We have discussed this possibility in the past, but now the issue is real and urgent—not just for me, apparently, but for the organization as well. Your request is well timed and duly noted. I need to reflect on these matters. I cannot put these decisions about my estate and legacy off much longer."

Kreuz is visibly relieved that I have not taken offense. "Thank you so much, Herr Álvarez. For your understanding. We are grateful—even just for the consideration."

"That you have. Now, I am a little tired. I should probably lie down before dinner. Is there anything else?"

The assistant rummages in his bag and retrieves a gift beautifully wrapped in silver-blue paper. He hands it to Kreuz, who in turn holds it delicately in his meaty hands, before saying, "Do you recall meeting an Icelandic doctor when you were touring our field operations in Sarajevo? This was many years ago."

"I do. The eye specialist. Dr. Einarsson. We discovered on that trip—as mortars were flying all around us—we both fished the same salmon river in the northwestern corner of Iceland. It was quite an extraordinary afternoon we had together."

"Yes. Exactly. Dr. Einarsson has since become an international star and a great ambassador of our work. He famously perfected a low-cost cataract operation, with a portable laser he invented and patented. His discovery has been licensed to Alcon, and he is donating half of all his royalties to our organization."

"A fine man. I knew that already back then."

"Well, I am glad you remember him, because he certainly remembers you. In fact, when Dr. Einarsson heard that you were fighting late-stage cancer, he asked me to give you this small gift."

Monsieur Kreuz solemnly hands me the package, the Japanese way, with both hands.

"Thank you very much. I'll open it upstairs. It was very good of you to come to remote Ägeri to see me. Now, let me show you out."

I get rid of them and wearily climb the stairs. I hear Lisa in the kitchen, and, wanting privacy, go all the way up, to our bedroom upstairs. I unwrap the gift on the bed. It is a series of three unusual salmon flies, framed under glass, which Dr. Einarsson has created. The flies are, his attached note says, particularly productive at catching fish on the Kjara, our favorite river. He draws my attention to the middle fly, which has a sleek black body, silver tinsel, and a touch of jungle-cock and partridge feather near the hook's eye. It looks lethal.

Dr. Einarsson has named the fly "The Professor."

The Professor is my nickname in Iceland, bestowed on me one summer by a ghillie after I broke the record of fish caught in one day on the Kjara River—three years in a row.

I am moved beyond words. I don't know how to respond to this thoughtful gift, this homage, from a virtual stranger.

It's almost more than my own sons would do for me.

It is late September and the last day of trout season is here. I rise early, pick up my favorite trout rod from my study, and stick a few boxes of flies into my fishing vest. I leave a note for Lisa, sleeping late, as is her habit, letting her know I won't fish the whole day, but will be back to have lunch with her.

The morning is fresh. I contentedly head, however slow of pace, toward the garage, sticking the magnetized rod holder on the roof of the Volvo. I secure my Hardy trout rod, and then throw waders and a fishing vest in the trunk. I let Alfredo out of his pen and he vigorously wags his stubby tail, repeatedly licks my hand in thanks, before lifting his great leg and peeing on a flowerpot. He then trots over to the Volvo and looks back at me with his bearded face, urging me to open the car door.

We drive to the Lebensbach, my favorite stream on the other side of the Rippenseite mountain. The day is cool but sunny, with a light wind rippling through the birch. Cowbells clank and the air smells rich. The country road turns to dirt and we pass a cluster of old farmhouses and barns, not quite a village, named Brunnenhof, because of the stone fountain gurgling at the crossroads of the dirt lanes. The brown cedar of the central farmhouse is so battered by age and weather the shingles are almost black, and as we drive by, an elderly woman in dreary skirt and blouse comes from around the side, a pitchfork full of hay raised high above her kerchief-covered head.

Alfredo leans against the door, looking out the window and smelling every barnyard animal that sweeps past, his ears pricking up if a dog barks or a cockerel cries. We pull down a dirt track that a logger has made along the river's edge. Next to a shed—municipal warnings about rabid squirrels and foxes and poisonous mushrooms hammered to its wooden walls—I pull the car hard against a spruce, its low-hanging branches lightly brushing the side of the car.

Alfredo is panting, ready for the hunt.

I pop open his door. "*Vámonos, Alfredo. Pescado para Dios.*"

Fish for God.

Funny, that. It's an expression I haven't thought about in seventy years. My father used to say this prayer, with much feeling, every time we went fishing. He'd ritualistically spit on his fly, piss his horse-stream into the river, and then roar

"*Pescado para Dios!*" as he threw his first cast with the power that came from his huge frame.

Alfredo snuffles through the underbrush as I fuss about in the back of the Volvo. With grunting effort, I pull on my hip waders before shrugging on the vest filled with flies and spools of filament. Around my head I hang the eyeglasses with the magnified bifocals that miraculously allow me to still tie flies at my advanced age, and then clip into place the Polaroid shades that enable me to see fish below the glare of the river's surface. Finally, I sling around my back an old wicker fishing basket from Galicia, a family heirloom with oft-repaired canvas side bags in which I store a bottle of water and a stick of salami, in case I feel weak.

Alfredo looks pleadingly at me, whines under his breath.

"I'm coming."

I slam shut the back of the Volvo, lift my rod from the magnetized holders, and together we take the nearly invisible path down through the trees. Alfredo trots ahead but always turns around to see if the old man is still following.

He is—but tediously. Some thirty tottering and stumbling minutes later we circle a large boulder, covered with moss and a few ash and elm seedlings that have taken root in its crevices. I have to stop and catch my breath. I feel a little weak. But I can hear the roar of the waterfall on the other side of the boulder, and as we slowly round its stone edges, its drifting spray comes through the spruce and refreshingly moistens my face, giving me a second wind. More importantly, I smell fish. I click my tongue at Alfredo, warning him not to run ahead, and he instantly falls into position, ears pricked up, one paw gingerly placed before the other, two steps behind and off to the right of my heel.

We come slowly down through the trees. I am at that age where I can no longer jump that last bit of slope, so I slide down on my backside, through the moss and fern, my boots finally landing solid on the rock below. I stand, panting and shaky and undignified. But I've done it. The old man has returned to his favorite fishing spot, even if his backside and pride are a little bruised.

The waterfall and pool appear luminescent in the dappled light. I gently slide the wicker fishing basket from around my neck, place it in a bed of pale ferns, and tie a stonefly onto the end of a 2.5-kilo leader. From a vest pocket, I pull out a rattling packet, and after sliding open its plastic door, retrieve a tiny bit of shot that I clamp to the leader.

The pool is fifty square meters and black-green in color, created by a powerful funnel of gin roaring over the top of a granite ledge. From the short distance away, where I am standing among the ferns, the waterfall could almost appear as wispy as the white-lace train of a wedding gown, but the river's throaty roar and the spray of mist the falls unleash quickly make it clear this is no dainty amount of water, but a deep pool.

I quietly inch my way forward. Alfredo follows, one paw up, his stubby tail straight. There is a mossy rock to the left of the waterfall, and I cast into the calm pocket of water behind it. Alfredo stands rigid to my right, ears pricked and alert. The current pulls the fly, but the shot and sinking line keep the fly down, keep it from bobbing to the surface, and it is pulled deep through the pool.

Nothing. I try the other side of the rock and the fly instantly hits a snag, probably a broken branch. I curse, pull at it, and as I do so, a silver bar flashes deep down in the black water.

Not a tree limb. A fish.

The reel cries, Alfredo whines. I step back as the fish runs into the hardest part of the falls, trying to shake the hook.

"Ha, Alfredo! The old man still has it!"

Three times I bring the trout to the surface, and three times the cock fish flips its tail, turns, and heads back down into the pool. Then he tries to run around a jagged rock, to break the line, and the ebullience I feel at hooking him gives way to a grudging respect. And so we continue—me pulling one way, he the other—until, weary of fighting for life, he finally rolls onto his side, and slowly comes to my feet.

It is a wonderful rainbow trout, almost three kilos. Its flank is a delicate mesh of silver scales, but with pink-and-blue hues glinting even in the forest's low light. He's on his side, his gills working furiously, gasping for breath. His head is lifted slightly by the taut line and rests on a rock, while his flank bobs in the water. But he defiantly flaps his tail, again and again, still trying to dodge his fate.

The one black eye, facing up, stares fiercely at me.

This may be the last fish I will ever catch in this world, and the courage with which the trout has fought for his life, it moves me. I was never one of those *maricones* who preached catch-and-release; it's just modern decadence, in my opinion, to torture fish and return them, rather than eat the fish you catch as God intended. But, before I know what is happening, I have bent down and am releasing the hook. I let the fish recover in the shallows, and eventually he pulls away, slowly swimming back into the deep belly of the pool.

I drop my rod, sit down heavily on a rock, my arms and legs suddenly too weak to hold me up. Alfredo looks at me as if I am insane. He backs away, keeps a wary distance, unsure what it all means.

As I sit slump-shouldered and staring blankly at the pool, I remember the time I came to this exact spot with my sons, when they were mere boys, to teach them how to catch trout with worms. Sam was around ten years old and, as I stood by his side, a nice-sized brook trout took his bait. John and Rob sat hushed on a mossy rock behind their older brother, as I whispered to Sam he should let the trout run with the line and fully take the worm. When enough time went by for the trout to swallow the hook, I told him it was time to pull up hard, and in one arc of bent rod he hauled the trout out of the pool and sent it flying over our heads to the bushes behind us.

Sam was shivering with excitement and chattering nonstop as we pulled the flopping trout from the bushes and I taught the boys how to kill it in a clean and manly way. We then gutted the fish and that night wrapped it in bacon and roasted it in the oven—and how we all agreed, as we sat in the chalet's dining room, that it was the best meal we ever had in our lives.

And as one memory leads to another, I remember another day, in the same dining room, having dinner with my handsome sons, then in their late teens and early twenties. That night I repeated to them, without really thinking about what I was saying, what my father had told me— that they were expected to take over the Álvarez family bank one day and run it well and pass it on to their children. The boys at first sat stone-faced in the shadows of the dining room, but then the

American in them rose up and violently declared their independence from me. Sam talked back and the other two quickly joined forces with their older brother. I am ashamed of my response now, but I couldn't stop myself at the time, and things ran away from us, undoubtedly because below the surface of our rage there stood a great deal of unspoken shame, disgust, and disappointment—in me.

Eventually we were all yelling at each other and Lisa was crying. When I was midsentence and smacking the table to make a point, the boys walked out on me—united as one.

The pain of this memory, it's unbearable—

How did you go from that young father standing joyously with his boys at the edge of this pool—to an old man nearing his end and alone at the same pool, with nothing to show for his life but an indifferent relationship with his sons?

I am a failure. A failure.

Alfredo whines, cocks his ears, and his quizzical look says it all—*Who are you?* When I see this, I am ashamed of my weakness, and pull myself together. I hold out a hand for the dog to sniff.

"It's all right, Alfredo. *Qué sé yo.* It's me. Just me."

He comes forward, licks my hand—and I find myself standing at the edge of the Atlantic as the tide comes in, my face wet with salt air.

Part II

1959

RIBADESELLA, NORTHERN SPAIN

THREE

The brown-sugar sand below Miramar, our summerhouse in Ribadesella, was getting a good pounding from the Atlantic Ocean that day, and the stiff breeze carried just enough spray back in our direction to moisten our skin and make our faces tingle with sea salt. I was sixteen, Papá had a hangover, and the two of us were out on our gravel drive, studying the men in threadbare black suits that were lined up along the coastal lane running between our house and the beach.

Little did I know then that I would never be happier than that summer of my youth—or that everything I experienced later in life flowed directly from that fishing trip. All I knew then was that it was spring and the fishing season had started. Some of the rough-looking men before us had shotguns hanging from leather straps off their shoulders, while others had pointers at their heels and were smoking yellow-skinned cigarettes—but they were all, every one of them, farmers who doubled as fishing guides and river managers.

Papá hacked up phlegm. His head hurt and he was shielding himself from the morning light with dark sunglasses. Papá was always meticulous about the way he looked, no matter what had transpired the night before, and he was dressed in a green tweed country suit, his usual monogrammed handkerchief poking out of his breast pocket. The light was, for some reason, making his Roman nose and formidable jaw look like it had been carved out of soft and salty butter, and his love of red wine and pig roasts was manifesting itself in a growing double chin bulging slightly above his wire-haired chest.

"*Bueno*," Papá said gruffly. "Let's start the show. Are you ready, José?"

I held a wicker basket filled with white envelopes, and his essence of stale whisky and Suavecito hair pomade and cigarette smoke was coming to me in gusts on the wind. I looked up at him and nodded. "*Sí, Papá.* I am ready."

We stepped forward. Papá began the annual ritual with Señor Guiterez, the head ghillie of the mightiest of Spanish salmon rivers. He was, according to custom, first in line, his panting and saliva-flecked collie seated obediently at his feet.

Papá held his cigarette like he was socializing at a tapas bar, its smoke curling up and above his rose-gold pinky ring stamped with our family crest, and after the usual exchange of pleasantries, he said, "So tell me, old friend, how are things on the Narcea?"

"This run could be the best we've ever seen, Don Jesús. Last year we had a record number of first-year fish returning to the river to spawn, but now we are seeing the second-year fish—monsters all above ten kilos—coming in large waves."

"*Joder. Muy bien.*"

Señor Guiterez was beaming at Papá with such self-satisfaction we could see every one of his silver teeth, plus the tobacco-stained ivory stubs left over from what God had given him. Papá turned to the basket I was holding, retrieved an envelope, and handed it solemnly over to the ghillie.

"Thank you for your friendship, Señor Guiterez. It is good of you to come this long distance to visit us."

"We hope to see the Álvarez family fishing the Narcea soon," Guiterez said, pocketing his envelope. "It's been too long."

"*Hombre*! We would like that very much. We love the Narcea, particularly the upper beat. But, as you know, God chooses where we fish."

The men laughed. It was an open secret in these parts of Spain that my father had an unusual method for picking the rivers our family fished. Every spring and fall, Spain's head of state, Generalísimo Francisco Franco, returned to Oviedo in Asturias, where he had first met his wife and been stationed as a young battalion commander of the Regimiento de Infantería del Príncipe. From his wife's country home, La Pinella, Franco staged lightning-like raids on the salmon in the rivers of the surrounding countryside, just like he massacred Berbers in the Rif Mountains of Morocco a few decades earlier.

He did so, of course, with the odds heavily stacked in his favor. Whenever Franco chose to fish the nearby Narcea, Nalón, or Navia rivers, the authorities in Madrid closed down the entire river three weeks before El Caudillo arrived, so the fish were rested and ready to take the old man's lure. He fished with spoons or prawns, a common and coarse approach that my fly-fishing father and uncle privately ridiculed, but all Franco cared about was laying a string of dead fish out on the riverbank, and this he did with great efficiency.

Of course, the first commoner to know that El Caudillo was coming to fish a particular river was the water's head ghillie, who, a month in advance, would be personally notified by Madrid's Minister of Agriculture and Fisheries to close down the river. That would then force the ghillies to chase off any fishermen who had licenses to fish the river during those weeks. My father and uncle had been repeatedly bumped off their fishing beats in this manner. They were not pleased.

So, starting in 1953, Papá quietly put the head ghillies of Northern Spain's salmon rivers on his payroll. The arrangement was simple: the Álvarez family—originally from these parts, before the family bank was moved to the wealthy Basque city of San Sebastián—would lease the best river beats immediately after El Caudillo concluded his vacation. We would fish "in God's shadow" was how Papá explained it. My father figured that one old man could not properly fish an entire river, particularly after it was rested for weeks before the old man even arrived, which meant our family would in this way be guaranteed the second-best fishing in all Spain, after Franco himself, of course.

But the head ghillies had to be financially rewarded for their efforts on our family's behalf, which was why, on that spring morning, they were lined up to receive our "tokens of appreciation." Papá loved the annual ritual and he moved to the next man down the line, like a general inspecting his troops, warmly shaking the fellow's hand and passing him a cash-filled envelope. The white-haired ghillie bowed courteously.

"*Gracias*, *Don Jesús*. May Saint Peter ensure you and your family a great catch this year. I hear you will be fishing the Sella."

"Yes. Apparently, God has become rather fond of the Bridge Pool in Omedina."

The men up and down the lane laughed. When the last ghillie had received his envelope, our manservant, Jorge, came out with a silver tray filled with blanched almonds and shot glasses of Fanjul, the local apple-cider liquor. I looked down at the basket and the last and fattest envelope left, which would go to Ignacio del Toro, the head ghillie of the Sella. We raised our glasses, drank to each other's good health, and returned them empty to Jorge's tray. "Now, please forgive us, gentleman," Papá said. "My son and I have to run into town for our supplies. May God be with you and your families in the coming year."

The men roared their well wishes, and Papá and I returned to the house. We found Uncle Augustin seated in a living-room armchair, reading the local paper through a pair of gold-rimmed bifocals as he waited for our return, while from the back of the house came the industrious clatter of Conchata, our cook. Papá and I needed to freshen up before we headed to town, and so climbed the stairs two by two, heading to our respective rooms.

As we turned into the landing on the next floor, there was a movement behind a slightly open door, and we both turned our heads in its direction. My younger brother, Juan, just fourteen, was standing naked before the full-length mirror in Mother's bedroom. His back was to us and he was staring at his body, flexing the muscles in his right arm, his left hand reaching down to pull at his dick poking from his pubic hair, trying to make it look longer. He had doused himself in Suavecito, and the smell came to us, thick and pungent in the hall. Just then, Juan twisted his upper torso to look admiringly at his butt.

Papá laughed as we passed and said, "He is going to create trouble, our Juan. The girls better watch out. Mark my words. That's Don Juan in the making."

Juan and I went to the seawall at the end of Ribadesella, and stood on our tiptoes, peering into the sea, as Father and Uncle Augustin foraged in town for supplies. The Atlantic was rough that day, a slip-sliding surface that shifted somewhere between milky blue and icy platinum, until the water thundered foamy white against the blocks of brown rock. Curve-necked cormorants stood on the marlstone and peered intently down into the water with their angry-yellow eyes, fierce hunters standing in between the seaweed toupees that here and there were plopped haphazardly atop the bald and barnacled rocks.

A bar of silver flew out of the water a hundred meters off, before plunging again. It was a krill-fattened salmon shaking loose the sea lice that were dying in that sweet-salt water where river mouth and ocean met.

"Look," I said, pointing out at the water. "They are there, hovering, just below the surface."

"*Cabrón.* I am not stupid. I have eyes in my head, you know."

My brother was leaning far over the wall,

staring deep and pensively into the water, the zipper end of his blue windbreaker flapping in the stiff breeze. The blue light that day caught his delicate skin, his curly brown hair. He had the family's black eyebrows, set like a pair of grammatical tildes above burnt-flan eyes, and they were fierce and furrowed with concentration.

"Hey, stupid," Juan said. "You're missing the action."

My brother pointed as another salmon jumped—and another. It was like an electrical current under the sea was sending fish flying up into the air, and the seagulls hovering above us cried with excitement at the sight. According to the farmer's almanac in the pocket of my peacoat, a silver peseta of a full moon would that night draw in the month's highest tide, and with it would come large numbers of Atlantic salmon making their egg-and-milt dash up the River Sella to spawn in the water that originally gave them life.

"This year I am going to catch *salmones* much bigger than yours," said my brother.

"And how are you going to do that?"

"*Coño.* By fishing better than you, than Papá, than Uncle Augustin. You'll see. And if I don't, I'll just steal one of Papá's fish, and tell you I caught it. You're so gullible, you'll probably believe me."

I ruffled his curly hair and he angrily pulled

away from me, and carefully combed his locks with his fingers, already, at fourteen, meticulous about his appearance, just like Papá.

The Roman town of Ribadesella strategically grew up in a protective bend of the Sella River, right before it entered the Atlantic, its port just a few hundred meters to the left and behind us. The salmon river originated in the Picos mountains on the horizon behind us and, after its journey to the coast, unfurled itself into the crashing sea before us like a flamenco dancer might unfurl her curled palm out flat toward a group of unruly and drunken men.

The warm and salty air of that spring was imbued with that special light of youth, and as I looked across the river, to the bay, I spotted the gray towers of our summerhouse. "Come," I said. "It's time for us to get back. Papá said we'd have lunch in town before we went back to the house to finish packing."

We turned just as two fishing vessels entered the river mouth and made their way to the port's fish market. Salmon hooks dressed in a tangle of meaty prawns and worms, a method of fishing unique to the Sella, sailed through the air. Old men and boys had created a gauntlet along the river wall and were casting painted cork bobbers into the string of pools that fed into the sea. Sacks filled with *jamón* and sheepskins full of wine were at their feet. A large number of growling feral cats were slinking between the fishermen's legs, while yellow-legged gulls surfed the air, crying in anticipation of the approaching fish slaughter.

The brass bell hanging at the top of the wall was rung each spring for the *campanu*, the first salmon caught of the season, and the wind gusts that day occasionally produced from it a dull clang. Juan and I began following the wall back toward the center of town, as a mud-splattered farmer and a bony donkey, pulling a cart of turnips, came up the cobblestone river road, and a half-mad monk in coarse habit crossed to the other side, muttering darkly to himself. A cry went out and Juan and I looked back at the line of fishermen along the wall.

A man in a black beret was stepping back from the wall, his bamboo rod bent in two, his line screaming from a clunky steel reel. His *compañero* stepped forward and rang the brass bell announcing the *campanu*, and the wall revelers roared in celebration. Several tipped back their heads to take the wine from the *botas*, the sheepskin bladders held aloft that sent a stream of wine-piss soaring through the air and directly into their opened mouths. But we had no time to stop and watch the festivities, and reluctantly turned just as the fisherman's half-drunk friend plunged a gaff into the salmon's head and hauled it up the stone wall, the shuddering fish spouting blood like a punctured wine barrel.

Below the older men, teenage boys and younger were fishing the river with hand lines and sand eels and ribbons of squid. We could just make out shoals of gray mullet moving down the pebbly riverbanks, sucking in plankton, dead plants, and scum. Here and there the tails of brill and bream poked up from their tin buckets.

"Rich boys," one local called out. "Buy our fish."

"No chance," Juan retorted. "They smell like your stinky butt."

There was a roar and some of the village boys jumped up to fight. I grabbed Juan by the nape of his neck and steered him straight ahead, forcing him to look at the Guardia Civil in his olive-green cape and black tricorne hat, heading in our direction. The policeman glared at us over the hood of a dusty 1930s Packard coming down the street, and the local boys, who also saw him coming, quickly stepped back to their river perches, dropping eels over the side.

The air that day smelled of the Arabian jasmine curling lasciviously up the town's Roman wall, just starting to flower in April's warm breath; and of donkey manure attracting swarms of bluebottles and starting to cook on the cobblestone skillet; and of maturing cod, packed in the diamond-dust of rock salt and stored in oak barrels outside the riverside fish restaurants.

Up ahead, at Ribadesella's central port, the two

fishing vessels had docked and were unloading trays of red snapper and whiskered San Pedro. Uncle Augustin and Papá were sitting at a sidewalk table next to the port, under the bronze and watchful stare of a Franco statue, and studying the catch coming in at the fish market. They spotted us and impatiently waved at us to hurry up and take our seats at the table. Even from that distance, Juan and I could feel their eagerness to start fishing.

Our bachelor uncle was slight in comparison to Papá, a good five centimeters shorter than his older brother, but lean and muscular as a matador. He was dressed in a hunting jacket of brown wool and an open white shirt that revealed a gold cross and chain in a tangle of dappled chest hair. Uncle Augustin smiled kindly at me, from below his well-groomed mustache, and patted the chair next to his.

The pretty daughter of the proprietor brought out a bottle of white wine and a dish of fried baby eels to the table. Papá followed her hungrily with his eyes. We reported what we saw at the seawall, while quickly reducing the eels to an oily paste on our back teeth and washing it down with the wine. When I looked up from my plate, an elderly man in black suit and narrow tie stood silently under the Franco statue, waiting to be noticed. I nudged Uncle Augustin.

"*Hola, Ignacio!*" he said. "Come. Have a glass of wine with us. Are you hungry?"

My father yelled at the waiters to bring a chair, glass, and plate, and for a moment there was a flurry of white aprons as they fought over who would bring over what. Ignacio del Toro, the head ghillie of the Sella River, carefully slung his shotgun over the back of the wooden chair placed before him, and sat by our table, a respectful distance back, ever mindful of his place. He held up his glass of wine to my father, formally and sonorously intoning, *"Salud, Don Jesús.* To your health and the health of the entire Álvarez family."

Papá handed Ignacio his envelope, piled his plate with eels, and warmly asked about his health and the state of his farm. The aged ghillie returned polite, taciturn responses, in between lowering his head over the fish platter, until Father finally blurted out, *"Qué pasa, hombre*! Come on. Tell us what's happening on the river. How did Franco do?"

The aged ghillie paused, put down his fork, and slowly began telling his tale. "El Caudillo arrived last week, with half his cabinet, his security detail, and a large number of horses. All appeared as normal. But he was on the river less than a day, up near Omedina, when his chief of staff arrived from Madrid. After they talked, Franco came up to our farm to take a phone call. *Pfft.* It was all over. Franco and his entire cabinet returned immediately to Madrid after the call."

My father squinted suspiciously. "*Por qué*? Franco never gives up his fishing."

"One of the officers told me they had finally caught Dr. Azel Echeverría, the Basque separatist. El Caudillo and his cabinet took off back to Madrid, to figure out how to get the most out of the terrorist's capture."

We all looked at each other.

"So," Augustin finally said. "Franco never fished the Sella. It's been resting for five weeks and still hasn't been fished?"

My father roared with laughter and gave my brother's neck a gentle shake. "Juanito! You will catch your first salmon on the fly this year. I can tell. *Coño*. What a slaughter we shall have."

"The river is so full of salmon you can walk across their backs sticking out of the water," the head ghillie said in his unhurried way.

"Eat up, boys. The Sella is calling us."

Uncle Augustin turned to impatiently signal the waiter we were ready for the next course, at the exact same moment my brother turned in the other direction, to glower at one of the riverbank boys who was walking close by and clicking his tongue at us. I remember the eyebrows, the noses, the intense and wiry energy of uncle and brother—they were Álvarez mirrors of each other.

We returned to Miramar. Our manservant, maid, and cook had used the time to pack our luggage, but we still had to pack our fishing gear and went directly to the low-slung and windowless side shed that was once used to dry apricots and cure sausages but now stored our rods and fishing equipment. The pile on the floor of the shed grew larger and larger: duffel bags and reed baskets filled with fly reels and fly boxes; canvas bags to carry dead salmon down from the mountains; leather-laced boots, shin guards, and high-water wading sticks. As we came to the end of our packing, Jorge and our chubby-faced cook appeared at the hut's door. *"Perdóname, Don Jesús,"* Conchata said. *"La Doña.* She is on the phone and asking for you, sir."

Papá went off to take the call while Uncle Augustin had my brother and me relay the fishing equipment to the driveway, as Jorge backed the Hispano-Suiza into position. The duffel bags were packed tight in the rumble seat, then covered by a canvas tarp, and secured with leather straps. A half dozen leather canisters contained our rods, everything from locally made trout rods as agile as the birch switch our Jesuit teachers used to whip us with, to the long and heavy two-handed Hardy salmon rods made of split bamboo, lacquered and lashed with silk thread to a center rod of galvanized steel. Jorge climbed on the running board and pulled tight the straps securing our rod canisters to the car's roof.

I had to pee and ran inside the house. As I

made my way down the waxed corridor, to the ground-floor bathroom tucked off the library, something strange in Papá's voice made me turn my head. He was in the living room, standing by the ruched silk curtains. One hand held the phone tight to his ear, while the other absentmindedly toyed with the brocade couch. His profile was pure Picos de Europa: the mountainous forehead, the black brows, the large and noble nose, the fat and sensuous lips underneath. He stared out to sea, the look on his face so intense it looked like he could see his future in its waves.

"Isabel. You are right. Totally unacceptable. I am deeply sorry she came by the house. Don't worry. I'll take care of her . . . Now, don't cry, my dear. She means nothing to me. You know that. A diversion. That is all. *Pfft.* She is nothing. I love only you and the boys. Please. Don't cry, my sweet."

He absentmindedly brought his hand down with a smack, squashing a fly against the back of the couch, and I turned for the bathroom. When I came back outside, Papá was already sitting behind the wheel of the Hispano-Suiza, intently studying me as I stood at the top of the stone steps. I hesitated. Jorge and Conchata were climbing into the SEAT, ready to follow us upriver.

My instinct, at that moment, was to create a distance between my father and me, and I looked to the back of the Hispano-Suiza, but Uncle Augustin was already sitting there with Juanito. My father, still studying my face and without a care in the world, or so it seemed to me, leaned over and popped open the door. I slid silently into the passenger's seat next to him.

Papá lit a Ducados and then, with two fingers, deftly slid the Hispano-Suiza gearshift into first. "Are we ready?"

"Ready!!!" we cried.

"*Entonces*. Let us pay our respects to *El Rey Salmón*."

FOUR

Conchata rose early the next morning, and soon the fishing lodge, a converted sheep's corral on the banks of the Sella River, was filled with the smells of a Spanish tortilla in the pan and a metal pot percolating coffee on the stove. My brother and I came stumbling from our cots.

Uncle Augustin was fully dressed in corduroy and flannel and sitting at the dining-room table. "Good morning, nephews," he said softly, as he reached for a plate of *manchego* cheese and fig jam.

Jorge came barreling through the front door, sending a gust of wind swirling around the stone floor. *"Hombre,"* he said. "There's a chilly drizzle coming down from Los Picos."

Papá emerged from the toilet, his suspenders still dropped and dangling around his knees. He sat down at the head of the dining-room table and pulled the iron skillet of tortilla in his direction. Jorge pulled from his jacket pocket a few straws and silently laid them on the table by my father's elbow. Papá shuffled them, held them up, and we pulled straws to see who would fish what stretch of river: I got the top and, at this time of year, worst beat.

"Juanito," Papá said. "You are fishing with me

this morning. We'll take my small fly rod. You can manage that now. It's time you caught a *salmón* on the fly."

"But we'll take the worm rod, too, won't we? Just in case."

"Aaah. You have been defeated before you started. You must go fully committed to the fly, Juanito. Trust me. You will catch a salmon on the fly this morning. If you work at it, have confidence." He made a face, like he had a taste of bad milk in his mouth. "Worm fishing is for farmers. Gentlemen fish with the fly."

But things changed once we went outside. Out on the gravel drive, my brother was circling our father, parrying his fly rod like it was a fencing foil. Papá was sitting on the stone bench and had his head down, peering through his bifocals as he tied his leader to the fly line.

"It's gray today," Juan said, "so I think I will use a bright fly—something red and yellow—to make the fish see it. What do you think, Papá?"

"Yes. Yes. That sounds good," my father said in a faraway voice, never bothering to look up from his line. "The fly boxes are over there."

I stopped what I was doing and turned in their direction. On a dark day you use dark flies, and on a bright day, bright flies—every serious fisherman knew this. My father, failing to correct my brother, was condemning Juan to a day without fish.

I studied my father—how he peered through the curling smoke of his cigarette, how those beefy and fluttering lids masked his true thoughts—and saw for the first time he was totally bored with his younger son and greatly regretting he had insisted they fish together. Papá, I knew, would spend the entire day running roughshod over everyone and anything getting in the way of his fishing, and in the end, my little brother, instead of experiencing his rite of passage, his day of joy, would somehow wind up paying the price for our father's self-absorption.

"Papá, I want Juan to come with me. I want to be with him when he catches his first salmon."

"Really?" said Juan.

My father was relieved—you could see he was, just below the lids of his eyes—and he said, "If you boys insist." Juan clapped his hands in excitement. I suspect he knew there was some unseen gulf between him and our father that could never be bridged, and, because of that, he preferred to be with his older brother on that special day.

The knowledge that Juan wanted to be with me flooded me with elation, a physical tingling that ran right down my arm to the very center of my being. The sensation was so overwhelming, in fact, that I had to turn away from Juan, lest he see how much the moment meant to me. Luckily, Ignacio's grandson, Felipe, assigned to be my fishing guide and just then coming around the side of the lodge, served as distraction. "My brother is joining us above," I said brusquely.

Felipe was nineteen, only three years older than me, but knew the surrounding land and river like it was the pear orchard outside his family farm. He was standing against the wall of the Sheep's Corral when we emerged from it for the last time, patiently waiting to take my brother and me upriver. Felipe wore a drizzle-dampened black cap, pulled over his curly hair and black eyes; a hand was resting lightly on the sheathed hunting knife hanging from his belt. We looked at each other, blinked an acknowledgment, and then lowered our eyes.

By 7:00 a.m. we were heading upriver, Felipe leading the way. We passed through a field of persimmon trees, planted by Felipe's great-grandfather, before the rough track led down a hillock and through blackberry bramble. Juan trudged after us, contentedly humming "Hound Dog" to himself, an American rock-and-roll song that had recently invaded the state-run airwaves throughout Spain.

The blue-green river was to the left of us, curving around boulders at the bottom of the Dead Priest's Pool, a long and deep stretch of river named after the local monsignor who had drowned two hundred years earlier when he came home drunk one night from his mistress and slipped from the path. Ever since, the locals said, the waters here were haunted by the priest's penitent spirit.

Felipe made the sign of the cross as we passed, and when I gave him an odd look, he said, "The old women down in the village say the dead priest rises from the river and visits those who are near death."

Juan and I laughed at this ridiculous superstition, and Felipe, hurt that we should make fun of him, looked away.

Our breathing soon became labored as we ascended the mountains, tracing the river to its source. Felipe was an amateur *cantaor* and began singing an old country song, about yearning, and my younger brother, who spoke that language, too, joined in the chorus, the two of them creating a haunting cry that seemed to shimmer out into the warm embrace of the trembling oak leaves and the tinkle of goat bells.

Through the next brush, whinnying at our approach and tethered to a cork tree, stood three horses. Two canvas bags for toting fish hung from a branch. Felipe turned and said, in his usual unsmiling way, "I brought the horses up yesterday afternoon, so we could move quicker, fish longer, and waste less time walking. Not even my grandfather knows I took them. The chestnut was meant to carry our catch, but Juan can ride her." He smiled with his eyes, then, over the paper and tobacco shreds he was rolling into a cigarette. "I had a feeling you were going to wind up with the worst beat. Shit on them. We can't let the old men beat us."

Juan and I laughed and thanked him for his foresight. We mounted the mares and headed twelve kilometers up the stony goat path, sending rabbits scurrying into the hedges. A weed-tufted millstone from Roman times stuck half in and half out of the far riverbank, the marker that told us we had just reached the Mill Pool. We crossed the shallows with the horses, and crept up along the far field, carefully staying well back from the water so the fish wouldn't see us and get spooked. We tethered the horses to an oak. The animals began feeding on the silvery grass underfoot, as we walked our gear down to where the field and limestone met.

The jagged-peaked Picos and their crevice patches of blue ice hovered behind the yellow-flowered forsythia blooming in the foreground. We each took a four-piece rod from its case, and, rubbing the joint ends against our oily foreheads, slipped the greased male-female rod pieces together, starting with the cork and split-bamboo double-handed base.

I looked over at Juan. "*Coño*," he said. "It's not like I haven't done this a million times before. You don't have to keep checking on me like that."

We each screwed the heavy Hardy reels into the rods' cork bases, and then threaded the reel's wax-coated canvas line through the rod rings and out the top. Felipe reached inside his pocket for a spool of nylon, to tie on as leader. "Don't go lower than ten-kilo test," he said. "There are some big fish in the river this year. I saw one down at the bridge the other day. It was at least fifteen kilos. Almost shit my pants."

Juan laughed. I peered unsurely at my leather billfolds filled with flies, at the red-and-yellow feathers, the florid spread of jungle cock, the dyed bits of tufted wool and tinsel tied to the high-water hooks. I chose a No. 6 Carmela, its black-and-yellow body and multicolored wings hand tied by Uncle Augustin, and handed Juan a blue-and-red Primorosa. "Good choice," Felipe said.

We turned and faced the river. A side stream came fast down the steep mountainside on the far bank, a series of waterfalls that fell over moss-covered rocks, entering the Sella just after a gravel bar squeezed the main river current into a white-water run.

High above, a hawk circled, hunting for rabbits and mice. "I'll start, you follow," I said to Juan. "If I catch a fish, then you move ahead of me and start fishing first, until you catch a fish. Then we switch again, with me going first."

Juan, usually so bold, licked his lips. "I'm not

that good. I might spook the fish, the way my fly comes crashing down on the water sometimes. It drives Papá crazy."

"So be it. We share our fate."

My brother and I looked at each other, nodded, and went down to the river's edge. As was the custom then, we spat on our flies, pissed into the river, and made the sign of the cross. Felipe stood still between us, talking quietly. "José María, start first in the top basin hollowed out by that stream. Sometimes, when the fish are running, you can catch one or two in the fast water there. But use the sinking tip in that fast water—and don't waste too much time. The real action is down below."

I switched rods, after fishing the fast water, and made my way, with the floating line, centimeter by centimeter through the calmer water. First came the backward cast, the swirl of green line rising in the air, like I was a medieval monk drawing letters in the sky with a quill. Then the forward thrust of the heavy rod, which reversed the line's course, the looping forward momentum shooting the tapered green line straight and hard to the far side of the river. The fly shot to the end of the line and then hovered for a brief second, just a few centimeters above the water, before gently sinking with a sigh to the watery deck, only a raindrop plop to show where the fly had entered the river.

The current tugged at my line and swept the Carmela, just below the surface, on a diagonal race across the river, across a thousand different underwater currents stirred up and twirling, complicated eddies created by gravel and boulders and old branches felled and cast into the river by hard storms past.

I stripped my line, cast again, swept away by the sound of the running water and chirping finches in the brambles and the buzzing flies and the horses' rhythmic tearing of grass behind me; by the pull and cast of the line, like a steadily pulsing heart; and by the river itself, as clear as *aguardiente*, making us all drunk.

Pulled up short, after reaching the end of the line, the crossing fly swung through the water to my side of the pool, that sudden change in direction sometimes so enraging the salmon that they darted forward to kill it. But still no takes. The only sign of life was the black tobacco smoldering in Felipe's stained fingers and the aromatic wafts of sweaty horse flanks that came to me on the wind.

Felipe was gently telling Juan where to drop the fly. My brother, not wanting to disturb the fish, was fishing well, his line straight. Juan unexpectedly filled me with pride, the way he was fishing, and, sensing my every move, he turned to look in my direction and shook his head.

No rise. No sign of fish.

I made a poor cast a good two meters above the pool's last big boulder.

The steel hook hit the river's surface and the water boiled as a salmon rose furiously in a roll of white water, brutally bringing down the fly. I gasped, took a half step back, and raised my rod, sinking the hook into the fish's jaw. The salmon instantly shot hard upriver, the reel screamed, and Juan and Felipe scrambled out of the river, to get out of the fish's way.

"Keep your rod up!" Felipe barked.

"*Ayyyyy, hermano!*" Juan yelped.

The fish headed downriver, back up again, jumped twice. Then it made a run for the white water that led down to the next pool. I bore down hard on the line, trying to hold the fish before it reached the rapids. It turned just before the river erupted in boils and white froth, and I walked the fish back up to the deepest part of the pool, the flashing salmon coming in, running out again, jumping again on the far side of the current. It was tiring, and I carefully walked backward toward the field and snorting horses behind me, slowly bringing the fish up onto the riverbank.

Felipe, ankle deep in the shallow water, unclipped the gaff on his belt. The fish was now in the shallows, shaking its head, trying to drop the fly. Felipe's arm darted out, quick as a picador, and came back with the salmon's head gored at the end of his gaff. He straightened his back and almost languidly came in from the water's edge, his elbow up, the silvery fresh salmon shuddering and flapping and pouring blood from the gaff hole just below the pectoral fin.

"A fresh fish," he said. "Four and a half kilos."

Juan clapped me on the back. "Our first fish, José! You broke our streak!"

"Get in there, Juanito. It's your turn. There's more where that came from."

Juan eagerly walked down to the water with his rod, as I turned back to the gaffed salmon. It shivered death. Blood was still pulsing down its flanks, splattering the smooth pebbles and stones below our boots. I was shivering, too, elated, high, pumped with adrenaline.

Felipe gently removed the gaff from the twitching hen fish. She was bursting with orange eggs that would never produce life.

"She came in last night. Look how fresh." His knife poked at the four black sea lice clinging just below the fish's adipose fin. "The heads of the lice haven't dropped off yet, which means she hasn't been in the river twenty-four hours yet. We were right to come this far upriver." He pointed at the water. "The fresh fish are here."

I lit a cigarette with a trembling hand. With a thrust and crunch, Felipe cut through the wine-red fan of gills, a bloodletting that entirely drained the fish and allowed the meat to taste extra sweet, with no bitter clots of coagulated blood marring the salmon's flavor when it was cold smoked.

Felipe then grasped the fish by its tail, just above the caudal fin, and, for a moment, the silvery salmon caught glorious the sunlight. He took it to a side stream and lovingly washed it of blood, like it was a baby in the bath, before carrying it back toward the horses and gently laying it to rest in the canvas body bag spread out in the cool shadow of a tree.

"Bueno," he said. He stood and finally came over to formally shake my hand. "This calls for a toast."

Under that spring Asturian sun, we held the *bota* up high, like a biblical horn, the blood-red wine pouring in an arc across the sky and splashing deliciously into our mouths. Just then, a fish took Juan's fly, only a meter below where I had caught mine, and he roared for help. Felipe and I flicked away our cigarettes and went to stand by my brother, as he played the fish.

"Cabrón. Cabrón," he kept saying in a high-pitched voice. The four-kilo fish came into the shallows, again expertly gaffed and lifted ashore by Felipe, and my younger brother burst out in an exultant whoop, for he had finally caught his first salmon on the fly.

In our family's books, Juan had just become a man.

"Congratulations, Juanito," I said. "It's official. You're no longer a virgin."

Juan grinned, crouched by his fish, and stroked it with his palm. He looked up. "If I had been fishing with Papá, this would never have happened. I only caught this salmon because you found the fish and then let me fish the pool."

"*Claro*! What is mine is yours, Juan. We share everything."

Juan jumped up, threw his arms around me, and kissed my neck. I laughed, patted his back. "I'm proud of you. But now, Juanito, the Sella must claim its ritual."

Felipe smiled, took out his knife, and cut the small and rubbery dorsal fin off the fish. He handed it to Juan. "Everyone who catches their first *salmón* on the Sella must eat the fin. Raw. If you don't, you will have bad luck fishing for the rest of your life." I went to the rucksack, pulled out a small flask of apple brandy, and handed it to Juan. He made a face, as he ground the fin between his teeth, swallowed, and then quickly washed it down with an eye-watering swig of the liqueur.

"That is just disgusting! Who thought up this bullshit?"

Felipe and I laughed, ruffled his hair.

Juan was emanating a force of pure adrenaline and joy. "Go on, José, it's your turn to catch one. But hurry up. I want to catch another. The fly finally clicked. I am getting a feel for it. So much more fun than catching fish with the worm."

Soon thereafter I felt that solid tug—a slow, deep glide into the center of the river that told me, here was the greatest fish of the day. The eighteen-kilo salmon took over an hour to bring ashore, after it took off downstream and sent Felipe and me yelling and stumbling after it, down a kilometer of rapids, the monster fish taking out almost all the white backing of the reel's line. But still, miraculously, the fly stayed grappled to the fish's jaw, and eventually the beast went belly-up and we could gaff it in its massive steel head and drag it ashore. Juan, left alone at the upper pool, wasted no time, and by the time Felipe and I got back up to the Mill Pool, he had two more salmon on the riverbed.

When we stopped for lunch we had thirteen salmon on the banks, the smallest of which was four kilos. Drained by the morning's events, we sat down on the swayback of the riverbank, near the grazing horses, and raided our canvas rucksacks for food. While we were chewing greasy slices of *jamón de pata negra*, Felipe looked out across the valley, blinked, and said to me, "You fish better than your father and uncle. You feel the fish."

This compliment, from this terse farmer's son, welled up inside of me, grew into a glowing ball of preening pride, so full and swelling and all-consuming that only a Spaniard can fully understand it.

"And you, Juan. Not bad to beach two fish by yourself on the first day you ever caught a salmon on the fly. There's a master fisherman there, like your brother, waiting to emerge." And the look on Juan's face—I will never forget it—the way it perfectly reflected the finest day of our lives.

The sun was dropping and the sky was the color of a shrimp fly, when we arrived back at Sheep's Corral in the early evening. There were four silvery salmon already hanging from the lodge's gabled support. Swallows darted low, this way and that, as they swept through the mosquito thrum, scooping up their dinner.

Papá and Uncle Augustin heard the approach of the clopping horse hooves and came out of the front door carrying tumblers full of scotch.

"Papá! I caught my first salmon! Nine of them!"

"Well done, Juan!" said my beaming father, patting his son's leg jammed into the stirrup. "You salmon killer! Fantastic news. Congratulations. Very proud of you."

We dismounted, and Uncle Augustin, wearing a bemused smile just below his groomed mustache, held up his glass in my brother's honor, and in his courtly way said, "To Juan, a young man of great courage and talent and promise."

There was something in that moment—about my brother and me, my father and his brother—like our fraternal fates were at that moment sealed in the shadow of our fish slaughter, a moment that came to us as the setting sun hit the flanks of the salmon hung from the gills in front of the cottage door.

Papá, perhaps sensing something in this moment as well, turned slightly in my direction and said, "You're awfully quiet, José María. What's up with you?"

"This is Juan's day."

"How'd you do upriver?"

Felipe was unstrapping our fishing gear from the horses when I said, "Not much. We saw a few, which we stalked. That's how Juan caught his nine. But the fish really haven't moved upriver yet."

Felipe glanced at me over the backs of the horses.

"Aaah. That's too bad," said Papá, scratching his crotch through his front pocket, his expression unable to conceal how delighted he was he hadn't been stuck with the upper beat. "Well, down here, it was fantastic. You'll have your chance tomorrow. I caught eighteen fish. Your uncle, the *cabrón*, caught twenty-one. This is the best fishing we've ever had on the Sella. Am I right, Augustin?"

"You are right, Jesús. These are the best of days."

My father and uncle stood on the gravel, swigging their scotches, and traded stories, each advising the other for their next beat rotation, occasionally putting a patronizing hand on a shoulder or arm to make a point.

"No. No. In the Finger Pool, the fish are not where they were last year. The spring flood must have changed the river, because the fish do not lie to the right of the boulder anymore, but are lined up in a straight line, to the left . . ."

I stayed close to my brother. We sat on a stump, poring over my leather pouch of salmon flies. Juan leaned against my flank, watching what I was doing, and I silently handed him the Carmela, my good-luck fly that had caught the eighteen-kilo salmon.

"Here, Juanito. Try this tomorrow."

Ignacio and Felipe came out from around the shed, a birch-tree pole resting on their shoulders. Eight salmon with twine running through their gills and gaping mouths hung from the pole. The fish ranged from 6.5 kilos to 11 kilos and were as long as a man's leg.

"That bastard brother of mine caught those beasts," Papá roared at us. "My biggest was nine kilos." Uncle Augustin, seeing his fish like that, made the sign of the cross, and, swaying slightly with liquor on an empty stomach, followed the fish a short distance. When a horse whinnied, he swiveled to stroke its neck, and finally spotted the bulging canvas bags of fish hanging from its far flank.

"José María! What have you done?"

Papá and Juanito, Ignacio, José, even Conchata from the kitchen, were instantly drawn by my uncle's cry. They all made their way over to the horses, as a grinning Felipe unpacked the twenty-eight massive salmon I had caught. He laid them out across the grass, the largest in the center, pride of place.

There were incredulous roars and cusses and backslaps and laughs. It was a river record and I had finally overtaken my father and uncle as a fisherman, and, for the rest of the night, Papá called me "Prince of Asturias." The bottle of Johnnie Walker was fetched from inside and more swigs of scotch were taken from glass tumblers, even, my father allowed, by Juanito, "Now that he is a man."

My tipsy brother ran giddily back and forth between us, eventually falling to his knees before the big fish nicknamed, by Papá, *El Gordo*—the Fat One. Papá, meanwhile, emerged drunkenly from the lodge with a brown-leather-encased Polaroid around his neck, a newfangled American invention that looked like a box but spat out photographs on a kind of sticky flypaper. He ordered Ignacio and Felipe to lay out on the grass all the seventy-six salmon we had caught that day—half of a ton of fish, a seemingly endless abundance of nature harvested—for a photographic record.

Those black-finned ingot bars, like silver deposits in the bank, were displayed across the grass, just as the sun was dropping behind the mountains, and the air around the fish was, for a glorious moment, imbued with a pink-and-blue rainbow shimmer. Papá, Uncle Augustin, Juan, and I—the del Toros and Conchata hovering shyly in the background—were caught standing behind the day's catch, drunk with fish and scotch, swaying contentedly in the setting sun as Jorge took our picture. Juan never looked more radiant and alive and full of hope for the future. One hand was lightly but possessively touching the flank of the first salmon he ever caught on the fly, but his other, it must be said, was wrapped tightly around my shoulder, pulling me close toward him.

FIVE

A profound exhaustion hit us on the third day of
our fishing trip. At dinnertime, Juan put his head
down on the table, before the dessert came, and
fell asleep. When Jorge began to pick him up, to
carry him to his bed, my brother woke, barked he
wasn't a baby anymore, and furiously stomped
off to his cot. Not long afterward, Uncle Augustin
fell asleep in front of the fire, snoring loudly,
head nodding, his brandy unfinished on the side
table beside the couch.

Papá was distant and dark with thoughts. He
never acknowledged the dinner conversation
we directed at him, but kept his head down and
his thoughts far away, as he shoveled food into
his mouth and dragged around bowls of boiled
cabbage and fish, heaping his plate with second
helpings. After the last plate was removed,
he stuck a toothpick in his mouth, stood, and
gathered his cigarettes and lighter from the
table. He was making his way to the del Toro
farmhouse up the road, he announced, to call
both our mother and his secretary.

"Let's see if things are still holding on the home
front," he said, before heading out the lodge's
front door.

So, for some time, I sat alone in the gloaming of

the lodge living room, the dying fire in the grate occasionally sparking when a log fell apart. A loud crack from the fire finally woke up Uncle Augustin.

"Where is everyone?"

"Papá left. He couldn't sit still."

"Aaah. He's gone hunting."

"I will be loyal to my wife," I hissed. "I will marry for love. Forever."

The fierceness with which I said this surprised us both, and Uncle Augustin looked over at me, quickly, and then just as quickly glanced away. He drained his brandy.

"The hungers of the heart are not polite or predictable," he said. "They have a force of their own. You'll understand one day. When you are older."

"Why didn't you marry, Uncle Augustin? Have you never been in love?"

"My God, where is this coming from?"

"Well? Have you?"

"Yes. But the woman I love is taken."

Uncle Augustin stood up from the couch. "Now good night, nephew. No more. I'm tired and off to bed. You should do the same. Tomorrow is another day of hard fishing."

We both stepped to the back of the shed. Uncle slipped into his chamber, without another word, and I quietly opened the door to my room. The light that came in from the hall fell across Juan's cot. He was tangled in the sheets, facing the wall, one leg out of the cover, his underwear riding halfway down his backside. Juan's steady breathing produced a boyish snore, and his curly hair was squashed against the pillow, but the hall light caught his tangled blond highlights, and there seemed to be a kind of luminous ring hovering lightly around my brother's head.

I eased shut the door. I was still too restless to sleep and went outside for fresh air and a smoke. The night was river moist and filled with the sharp smell of sap and the smoldering wisps of the dying oak embers rising from the cottage chimney. The air sang with the sounds of chanting crickets, bullfrogs, and strange underbrush snuffles, while the large yellow flowers of the persimmon tree were eerily aglow in the moonlight.

Muffled voices came from the dirt path that led up from the village.

"You are delightful, my dear."

A young woman giggled.

I called out. "Papá? Is that you?"

My father ambled forward, into the light, like a bear coming out of the woods to tear open the garbage bins behind a restaurant. "José, come. Meet my friend Sabrina."

Papá waved vaguely toward a willowy figure standing off in the dark woods.

"Come. Let's all go for a ride. I have to take Sabrina back."

• • •

The Hispano-Suiza took off with a drunken lurch, through the woods and along the river. I turned to look at the woman in the back seat. She was sitting in the far corner, staring mesmerized out the window, like driving in a fine car was a rare treat.

She was in her late twenties, I guessed, her gauntness magnified by a too-large and rather old-fashioned blue evening dress that, even through the dark, revealed the luminous glow of white skin and pert breasts. Her hair was her best feature, long and silky, and I suddenly imagined her wrapping it around my father's feet—an image, involving my father, that both revolted me and made my pulse race.

She stared boldly back and said, "Do you like what you see?"

I blushed and looked away. My father laughed.

Papá drove us to a dreary two-story house in Ribadesella, its bay window blacked out by brown-velvet curtains; yellow light still shone through the curtain folds not quite pulled tight. "Run along now, Sabrina," Papá said. "Tell Madame Christine to give you a proper dinner and put it on my bill. We'll be in shortly."

The young woman ran up the stairs and knocked twice on the black door. It opened, Sabrina slipped inside, and it quickly shut again. Papá pulled a Dominican cigar from a leather case tucked in his inside pocket, and lit it with a flurry of puffs and leaping flames. "Madame Christine doesn't allow cigars to be smoked inside," he drawled. "She says they make the curtains smell. Such nonsense. You'll see. The women inside smoke like fiends."

"What are we doing here, Papá?"

"Do you really not know, *hijo*?"

I blushed and looked down. "*Sí. Lo sé.*"

The end of his cigar glowed orange in the dark. "Josésito, please do not be embarrassed by the sensual pleasures of life. It's such a waste of time—and so unproductive."

"I want to be a good person. A just and righteous person."

Father waved his cigar in the air, instantly reducing my remark to nothing.

"José, listen to me. There will be times in life when, as a man, you will be overwhelmed by your responsibilities. They will weigh on you, crush you if you are not careful, and when such pressures come barreling down, you'll be fighting just to survive. The real responsibility for a man in such moments is beyond family and what polite society considers right and wrong—it is much more fundamental. At such times, it is simply about finding your inner strength so you can carry on the fight. It's a question of survival. Do you understand me, José?"

"I think so, Papá."

"Good. Well, sex brings me back to my center, brings out the best in me as a man, and it gives me the inner strength I need to carry on another day. *Comprendes*, *hijo*?"

"*Sí*, *Papá*. I think so."

"*Bueno*."

Papá threw his half-smoked cigar on the ground and draped his arm around my shoulder. "Come then, *hijo*. All this talk—it has whetted my appetite. Let us be friends and taste what is on offer at Madame Christine's tonight."

The house was, as my father promised, filled with the milky haze of cigarette smoke, but still, underneath it all, I smelled fried onions, wilting gardenias, and a rotting crab-shell musk that I later realized was spent lust.

Madame Christine emerged through the front corridor's haze, covered in wrinkles and clouded diamonds and an ancient, chin-to-ankle black-lace dress. The wan maid stood flat against the wall, to let Madame Christine pass, and the ancient Frenchwoman hobbled unsteadily but determinedly toward us, the narrow hallway filling with the clack of her metal-tipped ebony cane smacking on the herringbone floor between us.

"Señor Álvarez," she croaked. "Welcome back."

"Good to be here, as always, Madame Christine. I brought my oldest son."

Madame Christine, suffering from emphysema

and gasping for air, stroked my cheek with her arthritic knuckles. Her hands were monstrously swollen and veined, but, despite her immense age, she worked hard at maintaining a feminine aura through a coquettish amount of perfume, lace, and dyed-auburn hair packed into a matted cocoon atop her head.

"Your son is so handsome, Don Jesús. So handsome. The girls will eat him up."

"He is. And a very fine fisherman to boot."

"A gentleman—just like his father. Tonight, on his initial voyage into our world, we shall let José María pick first. Don't you agree, Don Jesús?"

"I do. Excellent idea."

Papá rested his hand above my elbow, almost like he was guiding a first date to a romantic corner table in a restaurant, and led me through the oak hall door to our right. We were in the main room of what was probably the original shop and where the brown curtains against the windows were drawn.

Half a dozen women of various sizes and ages were sitting in brocade chairs and lion-footed love seats. There was an immensely fleshy woman in the corner, with bulging bags of cottage-cheese skin erupting from her slip. She had a dark mole that sat in bas-relief against the whiteness of her blue-veined breasts. There were three young and pretty women of identical delicate sizes and height sitting on a heavily stained couch, like three muses in matching pink, baby-blue, and lavender panties and slips. They shared a common aura, but for their coloring— one was a fair-skinned blonde, of the dyed sort; the other a brunette with boyish freckles; the third had such dark and shiny skin, she looked like a black olive sitting in oil.

A flat-chested girl with thick glasses and a startled look sat at the far side of the room and smiled eagerly at me, while a chain-smoking older woman with red hair, lighting one butt off the other, never looked up from her game of solitaire at the card table pushed against the wall. Sabrina came through a curtain, drifted aimlessly into the salon while ferreting between her teeth with a toothpick. She had changed into a sherbet-colored slip—the house uniform, apparently— and plopped herself down on the other side of the card table, to watch the old whore's solitaire.

My eyes drifted back to the black woman, who puffed a cigarette while restlessly jiggling a Moroccan slipper from her archly extended foot. She stared out into space, her pensive expression and knitted brows suggesting she was anywhere but there. But maybe that was just a ruse and she was intently aware of my interest, because she suddenly flicked her ironed black hair back across her shoulder and scratched her nipple, which, at that moment, was pertly poking through the lavender slip that had one spaghetti strand seductively sliding down the shoulder.

This touching of herself—it instantly made my pants tighten. I was confused and flustered by all the emotions inside of me—the trembling, the shame and disgust, the sweaty-palm excitement, the weirdness of having such intimate thoughts in my father's presence, the overwhelming and oddly stirring sensation that all my nerve endings were alive and firing at once.

I looked down at the floor, my face red with shame.

"Excellent choice," Papá said. "She's a fire-cracker."

"Carlotta," said Madame Christine. "Take the young man to the green room. He already has a tent pole."

Carlotta went down the basement stairs first, reaching back with one hand to hold my forefinger and lead me into the cellar. Her lingerie made a wet and slippery sound as we descended the stairs.

The wall lamps in the musty basement were draped with red scarves, casting a blood-orange hue over us. Carlotta opened a small door, and I ducked under its low frame and entered the windowless room painted olive green. I had a vague sense there was a lamp in the corner, and a sink and mirror, with towels for washing, plus bottles of massage oil, medicinal ointments, and condom foils, neatly stacked on the mirror shelf.

I am also sure there were a couple of wall hooks and a green-painted stool for undressing. But the only thing I really saw was the huge bed, high as a throne. It had a wrought-iron headboard, from which two sets of medieval-looking handcuffs dangled.

"I don't know if I can do this," I stuttered. "It's too much."

Carlotta saw what I was staring at, smiled, and lightly ran her fingers through my hair. "Oh, sweet boy, don't mind the restraints. They're not for you." She unhooked the handcuffs and shoved them into the side table's drawer. "You're a virile young man. You don't need such activities to get you aroused. For you, simple touch should do the trick."

I could smell her cocoa-butter skin cream. She had me perch at the edge of the bed, but I couldn't relax and sat upright and stiff as she crouched down at my feet, taking off my shoes and socks.

"Go on. Close your eyes."

I reluctantly did as she said, felt her brown fingers unbutton my shirt and slide it off my back. There was something soothing about being undressed like that. Her warm palm gently pressed against my chest, forcing my torso to drop back slowly to the bed, while my feet remained firmly planted on the floor.

I relaxed a bit, as her fingers expertly undid my

belt, unbuttoned my fly. I felt her reach inside, probing my underwear, her fingers cupping the tip of my cock. I groaned, came immediately.

I sat bolt upright and stuttered profuse apologies. Carlotta laughed and pushed me back to the bed again. "Don't be silly, *guapo*. That's normal with young men. It's good to get the eagerness out of the way. Now, we'll just give you a little rest and start again. Madame Christine told me to give you the royal treatment."

My eyes were tightly closed—with self-loathing and an unbearable sadness. I silently recited the Lord's Prayer. I heard running water. My pants were removed and then I felt a warm cloth wiping my midriff of semen, and my cock, that cursed thing, it was again standing to attention.

Juan made huge strides as a fisherman that week, the simple act of catching fish that first day boosting his confidence. From that moment on, he followed hard in my footsteps, fishing with single-minded purpose, eager for his skills to catch up to those of his brother, uncle, and father. One afternoon, with the help of God and Felipe, Juanito landed a twelve-kilo fish. News spread, and Papá came down to our beat at the end of the day to closely observe Juan fishing on the far bank. He saw instantly that Juan was a true Álvarez—no longer slapping the water like an impatient boy, but precisely bringing his rod back with that unique mix of strength and gentleness, before sending his line straight across the river with a serious and manly intent. He stood and watched my brother and smoked a cigar.

"Juanito," Papá drawled at dinner, "you'll fish with me tomorrow."

"That's all right, Papá," I interjected. "Juan can stay on my beat."

"That was not a request. It was a father's command."

Juan was sitting to the right of Papá, and his hand suddenly shot out, snatching the piece of roast lamb Papá was trying to spear for his own plate.

"Aren't you worried I will snatch all the fish from right under your nose?"

We all laughed, Papá loudest of all. He gently rapped the back of my brother's head, his eyes filled with that special love and affection Juan evoked in all of us. But Papá's face stiffened when Juan said, *"Gracias, Papá,* but I will just get in your way. I'll keep fishing with José María and Felipe. He's incredible, our ghillie. I am learning so much."

Father reached out for more lamb.

"As you wish, Juan. Do as you like. I don't care."

"Gracias, Papá. I will."

The next day, rotated back up to the highest beat of the river, we were visited by unseasonably warm weather. Smells of lavender, rosemary, and ripening black cherries fluttered like ribbons in the air. Hatches came out, dotted the river. All day we saw natural rises as irritated salmon took down the annoying flies buzzing on the current's surface. By late afternoon, we couldn't beach any more fish; the canvas bags were so full with salmon they were in danger of tearing apart at the seams.

"The heat," Felipe said. "It's not good for the fish. We should head back a little early and get them on ice. Do you agree?"

"I do." I reeled in my line. "Let's go."

The horses were excited to be going home, to the bag of oats that they knew would be their reward at Sheep's Corral, and they trotted down the goat's path at a hard clop, every now and then breaking into a half gallop.

As we came around a bend in the river, Juan roared out in pain and slapped his neck hard, involuntarily digging his heels into his mare. She bolted and shot past my horse. The excited other horses, not wanting to miss out on the oats, began to gallop after Juan's hard-charging mare.

"Hold your horse! Hold your horse!" Felipe yelled.

Juan swore and pulled hard on the reins. The mare's head swiveled this way and that, and then she came up short, snorting furiously and whinnying. In one fluid motion, Juan jumped off, tethered her to a willow branch, and yanked off his shirt. A crushed bee fell from its folds.

"Shit on the milk!"

Juan turned to show us the angry red boil on his neck. "What does it look like? It's killing me!"

"Quick! Jump in the river!" Felipe said. "The cold water will help with the swelling."

Juan unbuckled his pants, yanked down his underwear, and hopped around on one foot, cursing as he pulled one boot and sock, and then the other, in one smooth motion pulling the entire tangle of corduroy pants, underwear, and socks from under him. His neck was a leathery column of sun brown and angry red that haloed out around his shoulders, before giving way to a strong but hairless torso white as sheep's cheese. Juan turned and ran full force off the riverbank, landing atop the water's surface in a loud belly flop, his moonlike butt cheeks last to disappear under the surface.

Felipe and I were roaring with laughter at his belly flop when Juan's head finally came up to the surface, his sigh and face the picture of relief. "You assholes," he yelled from the river, splashing water at us, even though we were too far away to get wet. "Come here if you dare!"

Felipe and I exchanged glances and, without another word, stripped naked and similarly ran hard off the river's bank. For the next half hour we horsed around, swam a little out into the current, and then drifted off into the rocky shallows, again talking about the fish we had caught that day. A sheer wall of black rock rose on the far side of the pool, pocked with the odd cliff-clinging sapling.

High up, in the top ledge of forest overlooking the pool, a tiny chapel was catching the day's late light. The plaster shell was painted a faded pink. A naïve painting of a friar, his hands clasped in prayer, stood at its center, behind the simple wooden crucifix. Someone had recently lit candles and left a jam jar filled with lemon-yellow wildflowers.

We were in the Dead Priest's Pool, I suddenly realized.

The sun was low, its slanting rays pouring over the riverbank bushes, and it left the pool partially in a golden light of swirling motes, partially in a cool, wine-bottle-green shadow. I looked downriver at my brother and Felipe, who were sitting on rocks in the sun and dangling their legs in the water. Felipe suddenly waded to the riverbank, plucked some broad and furry leaves from an unassuming bush; he carefully split the leaves down their center vein and they instantly oozed sap. He waded back to my brother, talking to him in a low voice. Juan looked wary, but did as he was told, lifting the hair off the back of his neck and bending forward, so Felipe could rub the soothing leaf ooze onto his bee sting.

I stood still as the river lapped my midriff.

I was mesmerized by the care in Felipe's gesture, as he administered the balm; at the submissive bend of Juan's exposed neck, as he pushed away his hair and offered up his bee sting; at the luminous way the two of them were cast in the glow of the day's fading light; at the way the pool beside them looked at that moment, deep and green and full of mysterious life. I drank the scene in, like a man parched, and it felt like God himself had just entered me, had come into my life, and I silently prayed that I could stay in this moment forever and ever, amen. I loved my brother beyond all else, loved him far more than my own parents. He was the only real friend and ally I had in this world.

Our week fishing was coming to an end when Felipe and I made our way at 7:00 a.m. to the Bridge Pool in Omedina, the river's most famous stretch of water. More fish were caught from this one pool than any other part of the Sella.

Juan was missing, having finally given in to the pressure and joined Papá on his beat, and his absence left a hole in our day. But I ignored that anxious knot of loss sitting in my stomach and focused instead on the task at hand: pulling fish out of the Bridge Pool. A few villagers stood on the bridge overhead, looking down at me as I made the first few casts, getting line out with a tufted San Martin. The fly finally landed a centimeter off the limestone cliff on the far side of the pool, just where I wanted it, and a salmon instantly rose to the bait.

On almost every cast, a salmon went after the fly or came on to the line. By 11:00 a.m., the bridge was filled with a few hundred excited locals from as far away as Beleño and Panes, all chattering about that Álvarez boy down below, who all week long was breaking record after record on the Sella River. At one point, the noise grew so loud, Felipe had to climb the riverbank to have a word with the two Guardia Civil officers, one of whom was his cousin. The officers hushed the crowd and told them not to spook the fish or disturb the gifted young Señor Álvarez fishing down below.

Felipe and I, focused on beaching the next fish, never fully registered the two black sedans pulling up on the far side of the bridge and disgorging four men in black leather coats. One of them returned to his car and spoke into a radio. Then a motorcade of BMW motorbikes and army trucks, surrounding a bulletproof Cadillac with tinted windows, rumbled into town and stopped just short of the stone wall. I was playing the small salmon in the gravelly shallows when El Caudillo emerged from the back of the Cadillac and a roar went up from the crowd.

Felipe and I, startled by the noise, looked

up. Generalísimo Francisco Franco, the man who had slaughtered his opponents during the Spanish Civil War and turned our country into a fascist dictatorship, was looking down at us in a billowing rain slicker and porkpie hat, his face hidden by large sunglasses.

My first thought—*He's the shape of a Bosc pear!*—was an utterance that, had I spoken it aloud, could very well have had me thrown in prison.

Several men and women were trying to kiss Franco's hand, while the mayors of nearby towns pushed themselves forward and bowed and scraped and uttered excessive and repeated welcomes in such flowery language that even their wives blushed. Franco pretended to listen to the local dignitaries, but kept glancing over the bridge in our direction, until his chief of staff, sensing Franco's growing impatience and anger, extracted his boss from the crowd.

The captain of the Moorish Guard, his chest full of ribbons, was first to climb over the stile. He was followed by military officers, the minister of agriculture and fisheries, and Franco's chief of staff. Sergeants were ready to catch the diminutive Franco as the great man himself came next over the stile. A handful of secret police followed, as did an eighteen-year-old cadet who did nothing but carry around the "Hand of Saint Teresa of Avila," a relic that Franco had seized during the Civil War and that he now took with him wherever he went, a talisman to ward off evil and to assert God's divine command that he rule all Spain.

Felipe and I stood open-mouthed as Franco's train of officialdom followed the goat trail down through azaleas and Spanish gold broom. I had lost the fish; my fly line was left dead and drifting in the river. When Franco and his men finally landed with a thud on the gravel bank, their suits were dusted with orange pollen.

Felipe and I repeatedly dipped our heads, our tongues frozen.

"You have done well this morning, boys," Franco said. "El Caudillo is impressed by your fishing skills. Whom am I speaking to?"

I gave him my name.

"Aaaah, yes. I have heard of you already. Your reputation as a fisherman precedes you. I know your father, Don Jesús, and of course the family's Banco Álvarez in San Sebastián."

I again lowered my head.

"It is the only bank in San Sebastián not owned by Basques," Franco said to the hills. He smiled slightly, from behind the sunglasses. "Your family is providing the nation a great service." He turned toward Felipe and barked, "You are Ignacio del Toro's grandson, are you not?"

Felipe was clutching his hat and visibly trembling, while staring resolutely at the ground.

"*Sí,, Generalísimo,*" he whispered, not daring to look up. "Felipe del Toro."

"Look up, boy," Franco said before adding, a little more gently, "You have an honest Spanish face."

Franco turned back in my direction. "You've had some excellent fishing this week. I was supposed to have fished the Sella. But you know that, don't you?"

"*Sí, Caudillo.*"

He looked longingly at the river. "The duties of state, you know . . ."

I glanced at the gravel underfoot, looked contrite.

"This is my favorite pool on the Sella," he continued. "They usually take there, in the current against the far rock wall. Is that not so?"

"Yes, El Caudillo."

"Young man, do me a favor. Tell your father I know what he is up to—booking the river after me." Franco chuckled in a way that sounded like a dry cough. "I am amused by your father's antics, both on the river and in business. He's always entertaining—and, we concede, very clever."

I was not sure how I should respond, nor what the true meaning of these remarks was. Franco looked at his watch. "Well, I have to be off. I have a meeting in Oviedo. But first, José María, humor an old man. Show me what the river has yielded today. There are some monsters here on the riverbank, no?"

I led Franco and his procession downriver, to where Felipe had bled the fish and laid them out in the moist grass under the trees. I had caught nine salmon that morning, the largest of which was eleven kilos, but none smaller than five kilos. El Caudillo slowly walked the entire length of fish with his hands behind his back, like he was inspecting his troops on the boulevards of Madrid.

"*Sin novedades en el Alcázar, mi General*," he said.

There was a gasp. We all knew that line, had learned it in school, perhaps the most famous uttering of the Civil War. It was spoken when Franco's battle-hardened African Legion marched into Toledo in the fall of 1936, to rescue the Nationalists and Falangists holed up in the Alcázar castle and surrounded by Republican soldiers. The African Legion marched into the city singing their anthem, *El novio de la muerte*, "The Bridegroom of Death," their unified voices unsettling the Republicans' ragtag army of laborers armed with old shotguns and pistols.

That day Franco's troops slaughtered everyone they saw: whole families, even entire apartment buildings of people, were left in dead heaps on the cobblestone lanes, rivers of their blood running through the gutters. Even the wounded

Republicans were dispatched by lightly tossing a few hand grenades into the local hospital. It was a massacre.

The next day, the African Legion's General Varela laconically reported back to Franco, "All quiet in the Alcázar, my General."

This was the famous line that Franco repeated to me that morning, when he saw my salmon laid out on the riverbank, like bodies in a morgue. I didn't know what to say. He took off his hat, wiped the sweat from its band with a linen handkerchief, and replaced it.

He smiled dryly, and absentmindedly patted my cheek.

"*Bueno*. It was a pleasure meeting you, José. You are a fine young Spaniard. But I must go now." Franco formally shook my hand, and said, in the most officious and florid language, "Please extend my regards to your father, Don Jesús, and tell him the nation is grateful for the banking services he is providing our modern state."

Felipe and I again bowed repeatedly. The old man's rain slicker flapped around his body like a loose wrapper, as he got ready to scrabble back up the goat path to the stile. But, as he turned, he also said, clear enough for everyone to hear, "Pack up El Caudillo's fish. We will eat the *salmón* tonight at the Automobile Club banquet."

It was said, I suspect, for the benefit of the villagers staring down from the bridge, a clear reminder of who ruled Spain—even the fish in the rivers belonged to El Caudillo, particularly when he himself should have been fishing the beat. But I suspected it was also a public warning to my father and me: Using our skills and smarts to bring in great catches was tolerated only to a point. Cross Franco's invisible line—and there would be a price to pay.

The Moorish regiment above began clearing a path for Franco, as the drivers ran back to their cars and fired up engines. Franco and his cabinet scrambled up the goat path, as the two officers left on the river took out long knives and cut down a tree branch and began stripping it. They strung all the fish on the bald pole, hoisted the sixty kilos of swaying salmon to their shoulders, and then made their grunting way up the hill and over the stile to the lone military truck waiting to take them and the fish to Oviedo.

When I got back to the lodge and feverishly gave my father a full account of what happened, he listened intently and then dryly said, "*Relájate, José*. Let's eat. Tomorrow we return to San Sebastián—and your mother."

I understood, in a way, what he meant. *Let's keep Franco in perspective,* he was saying. Mother was a great force—and potentially more unpredictable and dangerous than our nation's head of state.

SIX

The most honest conversation I ever had with my mother took place when I was eighteen, on a dismal June day, when we were walking home from church along San Sebastián's Paseo de la Concha.

Mamá had just spent an inordinately long time in the confessional in the back of the cathedral. Afterward, she bent her knees and bowed her head, whispering a seemingly endless string of penance into the ebony rosary clutched in her hands.

She finally came out of the dark, into the gray light of the day, and we began walking home together. I glanced in her direction, not sure what I should do. The penance and prayers did not seem to help her at all that day. She was wrapped up tight in her black shawl and dark thoughts, pulling at the shawl's tasseled ends like a madwoman in an insane asylum might pull at her hair.

"Why did you spend so long in the confessional?"

Mother was startled by the sound of my voice. "Did I? I suppose it's because I have so many sins to atone for."

"You mean your drinking."

She flinched.

"I don't regret the drinking. I do regret the decisions I make while I am drinking—and how I hurt you and your brother at such times."

"Please, I beg you again, stop drinking. It doesn't help—just makes your sadness worse. Please. All Juan and I want is for you to be happy."

Mamá stopped dead still. She was fighting back tears, trying to hold herself together. She smiled and placed her hand on my cheek.

"My beautiful boy. My special son. It's not quite as easy as it sounds. Being happy."

"I am not special. Stop saying I am special."

"You are to me."

"Why don't you leave Papá? *Es una auténtica locura.* All you do is torture each other."

"Aaah," she said, turning from me and starting to walk again. "Your father is my strongest drink."

She sensed my increasing fury at her evasive responses, however, and after a while she said, "Weakness, José, is one of the greatest sins. I pray for God's strength to enter me and make me whole. But even my prayers are weak—and that's the most terrible sin of all. God will punish me for that one day."

At the time, I didn't know what she was talking about.

One afternoon, a month later, a phone rang at the front of Banco Álvarez's counting hall, shattering the silence that filled every corner of the cavernous room. Señor Domingo, the bank's cigarillo-thin chief accountant, picked up the phone and talked briefly to whomever was at the other end, then stood up from his desk and began walking the hall, his hands clasped behind his back.

Domingo was, unusually for men of the accounting profession, as fashionable and high-stepping as a coiffed poodle out on a ramble along the port, and he was dressed that day in a blue serge three-piece suit with a gold pocket watch and fob stretched across his flank. He made his unhurried way in between the desks crammed with his staff of thirty-two accountants. They all had their heads down over eight-column ledgers and were intently scratching away at numbers, hoping he wouldn't stop and grill them. But Domingo headed straight to the back of the room and stopped only once he reached my desk. It was the summer before I started university in Salamanca and I was working as an apprentice at the family bank.

"*Señor Álvarez Junior.* Have you finished?"

"Almost, *Señor Domingo*. It's the last file."

He looked over my shoulder as I matched pink buy-and-sell order sheets from the Bolsa de Madrid with the sums deducted or deposited from clients' accounts. "Give it to me," he said. "I will finish up. Your father's secretary just called. He wants you in his office."

Papá's corner suite, on the upper floor, smelled of roasted coffee, Ducados, and the whisky trolley that rolled by every day at 4:30 p.m. He sat beetle-browed behind his desk, under the oil painting of my great-grandfather, pensively smoking a cigar as he tipped back and forth in his chair. Uncle Augustin smiled warmly over his bifocals when I entered the office suite, and asked me when I was going trout fishing with my friend and neighbor, Manuel.

Alfonso Gorrindo Campo, the bank's lawyer and my father's most valued advisor, sat in the other leather armchair. Gorrindo was a big and burly Basque with a handlebar mustache and a booming laugh. When my brother and I were young, he always kept a handful of boiled sweets in his pocket to slip us when our parents weren't looking.

"*Hola, chico malo*," he said.

"*Hola, Tío*," I replied, using the affectionate term for uncle.

"How is Carmen?"

"We are no longer together. She said I don't talk enough. She found a new *novio* that she prefers."

"Aaah. The painful affairs of the heart. Well, good riddance, I say. Go unencumbered to Salamanca and roam the streets. The rest will come in time."

Papá buzzed his secretary to "send him in." When I looked at him quizzically, he said, "Sit. This, too, is part of your education. We are getting paid a visit."

The bank's head porter stood timidly in the

129

doorway. Father gestured he should take a seat and asked him warmly about his family. "Now, tell us what is troubling you, old friend. I can tell you are upset."

The elderly porter recalled, with a quavering voice, how a leading member of the underground Basque separatist organization, ETA, had approached him in the street, demanding he pass a message on to my father. He said the man's name. Papá knew him. They had been in elementary school together.

"He insisted it was important the Álvarez family understood the changing circumstances of the Basque nation," our head porter said. "That while you and your family were not Basques, you owned one of the most important commercial banks in the entire Basque nation, and ETA thought it was appropriate, as a guest in their country, you pay a tax to their organization . . ."

"*Entonces*," Father said, stubbing out his cigar. "We are at the crux of the matter."

The elderly porter slid a quivering piece of paper across Papá's desk. ETA's conditions were precisely outlined: they wanted a dozen fictional "men" put on the bank's payroll, each paid twenty thousand pesetas a month.

"Think of the boys. Your boys!"

My parents' drunken yelling pierced the walls of their bedroom.

"*Mujer*! Stay out of things you don't understand! If I pay off ETA and Franco finds out, we are finished. And if I refuse to make the payments, ETA will cause a strike or worse . . ."

"It's unconscionable. Always that bank before your own family!"

I winced at the sound of the slap and her sudden cry.

"How dare you say I neglect you and the boys! Everything I do is for you and our sons! The money that pays for all your goddamn charity work comes from that bank. Don't give yourself such pious airs, woman."

My brother and I had witnessed such wine-fueled brawls many times before, but there was something different in the air that night, and when Juan came down from his bedroom next to theirs, he was pale and trembling and biting his cuticles.

"This is a bad one. I think he just hit her."

"Yes. They're more drunk than usual."

Juan stood shivering by my side, stripped of his usual bravado. I put a hand on his shoulder.

"If they come down here, I will distract them. Take yourself away. Go see Manuel next door and tell him I sent you—to sleep at his house tonight."

My brother was quiet for some time and then said, "When he hits me, it hurts and then it is over. When she lashes out, the sting in her words lasts for weeks."

The upstairs door suddenly slammed open, and my father came pounding down the central staircase. Mother came flying out after him, still in the sparkly evening gown she had worn to the annual Knights of Malta dinner. She leaned unsteadily against the upstairs banister, a glass of wine clutched in her hand.

"Go," she hissed down at my father. "Go to your whores."

Her neck and chest were flushed and mottled, like she had a fever working through her system, and a nasty red mark, where he had slapped her, was starting to emerge to the right of her cheek.

My father stopped short when he saw my brother and me standing in the shadows of the foyer. "It's nothing," he said thickly. "Your mother and I are just having a talk."

Mother laughed incredulously, said something cutting, and Papá turned his attention back to the upper landing. But our presence somehow changed something inside of him, turned down the rage, because now he spoke to her in a world-weary tone.

"For all your charity works, Isabel, you have a cold heart. No one blames me for seeking warmth elsewhere."

It was like he had hit her again. Mamá burst into tears and fled back to her room, as Papá left the house. Juan and I stared at each other, wondering if Mother would come down to try and win us over to her side, as she often did when she drank. But that night, much to our relief, she drank alone in her room.

I slept badly and got up early. I went directly to Conchata in the kitchen, grabbed coffee, and sat by her, as she moved about the counters. She was reassuringly warm and kind as always: flour dusted and singing under her breath as she baked an onion pie for lunch. Conchata stopped her bustling for a moment, stroked my face with her chubby hand, and said, *"Pobrecita"*—poor little thing.

I heard the click of the front door and turned to look down the corridor that led from the back kitchen to the front foyer. Papá was swaying uncertainly under the front lobby's chandelier. His tie was loose and untied around his neck, and great sweat stains fanned out from his armpits. Papá looked so bewildered, I momentarily felt sorry for him, and went out to help, just as Jorge similarly emerged from his room to assist his master.

"Come, Papá," I said gently. "I'll help you to bed."

"You should have come with me, Josésito. I missed you."

Papá was slurring his words so badly I almost couldn't understand what he was saying. Jorge took Papá's other arm and together we moved toward the stairs in an effort to get him up to his bedroom. Papá, draped over us, engulfed us in his sour smell of sex and alcohol. We laboriously put a foot on the lowest step, but there was movement in the air above us and we looked up.

Mother was standing at the top of the stairs in her blue-silk bathrobe. She looked down at us and spoke in a cold and imperious voice, almost sober sounding despite the fact she, too, had been drinking through the night.

"I hope you had a lovely evening. Just one question, *marido*. Are you sure Juan is your son?" She did not wait for the effect of her remark, but turned and unsteadily walked back to her room.

My father held on to the banister. He could not move. But his face said it all.

Enough of this *mierda*, I thought. I let go of Papá's arm and climbed the stairs to pack my bag, determined to leave for Galicia that very morning. But as I was angrily pressing socks and underwear and rain gear into a duffel bag, Juanito, still in his pajamas, slipped into my room and sat on the edge of my bed. Just one look told me what I had most feared—he had heard everything through his bedroom door.

"Where are you going?" he asked.

"Fishing. With Manuel."

"Can I come?"

"No."

Juan lowered his head, looked at his hands.

134

"You're going to leave me alone with them. Please. Let me come fishing with you. I won't bother you." The sadness in his voice was unbearable. I stopped packing, went over, and put my arm around his shoulder, pressed my temple against the side of his head.

"Juanito, look, I love you. But right now I have to leave and be alone and get away from anything that reminds me of all this. I can't breathe. I need to be alone."

"And what will become of me?"

"I don't know. I'm sorry. Stay in your room or go be with your own friends. That's your choice. I am leaving."

He turned away from me and for a few moments stared out the window.

Then he got up and walked from my room.

"Have fun," he said on his way out my door.

My best friend, Manuel, and I headed west in his mother's Fiat 500 Topolino, the tiny car crammed with our fly rods and nets and silver-tinseled sea-trout flies. We camped in a farmer's field along the River Eume. For those ten blissful days, I forgot about everything going on back in San Sebastián. We cooked sausages and toasted bread around the campfire in the predawn; we stood on the gravelly riverbed, as the sun burned off the mist, working the river pots with our flies; and during the heat of the day, we napped in the stifling, fly-filled tent, resting up for the next high tide and the sounds of night pouring into the valley, when our second shift of fishing took place.

The moon was already visible, fizzy and bright. We followed the sound of gurgling water down the path, our feet landing on the crunching gravel bed. Swarms of gray bats dropped from the tree branches across the river and soared out into the night, greedily gulping down mosquitoes and gnats. In the water near our feet—black as coffee but laced with silver ripples as the full moon caught the edges of the current—I could just hear little sucking sounds, plops, and splashes. There, under the moon, we cast with short lines for the sea trout—and all was good with the world.

I had a dream the night before we returned to San Sebastián. My brother and I were sitting in the living room of the family house, watching our parents drink and attack each other. Jorge came into the room holding a silver tray heaped with fish bones. "It's not what they say," he whispered in my ear. "The truth is the silence that hangs like tombs between the words."

Manuel and I drove back to San Sebastián after we caught a record 712 sea trout. We sold them, along the way, to the best restaurants on the coast, ending our fishing holiday with all our expenses paid and a 13,700-peseta profit. News of our catch spread, and a newspaper photographer took a photo of us as we sold the last three-dozen fish to the popular seaside restaurant Salinas. The next day, the afternoon paper in Santiago de Compostela came out with a photo of Manuel and me, unloading from the Topolino our last box bulging with fish.

When we pulled into the family house, Guardia Civil sentinels with carbines stood duty at the gates of our driveway, leaning through the car window to ascertain who we were. We handed them our papers and they waved us in.

So that's that, I thought. Papá has refused to pay off ETA and even informed the authorities. Manuel, sensing my upset, clapped me on the back. "Don't let them get you down, José," he said. But then Manuel quickly backed out of our gates and pulled into his driveway next door, almost like he couldn't get away fast enough from the tension emanating from our house.

I stood for a few moments in our hall foyer, reacclimatizing myself to the cold and familiar silence—and the sickening feeling that was once again filling my stomach. The hall smelled of beeswax and roasting *dorada*.

Jorge came out of his room off the central hall.

"*Hola, José María.* Welcome home. Was the fishing good?"

"Yes. Very good. Are they here?"

He took my fishing gear. "In the parlor." He knew what I was thinking and smiled kindly. "All is calm at sea. Dinner will be ready in twenty minutes."

Papá was smoking in his wingback near the fireplace, reading *El País*. Every now and then his hand reached out from behind the paper, to lift a tumbler of scotch. Mother sat across from him, erect on the couch, her legs folded to the side. She had her head down over her embroidery, her hand rhythmically weaving the blue-silk thread through the linen held taut by the wooden frame.

She wore, as usual, her hair in a tight black bun at the back of her head. A glass of carbonated soda, for her digestion, stood next to her on the coffee table. I walked warily into the room, gauging the mood, but sensed instantly that Mamá was back to her kind and sober self. She looked the most tranquil I had seen her in a long time.

Mother had a long neck like a flamenco dancer, her skin as pale and glowing as a side of turbot. Her aristocratic nose pointed severely down at the work in hand, as if her body was reminding her that in such humble work God would be found. She looked up from her embroidery—and smiled. I went over and kissed her on the cheek and sat next to her. She reached out and patted my hand.

"*Hola, José.* Welcome home. You look so handsome and brown."

Papá lowered his newspaper. "*Hola, hijo.* How many?"

138

"Seven hundred and twelve."

"Incredible. The Prince of Asturias has struck again. You can coax the fish right out of the water. Like Saint Peter himself."

"You are our special child."

"I'm not that special, Mother. I wish you would stop saying that. It is Juan who is different and special."

My mother froze stiff for a moment and then returned to her stitching. There was an electronic hum coming from across the room and I looked over. My parents had recently purchased a modern American refrigerator, a new and coveted import to Spain, and while I was away they had installed the white-enameled GE device in the living room, so visitors to our house could see how fashionable we were.

Outside the bay windows, across our crescent driveway, San Sebastián's scalloped bay was lapping against the caramel sand. Maids and mothers and boisterous children passed through the frame of the window as they promenaded along the seawall, a strong breeze fluttering their hats and dresses.

Juan, normally out in the middle of all that sand and summer activity, was stuck upstairs in his room doing his homework. He was behind in math at school, and our English governess was tutoring him over the summer. I could hear his chair scraping across the wooden floor overhead, as he finally finished his assignment for the day. He came thumping down the stairs in a foul mood. "So, how's the 'golden one'?" he sneered.

"Pretty well, thank you. Smart enough to know it's better to do your work in school than spend the summer indoors at a desk." Juan gave me a withering look and then sat down in a corner armchair. He picked up *Biggles' Second Case*, one of his adventure books about a British flying ace. His foot jiggled impatiently as we waited. After what seemed forever, but was probably only a few minutes, Jorge announced the Sunday dinner was ready to be served.

A porcelain soup tureen sent a fragrant steam of leeks up into the air of the dining room. Jorge, now wearing white gloves, silently moved around the table as he served us. He stood quietly next to Mother with a bottle of Albariño in his gloved hand, a quizzical expression on his face.

"Go on," Papá said. "Have one. I hate drinking alone."

"Yes. I think I will. Thank you, Jorge."

Jorge poured my mother her first drink of the day, and my brother jiggled his legs under the table like he was a combustion engine ready to explode. There was a cold and leaden feeling to that meal, as the clock on the mantelpiece slowly ticked the minutes. Juan and I both kept our heads down, pushing the sea bream back and forth across our plates, intent on not provoking our parents, who were, as the meal progressed, getting increasingly drunk.

"I can't stand it," Mother said, holding out her glass for a refill. "No more about the bank. Please. Just one meal without talking about the bank . . ."

Papá poured her the last glass from the bottle. "What are we doing for Big Week? Rinaldo de Ribeiro Suner invited us to his farm. For a partridge shoot . . ."

"Juan! Your manners! Stop playing with your food . . ."

"Jorge!" Papá bellowed. "Get the forty-seven out from the cellar."

I announced I was tired from the trip and asked permission to go upstairs to my room. "Of course, José," Mother said, her neck already mottled red. "Sleep well."

I went and kissed her good night. Papá waved at me dismissively, for he was suddenly focused on Juanito, grilling him on how the math tutorials were going. I will always remember the look of anguish on Juan's face, as my father poked his wrist and lectured him on the skills needed to come work at the bank, when he was finally mature enough to take on the responsibility.

I should have stepped in, should have protected him, but instead I went upstairs, down the corridor that was lined by medieval armor and the sixteenth-century linen closet that once belonged

141

to our relative, the Archbishop of Bilbao. Finally safe behind the door of my bedroom, I went to the windows that faced the street and threw them wide open, to let in air.

Manuel lived in the house next to us, and, at that moment, his family's uniformed maid was leaning from the roof garret window, her golden hair catching the light from the attic's overhead bulb. She was smoking a cigarette and staring wistfully out over the rooftops, at the ships heading into the night-blackened sea. I sensed her loneliness, her craving to escape her life, and I was suddenly filled with a similar ache.

It was Monday and we were all back to our normal routine. I came down to find my parents sitting around the breakfast table. Papá was dressed in his blue suit for the bank. Mother's white gloves and matching hat were resting on the sideboard.

"Today we are discussing a new dorm for the orphanage," she said.

"How much is this going to cost me?"

"Don't be so cynical, Jesús. If the monsignor approves the plan, I will launch a fundraising drive . . . Jorge, please remind Conchata that we will be out for lunch."

"*Por supuesto, Doña Isabel.*"

Father shoveled some cooked mushrooms into his mouth. "What lunch?"

"Augustin invited us to lunch today. At the beach club." She looked at Papá, flatly. "I put it in the book weeks ago."

"I don't recall seeing it. But, either way, I can't go. Augustin may have time for languid lunches, but I actually have to work. I'm off to Vitoria this morning, to see our bank manager there. I will be back by dinner. You go."

"Oh. How disappointing . . ."

"It's maddening. Augustin never does any real work anymore. I have to have a talk with him. He's either having long lunches or off shooting with the clients." My father looked up from his blood sausage and said, "José María, join your mother and uncle for lunch. And bring your brother."

"I have plans . . ."

"Not anymore."

My mother gave me a warm and understanding smile. She looked back at Papá and touched his hand. "Jesus, don't be like that. He's off to university soon. Let him have a little fun his last summer of childhood."

"You're not dining alone in public with a man, even if he is my brother. All the hens of San Sebastián will be clucking."

Mother dropped her head and dabbed her lips with the serviette.

When my lunch break at the bank rolled around, I took a taxi home, so I could walk with Juan the short distance to the beach club. Our bodyguard—hired by Papá to watch over us the day he dismissed ETA's demands—was dressed in a tan summer suit and followed us out of the driveway at a discreet distance.

It was still and hot, with little breeze coming off the preternaturally calm Atlantic. The smell of roasting almonds from the vendor at the corner of the Paseo de la Concha mingled with the hot shimmerings of the black tar and the diesel fumes of the trucks rattling by with hauls of furniture and cabbage.

On the boulevard, Señor Domingo, the bank's chief accountant, came out of Don Pedro's jewelry store and almost bumped into us. He looked startled for a moment and then politely doffed his Panama hat. "Good afternoon, gentlemen." He appeared to have just purchased a gold identification bracelet, which dangled brilliantly in the sun on his raised wrist.

"Señor Domingo," I said nervously, as if I had just been caught playing hooky. "We're off to have lunch with our mother and uncle."

"How lovely." He bowed slightly. "Give them my warmest regards. Good day. I will see you back at the bank. Don't be late."

Uncle's beach club was a two-story art deco building that appeared like a Baked Alaska cooked right into San Sebastián's seawall. One set of stairs led down to the cool and dark changing rooms, umbrellas, and the wooden-slat walkway that headed through the sand to the sea. Another set of stone steps led up to the potted palm on the upper terrace, and the ornate iron-and-brass door of the club restaurant. Candy-striped umbrellas and cast-iron tables sat out on the terrace, providing wonderful views of the Bay of Biscay.

The club doorman, standing in uniform under the sidewalk umbrella, nodded at our approach and went to open the glass door for us. I looked up and saw Mother and Uncle Augustin already sitting out at the corner table of the upper terrace, the best spot to catch whatever breeze was available that day.

Mother was fanning herself with the day's menu, and was talking earnestly and fervently with Uncle Augustin, as if she had so much to say in a short time. She had a slight smile on her lips. I remember her pleasure and I remember thinking how rare it was to see her looking that way and how happy it made me feel.

Right then, her hand stretched forward and delicately touched my uncle's hairy wrist.

His forefinger lightly caressed hers back.

I stopped in my tracks. My brother was looking in the other direction, down at the beach, a hand cupped over his eyes, searching for friends. I saw it then, in his face, in the silhouette, as clear as day—my brother was the spitting image of my uncle.

The wind turned. Uncle Augustin swiveled his head slightly to the left and peered down the promenade. We locked eyes and he quickly pulled his hand away from my mother, who, sensing the danger, turned, a smile frozen across her face.

She waved at us, gestured we should come join them up on the terrace.

"Juan. You go."

My brother turned his head.

"What? Aren't you having lunch?"

"I'm not feeling well. Tell them I am going home to lie down. Conchata will make me some soup."

"Don't be such an old woman. Come."

"Go, you little shit. Go before I smash you in the face."

I shoved him in the chest.

I had never done this sort of thing to Juan before, and he blanched at my attack, stepped back, swiveled, and ran hard, trying to get away from me, straight across the Paseo de la Concha.

There was a screech and shudder and thud as my brother flew through the air, his limbs at odd angles. His head bounced on the cement and then disappeared under the wheels of the rusty truck hauling onions. The sea roaring in my ear was deafening. I could not immediately hear anything. All I could see were the round, open mouths of anguish, belonging to my mother and

Uncle Augustin and the doorman, as they leapt up, shocked and straight and immobile, from their positions on the club's terrace.

Our bodyguard was the first to move. He ran across the street and cradled my brother's pulpy head in his hands. Blood leached into his summer suit, as he tried to determine if life was still there. Then the truck driver jumped from the front seat, bellowing like a madman, and ran back to help, just as Uncle Augustin finally found his legs and came clattering down the club's stairs as well.

I still could not move. But I could hear again. As I filled up with the horror of what had just happened, I heard a laconic baritone, without a trace of upset, calmly say, "All quiet in the Alcázar, my General."

SEVEN

Mother sat in the corner of her bedroom, on a cream divan, staring out to sea. She was still in her shift and gown, and although we were alone, she wouldn't look at me.

"Mother, I need to talk to you. To tell you something."

She didn't acknowledge that I had spoken. She was so still and quiet, it was like she had even stopped blinking.

"Mamá, I killed Juan. I yelled at him, pushed him, and he ran across the road."

She finally woke up, blinked rapidly, and turned ever so slightly from the sea.

"Promise me," she finally said, her hands clasped tight in her lap, two fingers held by five. "Promise me you will hear what I am about to tell you."

"*Sí, Mamá.* Anything."

"You are innocent."

"You didn't understand what I just said."

"You have nothing to do with this. Nothing. I alone am to blame for Juan's death. This is God at work, punishing me for my sins."

"I was angry. About what I saw between you and . . . I pushed him."

She shook her head.

"José, please understand. God was working through you. It was not you. God is punishing me for my wickedness, through my children."

She turned then, all the way in my direction, and looked me square and earnestly in the face. "If I give you anything in this life, José, let it be that you understand you were not to blame for Juan's death. It was me. Entirely. It was my sinful behavior that killed Juanito, just as if I gave birth and then strangled him with my bare hands."

Her speech was so forceful it made me sit down hard on the embroidered footstool at her feet. She reached out and caressed the back of my head.

"Remember, José. Remember. You are innocent."

She kissed my hair. Even then I knew that this attempt to absolve me of the guilt that was mine alone and not hers to forgive—it was the purest and most decent thing my mother ever tried to do for me.

But life continues relentlessly for the living. Mother's maid returned to the room, carrying a black dress wrapped in tissue, and gasped when she saw my mother bent over and weeping into the back of my head.

"Oh no. None of this. Not now. We have to get ready." The maid looked crossly at me. "José, stop upsetting your mother! She's got to get dressed. The car is leaving shortly. Leave now, please. So I can get her dressed."

I stood and Mamá sat up straight. She wiped

her eyes with a handkerchief, and then turned, surrendering herself to her maid.

On the way back down the corridor, I glanced left into my brother's room, and through the crack in the door, I saw *Biggles' Second Case* splayed on its binding in the middle of his bed, just where Juan left it the day he died. It was like he had just gone off to the bathroom a few moments earlier.

I somehow managed to get back to my room. I stared at myself in the closet-door mirror, while attempting to tie my tie, asking the same questions over and over again—

Why didn't I let you come fishing with me in Galicia, Juanito? Why?

Papá came to my room with a black armband clamped between his damp fingers, like he wasn't quite sure what to do with it. His face was gray, racked with pain. He wandered aimlessly about my room; he picked up a book on trout flies, put it down again, listlessly spun the globe. "We have to help your mother get through the day," he said, but he could not speak further. His lip was trembling. I reached out and helped him secure the black armband, which he did for me, both of us using the armbands as an excuse to cling to each other.

Jorge appeared, his chauffeur's hat in hand, and told us the car was ready.

Mother was waiting for us in the foyer

downstairs. She wore the black dress, her face hidden behind sunglasses. When she saw us coming down the stairs, she lifted the shawl from her shoulders and covered her head, so that her face was entirely blotted out by a wall of black lace.

"It's time, my dear, to put Juanito to rest," Papá said.

Mamá did not say a word, but stared at the front door, her ebony rosary and an embroidered linen handkerchief clutched fiercely in her hands. We saw then that she was incapable of moving. Papá and I stepped forward, gently lifted her to her feet, and guided her out the door.

The sun was shining harsh and bright, and it took us some moments to adjust from the gloom of the drawn-curtain house. The Hispano-Suiza was glinting chrome out front, behind the flower-bedecked hearse sitting farther down our crescent drive. A Guardia Civil motorbike escort and our family friends were waiting in a long line of cars just outside the house gates. Papá had insisted we bury Juan in our ancestral town of Oviedo, and as we pulled out of the pebbled drive in the Hispano-Suiza, the train of cars fired up and fell into line behind us.

Papá kept one lifeless hand in his lap, while the other held aloft a Ducados, which he periodically puffed from the side of his mouth, blowing smoke in the direction of the half-open window. We drove almost the entire six-hour trip in silence. Mother was pressed into the far dark corner of the red-leather seats, her face in shadow, unable to look at any of us. We passed lush green fields of maize and brown dairy farms. We passed pine trees standing sentinel atop the cliffs, circled by eagles, as the waves below crashed upon the rocks.

Jorge whispered to me under his breath, so my parents couldn't hear. "The sun should not shine on such a day. It makes things worse."

It was late afternoon when we finally pulled into the Oviedo cemetery. The Bishop of Oviedo, a distant relative, stood regally in his miter and green chasuble laced with gold thread—and gathered us around my brother's casket under the cork trees.

Uncle Augustin came separately and on his own. I watched him in his black suit come quietly up the left side of the cemetery drive, light on his feet and with his head down, as if he didn't want to leave a firm impression. Mother had refused to see Augustin back at the house, when he came calling, and this now was the first time I had seen him since that fateful day at his beach club.

Papá was standing on the grass, thanking all our friends for coming this long distance to bury Juanito. He was the picture of manly rectitude, but the moment he saw Augustin, he threw his arms around his brother and openly wept on his neck. My uncle, his eyes closed, patted my father on the back, whispered in his ear.

It was amazing to me that Papá—who was so wily and good at the shadow game of business and viscerally understood the subverted reasons why people did what they did—was, in this case, totally blind to how his brother had betrayed him.

But I knew, as did my mother, and when Uncle Augustin turned to Mamá, her face was entirely blotted out by the sunglasses and black lace. But you could still sense, even through this impenetrable black mask, how coldly she was surveying her former lover.

"Isabel, it is me," Uncle Augustin said softly, bending forward to kiss her. "Just me. I have been sick, thinking of you nonstop. My heart is broken . . ."

Mother reared her head back to avoid his kiss. Augustin blanched and stood awkwardly for a moment, holding his homburg in his hand, deciding what he should do next. He finally bowed at her, deeply, and came toward me.

When I saw that pig of an uncle heading toward me, I was filled with our family's shame. I could only think about how the memory of my brother, if this ever came out, would forever be tainted by this horrible truth, and that the true person that was my brother would be entirely lost to the world. This could not happen, and in that moment I swore to Juan, on his grave, that I would keep the family secret—his secret—until the day I died.

"Nephew. I am so sorry. We will miss Juanito."

"How could you betray Papá like that? You, the man he loves most."

Uncle Augustin looked like he might get sick. He was white and trembling and clutching the rim of his hat. But he gathered himself. "Affairs of the heart are not so simple, José," he said under his breath, looking over at Papá, who was greeting some latecomers from San Sebastián. "Perhaps you will understand this one day."

"I understand you are a coward and a hypocrite and not to be trusted."

He pursed his lips. "Are you going to tell your father?"

"No. I couldn't do that to him. But it's over. I don't want you anywhere near my parents. I don't even want you in the same city. That's my price. Figure something out. Why you have to go away."

Uncle Augustin looked at the white lilies resting atop Juan's mahogany casket, and you could see, in his face, that he had given up. "*Bueno.* If your mother wishes it."

"She just gave you her opinion on the matter."

I was about to leave, but as I turned away, Uncle Augustin said, "Goodbye, nephew. I suppose you will never talk to me again. Just remember. I saw how you pushed Juan into the road. We are both, each in our way, responsible for hurting our brothers."

He hit me where I hurt most, and I was shaken, but I did not want to give him the satisfaction. "No, we are not, Uncle. What you did was pure deceit, deliberately plotted, and all you are worried about now is that your secret will come out, even though my brother, your son, lies dead in front of you. You are despicable."

"You have no idea what is in my heart," he hissed angrily. "How heavy . . ."

I walked away from him, took up my place next to Mamá. Papá was on the other side of her and solicitously holding her elbow, in case she might faint. A short while later, Uncle Augustin, his face set in stone, took up his position next to his brother.

Thuribles were swung, the bishop began his doleful lament, and the air filled with the smells of smoking myrrh and lilies rotting in the sun. A few minutes after the service started, however, a roar and commotion rose from the mourners in the back of the gathering. The bishop, looking irritated, stopped his funeral oration. We all followed his gaze.

El Caudillo, in his bulletproof Cadillac, surrounded by his African Corps bodyguards, was coming down the lilac-lined cemetery drive.

To come to a boy's funeral—it was an unheard-of

thing—and there were excited murmurs. Franco emerged from the car in formal blue-and-red uniform, with ribbons and medals attached to his breast, the embroidered cap and trademark sunglasses hiding his face. The mourners bowed their heads and parted as Franco walked up the path to the front, where Papá, Mamá, and I were sitting in front-row chairs, clutching handkerchiefs to our brows and upper lips.

We stood and El Caudillo embraced us.

"The burden of the mother is great," Franco said, kissing blank-faced Mamá. "I am sorry for your great loss, Doña Isabel.

"To lose a son is an unfathomable tragedy," Franco told Papá. "You have given so much to *la Patria*, and the state shall not forget your sacrifices. We shall find a way, one way or another, to give back to your family."

Papá murmured some response and turned to introduce us, but El Caudillo had already moved on to me. "Yes. Yes. José María. We met before on the Sella. And I of course read about your recent sea-trout catch in Galicia. Quite a killing."

"*Sí, Generalísimo.*"

He made that odd chuckling noise, like a cough, and reached out to pat my cheek. "You are quite dangerous to Spain's fish stock, young man!"

At that moment the bishop, surrounded by the young priests swinging smoky thuribles, cleared his throat. El Caudillo, remembering where he was, walked over and stood in front of Augustin. It was almost like he instinctively knew Uncle Augustin had, through his actions, relinquished his position of respect in our family. Franco waited expectantly, until my uncle gave up his seat and shuffled down the line. El Caudillo made the sign of the cross and nodded at the bishop to continue with the service.

Mother and Father, heads down as they shook and wept, shoveled dirt onto Juanito's casket. I had brought a small jar of sand from the beach of San Sebastián that Juan so loved; I emptied its contents onto his casket. The feelings I had suppressed since that fatal push suddenly welled up in me, and I could not stop crying and shaking. I felt arms around me, Papá's and my friend Manuel's and his mother's—never my own mother's—but there simply was no consolation to be had.

When I finally looked up, I saw that El Caudillo had been observing me closely, without comment. As soon as we made eye contact, he dropped his head, almost like he was shy, and then abruptly left. I watched Franco retreat, but my mind was entirely elsewhere. I turned back to look at my brother's grave.

Why didn't I let you come fishing with me in Galicia? Why? I would do anything to fish the Sella again with you, Juanito. Please, God. I ache for that.

• • •

Papá and I were sitting in the library at home in San Sebastián. He was behind his partner's desk, a stack of letters and bills to his side, toying with the paper knife. The Thomas Cook envelope with the airline ticket was on the table between us.

I wouldn't touch it. "I don't want to go."

Papá sighed. He picked up his soft cigarette pack and offered me one. I shook my head. I didn't want anything from him.

"You should really look at this as an opportunity. I thought you wanted to explore the world, fish other rivers."

"Not like this. Not while everything has fallen apart."

"You're driving me crazy. You're worse than your mother."

I thought I might leap across the table and choke him.

"José, it's time for you to stop this childishness. Franco has given us one of only two private-banking licenses in all Spain. We'll make a killing, helping all these newly wealthy Spaniards get their money out of the country and properly invested in safe havens. *Hostia.* Imagine the possibilities."

"Ask Augustin."

"That *cabrón*? He's moving to Mexico City. Says he's tired of working for me, always under my thumb. I don't know what has gotten into him."

158

"There are others."

"No. No. Go to New York, get your degree at Columbia University as we discussed, and then start your training with the Swiss Federal Credit Bank. It's all been arranged."

He impatiently blew a column of smoke heavenward.

"Do you know how many young men would kill for this opportunity? To be under the personal patronage of Francisco Franco and to live in New York? *Joder.* I would have jumped at the chance, if I were your age."

"Then you go. How can you pretend nothing happened?"

"Don't be so fresh. I am not pretending. I think about Juanito and your mother every day. But, *coño*, that doesn't mean we give up on life!"

I looked down at my lap. "I am afraid."

"Well, of course you are, José," Papá said gently. "That's normal. Only an idiot wouldn't be afraid. Matadors are most afraid just before they step into the ring. But what makes the man is that he still steps in for the fight."

I looked up, exasperated. "You don't understand. I'm afraid I will never see Spain again. That I will go into exile and never come back."

"*Oh Dios mío.* What shit."

Papá leaned across the table and pushed the envelope at me, the ticket that would take me to the pink continent on the globe in my room.

159

"Pick up the fucking ticket and go to fucking America already! Go on now, José María. *Qué mierda.*"

A simple wooden crucifix hung above the metal cot in Mother's room in the psychiatric ward. Her window overlooked the hospital's grounds. When the nun took me in to see Mamá, she was sitting in her usual way, two fingers clutched by five, staring out the window at the lawn lined by rosebushes. Her side table was covered in rosaries, a large collection of beads in everything from ebony to amethyst, laid out neatly in a line across the table.

"Doña Isabel. Your son is here to see you . . . Do not upset her, young man. She has her exercises in twenty-five minutes."

"Let him stay longer, Sister. He is my only son."

"You know the routine. We must stick to the program. It is the doctor's order."

Mother smiled at me and patted the chair next to her.

"Then we must take advantage of the time we have together."

When the nun retreated, I asked Mamá how they were treating her.

"Very well, José. I feel much better. Did you bring me the rosary?"

I dug into my pocket and retrieved the rosary

160

that had belonged to her late great-uncle, a monk with a famously large appetite for life. The rope and beads were outsized. He wore the rosary as a belt, tied around his plump waist.

Mamá took my offering and lovingly and carefully laid it across the side table with the other rosaries. "Thank you, my sweet boy." When she patted my knee, I saw the thin red scars, up and down her wrists, were still healing.

"Come home. I miss you."

Mother's eyes were large with fright. "But I don't want to, José. I just got here. I don't want to leave."

"I mean when you are ready," I added hastily.

"It is very calm and soothing here. I have time to be alone. Time to pray and think. Without all the noise."

"That's good. Rest is good."

"Your father. He is so loud. So full of energy. There is no peace and quiet around him. No room to breathe. He fills every space he occupies. The quiet here is quite special. You can hear yourself think."

"That's nice, Mother. But I came to tell you something important."

She turned her head and looked out the window, clutching her fingers again, as if she were steeling herself for another blow. "Yes?"

"I am probably going to America. To university. It's an opportunity for me."

161

She never turned her head from looking out the window. This I expected. But the vehemence with which she spoke next stunned me, and finally made up my mind about what I should do.

"Look at what I have become, José. Look hard. This is your fate if you stay. Get away from all this. Run as far and fast as you can."

It was raining the day I left Spain. Papá and I were escorted to the VIP room in the back of the Bilbao International Airport, which we had entirely to ourselves. He poured us both a scotch from the lounge's side cabinet and then collapsed on the brown-leather couch beside me. He was constantly squeezing my right knee, reassuring himself I was still there.

"Forgive me," he said, his voice quavering. "But seeing you like this, a man heading out into the world—I keep thinking of your mother and brother."

I stared straight ahead, dry eyed. Papá was so obviously feeling sorry for himself. I was the last representative of his family, his first family I should say, and now I, too, was leaving his side. But Papá could never be alone, and we both knew, without any words exchanged, that he would have his marriage to my mother annulled and be remarried within a few months—to one of his many mistresses. He was always one to keep moving forward with life, never looking back.

The door to the lounge swung open and Franco's minister of fisheries and agricultural affairs strode into the room, his aide carrying his briefcase. Papá and I instantly stood, shook the minister's hand.

"I'm off to Barcelona and heard you were here," the minister said. "Just wanted to come in and personally wish you best of luck, José María. And also tell you, on behalf of El Caudillo, how proud Spain is of you—and what you will do for her in the future."

"Thank you, Minister."

"May God be with you, my boy."

My father thanked the cabinet official for his visit, in his formal and courtly manner, but as soon as the white-haired fisheries minister left, Papá exploded, smacking his fists together.

"I am not sure why you are getting so worked up," I said. "I thought it was very decent of him to come say goodbye."

"You need to get better at chess."

"What's that supposed to mean?"

"That little shit didn't come here out of his own choice. No. No. Trust me. It's Franco who sent him here. He was ordered to come see you."

"That's ridiculous."

"José, Franco sent his fisheries minister here for one reason—to personally verify you got on the airplane and actually left the country."

"But why?"

"El Caudillo doesn't want you fishing his rivers."

"What are you talking about?"

"When I was in Madrid the other day, the minister of minerals and mining, my old friend, pulled me aside and told me why Franco gave us the banking license—and why all these strings were pulled to get you into Columbia University in New York and the Swiss Federal Credit Bank's trainee program in Zürich. It's not just to modernize the nation's banking industry and reward me personally for my services to the nation. It's because Franco is obsessed, absolutely livid, about how much fish you catch. This way he gets you out of the country and as far away as possible from his rivers. That's what he has wanted all along, ever since he saw you fishing the Sella's Bridge Pool."

For a few minutes I couldn't actually speak. "So," I finally said. "I am being sent into exile. I might never see Spain again. I was right."

Father looked sheepish for a moment. "Not if I can help it, José. We will fish the Sella together again. This, I promise." He tossed back his scotch.

My flight was boarding. Papá and I followed our escort down the hall and began crossing the wet tarmac. It was early September, 1961, but the air had already turned to fall, and gusts of rain were getting driven down the runway in our direction, partly from the turning propellers.

We reached the bottom of the gangway stairs. I looked back at the airport terminal, and saw the white-haired minister of fisheries and agriculture at the window, watching me board the DC-3 to Madrid and New York. Somehow I knew, even then, that I was finished with Spain. I never wanted to see her again. I wasn't being sent into exile, I thought with defiance, but voluntarily leaving her borders. There was nothing left for me in that country anymore.

I turned back to Papá, to say my final goodbye, and felt the loss of what was happening. I took in his handsome if overweight face, his sad eyes and proud nose, his pinky ring and smoldering cigarette, the smoke and lavender that were my father's essence—and this time I choked up.

"Goodbye, Papá."

"Goodbye, José María. I love you. Make me proud. Now go. Tight lines."

Part III

2019

CANTON ZUG, SWITZERLAND

EIGHT

"José María."

Ignore it. Maybe it will go away.

"José!"

There is a blurred face looming in front of me. Behind the face, I catch glimpses of trees, swaying branches and leaves, patches of pale, filtered light.

Why am I so sore and stiff?

With effort I focus on the round face, and it emerges pink cheeked, round, mustached—and concerned. There is something kind in the eyes. His big hands, coarse, hold out a water bottle.

"José, drink this," says Walter Iten, my friend, the village fishmonger.

"*Hostia.* It's you, Walter. You scared me."

He squats, looks intently at me, serious and grave, looking for signs of bruises and scrapes. He reaches down and pats Alfredo. The dog licks Walter's hand and wags his stubby tail, visibly relieved a sane person has arrived.

"Are you all right? Did you hurt yourself? Fall?"

"Of course not." I point at my favorite pool, where I just released the big rainbow trout. "I've been fishing."

"*Ja, du!* You have been gone ten hours, José.

169

You told your wife you would be home for lunch. She has been very worried. This is quite a thing. The police, villagers, they have been out looking for you."

"How ridiculous. I am perfectly fine."

I look at my watch. It is just past 5:00 p.m. "Good heavens."

I drink deeply from the water bottle. I had no idea I was this thirsty.

Walter studies his cell phone. "There is no reception here. It is why Lisa could not reach you." He reaches into his inside pocket and pulls out a walkie-talkie, from his role as one of the village's civil protection officers. It crackles alive.

"*Schatz, ich han José . . .*"

Walter tells his wife, Susi, he found me, I am safe, and that he's bringing me back to their cottage. Susi should call Lisa, to let her know I am fine and that she can come pick me up. Then his wife should contact Ägeri's police chief, so he can call off the search party.

I have been found.

"What about my car?"

"My son will come later and drive it back to your house. The keys?"

I dig into my pocket and hand them over.

"What a ridiculous production. You're fussing over me like an old lady, Walter. It's annoying. Really. I am absolutely fine."

But when I try to stand, I almost fall over. Walter grabs my arm and steadies me, and we make our way through the moss and fern and out of the darkening woods.

Walter opens the front passenger door of his Volkswagen station wagon and makes me sit inside. As I take another drink, he expertly takes apart my rod, lays it carefully in the car's trunk, along with my wicker creel and my fishing vest.

He tells Alfredo to get into the back seat.

Walter plops himself down behind the wheel.

"Now everything is fine again. Tip-top."

The Itens' cottage is tucked away in a twenty-five-hectare forest carve-out, where the wooded slopes come down into a pass of buttercup meadows, populated by bell-clanking cows and rimmed by a spring-fresh brook called the Zauberbach.

As we enter the eastern end of the pass, my phone begins to shake and vibrate. I look down. I have twenty-two calls and fifty-eight text messages. I dial Lisa.

"Are you hurt?" Her voice is tense.

"No. I was fishing and lost track of the time. Walter found me. We are heading to his house."

"Was it a blackout?"

I am about to say no, but when I open my mouth, I find myself saying, "Possibly. I got lost in memories of my early life in Spain. Many I had forgotten—for good reason. It wasn't pleasant. But I couldn't find my way back here."

There is a deafening silence.

"Lisa, please, I am fine. Just come and pick me up."

"I'm on my way. Do you need me to bring anything?"

"A sweater. I'm cold."

I turn to look out the window. We're at the bottom of the pass, driving along the rim of the bog-and-birch basin. In the spring, the marsh ponds here are alive with frogs, croaking and moaning their love. Every year Walter invites me over in the evening for spring's ritual frog hunt. I remember, then, the first time he invited me on the nighttime hunt, some twenty-five years ago.

We started in his cabin with a shot of eau-de-vie, to sear our innards and fortify our spirits, before heading out into the night with flashlights and small mesh nets. Our Wellington boots made a squelching sound in the sponge-like turf. An imperceptibly slow-moving stream, passing over the mossy carpet, was feeding fresh water into the shallow bog ponds alive with croaks.

Our flashlights began to pick up the blue-green incandescent discs that were frogs' eyes. Before the blinded could blink and register our presence, we quietly stepped forward, dropped the nets into the reeking water, and scooped the frogs up. They were mating and, even when lifted in the net, they clung to each other in an amorous embrace, gulping with passion, their eyes bulging, fingers spread wide in astonishment. How touchingly and imploringly the red-throated males grasped the plump females, their lusty purring the music of the night.

We had, within an hour, seventy mating frogs plopped into the green-metal tank of sloshing water that Walter had strapped to his back. We returned to the cottage, its stone chimney sending up into the starry night undulating curls of birch smoke.

Sensors tripped the lights as soon as we came up the property's front-facing rhubarb patch, flooding in bright light the trapdoor fish tank in the front grass and the glistening stone patio at the back of the cottage. Susi Iten had brought out to the patio sharp knives, wooden carving boards, and glass bowls filled with egg yolks and flour and parsley bread crumbs. Everything we needed for our feast was carefully laid out on the round table lit up by the nightlight.

Husband and wife exchanged the local Swiss-German patois, as Walter gently dropped the leather straps from his shoulders, easing the tank full of frogs onto the flagstone. He popped open its metal top and stuck a hand inside, emerging with two frogs, still locked in an amorous amphibian clasp and refusing to part. I stuck my hand into the tank and followed suit.

We held the frogs tightly by their hind legs, swung them up in the air, and then brought their heads smack down against the stone back wall. We bashed them a couple of times each, just to make sure the job was decisively done, and with each crack of bone and stone, frog blood splattered across the feldspar. Our arms twirled through the night air like we were Olympian discus throwers, rhythmically smacking the green heads down against the sharp-edged stone, and by the time we finished forty minutes later, Jackson Pollock splatters of red had been sent out in every direction of the black night.

Finally, it was over. I was sweating and panting slightly from the exertion, but the hunt was a success. Our platter was heaped high with dead frogs. A few legs still twitched, sinewy nerve endings that refused to register the life gone.

I gently placed a frog on the wooden carving boards laid out on the patio table, and made a small surgical cut in its green back. I poked my fingers underneath the skin slit, in both directions, and then pulled off the sheaf of amphibian hide. It felt like pulling duct tape off a storage box.

We chopped off their hind legs, carefully cut away any remaining viscera that was still stubbornly attached, and then cast away their upper torsos. A downward crunch of the blade severed the clawed and webbed feet from the naked legs, before we gave them a final, ritual bath in fresh water and blotted them with paper towels.

In no time, we had a platter full of frogs' legs—tiny bones, translucent membranes, stringy pink muscle. Into the flour the skinny legs went, then the egg, followed by the coat of crunchy bread crumbs. They were ready for the pan.

Susi hosed down the patio's back wall, erasing all traces of our sins.

"*Also.* We are here."

I come back. We are at Iten's cottage.

"Why are we here?"

He furrows his brow, looks concerned again.

"We are waiting for your wife. She is coming to pick you up."

The Swiss flag snaps smartly on the flagpole outside the cabin, as Walter pulls the Volkswagen station wagon under the tin-roofed carport. I have a little trouble lifting my legs and pulling myself out of the car, but I feel better as soon as I stand on the solid tar.

Terra firma.

Walter hovers at my elbow, ready to steady me if I should wobble. I can see he is eager to get me inside the house, so his wife, a nurse, can look me over.

But I stand stock-still in the path leading through the rhubarb patch. Alfredo turns to look over his shoulder, as if to say, *Now what? It's dinnertime.*

"Walter. The tank."

"Not today, José. You must come in and have a Café Lutz, to warm you up and revive you. I think you have a bit of shock."

"Today is no different than any other. I won't move until you show me."

Walter, perhaps reassured I am not in such bad shape as he initially thought, kneels on one knee, next to the gray-green trapdoor buried in the grass, alongside the cottage's stone path. He pops the lock and lifts the door, so I can peer into the stone-lined tank, fed by an underwater spring.

The biggest fish that day—silky and sulking—is a three-kilo pike with long gray body and round nose, sitting at the bottom of the tank. Around the pike, a few zebra-striped *Egli*, mountain perch; two nice-sized *Felchen*; and a half dozen brook trout Walter's oldest son had caught with grasshoppers in the Zauberbach.

"Beautiful fish."

"The pike is very small. All the big fish have gone."

It is always so. Walter's constant lament is how the fish are all disappearing. I have heard him go on in this way for the last thirty years.

"I remember, when I fished the Lake of Ägeri with my father, we never came home with pike below ten kilos. But those days are over."

"*Ja hallo. Wieso chömed Ihr neut inne?*"

Susi Iten is standing in her floral housedress,

hands on hips, demanding to know why we aren't coming inside. Walter eases shut the trapdoor.

"What haf you been doing, José?" Susi snaps at me. "You put a big fright in your wife bosom."

"I am sorry to have caused such theater. I am fine. Just been out fishing."

"*Ja du!*"

She stands back to let us through the cottage's small door, and as I pass, she barks, "Let me look at you." To my shock, she begins to squeeze and poke my arms and sides—"Does ribs pain?"—like I am a market chicken she might buy.

I have to fight an impulse to turn around and slap her.

"Please stop that. I did not fall. As I said, I am perfectly fine."

But right then a wave of wood-heated air hits me, so warm and comforting that I sag at the knees. Susi and Walter lurch forward to grab me and guide me to the reclining lounge chair inside the cottage. They tilt the chair back, like I am at the dentist, and I am half looking at the ceiling.

Susi bustles about in the kitchen, filling a glass with water from their well, and putting the teakettle on. Walter turns to the glass-fronted cabinet and pulls out a bottle of homemade *Pflümli-Wasser*—a firewater made from plums—and pours a couple of fingers into the bottom of a ceramic mug, to which Susi adds hot tea from a small pot. They bring me the drinks, along with

177

Bündnerfleisch, paper-thin cuts of beef dried in the mountain air, plus wedges of Gruyère and hard-crusted buns called *Bürli*.

"Eat!" Susi barks.

The protein of the meat and the fat of the cheese and the hot tea with spirits—it does, just as they said it would, make me feel better. I am less light-headed.

I must have dozed for a while, after the food and drink, because when I open my eyes again, Walter and Susi have taken their concerned looks away from me and are silently going about their chores in the small cottage.

Susi is in the open kitchen at the back. She is moving along the counter, between bowls and knives and platters, preparing the night's dinner of pan-fried pike. Across from her, under the lamp hanging low over the wooden dining-room table and the curved bench, Walter has his head down, repairing a reel.

The reel's barrels and drums and springs are laid out on a cloth, and his thick fingers are inside, with fine rag and oilcan, cleaning out sand and relubricating the gears and joints. The smell of birch wood is in the air, as the potbellied stove in the corner crackles with fire. I look at the Swiss couple, each unselfconsciously at ease in their corner, and my tumor-pressed mind begins to pulse.

This is their home. This is their home. This is where they belong.

It is dark outside and car lights sweep the front path.

Walter lifts his head, like a dog listening for his master coming down the lane. He slides from behind the table and is out the door. I look out the cottage window, past the rhododendrons, and see Walter heading down the cottage path, tripping the lights, as Lisa comes up from the carport.

They stop, face to face, and look at each other. My wife then slowly drops her head against Walter's chest. He puts his arms around, tenderly, and caresses her back. They stand like that for a few moments, hugging, giving comfort to each other.

"Drink!"

Susi is thrusting another glass of water at me.

"You are dehydrated. Make you light in the head. Drink!"

And then Lisa is in the cottage. She is magnificent, like an avenging spirit coming to retrieve me from this dark forest and bring me back into the light of our life together. Walter and Susi stand respectfully and silently to the side, as Lisa strides full of purpose, in jeans and quilted Barbour vest, across the entire length of the cottage. She possessively places a gold-bangled hand on my shoulder, bends down, and kisses me, hard and full on the lips, like she needs to taste

179

that I am really here and have not yet left her.

I am so relieved, so relieved to see her. I reach out and hold her as tight as I can.

Lisa whispers in my ear, so the Itens can't hear. "Let's take you home, José. Where you belong."

I cannot speak, when I hear the love and concern and tenderness in that voice. All I can do is nod, nod like a child, and gratefully clasp her hands back. And in that moment, I give myself entirely over to my wife, in the hope of hopes she can, as she promises, take me home.

I sleep a solid ten hours. I haven't done that since I was in my forties.

I shuffle in my robe and slippers, slightly dazed, to the informal living room adjoining the kitchen. Alfredo is half asleep in his basket, but his tail stump works furiously as soon as I come into the room. He licks my hand when I pat him.

Lisa has been up for hours already, a complete reversal of our usual habits. She is reading the *International New York Times*, her feet up on the couch. Lisa has my breakfast laid out in the breakfast room, along with the stack of pills and vitamins that are now my daily regimen, and she rises from the couch, kisses me full on the lips, and then steps into the kitchen, to fire up the espresso machine.

"How did you sleep?"

"Like I was dead."

Lisa has her back to me, through the kitchen doorway.

"Well, you're not. Not yet."

I change the subject, ask her what's in the paper. We talk about the things far removed from our little world: about how another EU member state is desperately trying to hold its national borders together, as yet another of its cities demands independence and declares itself a twenty-first-century "City State" with direct representational links to the EU; and about the dangerously escalating Chinese-Russian-US naval skirmishes over the rights to fish for black cod in the Bering Sea.

We move into the breakfast room. Lisa has set me a place, with linen and silver and the indigo-and-gold demitasse that I bought her years ago in Paris. We sit for quite a while, husband and wife, sipping coffee at the table.

There is good reason for my silence. There's an interesting development in my mental state—and it's hard to avoid. That young man I saw at the church in Zürich, his long hair smelling of Suavecito, is in the farmhouse, sitting in the armchair in the corner of the breakfast room, next to the antique linen closet. He is half in darkness, just watching me with his black eyes. I cannot look at him, but even with my head studiously averted, I can smell him, that smell of pomade, like flowers decomposing in a vase.

A cloud must have passed somewhere above the pear tree outside, because a rectangle of light comes pouring in through the window, bright and clear, illuminating my wife. She turns the angle of her chair, so she can feel the sun on her face, and lazily asks, "What d'you want to do today?"

"I will take Alfredo for his walk. And then I will clean up my study, like you have long asked me to do. I think it is time I threw some stuff out."

"There was a time when I would have been happy to hear those words. Not so much now."

I don't say a thing. Just slice my pear.

"Were you serious about moving out of our bedroom and down to the study, like you told the hospice director? I mean, when it's time."

"Yes."

Lisa looks out the window. After a few minutes, she turns back and says, "Do you want help cleaning out the room? I could help."

"No. I must do this myself. But I'll need some garbage bags."

The look of hurt in her face, it is almost unbearable.

She turns her head from me, stirs her coffee. "This is what you always do. To all of us. The boys. Me. Any of us who care. Shut us out. You are always so secretive."

I look down at my hands. "*Mujer.* It is the way it is. Even with the best of intentions, you cannot take this trip with me. This—we all do alone."

"You don't get it. You just don't get it."

Lisa stands and carries our plates to the kitchen sink.

I stand myself, to go downstairs to my study, but the young man is suddenly standing in the darkness of the doorway, his arms crossed, looking darkly at me. He is blocking my exit. His presence, it triggers both fear and an equally steely determination to push past him, but I falter after a few steps, lose my nerve. He is resolute. I see it in his face. He will not let me through.

He's waiting for a proper atonement. Like at the church. I feel it.

"Lisa," I say, my voice shaking slightly. "What I am going through, it is hard to describe. Strange things are happening to me, to my mind, and one day soon I probably won't be able to talk at all. I should say now what I might not be able to say in the near future."

I turn in her direction. She is still facing the sink, which somehow makes what I have to say a little easier. "I am not a man who expresses his feelings well. You know this better than anyone else. But please know how grateful I am to you—for creating such calm in this house, for almost single-handedly bringing up our fine sons. I have always loved you, even when my behavior at times seemed to suggest the opposite."

I move closer, whisper into her back. "Without

you—I would have been nothing. *Discúlpeme.* Forgive me. I beg you."

Lisa does not turn around. She is still facing the sink.

"There is nothing to forgive. I knew what I was marrying."

She bends down, to rummage under the sink, and emerges with a single black garbage bag. "It's the last one. I'll bring some more down in a few minutes. They're in the supply closet."

I stand at the threshold of my study, clutching the garbage bag, not sure how I should proceed. Alfredo ambles over to his rug in the corner and plops himself down as I take stock of my room: The marble-topped coffee table, made from blue-and-gray stone, matching the couch and armchairs in crushed velvet. They stand before the French doors leading into the garden. From the leather swivel chair, behind my glass-and-chrome desk, I can look out the French doors and see the stone fountain, the bird feeder hanging from the overhead eave, and the beds of Apricot, Falstaff, and Cherry Parfait roses lining the garden's flagstone path.

There are some eight hundred books on fish and fishing, a brass-railed ladder, and a nineteenth-century globe in the corner library. One panel of the library is a disguised door, and behind it is a full bathroom with Finnish sauna. Next to that, my vanity wall: framed photos of me fishing for trout in Canton Uri, high in the Swiss Alps; after sea trout in County Mayo, Ireland; Spey casting with double-handed rod on the Dee in Scotland; hunting sea trout in windswept Patagonia; with the boys on the Kjara River in Iceland, the banks behind us a killing field of slaughtered salmon; and on the Eagle River in Labrador, Canada, the bears across the river eyeing our fish.

I imagine myself spending my final days here, looking at the life buzzing outside the French doors, before I finally drift off. I write "to go" in black on the stickums and put them on the couch and coffee table, markers for when the movers come. They will make room for my deathbed.

I pivot to the other side of the office. Lisa calls the fly-tying workbench in the corner my "private altar." Tacked to the board above the workbench are the rumps and wings of fowl, everything from red grouse to a rare and illegal hide of the King of Saxony bird-of-paradise. There are also little baggies filled with the inexpensive and furry skins of voles and black squirrels; and spools of silk thread, in colors ranging from caviar-black to flamingo-scarlet, used to tie the feathers to the hooks.

I can't decide what to do with the fly-tying bench, and turn my attention to a filing cabinet on casters pushed under the desk. In the top drawer, I find dried-out pens, clips, calling cards;

I upend it all into a garbage bag. In the next drawer, there are letters and printed emails from my sons, wrapped in rubber bands and neatly stacked according to date.

I open one packet and read the first email. It is from Sam. "Dear Dad, Thanks for the $35,000 wire transfer. It arrived yesterday. This morning I gave the landlord the deposit for the two-bedroom rental, which is just a block from campus. I just discovered my new roommate, from Austria, knows the rivers of the Tyrol and tells me he mostly fishes for grayling. When I know him better, will pump him for information on what are the best rivers. Love, Sam."

I take another. It is a handwritten note from John that I have preserved in its original cream envelope. "Dad, I am getting married to Joanne, the woman I love, whether you like it or not. My brothers are all showing up in Vegas, proud to stand by me on our special day. I hope you and Mom make it. Please come. John."

John was always the son we worried over most. I return his letter to its rubber-band stack and decide to keep the letters. *Let them see what I kept.*

But there is something niggling in the back of my mind, a memory buried from another period of my life, and I keep searching the bric-a-brac, until my hands finally clamp down on an old cigar box of Montecristo No. 2, pushed to the far corner of the drawer. I pull the box out and gently lift its lid. It still smells of Havanas.

Amidst the papers inside, the high school grades and magnifying glass, I find a color photo that has yellowed with age. I excitedly take out the picture, so long buried in its cigar-box casket, and hold it in the light of the French doors.

It is a picture of me, in my forties, on a working vacation in Southern India. I am relaxed and happy and standing on a terrace in front of a teak bungalow, surrounded by jungle. Next to me stands a smiling travel companion.

Or so I remember. The photo has been mutilated. Someone has angrily cut out the young man's head, leaving behind just a headless torso in denim shorts. I sense instantly it was Lisa who found the picture and jaggedly cut out the head. I suddenly start shaking, feel like I might throw up, and I upend the drawer's entire contents, including the photo, into the garbage bag. I can't get rid of the picture quick enough.

But the shaking doesn't stop, and when I start jotting down on a stickum that the fly-tying workbench is a gift to my friend, Walter Iten, I find I can't write the sentence. My arm is trembling too hard. I look down at the limb, like it is something foreign, not a part of me. I have the coolness of mind to observe the tremors are just on the right side of my body, but they won't stop, and now I am seeing zigzags of light and am visited by an entirely new kind of searing pain.

I crawl on all fours to the crushed-velvet couch. I lie down and look out the French doors, at the roses, as my body shakes with the tremors and pain. As I lie there, clammy with sweat, waiting for it to pass or turn into something worse, images begin circling, silver shadows slowly coming up from the deep.

One of them morphs into the young man with the long hair slicked down with pomade. He is looking intently at me.

"It's not my fault," he says. "I never asked you to keep the secrets."

NINE

The room slowly reveals itself. There is a large window with a view of the Lake of Zürich. On the sill stands a glass vase filled with tiger lilies and Queen Anne's lace—and Lisa's poncho.

"Don't ever do that again," Lisa says. "You scared me so, José."

"Where am I?"

"The Hirschlanden Hospital. They came and took you by helicopter."

How much is all this costing me? Looks more like a hotel than a hospital.

There is tugging on the left.

A nurse in uniform and short-cropped silver hair is fiddling with the drip taped into my hand, and watching the heart monitor to the side of the bed.

"Can you understand me? What is your name?"

My head is pounding like I have been drinking *aguardiente* for a week. There is a Vaseline-like film over my eyes.

"José María Álvarez de Oviedo."

Lisa kisses the right side of my face, again and again. "You *are* back. Oh, José. You gave Alfredo and me such a scare."

Dr. Sutter strides into the room. "Aaah. You are alert. I see that already in your eyes,

Herr Álvarez. Welcome back. You had a nasty seizure."

The nurse and Lisa help me sit up, as Dr. Sutter takes a flashlight from his coat pocket and waves it before my eyes. "Nurse, take note. Pupils dilating. Responding appropriately to light stimulus."

The doctor and nurse speak then in Swiss German as they have me move my fingers and toes. My mind is too slow-moving to follow what they say, but I kept hearing the word *Hirn*, which I know means brain.

"Yes. Yes. We had here abnormal electrical activity in the temporal lobe, caused by the tumor. It was causing the seizures. We could see the activity on the EEG. But we have given you seizure medicine, similar to what we give epileptics. That seems to have calmed things down."

"I feel like I have been on a bender."

"Ha ha. A joke. *Ja.* This is good."

A scrape against my heel, with a steel instrument, and my toes curl involuntarily.

"Tell me what happened, just before you lost consciousness."

"I had a funny sensation. In my stomach. And then my arm began to tingle and shake. I remember crawling to the couch . . ."

"This is what we call a 'complex partial.' Did you have any visions? Hallucinations?"

I look out the window.

"Herr Álvarez?"

"Yes, I've had hallucinations. But it's not that simple."

"What do you mean?"

"The blackouts, they are not actual blackouts. I am reliving memories. They are very vivid, things that I have not thought about in many years and have actively tried to forget. But they are not hallucinations. It's like watching a film of my younger self."

"This is actually a good sign. There is frequently a loss of memory in cases like this, sometimes profound. With the tumor growing, it could all go, the memories. *Pfffft* . . . just like that. So this is reassuring. This deep part of your brain is still functioning, as it should. But we will want to do some more scans."

Bile rises in my throat. I begin to cough. I look frantically for Lisa and calm down once I realize she has shifted her chair to the back of the room, so the doctor and nurse can move around my bed.

"And the hallucinations?" continues Dr. Sutter.

"They happen when I am conscious and going about the day."

"Flashes of light? Noises? Or full hallucinations?"

"There are lights, sometimes, yes, but I am mostly visited by a young man. He comes to me, again and again. He seems as real as you are now."

"For God's sake, José!" Lisa exclaims. "Why didn't you tell me? How frightening that must be. Why must you keep everything a secret? Honestly."

"Is this figure someone you recognize? Someone real. Like with the returning memories."

"No. He's a man with long hair, and seems vaguely familiar, like I did know him once. But I really don't. I do recognize his smell, however."

"His smell?"

"Suavecito. It's a pomade the men in my family used to wear, years ago, in Spain."

Much scratching of the pen before he looks up again.

"We will get you a psychiatrist to talk to. He can perhaps help with this."

I shrug. *"No sé."*

I am filled with an almost unbearable sadness. I anxiously ask Lisa whether she has heard from our sons. Lisa does not respond. She sits a little taller in her chair in the back, her hands clasped in her lap, her eyes wide with alarm. She has an uncomprehending look on her face. I glance over at the nurse and the doctor, and they, too, are looking at me with peculiar expressions. Dr. Sutter puts a hand on my wrist. "Herr Álvarez," he says gently. "We can't understand you. You are speaking a foreign language. It has an old sound. Could it be Basque?"

I don't want to be stuck in the hospital—until I die.

So I concentrate hard, try to make it all look easy.

"Was I? Sorry. Slip of the tongue. Lisa, I was asking about the boys. Have they called?"

"Sam called and I told him what is going on. It just poured out of me. I'm sorry, but this isn't just about you anymore. I had to tell him. I need someone to talk to as well, you know, and since I told Sam, well, I of course had to tell Rob and John. So they all know." She looks at me, defiantly. "It was the right thing to do."

"*Bueno.* I am ready to see them."

"Well, thank God. Because they're all on their way here."

Dr. Sutter orders MRI scans, and then turns back to me a final time. "Staff will be coming to take you shortly to another part of the hospital for the scans. Afterward, we will start the rehab, to get the motor running again."

I grab Sutter's wrist and make him look me straight in the face. "I want to go home. If I need round-the-clock private nurses—*no me importa.* I will hire all the nurses and equipment you want. But I want you to send me home."

"Yes. Yes. I am aware of your wishes." He looks down at his wrist and I let go. "We will send you home as soon as we can, Herr Álvarez. But let us just conclude these tests, so we know how best to make you comfortable."

Again that fucking word.

Qué mierda.

· · ·

My wife and I are finally alone. We hold hands.

"Lisa. I am sorry. For everything."

"Please stop saying that."

"I have to talk sometimes. It helps."

"All right. What about?"

"The things that haunt me . . ."

"Look, José. We've all done things we regret. Sometimes we hurt the people we love most. It's a fact. I was just talking about this with my friend the other night. The analyst."

"Oh, God. What did *she* have to say on the subject?"

"She says, in her experience, the key is not to lie to yourself about the crimes you have committed, but to try and let in what you have done and why you did it at the time. That's the path to forgiving yourself."

"That's pop psychology."

"Well, if you don't forgive yourself, you also won't forgive others, and that means you're likely to commit the same crimes again and again. Is that what you want? I'm not sure what other options you think there are."

You don't understand. I'm not strong enough to face what I have done.

But I cannot say what is in my heart. She sees the pain in my face, however, and instantly softens. "Oh, dear. Let's change the subject. The last thing you need right now is a stressful conversation." She snaps open her purse, retrieves a tissue, and speaks cheerfully. "I have to tell you about your departure from the farm. It really was something. The helicopter landed in the field in the back of the house, and all our Swiss neighbors came out for a good look over the fence. Like cows. Herr Müller even came down our lane and asked me what kind of helicopter it was. Imagine that. Here's a woman whose husband is convulsing and fighting for his life—and this man is asking me what kind of helicopter the emergency service is using. Really. The Swiss are . . ." But she stops herself, looks down at her lap. "That doesn't matter anymore. None of it matters."

"No. It doesn't."

I hold her hand a little tighter. "I'm slipping away, Lisa."

"Yes, I can feel it."

"The borders of my mind are falling apart."

"I'm so sorry. I would do anything to help. It's difficult to watch."

Lisa rests her head on my stomach, her face turned so she can stare up at me, over the lumpy cover. She brings my liver-spotted hand up to her lips, to kiss it. I stroke her head. We sit like that for some time. There is a pattering sound on the windowsill. It is starting to gust and drizzle outside.

"I think it's time I speak with Hans-Peter.

Before it's too late. I need to finalize my affairs. While I still can."

Lisa sits bolt upright. She has been waiting for this.

"Yes, of course. I'll call him right now."

"Hoppla, Herr Álvarez."

I was sleeping. Emphasis on *was*. A nurse's aide, whom I haven't seen before, is standing in front of me. She is just thirty, I guess, and has purple-dyed hair, a ring through her nose, and a tattoo of a lotus on her neck. She is smiling in that forced way that infects health-care workers. She is trying to get me to sit up.

"Hoppla? Is this something I am meant to do?"

"Ja. Ja. Time for *Physiotherapie."*

With one yank she has the covers off and is swinging my legs onto the steps that help me off the high bed.

"You. Stop pushing. *Joder."*

She keeps on pushing, as if I haven't spoken.

"You! Goddammit. Stop it with the pushing!"

The nurse and I stare at each other.

She grabs my hand and makes me clasp the drip pole.

"My name is Ursula. Stop saying 'you.' It is rude. Call me by my name, Ursula."

We begin walking from the room, very slowly, out into the corridor. "Lock that cabinet," I say. "People are coming in and stealing my clothes."

"No one is stealing your clothes, Herr Álvarez."

But she locks the cabinet anyway.

We walk down the long hospital hall. It takes forever.

"What happened to your hair?"

"It is the fashion."

"*Oh Dios mío.* Do you have tattoos on other body parts?"

"Yes."

"That ring through your nose. It makes you look like a bull."

"Herr Álvarez. I respect you. Please return me the favor."

After what seems like an interminable long walk in silence through the busy hospital, we enter a studio, set up with blue floor mats, parallel bars, and leg pulleys attached to Pilates contraptions. There are three patients at work with physiotherapists, two white-haired and bent and looking worse than I feel; the other, a teenage girl, has braces on her legs and a helmet on her head.

"Sit in this chair. I want to see how you get up."

Oh, God. She's not a nurse's aide but my physiotherapist.

Cabrón! *Why did you have to say that thing about the nose ring?*

You're such an idiot!

It is utterly brutal. Worse than I expected. I am at Ursula's mercy for the next ninety minutes, and

197

by the end, I am panting and sweating from the ball passing, the balance exercises, the painful stretches.

But—*coño*!—I make it through the ordeal.

"I thought you were going to be difficult, Herr Álvarez. But you did your exercises well. You worked hard."

"It's the quickest way out of the hospital, isn't it?"

"Yes."

"*Bueno.* I am motivated."

She walks me back to the hospital's west wing, through a glass-walled corridor decorated with contemporary art, splotchy and cheerful with color. The hallway opens up into a large waiting room, where seats are taken up by Middle Eastern families, the women buried under the hijab; elderly Italians, their skin leathery from too many years in the Amalfi sun; and a couple of African men in shiny suits. There is one family that touches me: the Swiss couple that sits patiently with their two children bent and twisted with cerebral palsy.

We are all waiting. Waiting.

I stop.

"Herr Álvarez. What is it?"

Suavecito.

"Are you in pain? You are white."

I follow the smell of lavender. There, in the corner of the waiting room, his head down, the man with the long hair. His foot is crossed and jiggling furiously, like a combustible engine ready to explode. He is reading a book.

"Ursula. Please. Take me to that corner."

The physiotherapist looks uncertain, but she can see the need in my face, and so she gently touches my elbow and we begin walking to the far corner of the waiting room.

"Is this where you want to be? Near this plant?"

I stand before the young man. His head is still down. He is reading *Biggles*.

That's why he seemed so familiar.

My brother, as he might have been had he lived into his thirties, slowly shuts *Biggles' Second Case* and looks up at me. But still he won't speak.

"Juanito. What do you want? For the love of God, tell me what you want."

"Herr Álvarez, are you having an episode? Talk to me. I am about to call for assistance. You must address me. There is no one here. You are not making sense."

It is definitely Juan. He is there, in the young man's eyes.

Say something, Juan, please. I beg you.

He finally speaks.

"Come home, José María. It's time for you to come home."

There is frost on the window when Hans-Peter Grieder comes by. He brings me *Schocki-Stengeli*, the kirsch-filled chocolate sticks from Lindt & Sprüngli. It's a singularly odd gift, considering the amount of drugs I am on, but I don't say a word.

The alcohol-filled chocolates are my crack, as he knows, and I tear open the box. After I have had my fill, I say, "Let's get on with this." Hans-Peter hands me a napkin from the table, to wipe the chocolate off my face, before taking documents out of his briefcase. He recites what I had previously left Lisa.

"That's good," I say. "Now, additionally, I want the boys to get ten million Swiss francs each. It's enough to buy them some comforts—but not enough to kill their ambitions. They'll still have to work."

Hans-Peter scratches away at his pad, takes careful notes. "And the bulk of the estate? The shares in the bank?"

"I leave all my remaining assets, in trust, to Médecins Sans Frontières. It's an excellent organization."

Hans-Peter calmly writes my instructions down. He makes me sign and date his notes. But I have known him a long time and can see the flickers behind his eyes. He wants to say something.

"Are you shocked by my decision?"

"It is not my position to be shocked. This is your wealth. You must do with it as you see fit."

"Come on, Hans-Peter. Don't go all Swiss

banker on me. *Coño.* We are old friends. Speak your mind."

Hans-Peter looks out the window before answering.

"I am speaking as your friend, not as your banker. This money is what you leave the world, how you finally settle up the unfinished business of life, and, possibly, how you make amends and correct mistakes made while on this earth. Médecins Sans Frontières is an excellent organization, true, but I personally don't see its connection to you and your life."

"Well, I guess I asked for it."

"The decision appears to me, if I may say so, rather fractured and arbitrary and disassociated from your life and who you are. You could have just as well left your wealth to abused animals or battered women as Médecins Sans Frontières. I think you are missing a real opportunity here to make a statement about who José María is and how he marked his time on this earth."

"Christ. You don't hold back. All right, you said your piece. Let's wrap this up."

"I will get the paperwork executed and return in a day or two to have you sign all the documents. But there is one more thing I need to bring up. It's related to this estate decision."

"Go on."

"Word has got out that you are not well. I was invited to two lunches, back to back, with Rudolf

Schneider from Swiss Federal Credit Bank, and with Peter Stücki, on the Zürich Union Bank's board. They both expressed interest, on behalf of their institutions, in buying Privatbank Álvarez GmbH. Now Von Streubel has asked me for a meeting. The bank is in play, in other words, and, with so much interest, it could fetch a hefty premium."

"That's interesting. What do you think?"

"It would be foolish not to consider a sale. None of your heirs seem interested in running the bank."

"You are my heir."

Hans-Peter is clearly touched, in his bound-up Swiss way, that I would say something like that. But it's true. He has, in many ways, been more a son to me than my own sons have been.

"Well, you should at least consider the possibility of a sale. Interest like this doesn't come around every day, and the bids could be played off each other. We could fetch between one point five billion and one point nine billion Swiss francs for the bank."

"*Bueno.* Thank you. I will take it under consideration."

My old partner packs up, shakes my hand goodbye, and slips out of my room. I'm exhausted by the effort of giving away my life and grab a few more kirsch-filled *Schocki-Stengeli* from the box. I've earned them.

• • •

There is a God. Hallelujah.

Dr. Sutter is releasing me from the hospital. But not without giving me a little speech first. "All right, Herr Álvarez. I am satisfied you are stable enough to go home. But, from now on, you must be prepared that things will be different. You are entering the end stages. Do you understand?"

The important thing is you are returning to Ägeri.

The ambulance reaches the farmhouse. I am elated. But a battered blue Volkswagen Passat is waiting for us in the courtyard. That makes me suspicious.

What now?

The EMTs lower me in a wheelchair from the back of the ambulance, and a large white-haired woman, with massive forearms made for kneading bread, climbs out from behind the Passat wheel, clutching a file. She wears sensible tie-up shoes, a long floral skirt around her bulging midriff, and a billowy white blouse and cardigan.

She is smiling and waving at me in an overly familiar way.

"*Ja, Gruezi wohl Herr Álvarez!*"

"Hello," I say coldly. "Who are you?"

"I am Sister Bertha. From St. Agatha's Hand of Mercy."

"I see." I gesture at the bag on my lap. "You can bring in my bag."

She roars with laughter, as if that is the funniest thing she has ever heard.

"No. No. You are quite capable of helping yourself."

She grabs my arm and with great force hauls me up out of the wheelchair. She forces me to carry my bag in one hand, while balancing myself with the other on the pole that is dragging along my drip. Her own fist is clamped like a vise above my elbow, keeping me on my feet in case I stumble.

"It is good to work the muscles. If not, you become like a hard pear."

Lisa comes around the other side of the ambulance and finds Big Bertha hauling me around the courtyard, my drip rattling as I drag it across the cobblestone toward the front door.

"Oh. You've met. Sister Bertha is from hospice, José."

"*Ja. Ja.* Your husband and me. We are already old friends."

I look at my wife with pleading eyes. Her eyes let me know she understands my distress but there is nothing she can do. I am now in the nurse's care.

"Lift your feet," Bertha barks. "Lift your feet. *Ja.* That is better."

"Take this."

I am in my bed in the study, and Sister Bertha is

clutching a gray-and-white bottle in her massive fist and thrusting a spoon at me.

"What is it?" I ask.

"Stool softener. Go on. It will make you go caca."

Impossible woman.

I make a face.

"*Mein Gott, Herr Álvarez*! You fight everything. Constipation is side effect of opiates. You have been complaining. So, now, take the stool softener. Do you want to feel uncomfortable? *Verstopft.*"

It is true. I feel like I am going to explode. I open my mouth and she spoons the gray-pink liquid down my throat.

"Two spoons. *Ja prima. So isch guet.* Now rest. I will sit here and do my knitting."

She sits next to me, and pulls her red wool and knitting needles out of her bag. I close my eyes, try to rest, but I hear the clack-click of her fast-moving needles and they make me think of my mother. My eyes pop back open.

"What are you doing?"

"I am making woolen caps. For the poor souls with HIV and hepatitis C. They die of liver failure usually. Cirrhosis."

"Why woolen caps if their livers are falling apart? It doesn't make sense."

"In the end stages of those diseases, the patients become very cold. I make the woolen caps to help them feel warm. I am not sure it helps. But we have to do something to help the poor souls, don't we?"

"How in God's name does someone get all those diseases at once?"

"Unsafe sex and drugs."

"Oh. Of course."

"I once took care of a young man in Zürich. He was a prostitute. He must have been handsome once, but when I took care of him, when he was dying, he was not pretty at all. He was only thirty-six but looked like he was seventy. They give off a bad smell, from their breath, when the liver is failing. It is a very hard death. There is much pain in the joints."

"Sounds gruesome."

"But you know, some people, when they die, they are full of rage at what the world gave them. And some, it is the opposite. They are filled with God's grace. This young man was quite special. He was cold, so I knit him a cap. I finished it, he put it on, and then he died. He was in such pain, but he stayed alive just long enough to wear the cap he knew I was knitting for him. I could see it. Such a remarkable young man. We had so many interesting conversations before he died."

Sister Bertha gets choked up. She dips into her bag, retrieves a handkerchief, and wipes her nose after a good honk.

"*Ja*. Enough of this. There is a special place in heaven for the young men and women who sell their bodies. They suffer so much while on this earth. So I knit the caps, for when they come to me. But always in Miguel's honor and memory."

I am sweating and freezing at the same time.

"Where was he from?"

"Miguel? He was one of your compatriots. From Barcelona."

I look at her anew—and wonder.

Is this the hand of God at work?

Or am I hallucinating?

I awake with a jerk. I stare out the French doors at the fleshy red petals. I have come to rely on a single, surviving winter rose to ground me and remind me where I am. But the nauseating wave of pain that woke me makes stars flash before my eyes. I push the red button in my hand and am flooded with opiate relief.

I smell lime shaving cream and spearmint gum.

My brain is no longer functioning properly, but my sense of smell, for some reason, has become acute. I sniff the air again, to see if I am imagining things.

I am not.

I turn over on my side.

"Hi, Pops. You're awake."

Sam is a little grayer at the temples than I remembered, but still handsome and fit looking, sitting calmly in a tweed jacket and faded jeans in the armchair by my bed.

My eldest. He has come.

"Oh, Sam. I am so happy to see you."

I make an effort to sit up and he jumps to help. He plumps my pillows, kisses my forehead. I grab him back in teary gratitude, and bend as far forward as I can manage, to kiss whatever flesh and muscle I can find on his forearm. Sam stares at me blank faced, unused to seeing me so demonstrative and emotional.

Pull yourself together. Pull yourself together.

"Sorry. I am just so happy to see you. When did you arrive?"

"About an hour ago. You were sleeping. Mom told me not to wake you. I've been catching up with her upstairs."

"*Hostia.* She has undoubtedly informed you of all my affairs, sparing none of the details."

"Are you in pain?"

I wave a hand, dismissively.

"Comes and goes. When I get an attack, I push this little red button here and—presto—opiates flood the system. I finally got a taste of what all you boys were doing when you were teenagers."

"Watch out when John's here. When you're asleep, he might sneak in, unhook you, and attach himself to the drip."

"Ha ha. Yes, well, there are downsides, too. The constipation. I feel like I am packed full of toxic waste. Can't get rid of the damn stuff."

"Ouch."

I brush my bald spot, the invisible hair. "How do I look?"

"Honestly, not bad. A little thinner. The way Mom talked about you, I expected you to look much worse."

It is 11:30 a.m. Sister Bertha, in her dull gray dress and cropped silver hair, comes through the door. She is startled by my son's presence, but recovers and says, in her deep baritone, "*Gruezi wohl, Herr Álvarez Junior.*"

Sam responds accordingly and she formally shakes my son's hand, before turning in my direction. "Now is time for pills, Herr Álvarez Senior."

"Sam, this woman is here all day, torturing me."

"So amusing, your father. We should put him on *die Bühne*—the stage."

Sam smiles appreciatively at how she is handling me, and backs away from the bed, to give her room. "Thank you for all you are doing for my father, Sister. We can't thank you enough."

"Don't encourage her, Sam. I want her out of the house. Out."

Big Bertha smiles at my nonsense, hands me a glass of water, and makes me take three pills. Even I know I can't do without her.

You can't even remember what these fucking pills are for.

Bertha takes my pulse, checks the drip, and speaks again to Sam. "I am in the room next door. Always. Night and day. Just ring this bell if you need me. My relief, Sister Martha, works on the weekend."

Sister Bertha leaves, and my son and I find ourselves sitting in silence, our small talk already exhausted. Sam stares slit-eyed into space, rubs his temples, his right foot jiggling. I wish for Bertha to return.

There is movement in the corner of my eye.

Juan is sitting behind my desk, in the shadows, staring at us.

I turn back to my son. "So," I say with effort. "How is . . . ?"

Coño. *I can't remember her name.*

"Sharon. She's fine."

"And the girls?"

"Good. They switched boarding schools. They're in New Hampshire now."

"I see."

Another silence.

"Dad . . . I am sorry about all this. Truly. You don't deserve this. No one does."

We look at each other.

"It is what it is. Let's talk about other things. What's the latest with your Maritime Strategy Impact Fund?"

"We made *Barron's* list of the top fifty impact-investment funds again. We're ranked eighth."

"*Fantástico*. What an accomplishment."

I strain to remember everything I can about his fund. I recall it invests in for-profit companies tackling the environmental issues of our polluted oceans. I know one company he is heavily invested in, a Danish biotech firm, is trying to create enzymes and microbes that break down petroleum-based scum and other ocean pollutants. But beyond that, what he is doing is a mystery to me.

"What's your latest strategy?"

Sam's face lights up. He leans forward in his chair, makes a steeple with his fingers, his voice no longer wary. He goes on about how one warm winter day, passing through Reykjavik, Iceland, he sat at an outdoor café, next to a river that ran through the town. It was the first time in a while since he had been to Iceland in January, and there was just a smattering of snow, not the usual deep snowdrifts and frozen landscape.

In that moment, sipping tea, sun on his face, Sam had an epiphany. He realized that global warming had probably affected rivers near the Arctic Circle. Water that previously had been a frigid one to two degrees Celsius in the summer, too cold to sustain salmon, had in the last decade risen to five to eight degrees Celsius, the optimum temperatures for breeding salmon.

That meant, he realized, once icy and barren rivers in nearby Greenland could be turned—

with enough capital investment, for hatcheries and proper river management—into productive salmon rivers, collecting high rod fees from sports fishermen, and in effect turning a nonproductive natural asset into a major source of income for his fund and the impoverished Inughuit who lived in the area. And newly productive rivers would help replenish the world's dwindling stocks of wild salmon.

"Bringing salmon back," he says, smiling slyly, "while good for the environment, is also a huge turn-on to my investors, who, as you know, are looking to earn market-rate returns from positive environmental and social projects. The play, I realized, could massively increase our fund's credibility with impact investors and create a virtuous circle of bringing in more funding for our projects."

So that day, before others saw the opportunity, Sam was on a plane and quietly negotiating an "exclusive long-term river development agreement" with the Greenland government. Negotiations were drawn out and tough, particularly over revenue-sharing terms, but in the end the agreement was successfully concluded. A spin-off fund was jointly created with the Greenland government, and Sam has since raised $295 million in capital from new investors.

"You would love it, Dad. Our marine biologists

are now traveling through Greenland, identifying the rivers best suited to turn into new salmon habitat. It's not just river temperatures they are measuring, but also how much insect life lives in the waters, so the salmon parr born in the river, before they head to sea to feed and fatten up, actually have enough food to sustain them during those crucial early years of river life. Also, some rivers have natural geological impediments—a high waterfall that no returning salmon could climb, for example—so that, too, will factor into our decisions. In such cases we might want to build ladders, but that significantly raises development costs and it's very risky. Salmon, as you and I know, don't always like the man-made ladders. But it's pretty exciting and really fun to figure out."

And then, because we are both financiers at heart, he walks me through the numbers. How he figures it will cost on average $1.2 million to develop twenty kilometers of river, with an on-site hatchery costing an additional $2 million. He goes on, in great financial detail, but his calculations are too complicated, I cannot follow him, and I realize then, with great sadness, my mind is no longer up to the task.

"Payback to our investors should take place in year five. The returns could ultimately exceed sixty percent per annum," he says. Sam is spent by his speech, and he retreats to his temple-rubbing posture, with his eyes half closed.

I am so moved, so proud of him.

Such passion. Such brilliance. He is my boy.

"Sam, Sam. You should have taken over the family bank. What we could have accomplished together."

My son stiffens, sits up in the armchair. "Please don't start with that again, Dad. I just got here. We've done enough rounds on that one to last several lifetimes. Come on. I come in peace. Let's put it aside, take it easy."

"You know that Hans-Peter and I cleaned up the bank. We don't handle clients with tainted sources of wealth anymore."

"Yeah, after 9/11 and you had no choice but to clean up or get busted."

That remark hurts me and I can't help it—I get angry. "That's a distortion of the facts. You know full well that Hans-Peter and I began our new strategy, of only accepting onshore money, before 9/11."

"Don't kid a kidder, Dad. We both know you'd still be in the business of laundering money for crooks if you could get away with it."

"Why do you say such things?"

"Why did you bring the bank up again?"

"You act so superior. Don't forget that bank has allowed you to be a do-gooder."

Sam rolls his eyes. "Oh Christ. Here we go again."

"*Coño*. Don't be like that. I can't help it. It hurts. Our family bank has been run by an Álvarez for five generations—and all this now dies with my sons? Imagine how I feel. Like I failed. I can just see my father's face."

"Yeah. Whatever." Sam stands up. "I am going up to see Mom now. What do you do for lunch?"

I turn on my side and over my shoulder say, "Don't trouble yourself. Your mother brings me my lunch."

I stare at the ceiling. Shadows are shifting and moving.

My son despises me. This is my legacy.

Someone is coming down the stairs. I turn. It isn't Sam, but Lisa with my lunch tray. She silently and stiffly puts the tray down in front of me.

Uh oh. You're in trouble.

"What?"

"You know what. He hasn't been home in eight years and this is what you start with?"

"He's too touchy. Still a little boy."

Her lips are tight and thin—a bad sign.

"You never have the good grace to admit when you are wrong, José. Why can't you just let people be who they are? It's so sad to see a man reach this age and still not get it. Really."

I put my head down and take a slurp of pea soup.

"I am who I am."

"Yes, you are. And Sam is the way Sam is. Why should one rule exist for you and another for your sons?"

"*Joder.* You should have been a lawyer."

"We have raised fine, strong boys, who are decent and know what they want. I hope you appreciate what you have. Before it is too late."

I don't respond, but her remark, it sits in the pit of my stomach, with everything else that is already sitting there, and for the first time I really let in the possibility that I might have been wrong all this time.

Maybe this is what this mierda *is all about. Perhaps this death is providing me the time to process events and look at things a new way. Maybe I need to rejoice that the boys defied my will, became men in their own right, and found callings that brought meaning to their lives, not mine.*

"Tell Sam I am sorry. I won't bring up the bank again."

"No. I am tired of being your messenger. You tell him yourself."

I push the half-eaten bowl of soup away from me. I know I should nibble on a bit of cheese and apple, but my hand won't reach for the food. I have no appetite. Lisa is sitting on the stool, looking peevishly out the French doors.

"Take the tray away. I've had enough. When are Roberto and Juan arriving?"

216

She turns back in my direction. "I told you. They are flying in together tomorrow morning. Remember? We've discussed this a few times already. Sam is going to pick them up at the airport. He'll take the Volvo."

"Tell him . . ."

"What?"

"Forget it."

Green fire is leaping from Lisa's head, and when she stands to retrieve the tray, the air shimmers around her, like ripples of water lapping out from a lily pad. I don't know if I should tell Lisa that she is entirely green, wearing armor, and holding a scepter. It might alarm her.

Lisa is now all frog, and her long tongue is lashing the air. "We're going to have a special dinner in the dining room tonight, to celebrate the fact our oldest son is home. I don't want any trouble from you, José. Sister Bertha and Sam will help you get upstairs, and I don't want to hear anything about how you want to stay down here. You need to use your legs more or your muscles will atrophy."

I say OK and look down at the floor.

Lisa turns, to go back upstairs, and the Frog Queen steps out of her.

I am so relieved my wife has been restored. I could weep.

But for the rest of the afternoon, the Frog Queen sits squat and fat in the corner of the room, gulping, her large eyes feasting on me, a sort of embarrassed smile on her face. This I don't like, and I turn and face the French doors, so I don't have to look at her. I let the tumors and morphine take me where they like. But after a little while of floating aimlessly, I hear the Frog Queen shuffle closer to the French doors, see her craning around the corner to get a better look at me.

She is gulping, wide-eyed, somehow letting me know she isn't satisfied with my progress. This makes me angry and I turn, to talk back at her, when she smacks the scepter up the side of my head, catapulting me out of this world.

Part IV

1972

SAN SEBASTIÁN, NORTHERN SPAIN

TEN

Señor Fernando Fernandez, appointed the president of Banco Álvarez after my father died, called me in Zürich at 5:30 a.m. I was half asleep when he told me I needed to come immediately to San Sebastián, for a special board meeting. My former supervisor in accounting, Señor Domingo, had recently retired, and the new head of accounting had discovered his predecessor had systematically embezzled at least 620 million pesetas from the bank over the last decade of his employment.

The bank was now overrun with investigators from the Department of Finance and subject to a government audit. When the police went to Señor Domingo's apartment, he was nowhere to be found. But as soon as they opened his closets, they realized he had been living a lavish lifestyle. Bills they found from Church's on Jermyn Street in London suggested he had spent ten thousand pounds on shoes in the last year alone. Other letters they found indicated Domingo might be hiding with a friend somewhere in Colombia. The San Sebastián police had requested that Interpol issue an international arrest warrant.

"I will get there as soon as I can," I said into the phone.

A lot went through my head as I scrambled to head down to Spain. I had been back to San Sebastián only twice since I left for Columbia University and then moved to Switzerland. Once, to attend my mother's funeral; the next time, after I had graduated, for the bank's extraordinary board meeting, when we appointed Señor Fernandez the new president and CEO, after my father dropped dead of a heart attack.

Spain had no pull or attraction for me. But my absence had come at a price, I now realized. Without an Álvarez on the ground in Spain, looking out after the family's investment, the bank had been mismanaged and driven aground. I had made a huge mistake and now had to salvage what I could of my inheritance.

I asked Lisa to pack my bag and told my secretary to book my flights. I informed Herr Albiez, my superior at Swiss Federal Credit Bank, what was happening and why I needed time off. Then I got on the phone, my black address book open by my side, and called in every favor I could think of from New York to Zürich to San Sebastián and Madrid.

I needed information—the true currency of banking.

Not too many years ago the staff all greeted me when I walked Banco Álvarez's marble lobby, but now I slipped in through the glass doors unrecognized. In my father's day, the bank was alive with the buzz of commerce: discussions with clients, the sound of porters bringing papers in and out of the bank, boxes of cash on trolleys wheeled up from the vault and counted out at the teller stations.

Managers, with nothing to do, stared blankly at me from their desks. The only activity in the lobby came from a long line of silent and grim customers at the sole open teller, withdrawing their money. Even the giant rubber plants that grew up the walls on either side of the central staircase, once waxy green and jungle-like, were now sickly and yellow and covered in a film of dust.

I took the central staircase. Papá's old secretary burst into tears when I stepped into his former office suite. "What have we come to?" Louisa wailed. I hugged her, said something soothing, but also reminded her there wasn't time for hand-wringing since the board meeting was about to start. Louisa got ahold of herself and ushered me upstairs to the main conference room.

The entire board was waiting for me. Señor Fernandez, pale and dour as sour milk, came forward and ushered me to my seat. There were handshakes all around the boardroom table, somber greetings. I sat next to Alfonso Gorrindo, my father's trusted lawyer and advisor. I studied him. He was elderly now. His black and curly hair was white, as was the handlebar mustache, now streaked nicotine yellow from his years smoking. But his eyes were still piercingly blue, and, despite his age, he still looked as immovable and solid as the Picos de Europa.

"It is good to see you again, José, if not under these conditions," Gorrindo said quietly, kissing me on both cheeks. "A sad day. I keep thinking of your father."

"Thank you, *Tio*," I said, using the old and affectionate term for uncle, as I used to call him when I was a boy.

Señor Fernandez stood up to brief us on the bank's precarious state of affairs. Key customers, who had heard the rumors, were quietly closing down their accounts and withdrawing their money. Worse still, as the lines down below suggested, those in the know were, with every hour that transpired, steadily growing in number. The bank was currently hemorrhaging 250 million pesetas a day, and the central bank in Madrid had two days ago lent Banco Álvarez short-term emergency funds, so we could meet withdrawals in an orderly way.

But they had also parachuted auditors into the bank, to advise Madrid on next steps, if Banco Álvarez needed to be seized by the state. The forensic accountants were still unraveling Señor Domingo's fraud, but already they knew it was much bigger and more complex than first thought, with no end yet in sight. As to Domingo's motive, that, too, was a mystery. It seemed to be a simple case of greed. He had an unquenchable appetite for beautiful things. The amount stolen, so far, was 1.2 billion pesetas and mounting.

Fernandez cleared his throat and told us that worse was yet to come. That morning he had received a call from a reporter at *El Diario Vasco*, asking for comment. The reporter had clearly been briefed by someone intimate with the details, had all the facts, and wanted an official response before the newspaper went to press.

Fernandez had immediately called the paper's publisher, a member of his church, in an attempt to get the story quashed. But the publisher told him the truth could not be hidden from the public anymore—they had a right to know the bank was in trouble and that their life savings were in jeopardy—and not even God almighty could stop the article from going to the printer at this point. The piece would appear on the front page of tomorrow's newspaper. "We were told to brace ourselves," said Fernandez, his voice quavering.

At that moment, Louisa came back into the boardroom and announced that Señor Martin of Banco Central de Bilbao was on the phone and wanting to talk with me, the bank's majority shareholder. Every head turned in my direction. I stood with only one thought going through my head.

I am not equipped for this. I am too young.

The board chairman brought down the gavel and announced we would temporarily interrupt the meeting so that I could hear what Emilio Martin Senior had to say. I followed Louisa to her office and picked up the phone.

"*Sí? José María Álvarez de Oviedo aquí.*"

"*Buenos días, Señor Álvarez.* Thank you for coming to the phone," said the senatorial voice. "This is Señor Martin of Grupo Central de Bilbao. I am across the park from your office. In the back booth of Café Santiago. With my son. We'd very much like to talk with you."

"I am in a board meeting. This is highly irregular."

"We live in irregular times."

I paused. There was no point pretending. It was clear he knew everything already, even the time and place of this hastily called emergency board meeting.

"Give me a few minutes. I'll be there shortly."

I put the phone down on the cradle. I had this odd sensation that I wasn't on terra firma, that everything was unmoored and floating loose before me. But as I had learned to do, when such a thing happened, I closed my eyes and imagined myself standing in a river, fishing, and the bile that bubbled up into my throat, like mercury in a barometer, returned from where it came.

I strode back into the boardroom.

"Martin is across the park with his son and wants to meet in person."

The chairman suggested, due to my relative youth, I take someone with me to the talks. I looked around the room and settled on my father's longtime lawyer.

"I want Señor Gorrindo to accompany me."

Señor Emilio Martin de Sánchez wore his thinning strands of olive-gray hair slicked back with pomade. He was waiting in the back booth of the simple café, with his thirty-six-year-old son, also Emilio, who, eight years earlier, had joined the bank's executive board. He was, by all accounts, more brilliant and dangerous than his father.

Gorrindo and I slid onto the padded bench opposite them in the booth. Thankfully, there was little appetite for small talk, and shortly after the formal greetings and handshakes, Martin Senior forlornly waved his liver-spotted hand and came around to the purpose of the meeting.

"*Entonces.* Let me start by saying how sorry I am about all this. I greatly admired your father. None of this would have happened had he still been alive."

"No. He would not have let this come to pass."

"I knew that weakling Fernandez would destroy Banco Álvarez, although, I admit, I had no idea he would do so with such thoroughness and so quickly. It's probably the only thing he has done efficiently in his entire life. He was a terrible choice to run your inheritance, young man."

"I see that now. But there is no point in talking about that. It is too late to undo that decision."

Emilio Martin Junior looked up and studied me, like he was trying to decide what kind of person I was.

"No, you are right about that," said Martin Senior, pursing his lips.

The room was very warm and Martin Senior was perspiring slightly. The light was catching the film of oil across his face, and I couldn't stop staring at his thick lips, which looked like brown slugs crawling out onto a leaf in the rain.

"Then let us talk about the future," he continued. "We have an offer that will allow you a graceful way out of your predicament."

"I am listening."

"When the article comes out tomorrow, Banco Álvarez is finished. There will be a run and Madrid will immediately step in, take over, and nationalize the bank. They have all the pieces in place and it will be over in minutes—and you will have lost everything. Poof. Your entire inheritance will be gone."

"Yes. I gathered that from this morning's briefing."

"We propose instead that Grupo Central de Bilbao acquire Banco Álvarez. Today, even while there is much uncertainty. We will pay you one peseta for the bank, but assume all its liabilities, known and unknown. If the losses wind up below three point five billion pesetas, and we wind up righting the ship within the next three years, then we will pay you fifteen percent of the revived bank's net profits, for the first five years following its return to profitability. Your share of profits will be on a sliding scale, of course. If the losses exceed five billion pesetas—you get nothing."

"I see."

"Listen, young man," he said, tapping my hand and again adopting his grandfatherly tone. "It's really not a bad offer. At least this way you stand a chance to extract some money from this mess. I don't have to tell you, if Madrid takes over, you are guaranteed to get nothing. But you have to agree to sell us the bank in the next two hours. We will have to issue the press release today, before the article comes out tomorrow morning. Or else it's all over."

Martin then glanced sideways at his son, who opened a manila folder that had been resting on the table between us. One paper outlined the basic terms of the offer, as he had just told me, while the other was a press release. Martin Junior slid both papers across the table to me.

I read the documents quickly and pushed them over to Gorrindo, who stroked his white mustache as he read, never saying a word. The face-saving exit was contained in the press release. It would be the case of one great Spanish banking family selling to another great Spanish banking family.

I looked out the window for a few moments, to buy myself time. "I remember, how, when I was a teenager, you tried to buy our bank from my father and he politely showed you the door. It was not for sale."

"That is quite right. Your memory serves you well."

"I believe you were in on those talks, too, Alfonso."

"I was."

"At that time, Papá said to me, 'José María, if you ever play poker with the Martins, know they cannot resist lowballing. They never pay top dollar for anything. That is their weakness. Always on the hunt for the bargain, they don't understand that sometimes an opportunity comes along only once in a lifetime and it is often cheaper, in the end, to pay a higher price for a first-class asset than it is to pay a low price for a second-tier property.' "

Martin Senior smiled appreciatively. "That sounds like your father. He had a way with words. And he is right. We are hard negotiators. It is nothing to be ashamed of."

"Forgive me, Señor Martin, but the situation calls for straight talk. Banco Álvarez's retail branches and strong commercial lending unit are jewels in the crown and a perfect fit for Grupo Central de Bilbao. With one stroke, you will have extended your bank's footprint throughout Northern Spain, which has always been your ambition. This current problem, while I don't want to dismiss its significance, is short-term in nature. The assets we have—the branch network, alone—are extremely valuable to Grupo Central de Bilbao. All other bank acquisitions in the region will have major overlaps with your bank and force you to sell off valuable assets. We are the only perfect fit for Grupo Central de Bilbao. Let us not forget the value of that."

Señor Martin looked around the café like he was mildly interested in ordering a coffee cake. "That is true. I'll admit it. We do want the Álvarez branch franchise."

He then turned back to look at me, and now the kindly paternal look was nowhere to be seen. His voice was icy. "But you forget, young man, you aren't in a position to dictate terms. You hold no cards."

When he said that, my heart skipped a beat, and my insecurity must have been apparent in my face, because Gorrindo opened his mouth, as if he were about to take over our talks. But I got ahold of myself and touched the lawyer's arm, signaling I was still doing the talking.

I shrugged. "That is a matter of perspective,

Señor Martin. Every year, for decades, my father quietly parked a sliver of the family's banking profits in Switzerland, just for this sort of rainy-day occasion. So I am just thirty and already have more than enough capital in Zürich to start again. My life is ahead of me—as are life's opportunities. I have built many bridges in New York and Zürich. If Banco Álvarez collapses, so be it. My family and me, we will be fine."

"I don't believe you would let your distinguished family bank collapse," he scoffed. "There is only dishonor in that. Your father would be rolling over in his grave, if he heard the cavalier way you are talking now."

Now it was my turn to look careless and unruffled. "With all due respect, Señor Martin, I know what my father would be thinking better than you do, and he would urge me, in these circumstances, not to be overly sentimental. And so I am not. Our bank is about to be taken over. It will either be the state or Grupo Central de Bilbao that grabs Banco Álvarez. Make no mistake—to me, it is all the same. It is over for us. The Álvarez family is out of commercial and retail banking in Spain. So it's really you who has to decide whether you will accept my terms. My demands are reasonable. The question is, Will you, as my father suggested you might, lose a once-in-a-lifetime opportunity by trying too hard to get the lowest possible price?"

Señor Martin turned an alarming scarlet color as I was talking, and it was clear he was just about to storm from the table. No one talked to him in this manner, and certainly not an impertinent young man. But Martin Junior put a hand on the old man's wrist, calming him down. "So, what is it you want from us?" he asked.

"The basic financial terms for Banco Álvarez you outlined are acceptable to me, but for one modification. At closing, I get a nonrefundable advance of seven hundred fifty million pesetas on the fifteen percent of profits earned from when the bank has been stabilized. I keep this minimum payment whether it turns a profit or not in three years."

The two Martins exchanged glances and I could tell that the demand was not a deal breaker.

"Anything else?" said the younger.

"I also want the private-banking license, now sitting dormant inside Banco Álvarez. It is my birthright, what I have painfully earned by going abroad. Franco granted the license to Papá specifically for me, and it is valuable in its own right."

"We'll have to think about that."

"I haven't finished. The Spanish private-banking license will be spun out into a separate holding company called Privatbank Álvarez GmbH, headquartered in Zürich. Grupo Central de Bilbao will finance this private-bank holding company with an additional two hundred fifty million pesetas in paid-in capital, in exchange for ten percent of the shares. The remaining ninety percent of the shares will be owned by my family and me. The private bank will have branches and representative offices in Spain, but I will personally run it from Zürich, with the care with which my father once ran the retail and commercial bank in Spain. It will be a wise investment on your part. I will make you money. But you will also have to sign a contract stating you agree to steer all potential private-banking customers at Grupo Central de Bilbao and Banco Álvarez exclusively to our jointly owned private bank in Zürich."

"That's impossible," scoffed Señor Martin Senior. "You are too young and inexperienced. We work with Zürich Union Bank on our clients' private-banking matters. We have an agreement with them."

"Undo it. If you want Banco Álvarez—that's my price."

"And if we refuse?" asked Martin the younger.

"Very simple. The state gets our bank, you lose the valuable franchise you have wanted for so long, and . . ."

"And what?"

"And I inform the authorities that you have secretly been obtaining confidential information about Banco Álvarez from Señor Gorrindo.

Franco's new minister of the economy has declared war on corporate espionage, as you know, and he will be very interested in what I have to say about how Banco Álvarez was systematically plundered and undermined—from within and without."

All three men visibly stiffened, but they were pros, and their expressions fairly quickly returned to a neutral stance.

"Preposterous. But, even hypothetically, if you were to make such allegations, you'll need to produce evidence," said my father's old lawyer. His voice was dry and matter-of-fact. "Madrid will not go against one of the nation's great banking families on the basis of some outlandish accusations by a thirty-year-old, who really is, let's face it, no longer a true Spaniard."

I turned my head and for a few moments just stared at Gorrindo.

"People loved doing business with Papá, Gorrindo, partly because he had great gifts as a communicator. He was warm, made people feel good. I am shy and not so charming as he was. But I am a far better judge of character than Papá ever was. He believed in the people he loved. He could never imagine, for example, that his own brother or best friend would betray him—and yet they both did. I am a much better businessman than my father ever was. I will never make those mistakes."

"I repeat. You need evidence of wrongdoing to make such ridiculous allegations in public."

I opened my briefcase and took out a telex. "A new US Treasury regulation requires that all banks incorporated in the US disclose fees paid to third-party service providers. This telex is from a senior partner of the accounting firm Arthur Anderson. He states here that Grupo Central de Bilbao's US unit, located on Park Avenue, has, as required, filed the new 16-F disclosures in New York State."

"Yes?"

"Alfonso Gorrindo Campo appears on the 16-F disclosure as having received two point two million dollars in fees for 'advisory services.' "

My family's US accountants had uncovered for me this 16-F with Gorrindo's name, just before I flew down to Spain to salvage my inheritance. It was clear, by the look on his face, that Papá's aging provincial lawyer in San Sebastián was unaware of the change in banking regulations across the Atlantic Ocean.

"You are a paid employee of Banco Álvarez and on its board, Gorrindo. Even in Spain, receiving such a rich payment from Banco Álvarez's competitor—cash payments funneled through its foreign branch—will be seen as highly irregular and suspect, shortly before its takeover. Domingo, it turns out, was not the only one engaged in fraudulent misrepresentations at Banco Álvarez."

Gorrindo was a tough Basque, had nerves of steel, and he kept his gaze calm and steady. The only sign of agitation was the way he absentmindedly twirled his handlebar mustache as he pondered my telex.

He finally looked over at Martin Senior. "His cards are stronger than we thought, and, *coño*, they have been well played."

"This I did not expect," the old man said, sitting back hard in the booth. "But he's bluffing."

"I have seen this young man fish, Señor Martin. *Cuidado*. He has the stomach for the kill. It's not a problem for him. I advise you not to take that position."

"Tell me," said Martin the younger. "Is it true that Franco, after seeing your catch of salmon, said, 'All quiet in the Alcázar, my General'?"

"Yes, it is. And then he stole my fish. He claimed them as his own."

The Martins looked startled for a moment and then both roared with laughter, while Gorrindo and I sat tensely opposite, both of us awaiting our fates.

Martin Senior finally pulled a white hand-kerchief from his breast pocket, wiped his eyes and sweaty face, and then leisurely pushed it back into place. "El Caudillo certainly has his own ways," he said.

Martin thought for a few moments more, then leaned forward and held out his hand, grimacing with his white dentures. "*Bueno.* You have a deal, young man. You did your father proud today. He could not have done better."

His son held out his hand, too. "José María, *hombre*, if things don't work out with the private bank in Zürich, come talk to us. I am sure we can find an interesting job for you. But I have a feeling you will do just fine."

When Gorrindo offered his hand, I turned my back on my father's old lawyer and slid from the booth. "Gentlemen," I said to the Martins. "Please come with me now to the bank, so we can call my lawyer in Zürich and get this agreement legally drawn up and signed. It is, as you say, important we get the press release out this evening, before the article appears in tomorrow's newspaper."

I turned to Papá's old lawyer. I was elated, for having pulled off the deal with the Martins, but also murderous that my old *tío* had betrayed our family in this way. I could no longer hold in what I was feeling.

"Your services are no longer required, Gorrindo. You are dirt to the family who loyally paid your bills and helped you raise a family in comfort. If you ever see me again—cross to the other side of the street."

ELEVEN

I returned to Zürich, collapsed in my bed, and dreamt my father and I were fishing the Bridge Pool on the Ribadesella. It was like we were one. We raised our rods at the exact same moment, our forward casts sending the flies perfectly in unison to the pool's far wall. The green shrubs and the blue-green river were electric with life as we hooked fish after fish.

I awoke. Lisa was lying reassuringly next to me in the bed of our Tiefenbrunen apartment, while Sam was asleep in the nursery next door. I gazed at them as they slept, then put on my shoes and went to work.

My superior at the Swiss Federal Credit Bank had lunch with me on the terrace of Das Storchen, the hotel hanging over the Limmat in Zürich. Herr Albiez had been a great mentor, teaching me, among other things, that private banking wasn't really about managing assets, but the art of keeping family secrets, and when I looked over at the silver-haired banker sitting opposite me, I was unexpectedly moved and full of loss.

But the moment had arrived. "I cannot thank you enough, Herr Albiez. You have taught me so much, but it's time, as was always the plan, for me to leave the Swiss Federal Credit Bank and run my family's private bank."

Albiez returned his glass of dry white wine to the table. "I expected this after the Grupo Central de Bilbao announcement. Well played, Herr Álvarez. Every banking executive on the Bahnhofstrasse now knows of your existence. It's not often a feeder bank gets peeled away from the Zürich Union Bank. People have taken notice."

"Could I convince you to join me at Privatbank Álvarez?"

"Thank you for the compliment. But no. I'm afraid not. I am too old and prefer the security of the Swiss Federal Credit Bank."

We sat like that for a moment, both of us lost in thought and staring at the mallards bobbing along the river currents.

"But your instincts are right," he continued. "You will need an older Swiss banker to join you, to be the public face of Privatbank Álvarez. However gifted you are at seamlessly passing money back and forth across borders, without the authorities noticing, you are still far too young to be running a private bank in Switzerland. Private banking is all about projecting an aura of stability and security and timeless wisdom. Clients want to know that your institution can solidly provide them with the wealth preservation they need for generations into the future."

Albiez took another sip of wine, before

continuing in his blunt Swiss way. "Let us be honest. A private-bank start-up run by a young Spaniard? No. No. That just won't fly in Switzerland. This is not America. Wealthy European families won't give you their money. To have credibility in Zürich, you must have a seasoned Swiss insider by your side, someone who can open up closed doors."

"Yes. I know. I was hoping that might be you."

"No. But I have someone in mind who might be suitable. Franz Deutwiller at Julius Montblanc Group. They just took Latin America away from him. He's very unhappy."

"I know Deutwiller. That's a great idea. I will contact him."

Albiez and I, later joined by Deutwiller, plotted Privatbank Álvarez's strategy, a way my little family bank could survive among the Bahnhofstrasse titans of Swiss Federal Credit Bank, Zürich Union Bank, and the Schweizer-Deutsche Bank Gesellschaft. The plan was simple: Privatbank Álvarez would specialize in servicing Spanish, Portuguese, and Latin American clients who wanted to get their money out of their politically dangerous home countries and brought safely to Switzerland. We would target individuals—as we put it to the big Swiss banks, hoping for the crumbs they might want to leave on the plate—whose sources of wealth "are not of clear provenance and might prove difficult to process. Keeping the secrets of such families will be our specialty."

The first client that Albiez ushered out of the Swiss Federal Credit Bank headquarters and sent two blocks down the Bahnhofstrasse, to the just-opened Privatbank Álvarez, was Señor Herman Strauss of Paraguay. I promptly called up my former boss, discreetly asking for some background information about the trembling old cattle farmer in my office.

"One day," Albiez said, "there will be an uproar about how much looted Jewish wealth came to Zürich during and after the war. It will all be about the Jews, about how we Swiss bankers 'stole' all this money from the Jews."

He paused and then dryly added, "What they will never know—we actually took far more from the Nazis."

"Not far now. Just over the mountaintop."

"Can't wait," Lisa said sarcastically.

Lisa's perm was tied up in a blue-and-yellow silk kerchief, her big sunglasses blotting out her face. Every now and then she would swivel around, to check on Sam and John in the back seat, before remembering they were back in town with the nanny.

We drove up the pass in the Mercedes cabriolet, through the pine forest, and into the village of Unterägeri. Beyond the village's backstreets, dotted with smoke-belching chimneys, we came upon a 240-year-old farmhouse with a flagstone courtyard surrounded by pear trees.

The chalet's wooden sides were blackened with age, the shutters, green. Pink and white carnations were cascading from the window boxes. We pulled into the farm's courtyard. A gurgling stone trough stood at its center.

An old Swiss woman in black and wearing thick glasses came out of the barn and squinted at us nearsightedly. A few stalks of hay stuck to the kerchief she had wrapped tightly around her head.

"You've got to be kidding me," Lisa whispered. "I've got the creeps already."

The real estate agent from Zürich pulled into the court behind us and jumped cheerfully out of the car. She went to talk to the old woman, who, shortly thereafter, melted back into the barn and wasn't seen again.

Lisa was seven months pregnant with Rob. She was already huge and wearing a caftan dress favored by Elizabeth Taylor, a riot of concentric pink and orange circles that ballooned at the midriff. She pulled herself with difficulty out of the convertible's front seat. I rushed to help her and was again struck—even behind the face-hiding sunglasses and Hermès scarf—how everything about her was glowing. It was a sign, as they said in Spain, another boy was on its way, for a girl would have robbed her of her beauty.

"Please look beyond the décor," I said. "We will spend money modernizing it. Just look at the layout and rooms and feel of the space."

We went through the chalet's heavy main door, the small foyer with coat racks and shoe banks leading to the blackened-wood stairs heading steeply up to the first floor. The house smelled of rotten apples, sawdust, and a stale fish fry. Lisa held on to the banister tight, hauling her swollen and panting self up the stairs.

A speckled light poured in through the stained-glass window in the hallway, a scene of eleventh-century Swiss burghers fighting off the Austrians. Opposite this window stood a porcelain bank consisting of a stove and bench, for heating the house in winter and drying snowy outer clothes.

The agent opened the first door off the landing, and we walked into a light-filled kitchen. It had a cheerful breakfast nook with bench, under a set of wide windows overlooking a pear and apple orchard, and an elegant parlor and formal dining room in the other direction. Lisa grew quiet as we walked from room to room, each with its own little architectural surprise—a doorway arch, a potbellied stove with cheerful porcelain tiles, bedrooms beautifully paneled with good hardwoods and carvings.

"This is the only farm for fifty kilometers that foreigners are allowed to buy," said the agent.

We went downstairs again, to look at the stately barns and sheds and orchards out back, before saying our goodbyes to the estate agent. We got into the car and drove to the village of Ägeri. I held my breath, awaiting Lisa's verdict, but she wasn't giving anything away. I pulled in at Das Goldene Kreuz, the restaurant overlooking the village stream and canal.

The chef-patron sat us on the terrace out back, overlooking the waterway, the ducks, the young mothers with strollers coming down the towpath. We ordered drinks, some air-cured beef, and pickled onions.

"I still don't understand why you want to move us to a cow pasture."

I explained, once again, how Canton Zug, this province in Central Switzerland, had recently rewritten its corporate bylaws and lowered its tax rates so that it was now one of the best places in the world, from a cost perspective, to headquarter a finance company—and live.

I told her how Philips Brothers, Salomon Brothers, and Goldman Sachs were all relocating their global commodities-trading arms to the city of Zug, just fifteen minutes down the Gubel mountainside from Ägeri. That I had just met the local partner of oil traders Marc Rich and Pinky Green, and he had urged us to move here as well. He was fundraising for the American International School of Zürich, and the school's campus was fairly easily reachable, just over the hill. In short, our children would have a decent American school to attend, even from this seemingly remote outpost.

"Well?"

"You seem to have decided already."

"I would never make such a decision without you."

"Yeah, sure," she said dryly.

I studied my wife, looking for signs of what she was thinking. She was, in her way, as mercurial and difficult to read as I was. She of course had her own family secrets—a hard-drinking and abusive father, a weak and enabling mother—and I knew that a calm and conflict-free home was all she ever wanted in life. She had told me so many times before—and it is what I had provided her.

"Well, it's an amazing house. I have to admit."

"I'm glad you liked it."

"OK. I will do this on one condition."

"What's that?"

"We keep an apartment in Zürich, which we can go to whenever we want. If I have to wake up every day, knowing I will only be talking to cows and kids while you're off working in Zürich, I think I will kill myself."

"We don't want that."

She laughed. "No, we don't. I have a lot to live for. I have, for some reason, been blessed—by our boys and you and the peaceful home we have created together. I will do anything to preserve that. If buying this farmhouse will make you happy and keep the peace between us—count me in."

"The attorney general is here," said Frau Wollenweide, standing before me with the green leather folder full of letters she wanted me to sign.

It was 1978. Privatbank Álvarez's assets had been growing 30 percent per annum over the previous five years, and we were so busy and at capacity we almost couldn't poach staff fast enough. But with success came a whole new set of problems. "Bring the attorney general here, not the conference room," I told my secretary. "Let's make this informal. And go ask Herr Deutwiller to join us."

Frau Wollenweide sniffed and turned heel. She was twenty years my senior, and her constant frown made it clear she couldn't understand how a good Swiss woman who did everything by the book had ended up serving a young Spaniard.

She returned with Attorney General Abegg. We vigorously shook hands, exchanged the ritual pleasantries, before I asked if he would like a drink. He opted for a gin and tonic. Franz Deutwiller slipped inside and the room filled with the singsong of their Swiss cadence. The two old friends, stationed in the same army barracks in

Appenzell when they were young men in officers' training, spent a few minutes catching up with each other. Deutwiller looked at his watch—it was 4:15 in the afternoon—and said he'd have a beer. I retrieved a bottle of Feldschlösschen.

The three of us went out onto the Álvarez bank's penthouse terrace outside my office and sat on the cushioned iron chairs about the round table. A June breeze was lightly fanning our faces, and when we sat down, a flock of pigeons rose in unison from the Bahnhofstrasse below us, soaring across the jagged rooftops.

We talked about vacations coming up, where we were going with our families, and then the attorney general lightly said, "I came by your office because I have a formal request here from Mexico's attorney general."

He retrieved a letter from his inside pocket and gently placed it on the table before us. Deutwiller and I exchanged glances. Abegg took a deep swig of his gin and tonic and smacked his lips, while Deutwiller read the letter.

"The Mexican government is requesting that we, the Swiss attorney general's office, force you to disclose the ultimate owner of a Panamanian firm sending five million dollars a month to its numbered account at Privatbank Álvarez. The Mexican government believes the account belongs to a general in the Mexican army, suspected of being on the payroll of the Olviera drug cartel."

I glanced out over the copper-and-tile rooftops of Zürich, while Deutwiller pointedly asked, "And? Do they have evidence of criminal wrongdoing?"

Abegg waved his hands dismissively. "It is a fishing expedition. The Mexican government does not have a solid link between the general and the Panamanian company—which means we cannot allow you to disclose this information, particularly since they have not yet launched criminal proceedings against him. In fact, if you did disclose the ultimate account holder, you would be in violation of Swiss bank secrecy laws—and I would have to prosecute you!"

We all laughed at the absurdity. But I noticed something in his face and said, "Yet you still seem troubled, Herr Abegg. There is a reason why you are here."

"*Ja*," he said, studying a young secretary, in the office window opposite us, discreetly adjusting her pantyhose. "Things are changing. I am fielding more and more of these requests, as are our diplomats abroad, and there is a growing anger out there at how Swiss bank secrecy laws are shielding alleged wrongdoers in other parts of the world. Next month the US Congress is opening hearings on tax evasion and how Swiss banks are often used to hide money from US authorities. Imagine this. They are treating Swiss bankers like they are common criminals! The Zürich Union

Bank and Swiss Federal Credit Bank are furious their executives have been summoned. It is lost on the Americans that we are a sovereign nation with the right to make our own laws."

We tut-tutted over this state of affairs and then he said, "But the world is changing. Becoming more connected. Borders are not what they used to be. You know, Herr Álvarez, your friend in Zug, Marc Rich, I think the US authorities are starting to take an interest in his activities."

"Ah. Thank you. I will keep my distance."

Deutwiller put the letter back down on the table. "And what about this request from Mexico?"

"Well, they can't get the banking information they seek, of course. Not without proof of criminal behavior. Out of the question. We cannot have foreigners challenging our banking laws."

"Yes, but . . ."

"But it would still be good for Switzerland if we could turn down this official request in—how shall I say this?—a productive way. It would be helpful for everyone concerned if we could throw the Mexican authorities a bit of information that might help their cause to prosecute a corrupt and murderous general—without, of course, violating Swiss bank secrecy laws. It would earn us goodwill with the Mexican government that, quite frankly, we need for other diplomatic and prosecutorial reasons, which I cannot disclose."

I looked over at Deutwiller. He scratched his

jowls and said, "*Du, Peter.* Our clients come to us because we are utterly discreet. They know they are in safe hands. If word got out we were helping overseas criminal investigations . . ."

"*Gottes Willen nicht*! That would be terrible. We wouldn't want that. It would be very damaging to *Finanzplatz Schweiz*. You misunderstand me. I am just throwing out the idea—unofficially, of course—in case something comes to you. The attorney general's office would be extremely grateful to Privatbank Álvarez, if such a thing could happen."

He smiled lightly. "Who knows?" he said, glancing up from his drink and looking directly at me. "Maybe such gratitude by the Swiss attorney general's office will come in handy to Privatbank Álvarez one day."

I stood up and offered my hand.

"Thank you for coming, Attorney General Abegg. Excuse me now, but I have to drive back to Ägeri. I try, whenever possible, to have dinner with the family."

"*Ja. Ja.* Of course. This is important."

"Please feel free to stay, have another drink, and enjoy the view. Franz, will you please see our distinguished guest out when you are ready to close shop?"

I decided to go fishing. I needed the mental space to think this Mexican problem through. When I pulled into the farmhouse entrance, John and Rob were running toy cars through a speedway maze they had created out of Legos and tea trays. Sam was bouncing a ball against the side of the garage, while Lisa sat off to the side on a lawn chair, her eyes closed, her moistened skin worshipfully facing the setting June sun. Susi Iten's car was parked to the side of the far barn. She was upstairs, preparing dinner.

The boys—seven, eight, and eleven—stopped playing and looked up when I came out of the garage holding an empty duffel bag. Their round little faces, big black eyes, silently stared up at me.

"Hello, boys."

"Hi, Daddy."

I stepped over a fire-red Ferrari. The German shepherd puppy rose, wagged its tail, and came over to nuzzle my leg.

"You look upset," Lisa said.

"There's a problem at the bank. I've decided to go fishing in Andermatt for four days. To think things through."

Lisa closed her eyes again. "Just remember," she said sleepily, "we have the opera in Zürich on Wednesday. And the fundraiser for the school is on Friday. So you can't stay longer, even if the fishing's good."

"*Bueno.* Understood."

I went to the far barn, gathered my boots, nets,

and trout flies, and placed the gear in the trunk of the BMW. I came back out of the barn with wool socks, fishing vests, and waxed coats packed in the duffel bag, and then headed to the farm's main door, in order to finish my packing upstairs.

John was off to the side of the courtyard, standing behind the ornamental pot of carnations and studying a trail of ants. Sam was teasing the dog, bouncing the ball against the barn's far wall, as the puppy ran back and forth trying to catch it in his jaws. But little Rob was standing in my way, with his messy hair, clutching his gull-wing Mercedes Matchbox car and staring at me with his big black eyes.

"Daddy! Daddy! Stop. I want to ask you something."

"Not now, Roberto. I have to go."

I was already at the front door of the chalet, ready to shoot up the stairs, when Rob's plaintive and pleading voice rang out into the courtyard.

"Daddy, please. Can I come fishing with you? Please. I promise not to bother you."

Those words.

I am not sure how long I stood there frozen in time, holding tight to the door handle, caught somewhere between Swiss adulthood and Spanish adolescence. But I eventually turned around, came back, and kneeled by Rob's side. I hugged him.

"Of course you can, Roberto. *Claro.* I would

love it if you came fishing with me. It would make me very happy."

His two older brothers were staring at me, eyes wide with surprise at this remarkable turn of events.

"Listen up, boys. Who wants to come fishing in Andermatt?"

"I do! I do!" the boys yelled in unison.

We took the BMW and it roared us lustily down the highway to Chur. The boys held their breath in the tunnels and named all the foreign license plates they could spot. Germany, Italy, France, Netherlands. We started the hairpin ascent up the St. Gotthard pass, and at the final bend, the village of Andermatt became visible through a small opening in the mountains towering to the left and right.

We hauled our bags into the Hotel Sonne, the old inn in the center of town, with its weather-blackened wood exterior and rooms decorated with simple pine beds. The boys were in a large room with three twin beds and a breakfast table, and I had the adjoining room, accessed through an interconnecting door. I could hear the boys jumping on the beds as I unpacked. "Boys! Stop that. These beds are made of wood, not springs. You'll break the slats."

I must have barked because silence instantly followed. I felt bad. "Come here," I said, and they all came piling through the connecting door and clambered onto my bed. "All right, *chico malo*. First thing tomorrow we get our fishing licenses, which we do at the local barber. We'll have a quick bite to eat and then start fishing."

"Will I have my own rod?" asked Rob.

"*Naturalmente*. All of you will have your own rod."

"Yeah, doofus," said John. "What? You thought you were going to fish with your nose?"

"But I don't know how to fly-fish," Sam said.

"Not to worry, Sam. You've caught trout with a worm on the casting rod. This is not much different. We use a bobber and flies. It's just a little more delicate than worm fishing."

"I bet you I'll catch the first fish," said John.

"Yeah, with your stinky farts," Rob said. "You just have to cut one and all the fish will die." He grabbed his throat and made a face, like he was choking to death.

We marched together down the pebbly run to the high-altitude lake, flat and gray-blue like a marble tabletop. The wild Alpine grasses were shivering, and from the other side of the lake, we could hear the clinking bells of the cows sent in summer to graze in the high meadows. The boys followed me, in order of height, down a finger of land jutting into the lake, a little army of fishermen following their general. I showed them how to stand at the water's edge, cast the bobber out, behind which ran a line of three dry flies, and slowly reel in. They quickly spread out along the finger, ten meters or so between them. Sam staked his claim at the top of the peninsula, casting into the darkest part of the lake. John and Rob began casting into the coves on either side.

"I got one!"

"Me too!"

Sam's and John's bobbers were zigzagging across the lake.

"Don't play them so hard! Check the drag. Loosen it."

Rob and I ran first to Sam, and by the time we got there, he had a 15-centimeter Canadian lake trout near his feet. I netted it for him. I bent over, smacked the trout's head hard against the rock. It spit blood and shivered, and then went still. I laid its gray-blue-and-cream flank against the grass, kissed the top of Sam's head.

"Well done, Sam!"

He was beaming with that intoxicated look Álvarez men get when they beach a fish. I held Rob's hand and we ran giggling around the lip of land, to where John stood on the other side, still frantically yelling for help. We soon saw why. His trout was triple the size of Sam's and giving him a good fight. But the boy—I was so proud of him—was stern-faced with concentration and played the fish like the knowledge simply existed in his Álvarez blood. We got that fat fish into the net and onto shore and knocked her dead against an Alpine rock.

Rob made me give him the car keys. He ran up the hill, came back with my boxy Kodak Super 8, and began filming John holding his fish up and smiling. In the background, the Swiss Alps soared majestic. Sam yelled again as he hooked yet another Canadian lake trout, which had been fed into these frigid waters half a century ago and had somehow flourished in this high-altitude world. I told Rob to put down the camera. It was his turn to catch a fish.

I took my youngest boy by the hand, with his yellow-fiberglass casting rod, and we walked solemnly to another cove in the lake. I studied the glassy water and saw, within easy casting distance, a natural rise. It was the ring of a good-size trout, hiding under a pale rock and greedily coming up for flies.

"Stand here, Rob. Now see that cowshed on the far side of the lake?"

"Yes."

"OK. Stand here and cast as far as you can toward the cowshed, like you are trying to reach it."

Little Rob brought back his rod, and then swung it forward with all his might, but he let go of the line too soon and off to the side, and the bobber went flying in the wrong direction.

"OK. Reel it in slowly and we will try again. The lake is full of hungry fish."

"I got one. I got one . . . ooohhh."

"Never mind. It was just a small one. When you get a strike, don't pull too hard. OK, now let's try that again. Aim for the cowshed."

This time the bobber and flies sailed directly toward the cowshed on the far side of the lake, the bobber landing two meters past the white rock.

"Perfect. Now reel in slowly."

Just as the trailing flies passed the submerged white rock, there was a boil on Rob's line, and the large trout was hooked.

"Daddy! Daddy!"

"*Bueno, Roberto*! Now concentrate. Don't pull too hard. Let me check the break."

We got the trout on shore, a fighting cock fish, which I quickly killed. Rob was beaming bright light as I kissed him and congratulated him on his fine catch.

I went and knelt by a tiny tributary stream coming down the mountain and gutted the trout. I suddenly felt my youngest son's arms around my neck, his lips brushing against my stubbly chin, heard his little voice.

"Thank you, Daddy. I love you."

Before I could respond, Rob twirled around and ran hard in his Wellingtons, back to the water, to cast again, looking now for where there were natural rings in the water, signaling feeding fish.

When I packed Rob's fish away, and looked up again, all three boys had trout on at the same time. I never got to fish, but methodically went from one to the other, helping them bring in the trout, which I cleaned and slid into our plastic sack growing ever fatter with fish. Then John came timidly in my direction, handing me his rod, looking frightened that I would yell at him. His entire reel was a snarl of tangled nylon. I smiled, to let him know I wasn't angry, and told him to fish with my fly rod as I worked at unraveling his snarl, which took a good forty-five minutes and lots of swearing to sort out, even after a cutaway.

The mountain air temperature was falling rapidly, the sky darkening.

I looked at my watch and discovered it was already after five. I suggested we eat one of the fish we caught, an old Spanish ritual to guarantee luck, before heading down the mountain to our hotel and dinner. But we would rise early the following morning and start again. The boys hollered their agreement.

We hunted along the shore for any brush, bark, or wood we could find, and though there wasn't much above the tree line, we found enough scraps for a small fire. John was at my side the entire time, like a burr, carefully watching me as I found some sweet Alpine grass, a kind of wild rosemary and thyme, which I pulled, washed, and placed inside the trout's cavity.

"There. When we roast the fish on the fire, the mountain herbs will perfume the meat." John was wide-eyed, watching my every move as I stuck a twig through the mouth of the fish and down its cavity and used it to hold the trout and its crackling skin over the fire, turning the fish this way and that so it wouldn't burn.

He was so eager, so hungry, I let him take over the cooking. I looked up from our fire. Rob had the Super 8 trained on John and me, recording us as our heads were bent over the sizzling fish. Serious Sam, meanwhile, was down by the lakeside, almost in shadow, poking in a pool, studying the plants and bug life with a little flashlight he had brought along.

And I remember thinking—*One day they will be grown men and all working with me at Privatbank Álvarez.* The notion filled me with pride, that special, ruinous Spanish pride that only a man born on Iberian soil can really understand.

And it came to me then, how I would have Franz Deutwiller anonymously send the Swiss attorney general an address of a suburban house just outside Panama City, with nothing else on the note. If the Mexican authorities chose to monitor that nondescript Panamanian home, they might quickly discover what remarkable visitors were coming and going from the general's safe house.

It was not an easy decision. It went against every private-banker instinct in my body—to maintain a client's secrets was sacrosanct—but I would do this for my sons, so the family had a large deposit of goodwill in Switzerland's vault, to be drawn on if and when it was needed. Family always came first, after all, and we Álvarezes had our own secrets that needed protecting.

Part V

2019

ÄGERI, SWITZERLAND

TWELVE

Darkness has settled on the chalet and I can smell that dinner is ready.

Big Bertha clutches me on the left. She grabs me hard and barks instructions like a drill sergeant. Sam is on my right, holding me, as we inch our way up the staircase. I can hear Lisa breathing heavily behind me, as she drags my drip in our wake.

"Stop squeezing my arm so hard!"

They haul me, like movers with a large commode, and it takes us ten minutes to get up the staircase. But, finally, we are on the first-floor hallway, panting and catching our breath.

Bertha, my personal angel of death, is insufferably chipper today.

"See? Not so bad, Herr Álvarez."

"For whom?"

"Dad, relax a little. Please. Be grateful for what everyone is doing for you."

Lisa moves down the dimly lit hallway and opens the dining room's larch door. I want to get away from my hectoring son and the bossy Bertha, so I shuffle as energetically as I can after her.

The burl-yew oval table in the paneled dining room is covered in the best Swiss linen. Late-nineteenth-century Tiffany candelabras, passed on to Lisa from her grandmother, are filled with white tapered candles that cast their elegant and flickering light across the room. Cut-crystal vases sparkle in the light and are filled with African irises. There are three ceremonial gold plates around the table, on which sit smaller dinner plates in black enamel. The heavy Sheffield silverware from our wedding, engraved with Lisa's and my entwining initials, sits next to each plate. Even my mother's green-stemmed crystal wine and water glasses have been brought out of storage for the occasion.

"*Also wunderschön*," says the admiring Sister Bertha.

I have to agree. "You have outdone yourself, Lisa. We haven't done this in so long. It reminds me of Christmas, when they were all boys."

"Amazing," says Sam. "Let me take a picture. I want to send it to Sharon and my brothers."

Lisa is flushed with pleasure at our reactions.

"Come," she says, holding out a chair and making me sit in my usual place, at the head of the table, my back to the window. Sister Bertha, now that I am seated, excuses herself to eat in the kitchen next door. The wood-slatted drop-down curtain of the kitchen portico rattles up suddenly and Susi Iten sticks her head out.

"*Gruezi wohl, José*! We make you better with good Swiss food that erupt the strength!"

"Thank you, Susi. What was in Walter's net today?"

Their son, Walter Junior, whom we sometimes

266

hire to help us, brings out starters of gravlax and *nüssli* salad.

"Father had a good morning. Three pike. And seven *Felchen*."

That cheers me up. I try to shake out my linen napkin but have trouble, so Sam leans forward, snaps it open for me, and tucks it into my bathrobe collar.

There is something in the back of my mind I can't retrieve.

"I remember we had a family dinner party in the formal dining room. It was years ago. Something important happened." Lisa and Sam exchange glances, but relax when I add, "But I can't remember why or what happened. I can't recall the memory."

"Well, that's a blessing. You had an argument with the boys."

"Really? Was it that bad?"

Walter Junior stands at my elbow with a bottle of Rioja. "Wine?"

"No," says Lisa.

I hold out my glass. "Pour."

I look over at Lisa. "What are you worried about? It might kill me?"

Sam reaches out and touches my hand. "Pop, the combination—Oxycontin and wine. Not a good idea."

"I am just going to put the wine to my lips. Taste it."

I pick up my fork and lift, with shaking hand, a paper-thin slice of gravlax to my mouth. It takes forever to chew. A chant goes off in my head.

Make amends. Make amends.

"Sam, you're very talented. I don't say that enough. Your idea to turn global warming to your advantage and build salmon rivers in Greenland is really quite brilliant, I have to say."

I hold out my glass, to drink in his honor.

My son lifts his water to clink glasses and buy himself time, knowing he has just heard an apology. "Thanks," he finally says. "Appreciate it, Dad." He lowers his head back over the gravlax and brown bread.

The evening is pleasant. Lisa and Sam talk for some time about John and Rob arriving the next day, what we will all do together. My wife's voice is filled with spirit, for the first time in a long while.

I try to follow their conversation, but it's hard in my current state and I can't add anything of value to their plans. So I stay quiet, just content to be. Calf's liver is put down before us, one of Sam's and my favorite dinners, and we both make the proper noises of appreciation.

Susi's head pops through the portico again. "Eat! Liver is brain food!"

Lisa and Sam continue talking, accompanied by the sound of cutlery scraping plates, but Sam notices my silence after a while and tries to draw me into the conversation.

"So, Dad, I've been meaning to ask you."

I take a gulp of wine. "Ask me what?"

"Can you share with us what's happening to you? Can you articulate it? It might help."

"I'm dying of cancer."

"Umm . . . yes. But what else. What does it feel like?"

"I am going on a trip."

"What do you mean?" Lisa says.

"I am going on a fishing trip. There are choices to be made, routes to navigate, obstacles to overcome."

Lisa and Sam again exchange glances. Lisa dabs her lips with the serviette and then strokes my hand with her thumb.

"What obstacles, darling?"

I push away the plate. Can't eat any more.

"*Joder.* So many. My brother, Juan, he is very definite and clear. He wants me to go home with him and won't leave my side until I do. He says I need to get my house in order. That's all very good, I can handle that. But the Frog Queen . . ."

"The what?"

I look up. They both stare at me, eyes wide with alarm.

"The Frog Queen. She has other plans for me."

"Dad, what does the Frog Queen want from you?"

I shrug. "*No sé.* Juan is clear. He says what he wants outright. *Coño.* He's a Spaniard. But the Frog Queen . . . well, she's a mystery. Very enigmatic. But when I get the pain, the headaches, it's because she is banging my head with her scepter, like she is trying to beat something into my *cabeza* . . ."

Lisa stands, comes around, and puts a hand on my shoulder. She leans forward and says, with great feeling, "Darling, is this dinner too much?"

"*Sí, Mamá.* May I be excused? I am tired from the day's fishing."

The morning sky is bright blue outside the French doors. Lisa is sitting in a chair opposite, reading the local Swiss newspaper, *Zuger Zeitung.*

"What was that?"

"Sam. He just left for the airport to pick up John and Rob."

"Are they coming? Here?"

"Yes, José. I told you. They're coming home."

"But why?"

"To see you."

"We have to be on guard with John. He likes to steal my things. That *cabrón.* Whenever I turn my head, he's running off with my best fishing rods."

"You know that's not true."

"Don't be so naïve, Lisa. They steal, our boys."

"I am sorry. But I have to leave."

She gets up and slams shut the door.

I'm in trouble. She left the newspaper.

A few hours later, she is back. I open my eyes and she is again sitting in the blue armchair, slumped over the left armrest, staring out the French doors, listening to me sleep. Her cell phone is in her lap. Her face is as lined and weather-beaten as the granite of the mountain outside our window.

"Hello, my love."

She turns her head and tiredly says, "Hello, José."

"Have the boys arrived?"

"No. Not yet. But their plane just landed. Sam sent me a text."

I pull myself up and onto the pillow. "I am so excited to see them. Like a child. I haven't felt like this for a long time."

She smiles a little. "My husband is back."

"What do you mean?"

"Never mind."

"Thank you for bringing them home." I reach out and pat her hand. "I am just so happy that we will all be together again, without their wives. I know I shouldn't say that, but it's like Christmastime again, when the boys were young."

Lisa bends down to kiss my hand. Her affection, so genuine, it pains me. My breast is full of flutterings, tremors, and thumps of the heart. I am about to say something, but her phone buzzes, and she looks at her lap.

"Oh no. No. No. No."

"What?"

"It's Sam. He says they aren't coming right home. They've decided to drop by the apartment first. They're having lunch in the Niederdorf, before they continue on to the house. That means they won't be here until evening." Lisa lowers her head and begins to cry. "How could they? Don't they know how much we need them now? We've been waiting for them to come home for such a long time."

"Don't be upset, Lisa. Please."

Everything she has been holding in for so long suddenly erupts within her, and there is no stopping the rush of tears now. She puts her head down into her hands and weeps hard, pulling out the handkerchief she always keeps up her cardigan sleeve. I reach out, trembling, and manage to grab her hand.

I gently pull her to me. She comes, reluctantly, and sits at the edge of my bed. I make her put her head down on my shoulder. "Lisa, please, don't cry. It upsets me so. They are boys. They will do boy things."

"They are not boys! They are grown men. How selfish can they be?"

"*Pobrecita*." I stroke her head. "You've been so brave, for so long. But remember, the boys haven't seen each other for a long time either, and they just want some time to catch up and have fun, like they did when they were young, and before they have to come sit with their dying old man. Can you blame them?"

"Well, I'm sorry, but I think it is inconsiderate."

I imagine the three brothers, walking down the cobblestones of the Niederdorfstrasse, recalling when they, as teenagers, had been stumbling drunk on the very same thoroughfare and laughing and up to mischief on a Saturday night. And I am not sure why, perhaps because my own brother and I never got to experience those years, but I find myself happy and proud of them that they have taken this time together, before coming to the chalet.

"Sweet mama. We're home."

Alfredo jumps up and whines, his stumpy tail furiously wagging, looking back to see if I will open the door.

It is John's unmistakable voice in the hall.

I look at the clock. It is just past midnight.

"I'm in here."

They come through the door, grinning and red-cheeked, rolling their luggage.

"Hello, Pops."

"Hey there."

They are glassy-eyed drunk. They come and kiss my forehead, one by one. Sam stands back a little, allowing his younger brothers to step up to my bed, and it is Rob, the youngest, who darts forward first.

I check my memory, panicked for a second that I won't remember who he is, but I do remember, just in time, that he is the professional bass fisherman with his own cable TV show in America. Rob throws his arms around me, his car coat chilly and smelling of beer and fried *rösti*.

"Shit, Dad, sorry we're so late."

"Don't be. I am glad you had some fun. This is all grim enough."

John comes forward then, tall and lanky, the New Yorker with the midtown fish restaurant called Upstream. He bends down, like a giraffe, the diamond in his pierced ear glinting. His head is entirely shaved, like a misshapen billiard ball. I have not seen this look before. He wraps his arms around me, and I am engulfed in his smell, the shimmering fumes of cognac and sharp cheese.

"Dad, I have to say, you look like shit. Like you had a big one on and your fuckin' line just broke."

We all laugh and that, I realize, is precisely what I have been craving—male energy, a little gallows humor, less of the pinched and terrified female faces that have been surrounding me these last weeks. It makes me so happy. I am suddenly teary again. I wipe my eyes and John looks away, unsettled to see me so emotional. They are not used to seeing me this way.

"*Perdóname.* I am sorry. I can't tell you how much it means to me. To see you all here."

The door pushes open and Lisa, her face still stupid from half a sleeping pill, stands in the doorway, in her cotton nightgown and silk blue bathrobe. She is visibly trying to take it all in. The boys rush at her in unison, their arms out, yelping, "Mom!" Lisa disappears in their arms, a group hug of flailing limbs and pursed lips, and her face, so severe at first, melts in their embrace. Her blond tufts and heaven-looking eyes are just visible over their shoulders, and everything about her is beaming joy and light.

"I should smack you all."

But she is laughing and kissing each of them, hugging whatever flesh she can hold on to. Then it is over and they all stand awkwardly for a few moments, silent, at a loss for words now that the initial greeting has passed, and I have a sense that everyone is thinking about but not addressing the unseen visitor standing in the room—death.

"Well," Lisa finally says, wiping her eyes. "I am sure you are tired after your long flight, and your father needs his rest. Kamila has all your beds made up."

They turn back to their bags.

"So, what's on the agenda?" Rob asks.

"We'll talk about it tomorrow," Sam says, taking command now that I am incapacitated. "We'll draw up a list of tasks . . ."

"No control freakery, Sam," warns John. "First thing I am doing tomorrow morning is having a double espresso in a Swiss, up-to-my-chin bath. Dying for one."

"And I'm going to go for a run," adds Rob. "Maybe up to the Itens'."

Sam smiles at his brothers. They have the gift of making him relax. "We'll figure it out. It's just great to be together again."

And then they come and kiss me one more time, grab their bags and their mother's elbow, and disappear out the door and up the stairs.

It is sometime in the small hours.

I don't know what time exactly, but it's very dark and quiet.

Only the owl and I are awake. The garden is pitch-black through the French doors, so I can't see him, but I hear him insistently asking his questions.

"To who? To who?"

I turn my focus back to the room. Juan and the Frog Queen sit opposite my bed in stiff-backed chairs, mostly lost in the shadows. But I can see enough. Their expressions are grave and they are studying me with great intensity. Their looks make me uneasy. I feel my heart racing. They are judging me. I know it.

Say something, goddammit. Say something.

Alfredo, sensing I am agitated, gets up from under my bed and nuzzles my hand clutching the handrail meant to keep me from falling out of bed.

The Frog Queen opens her mouth, smacks her lips. "Men," she says, with a tinge of disgust. She is not really talking, but must be communicating through some form of telepathy, because both Juan and I can hear what she is saying.

"When men tell their stories, they always talk about how their business is doing. They never talk about how they are and what they are feeling—whether they are happy or depressed or manic or crazy or angry or frustrated. It's always all about their work."

Juan smiles sadly. "I know my brother. He will come through. He'll get around to it. I admit, he's a slow learner. But he'll get there eventually. Trust me."

"I hope so. He doesn't have much time left."

"Well, at least you're talking," I yell at them.

Alfredo whines, backs up, and scratches at the door, like he is trying to fetch Lisa. He lets out a muffled bark. The door flies open and a large figure in white comes billowing into the room. It is Sister Bertha and she is suddenly by my side, looking at my eyes, monitoring my pulse.

"*Was ha'mer da*? You are sweating, Herr Álvarez."

She puts a cool cloth on my forehead.

Her voice is unusually soft and gentle.

"Are you having a hard night?"

"Yes. Yes. I think I am."

She sits down on the stool beside the bed and takes ahold of my hand.

"I am here now, Herr Álvarez. I am here."

And I suddenly know, as I did when I discovered my confessor priest was a fellow Spaniard, that God has sent this particular hospice nurse at this particular time to enter my life.

It must be so.

"Tell me a story," I say.

"About what?"

"About the man."

"What man?"

"The man who waited for the wool cap."

"Oh, Miguel. What do you want to know?"

"Did he die alone? I want to know how his end came."

Sister Bertha studies me and then quietly says, "He died alone, as you would describe it. You would say he was abandoned and with no one but a silly hospice nurse by his side. But I know he died in Jesus's arms."

"What does that even mean? That's just Christian *mierda*."

"That is your opinion, Herr Álvarez. I'll admit Miguel was in a bad state the first month I was with him, wrestling with his demons all night and every night. He suffered greatly. But when Miguel was at his worst, a man came to see him, his only visitor the entire three months I was sitting by his side. It changed everything. He was almost ninety, I would guess. Miguel called him 'my Sweet Freak,' and I suspect he had been a client at one time. The man was wealthy and very ill himself. He came in a motorized wheelchair, with a private nurse and driver. He stayed for thirty minutes only, but you could see how determined he was to pay his respects, and he brought Miguel one hundred roses. When the old man left, Miguel wore a lovely smile and said, not so much to me, but to the universe at large, 'I was loved.' "

I fall deflated back into my pillow when I hear this.

"Toward the end, after Miguel dozed and had come back from wherever he was, he said, 'Do you know, Sister Bertha, that God is into threesomes? *Hombre.* He likes his sex wild.' I was both shocked and disgusted by this remark, that he should talk in this filthy way about God, but I tried not to show it and said, 'What do you mean?'

"He started gibbering then, making no sense at all, something about how there were times during sex when 'the son becomes the father,' which was also the exact moment when the 'third in the threesome joins the party.' "

Sister Bertha sees that the story has me riveted, firmly back on earth and among the living, so she gently lets go of my hand and retrieves her knitting from the canvas sack at her feet, before continuing with her story.

"Of course, this all sounded to me like the fevered talk of a deeply troubled homosexual who was dying. So, I tried to humor him. 'Really?' I said. 'And who is the third in this threesome?' *Ja.* I will always remember his answer. 'I think you know him as the Holy Ghost.' It gives me the chills, even now, just remembering how he said it. Such conviction. I totally believed him. And why not? When love is in the room, then God is in the room, and whatever happens there, it is not to be judged by us common mortals. It is in God's hands."

Sister Bertha yanks some blue wool yarn from the ball in the canvas bag.

"Such an unusual man. It is strange, but I think of Miguel all the time, to this day, even though I did not know him long. I have seen 'religious' people who prayed all their life completely lose their faith in the final approach to death. You can see the terror in their faces and twisted bodies. But I have also seen sinners filled with divine grace at the moment God carries them to the other side. It is hard to explain. You just never know what kind of death a man is going to have."

She looks up, puts the back of her hand on my forehead. "Are you feeling better, Herr Álvarez? You look better. Life is back in your face. But I can see you want to retreat now. Yes, that's fine. Go. Close your eyes."

Part VI

1983

ZÜRICH, SWITZERLAND

THIRTEEN

On the balance sheet of the soul, family secrets eventually have to be accounted for and reconciled—usually at a considerably marked-up price. My accounting started, quietly enough, that summer night when I was drinking Glenfiddich in the chalet's family room. It was Sunday evening, and I was in a morose and dour mood. Lisa was in her blue bathrobe, lying on the couch before me, reading the *Opera News*. I kept watching for that hand of hers, which periodically shot out and grabbed a wafer-thin square of Lindt from the box on the coffee table, before popping it into her mouth. I counted each trip. She was on her fifth chocolate. When she reached out again, I looked away. My teenage sons were half comatose and sprawled out on the floor, watching Wimbledon on the television, as spineless and shapeless as beanbags and dropping popcorn all over the floor.

When I met Lisa at the Columbia University mixer, so many years earlier, I knew this was the calm and kind woman with whom I could build a "normal" family life, the exact opposite of what I had experienced as a child—and we did build the home I always dreamt of. And she dreamt of. But that night, the family scene before me, the very thing I craved for so long, inexplicably filled me with rage.

Is this all there is? Is this what the hard work has been about? So she can eat chocolate and go to the opera—and they can watch fucking tennis on Swiss TV?

Luckily, a few days afterward, I was distracted by Deutwiller, who came into my office and announced he wanted to retire. It was a good time to restructure the bank, he advised. This corporate shuffling briefly gave me a new purpose in life, and I threw myself into the reorganization, burying in work the morose restlessness and depression that was slowly and steadily growing inside me. Over the next four years, Deutwiller retired, I bought out Grupo Central de Bilbao's 10 percent share, and groomed a sharp young Swiss banker, Hans-Peter Grieder, to become my second in command.

So the distraction worked—for a while.

My Venezuelan client turned, and for a brief while, I watched him, trailing cigar smoke, as he walked stiff-legged back to his suite at the Savoy on Paradeplatz. We had just eaten in an Italian restaurant near the Zürich Bourse. It was near midnight on a weekday, and when he was out of sight, I turned and walked in the opposite direction, back toward my apartment in the Niederdorf.

There was something in the deserted November air that night—in the wet mist, the rotting linden leaves—that made me profoundly sad, and I picked up my pace as I crossed the Rudolf Brun Bridge, trying to brush off my growing melancholia.

The city and its lights were bleakly reflected in the black Limmat River below, and this mirrored vision did nothing to cheer me up. Zürich seemed morbidly dead that night, and, somewhere in the middle of the bridge, I recalled the raucous nightlife of San Sebastián—the pavements filled with promenading families, the loud lowlifes drinking too much. What I had lost, by the choices I made during the course of my life, suddenly hit me full force, and a kind of grief accompanied my leaden footsteps across the bridge, as I headed deep into the buttoned-up Swiss-Protestant night.

It was dark, in the old quarter, but for the occasional cast-iron lamp clamped to the medieval stone walls rising around me. I took a deep breath, to calm myself, and then descended stone stairs. A cat walked a ledge just above my head.

At the bottom of the stairs, in the square below, I came across a linden tree, a stone fountain, an overflowing garbage can—and a young woman. She had blunt-cut, almost altar-boy hair, and hovered near the door of the Haifisch Bar. Her

Nautilus down jacket was unzipped and open, so the men passing by could see she wore nothing underneath but a yellow tank top and blue-satin hot pants.

A gold chain purse hung from her shoulder, and the platform shoes with cork soles gave the illusion she was tall. The way she puffed her cigarette, it all brought back the memory of that long-forgotten experience in Ribadesella's whorehouse—the thrill, the shame, the sensation of feeling intensely alive.

But I resolutely took the quickest route back to the family apartment, giving the prostitute only the smallest sideways glance as I passed. She wasn't more than twenty-five years old, I guessed, and was visibly trembling in the cold. There was something touching and awkward in her youthful movements, but I really wasn't giving her that much thought, was genuinely heading home, when the Haifisch Bar's door smacked open.

A portal to the underworld suddenly opened up, spilling light, smoke, and raucous chatter onto the square. Two laughing men fell out of the oak door. The girl, now in the bar's yellow seepage, looked up at the men hopefully, but they stumbled off, swaying arm in arm, and she turned disappointed back to the nub of her cigarette. The bar door pulled shut.

It was her pale and innocent face—the short

fringe of hair and the nails bitten down to the quick, but mostly the stud earrings caught momentarily in the bar light—that made me stop in my tracks. Those stud earrings were what baby girls wore at their christenings in Spain, and, as one thought triggers another, I had a vision of my brother, when we were just innocent boys and attending our neighbor's baptism in San Sebastián.

"Do you want a drink? It's a bit cold to be standing out at night in hot pants. Let's have a talk. *Coño.* I'm shivering just looking at you."

"Talk?" She looked me over. "Is that all you want?"

"Yes," I answered stiffly. "Let's start with talk."

"*Ja*, sure. I'll have a drink. It's a slow night. Can I have a bite to eat, too?"

"Of course. Come. Let's get you warmed up and something to eat."

We turned and she leaned on my arm, clutching me to her side. It wasn't an erotic gesture at all, but more like how a novice skater with weak ankles might reach out, without thinking, to clutch the nearest person for stability, as she wobbled unsteadily in her cork platform shoes, down the uneven cobblestones.

"What's your name?"

"José."

"Lena." She had a slight accent.

"Where are you from?"

"I am Swiss. From Bülach. But my father is Serbian."

We reached the covered archway of the Zum Saffron guild house, and stepped inside a smoky café, taking a table in the back. Lena ordered a peppermint tea and a salami-and-cheese roll. I ordered a Café Lutz, a coffee laced with apple brandy and sugar, although, truth be told, I really didn't need any more to drink.

"Are you married?"

"Yes. I have three sons."

"Where are they?"

I looked across the tables, toyed with my spoon. I didn't want to reveal too much.

"Central Switzerland. And you? Do you live alone?"

"Yes. I have a studio. Behind the train station."

"How old are you?"

"Twenty-four. And you?"

"Forty-five."

"So. Now we have that out of the way. No more discussion about age."

She took a bite of her salami *Brot*, chewed hungrily, and then said, in a hopeful and nervous way, "Would you like to see my flat?" like she was twelve and asking me over for a playdate. I looked at her blunt-cut hair and those earring studs and said, "Yes. I think I'd like that very much."

We quickly finished up, left the restaurant.

Lena took me by the hand and hailed a taxi. My heart was pounding and I could say very little, but she held my hand tight, determined not to let me go. The taxi stopped before a run-down apartment building from the 1900s, in the industrial part of town behind the Hauptbahnhof, which, very un-Swiss like, had not had a facelift or refurbishment for decades.

The brown wallpaper in the building's central staircase was ripped and soiled and scraped by the sofas and commodes that countless times had been carried up and down the turning staircase. The hall smelled of Turkish and Armenian stews cooked earlier in the day, their lingering odor left to hang stale in the cold hallway, like the smell of old socks.

I recoiled from the sordidness of it all and wanted out. But Lena's little hand tightly held mine, and we climbed the dimly lit stairs together, to the sound of her platform heels clunking on the steps. Her room was directly above the corner bar, and the roar from downstairs penetrated the wooden floorboards, as did the odor of spilled beer and stale cigarettes. But she had done the best she could with the room—there was a neatly made bed, a few celebrity magazines in a tidy pile on the sill, and a breakfast table with canine salt-and-pepper shakers.

Lena relaxed once she was inside her flat, stopped shivering, and seemed more mature. She kicked off her shoes and flung her purse onto the breakfast table. "Let me help you," she said. She took off my jacket, loosened my tie. A trembling heat was coming off me, through my shirt. I was confusingly filled with doubt, guilt, and a desire so powerful my breath was coming in gasps.

A voice inside chanted, *You swore you would never do this. You promised Lisa this was not you.* But my body was aching for me to take the other route, and my father's voice was forcibly roaring encouragement in my head.

Lena sensed it all, these riptides of conflicting feelings, and she put a finger to my lips. "Hush. Don't worry. It's natural to be a little afraid."

"I . . . I . . . don't know."

Lena surprised me then by quietly resting her head against my arm. She leaned against me, as if she were surrendering herself to me, and not the other way around. "It's perfectly natural. Men have hunger."

She guided me to the bed, murmuring comforting words. "Come here. Sit. We both have needs. You are helping me, too, you know. I need the money. And you are such a nice man. I can tell. This gives me pleasure, to be of service to you."

She talked quietly in this surprisingly honest way, making me feel quite innocent, and that it was just the natural order of things, this body exploration, somehow creating the illusion we were nothing more than innocent children playing doctor on the floor of a bedroom. I sat befuddled at the end of her bed, as she knelt before me and untied my shoes, gently pulling them off my hot and pinched feet.

She unbuttoned my shirt, slid it from my shoulders, before one of her hands—quickly, expertly—undid my belt, popped open the top button of my pants, and unzipped my fly. As each layer of clothing was removed, I felt myself stripped of the outer skins of my life—my roles as father and husband and private banker— until in the end I was reduced to my most basic essence, finally at rest with all my greedy flaws and imperfections, returning to a more brutish and primitive self, as the tip of my cock slid into her mouth.

It was morning. I heard the metallic sounds of the tram taking commuters to work, the crackling electricity from the overhead cables, the wheels underneath sending out a grating, skate-sharpening sound as the tram turned along the tracks into the station. The light was pink and pale and freshly innocent. I stared up at Lena's cracked and pocked ceiling for some moments, full of nausea and disgust, and then, unable to contain the self-loathing any longer, rolled off the bed.

Lena's eyes fluttered open. She looked pale and tired.

"Are you going?"

"Yes. Thank you for the lovely evening."

I left on her bedside table almost all the cash I had, four hundred francs. It was more than she had asked and her eyes briefly widened with excitement.

"Thank you, José. You are a nice man."

"No, I am not. But it is kind of you to say so."

I eased shut the door of her apartment and descended the stairs, behind an unshaven Albanian wearing a roadworks-orange vest, just heading out to work. The hall in the morning smelled of fresh winter stews again bubbling on the stove, and once outside, I grabbed a taxi and went directly to Hechtplatz, letting myself into the penthouse and the life that Lisa and I had built.

I went to the bathroom, dropped my clothes in a heap on the floor, and stepped behind the glass doors to take a boiling shower. I stood under the showerhead for I don't know how long, still trembling from the night, telling myself again and again that I had momentarily slipped, on a lonely and drunken night, but it wouldn't happen again. I stepped out of the shower, toweled off, and drove home.

"What is it?" Lisa asked.

We were in our living room in the farmhouse. I looked up from my paper.

"What is what?"

"That thing you are doing."

"*Mujer.* What are you talking about?"

"That thing that makes you so sweet and attentive one moment—and then cold and angry and withdrawn the next. It usually happens when you come back to us after a night at the apartment."

"I have no idea what you are talking about."

"Yes, you do."

She dropped her head, back to her sketch pad, and after a pause said, "Well, it's probably best I don't know. I should just focus on what I believe. That you love me, that you love us, and that you will never really jeopardize what we have built here." Her eyes were brimming and her voice trembled a little when she added, "Remember, we swore to each other we would raise our sons in a safe and kind household—that we would not let the madness of our childhoods infect *this* home."

For all her trembling, there was also steel in her voice, and her comment, it made me bleed inside. I could not speak. The scratch, scratch of her pencil across the paper was the sound of termites eating away at my insides. I was just about to confess all. Not just what had happened with Lena the previous night, but the family secrets I had so diligently hidden from Lisa during all our years together—that my brother was actually my cousin, and that, worst of all, I had killed him with my own hands.

But perhaps Lisa sensed a violent eruption was coming, because she looked up and said, "I think peace and tranquility are the most undervalued of virtues. I never understood why the 'truth' is always what everyone raves about—that it will set us free. Really? The 'truth' in my parents' house was used to bludgeon us kids to a bloody pulp. I don't have a problem with keeping unnecessary drama out of the home. I'm all for containment. Borders serve a purpose."

My wife, I realized then, believed as profoundly as I did that there were times when secrets must be kept. She was my soul mate. We were made for each other. I took a deep breath and said, "Lisa, I often forget how hard you had it while growing up. Unlike me, you show few scars on the outside. It is only during moments like this do I remember—and understand."

"Yes, well, let's leave it at that. No more of these dark discussions. Do you want some tea?"

My wet hands made the edge of the newspaper wilt and tremble. I folded it up quickly, to hide my sins, and smiled at my wife.

"What you made me last time. It was delicious. That smoky tea."

Over the following days, I could not stop thinking of Lena, the tilt of her ass, the back of her head, her creamy shoulders resting on my stomach. Erotic images of her thrust up into my consciousness at the most inappropriate moments. They came to me on the tram, in a meeting with a client, when standing with Lisa and the boys at the Migros supermarket checkout. Just the thought of Lena would moisten my palms and make my crotch tighten. It made me pant, feel alive.

One day, unable to stand the confines of my office anymore, too distracted by thoughts of Lena to work properly, I went for a walk. I came out of our bank building, turned left, and headed down the Bahnhofstrasse to the lake.

Seagulls surfed the air, coiffed women with wicker baskets were out shopping at the flea market, and the blue-and-white No. 4 tram was serenely gliding up the boulevard. I stared over the rail, at the lapping lake below, and tried to examine what was going on.

What was it I wanted from Lena? Just sex? What void did she fill?

I searched and searched my thoughts and came up with nothing that made sense. I couldn't understand what I was hungering after. Right then, however, I sensed a force present in the lake. I cupped my eyes and peered hard into the rippling water, and saw the toothy snout of a blue-gray pike poking out of a hole, waiting for prey to drift past.

The next foray into the night occurred a week later. It came much easier. A difficult work assignment meant I was again alone in Zürich, rather than driving back to the family and the farmhouse. It was 11:00 p.m. and I was in the penthouse, pouring myself a vodka tonic, restlessly flicking between the boring Swiss TV stations.

When I couldn't stand it any longer, I grabbed my coat and headed outside. I wasn't sure where I was going at first, but found myself walking the darkened backstreets of the Niederdorf, making my way, like a salmon smelling his way back to his river, to the same little square where I first saw Lena.

She was not there. An empty coffee cup, with a pink smudge at the edge, stood on the wall next to the garbage can. I picked up the cup, held it in my hand. I had no evidence Lena had left this cup, but I fervently believed she had, and it seemed, to me, the most precious object on earth at that moment.

I became more determined to find her. I arranged to be in town for the rest of the week, and for four nights in a row, I compulsively stalked the streets, hunting for her, late into the night. I hungrily fished every city pocket I could think of until I finally saw the back of her short-cropped head, this time down near Central. Her streetwalker's pose was unmistakable.

She was facing the opposite direction, in the same blue Nautilus down jacket, and was again puffing on a cigarette. I came in from behind and threw my arms around her. She was much taller than I remembered and I whispered into her neck, unable to cover up the longing in my voice. "Oh, you sweet thing. I haven't been able to get you out of my mind."

"*Hola, guapo. Qué quieres?*"

I was, for a moment, stunned, unable to grasp what had just happened or how to respond to this man turning, with a grin, to leer at me. Perhaps most disorienting of all was his remark—"Hello, handsome. What do you want?"—in my mother tongue, as if he knew exactly who I was already.

I reeled back, revolted, and angry. But I didn't walk away. My feet stayed firmly rooted to the pavement. There was something about the young man—something familiar, like he had known me all my life and perhaps longer.

"Forgive me. I thought you were someone else."

He coolly flicked away the nub of his cigarette.

It was an arrogant and dismissive gesture, so familiar to me, and it instantly brought to the surface a vision of Juan. It was not the vague baptism image triggered by Lena's stud earrings, but the full-blooded thing, so real a picture of my brother I could almost feel him there with us at the tram stop, close in age to when he died.

The man before me, in his late twenties, shifted his weight from his front leg to his back leg, and his impatient fidgeting brought me back. I looked at him, he looked at me, with his black and hungry eyes—and it felt like he was undressing me. I blushed.

"*Hombre*, it's all over your face. You're aching for a journey to the other side. I'll take you there, *guapo*. Come on. Let's have some fun."

He was smiling and his teeth flashed and dazzled white in the tram station's harsh light. He was handsome—his face chiseled, mottled with two days of stubble—but my eyes kept on returning to those flashing teeth.

"Yes, you are right. Take me to the other side."

"All right, then."

I looked down at the ground. "But I have no experience. I'm afraid."

He put his big hand on my shoulder, gave me a reassuring squeeze, and, again, produced that devastating smile. "Don't be scared, *guapo*. I am just the man to take you there. Trust me, we're gonna have so much fun."

He grabbed me possessively just above my elbow, told me his name was Miguel, and then began steering me through the streets of the Niederdorf, wherever he wanted, like I was a mere boy in the thrall of an older and experienced man, rather than the other way around.

Somewhere in the quarter's backstreets, we climbed the creaky stairs of a gray-stone building. At the top of the staircase, in the black-light landing, a bearded bouncer was wearing leather and studs. He was scowling down at us.

"He's with me."

Miguel turned in my direction, rubbed his fingers together, and I scrabbled in my pants for my money clip. He pulled fifty Swiss francs from my pile of bills and told me to put the rest away. The bouncer stamped my wrist from an inkpad, and stepped to the side, gesturing with his head that we should proceed. We pushed through the club's bronze-metal door. I figured that Miguel earned an under-the-table commission from bringing richer, older men to the disco. I didn't care.

The thump of the speakers, the dance floor moaning around the bend of a dark corridor, was a physical assault and I winced at the music's meaty presence. The music had the opposite effect on Miguel. His hands rose, like a flamenco dancer might raise his uncurling fists, his eyes half closed with music and lust.

"Donna Summer. 'She Works Hard for the Money,' " he yelled over the music. "*Hombre*, that's my song. Love it. *Tú tambien, guapo*?"

But I could not respond. I was frozen stiff, petrified, like I had just entered hell. I mustered all my strength, to turn and bolt back outside, but Miguel must have sensed this, because he quickly turned on his worn-down Cuban heels and pushed me hard against the wall. The sheer physicality of this—the scratch of his rough stubble, his body pushed against mine, our crotches pressed together like prayer hands—left me immobile, like a fly paralyzed by a spider bite.

Miguel was behind me now, a hand heavy on each of my shoulders, breathing and whispering in my ear, pushing me forward down the curve of the corridor. There was a stuttering strobe light, smoke, a thicket of men, and suddenly I was there, too, on the small dance floor. Miguel put his arms around my neck and began to grind his hips against me, his erection pushing against mine. "No," I said angrily and tried to pull away. But he laughed and held me tight, and Miguel's swaying hips, the music, the musky smell in the air, his hands around my back—it all swept me to the other side, filled that part of me where the dead normally sat.

"OK, you're ready," Miguel breathed in my ear. "Now let's get a room."

I rented a room for us at La Chinoise, a small hotel up on the high backstreets of the Niederdorf, where the lobby was fittingly red and whorishly lacquered. A black vase full of white lilies sat luridly on the reception desk.

Miguel stood back as I handed my credit card to the front-desk night manager, who efficiently checked us in with that discreet Swiss manner, his head down and facing the ledger, never up and gawking at what was so obvious.

We took the elevator to the fourth floor. The swing of that lacquered white door into the compact hotel room was sobering, and I became acutely aware that crossing this border would bring me into a lower ring of hell, a subterranean level so deep I might not ever emerge whole from it—if at all.

So I hesitated, stood back, and let Miguel pass first. But the young man was feral, had instincts like a dog, and he pulled me inside the room, once again silencing my inner voices with his arms wrapped tight around my back, so I was pinned and couldn't move, his lips hard against my neck, his breath in my ear.

"I am going to take you to paradise, *guapo*."

The next morning, I sipped my espresso with a shaky hand, puffed nervously on a cigarette. The glass-enclosed breakfast room atop the hotel was filled with morning light and giant palm fronds and white-painted wrought-iron furniture, like a Victorian winter garden had been transported to the high Niederdorf. I was still intoxicated from the night before and almost unable to talk, filled as I was with joy and guilt and shame and a few other emotions I had never experienced before.

Miguel was hungry and chatty. He tore open a hard roll and smeared it with quince jam. "That was fantastic. I slept so well, señor."

"*Coño*! Call me José."

"I tease you. It's a term of respect."

"It makes me feel old and disposable. Just call me by my name."

"So, how many children do you have?"

I shifted my weight. "I have three boys."

"You stud."

"What about you?"

"What about me?"

"Your background. What does your father do?"

"No idea. He walked out on us when I was six. Never saw him again."

There must have been something pained in my look, because Miguel stiffened and said, "It's OK. That was a long time ago. I am over him."

I reached over and squeezed his arm.

"Why are you doing that?"

"Just because. You touch me."

"You are *loco*, I think. *Bueno*, *guapo*. I have to go. It's my ten o'clock. The Sweet Freak."

"What do you mean?"

"Today is Wednesday. It's time for my regular."

"I mean, why do you call him the 'Sweet Freak'?"

"He's seventy years old and likes to sit on my lap in a diaper."

My revulsion must have been evident in my expression because he snapped, "What's that face, *cabrón*? Who are you to judge? You shouldn't be like that. He is absolutely harmless and quite sweet—and that two-hour session with him pays my rent for almost the entire month."

I could not stop my "journey to the other side," as Miguel called it, and six months later, the two of us were in India, following a porter down jungle-choked cliffs, our backs wet with trickling sweat. A Portuguese client had inherited a property from a deceased relative who lived in India, and I had to figure out a way to quickly and quietly liquidate the coconut plantation and get my client's assets out of India and safely into an offshore tax haven, without, he instructed, his estranged wife becoming the wiser.

Miguel jumped at the offer to join me on that trip to Southern India, his precise words—"Fuck yes, *guapo*! Count me in!"—making me laugh.

Those days at the resort in Kerala were, for me, heaven on earth, starting with that first moment when the porter took us down the cliff path that meandered gently through the orange-red flowers of pagoda plants and the intoxicating scents of the joy perfume tree. The house's low-slung roof and pagoda-like eaves gave us the delightful impression it was bowing at our arrival.

"*Coño*," Miguel said appreciatively.

Far down the cliffs, through the flowering jungle, there rose the cawing of strange and colorful birds, and through the branches you could just make out the caramel curve of a beach.

We could hear the pounding waves of the Arabian Sea, which, straight ahead over the treetops, stretched out platinum to the horizon.

A hammock hung in one corner of the shaded terrace, a simple wooden breakfast table stood in another, and as we marveled at the view, the porter unlocked the bungalow's carved door, as grand as any entrance to a temple. In its cool and dark interior, we found a library, a writing desk, a couch and tea table; in the corner alcove, there stood a massive teak bed dressed with white linens, under a mosquito net.

It was surprisingly cool. Rattan fans rotated overhead, and a breeze from the sea, coming in through the mosquito screens across the windows, wafted into the room the intoxicating smell of jasmine, sprigs of which were lying across each windowsill. A butler, in orange collarless shirt and black pants, came out of the shadows and stood by our side.

"Welcome, sirs. I hope you had a pleasant journey." He opened a carved cabinet, revealing a small and humming refrigerator. "Water is kept here. If it gets too hot, this is the switch for the air conditioning. And this is your bathroom . . ."

He flung open a back door, revealing a private walled-in courtyard and garden, open to the elements. A toilet and shower stood out in the open, but were protected from rain by being just under a set of roof eaves. The far stone wall was covered in vines bursting with dainty blue flowers, and below it stood a stone plunge pool the color of which—deep emerald, blue, gold—I had never seen before.

Miguel clapped his hands in delight. *"Oh Dios mío.* Thank you, *guapo*, for bringing me here. I've never been in a place like this."

"My pleasure."

I turned and tipped the porter. The butler tried to unpack our bags for us, but I said we would do so ourselves and tipped him to go away.

As soon as they were gone, Miguel was halfway across the room, dropping his pants and shirt and underwear onto the floor on his way out the back door. "I am going to spend the entire week naked," he yelled, lowering himself into the plunge pool. "This is amazing. Come on! Join me!"

We swam in the ocean, went shopping in the village, fucked a couple of times a day. We hired a car and driver who showed us the fish markets and then a temple devoted to Lord Ayyappa. We got out of the car and walked past a lake, in which a carved pavilion emerged from the middle of the water, a white-stone temple the color of fine ivory. Around the lake's perimeter, young men in loincloths and underwear sat on steel rails and washed their hair and armpits, cleansing themselves for the final steps of their religious journey.

We walked on and the town's streets began to throng with milling crowds, mangy packs of dogs, young girls selling marigold garlands from reed baskets, entire families sitting tight on a single motorbike, and oxen hauling carts of coconuts. Everywhere we came across large groups of men—with their oily-black hair and big bellies and hairy chests, offset by the colorful saffron-colored *mundu* wrapped around their legs—getting ready to enter the temple. And the air itself smelled of grilling pineapple and fried fish and burning incense.

The temple rose before us, like a powerful god's wedding cake, seven tapered stories of white stone, intricately carved with Hindu deities and thrusting high up into the azure sky. We were jostled, funneled into the temple's gated entrance. Miguel had, since we left the car, been chatting nonstop about his coming trip to Barcelona, but he suddenly grew quiet and unsure and looked like a boy.

A lean and unshaven guide in white loincloth appeared before us, offering his services, and I hired him. He told us to take off our shirts. We did as we were told, now bare-chested like all the other men around us.

The guide spoke unintelligible English, and though we understood only every third word— "pillar," "Lord Ayyappa," "Monkey God"—we walked quiet and awed and shirtless behind him, through a series of gates and into the temple's dark interior passageway. What little light there was came from feeble mine lamps bolted to the walls of the tunnel. Miguel and I exchanged nervous glances over the oiled heads around us, as the crush of overexcited pilgrims drove us forward, almost against our will.

Halfway through the tunnel, we could see an opening at the far end of the passageway, and from this murky portal arose strange chants and crashing cymbals and eerie groans.

Miguel stopped cold in his tracks.

"It's OK, Miguel," I said into his ear. "I am here."

Miguel instinctively reared back in the direction we had come, and I, grabbing him around the waist, leaned forward to where we had yet to go. I finally took a heavy step forward, and the way I was holding him tight against my flank, it forced Miguel to lumber forward with me, and the momentum of that step finally carried us down the entire last half of the claustrophobic passageway.

We were in the temple's stone-pillared inner sanctum. The cavity opened up, moist and airy and cool like an underground cave. White pillars and rich garlands of orange-and-white flowers slowly came into focus. The thicket of believers miraculously spread out and dispersed inside the massive inner chamber, each group heading to the statues dedicated to their favorite gods.

Carved stone statues and ropes of marigold and brass trays of smoking incense surrounded us, loomed up in the dark, then disappeared around the next corner. Across the sanctum, I could just make out some men prostrating themselves before Lord Shiva and Lord Vishnu, the male gods who coupled in order to give birth to Lord Ayyappa, their powerful son and the deity who was the protector of Kerala. Half-naked men, moaning and in ecstatic states in the dark, cruised around us, giving off a smell of feral heat, and I instantly had the blasphemous thought that this temple and the gay disco were somehow one and the same, just sacred and profane manifestations of the same hunger for transcendence.

"This is rare for foreigners to see," said our guide. "Come. You must witness."

He waved at us to follow him down a long walkway, lined on either side by pillars carved with stunning images of the mundane world. Their visions came at us as we followed our guide down the path—a lord reigning over a thief's execution; paupers begging, as hungry tigers behind them prowled the jungle; children playing with their grandparents in a flowering garden, three rearing cobras in the grass. But there were also the most intense erotic images— a man penetrating his wife, two naked women rolling in the dirt.

Miguel again stopped and this time his expression sent a shiver down my spine. I followed his gaze. Carved into a column was a tableau of a drunk man abandoning his family—a little boy was clinging to his father's legs, a desperate attempt to prevent him from leaving the family hut. But the man was mad with drink and was dragging his clinging son across the dirt, determined to flee his responsibilities. The carving was good—you could sense the tragic ending.

A look came over Miguel's face—I will never forget it—as his great wound, buried deep within, was suddenly torn open. At first you could see, in Miguel's eyes and frozen face, a herculean struggle to contain the rising emotions, but he couldn't keep the riptide at bay, and as the feelings of hurt washed over him, his mouth opened in a soundless cry.

My instinct was to shake him out of it. I grasped his elbow and said, "Just stop it. You're safe with me. Now let's get this over with."

I pushed him forward, forced him to take a step, and in this labored way we shuffled down past the remaining pillars, to our little gnome of a guide, who was energetically waving us on, perplexed as to why we were taking so long to join the ritual at that moment unfolding on the slightly raised dais.

The colorful statue commanding the back wall

was of Lord Ayyappa, a cherubic boy with a bell around his neck, leading a ferocious tiger through the forest. He was a golden child, a healer of the wounded, slayer of the evil demoness Mahishi, a granter of wishes. Believers, pressed hard against the raised platform, adoringly looked up at the priest and the idols, hands clasped in prayer. Their steepled fingers were raised high in front of their faces, their black eyes flinty and fiery and transported somewhere else. And in central position among the believers, the young man who had commissioned the ritual, his head bowed in prayer, desperate to find his soul mate.

The priest approached the young man dressed in his finest formal *mundu*, smeared his forehead with paste, and chanted extra prayers over his crown. Then he moved down the podium, handing out banana leaves smeared with a sticky-sweet rice lump and more smudges of the crimson paste he dabbed with his fingers on every believer's forehead. The air itself was filled with ecstatic awe, of hope and redemption and the possibility that love could be found on this earth.

I glanced over at Miguel. The look on his face spoke of an ache so deep, a yearning so powerful, I had to look away. A prayer unexpectedly rose to my own lips.

God, let me save Miguel, my penance for not saving Juan.

Let me in this way redeem myself before I die.

• • •

I did not sleep well Miguel's last night at the resort. I woke to the sound of the nuns and monks praying in the seventeenth-century Catholic monastery down below the cliffs, a half ruin originally built by the Portuguese. It was the lead-up to Christmas, and the Christian servants of God and a handful of devout villagers were singing their early-morning prayers. It was an otherworldly sound—half Gregorian chant, half Hindi pop song, the background crash of the waves keeping the music's beat—and it made my heart swell, pulled me naked from the bed, had me standing on the cold stone floor, looking back down at Miguel through the mosquito net.

Miguel was as usual naked and sprawled out across the sheets. His thick eyelashes were calmly pressed shut, his mouth and sensuous lips relaxed. He looked like a young god, asleep and at peace after a hunt in the woods. I let him be, pulled on a pair of drawstring pants, and padded across the suite, quietly slipping out the bungalow's carved teak door.

The terrace was moist and the surrounding jungle throbbed with chanting frogs and thrumming bugs and snuffling rodents and birds swooping through the branches. Above me, the stars were out in a squid-ink night sky, as was the silver moon, slivered like a shiny crescent pastry. There was a warm breeze coming off the ocean, suggesting the day would be very hot.

The nuns and monks were in their fifth verse, full of their love for Christ, and their otherworldly song rose up the cliffs to where I stood. I dropped into the hammock, but kept one foot solidly on the ground, rocking myself to the beat of their chant and the eternal crash of the waves. I don't know how long I was there, but the joy of that sound, the sight of the sun slowly rising across the Arabian Sea, spreading sorbet across the platinum water, it somehow made more poignant what I was feeling inside—the loss, the loss. Miguel would leave me in a few hours, without a backward glance, to fly off to Barcelona.

He ate his breakfast with his usual appetite, filling his plate with mango and yogurt and Indian breads stuffed with fish curry and rice balls studded with almonds and currants.

"I could eat an elephant. It was all that hot sex with you."

"You say that to all your friends."

"True, *guapo*. But with you I mean it."

"Who are you meeting in Barcelona?"

"No. No. No. Don't do that. You know our agreement. You don't ask questions about what I do when I am not with you. That's our deal."

"I can't stand it. Please. Stay."

"You are sweet. But no. That's not happening . . . Pass the marmalade."

We went back to the room and I morosely watched him throw his Speedo bathing suit, a few toiletries, into the bag and zip up. There was a bang on the door and the porter came in. "The taxi to the airport has arrived, sir." He bent down and, with one swoop, had hoisted Miguel's bag onto his shoulders and was slowly, methodically, crossing the terrace and climbing the cliff's stone steps.

Miguel came over and threw his arms around me.

"Thank you for the fantastic vacation, *guapo*. You are a good and kind man. I hope the work you have to do isn't too boring. If it is, just think of me in that plunge pool and jerk off. See you back in Zürich."

Don't leave me. Stay with me.

What I said, rather stiffly, was "Goodbye, Miguel. Thank you for the lovely time. Please stay safe."

"There you go again, going all formal and uptight and cold. Relax, *guapo*. Come on. Be cool."

He hugged me warmly one last time and then was gone.

I was alone.

I worked long hours, a form of penance for all my sins. I covered up my ache, pushed away every thought of Lisa and the boys and Miguel, and focused solely on the work. Day in and day out, I stayed inside the gray-walled office of the Trivandrum bank, under a turning rattan fan, working on my client's problem with a Chartered Sun Trust Bank manager and local lawyers, trying to figure out an innovative way to meet the client's mandate to squirrel away his inheritance.

The Indian heat was almost unbearable. It beat down on the bank's flat roof like a hammer, until my underwear was wet and soggy and chafing. I am not sure if it was the rising heat without, or the steaming and pressured heat within, but on the last day, unable to bear it any longer, I put down my pen, stood, and walked abruptly from the bank. I headed down the cliff, through the flowering jungle, to the beach and roaring surf. Here, I found a breeze and a cool ocean spray to moisten my face.

There was a line of blue-and-white fishing boats pulled up on the beach, and next to them stood two lines of sun-blackened men. There were a dozen fishermen in each line, and they were all wearing the little wraparound skirts called *lungi*.

The two orderly lines of chanting men were almost a kilometer apart, I guessed, and as I approached I saw that each was partaking in a relay of arms, pulling rhythmically at a net still out at sea, to the incessant beat of their song. I swiveled, cupped my hands to my eyes, and looked beyond the waves pounding ashore. Orange buoys marked the perimeter of the net, which, for all their pulling, still appeared to stretch over a kilometer out to sea.

A tall and skinny fisherman at the end of the line, shirtless and with a large silver cross dangling from his neck, broke off from the men, circled to the front of the rope coming taut out of the sea. He grabbed the thick hemp with two hands and then fell back with a hard tug and a grunt-chant, the force of his tug sending the entire line of chanting men behind him back another foot. The last man on the rope broke off, circled forward, and the relay started again.

Slowly, as the morning progressed, the two strings of men at either end of the beach, each tugging at one end of the net and dragging it forward through the wide sea, inched their way closer and closer together.

The bottom of the net was coming in; I could tell, because suddenly the pulled coil of curled net was making the beach reek of fish. The smell must have been a sign of sorts, because a shirtless man with a large belly tucked his *lungi* this way and that—so it wasn't hanging down as a skirt, but tight around his thighs like swimming trunks—and then unraveled his turban to tie the band of cloth around his waist, turning it into a belt.

He walked forward, solid as a rock, and then

dove headfirst into the water and swam hard, past the breaking waves, to the last bobbing buoy. He hung from the far side of the net and peered down into the water, looking for fish in the underwater basket. He waved his arm when he wanted the men to pull in one direction or another.

A fisherman broke off from the net and came to me.

"Hello."

"Hello," I replied.

"I am Simon."

"I am José." I pointed at the man in the water. "Who is that?"

"That is Peter. He is our foreman."

Before I could ask another question, there was a commotion and we both turned back to the water. Four younger fishermen dove into the sea and stood or bobbed in the surf, ducking when the biggest waves rolled in. They began smacking the water and yelling. They swam out a little ways, repeated their water dance, chasing the fish toward the back of the net and away from its open mouth at the beach.

The foreman swam back ashore. The two strings of men were now side by side. They hauled and hauled the last stretch of net, after three hours of praying and pulling, and the net came in quicker now, lying coiled and glistening in the sand. We looked and looked as the last beads of net were hauled ashore.

There were just two flapping fish, neither bigger than a child's palm, in the entire net.

The fishermen were silent.

"We are fishing in the wrong place," Peter said. "We won't fill our empty bellies this way. We are looking in the wrong place."

FOURTEEN

It was late July of the same year and the salmon were running. I stood on the ridge, just outside the fishing lodge, and squinted down at the wild river below, looking for my sons. The wind was blowing hard, as it always does in Iceland, but that afternoon the arctic sun was also bright in the sky, and it was making every wind-buffeted blade of tundra grass and shard of rock glint as if made from diamonds.

I snapped my Polaroid shades into place, and peered down at the Kjara River roaring through the ravine below. Devil's Gate was named for the frightening roar the water made as it poured hard through the funnel at the top of the gorge. The long pool, below the white water, was the blue-green of Murano glass.

Even from where I stood, I could see the silver glint of a salmon occasionally turning on its side, but I saw no sign of the boys, so I walked up the ravine another hundred meters and again stepped to the edge.

I spotted them. My sons had each taken one of the three branches of river threading through the plateau, and were methodically fishing every pot as they headed upriver, hunting for the salmon resting after an exhausting swim up through the powerful falls of Devil's Gate. I fished in my jacket for binoculars and zeroed in on the farthest figure. It was Sam, playing what looked like a one-year-at-sea grilse, on the outer branch of the river. Before I could swing my binoculars over to the other two boys, however, I sensed, in the momentary lull of the wind before another gust came barreling down the tundra, someone approaching me from behind.

Inge, the lodge maid, stood timidly, her blond hair fluttering wildly in the wind. We exchanged shy glances. That morning, on my way to the bathroom, I had seen Inge slink out of the married head ghillie's bedroom, and we both froze, embarrassed, before averting our gazes and continuing on our journeys.

"Señor Álvarez. Your wife is on the phone."

I followed her back to the lodge, wiped my feet on the mat. We passed through the beamed great room, its large window serving up a high-ridge view of Devil's Gate below. The dining room's long table, standing below the window, was already set for the 10:00 p.m. dinner. The lounge, on the other side of the great room, was filled with sturdy couches and leather armchairs, a coffee table covered in fishing logs, and a sideboard dotted with half-empty bottles of vodka, whisky, and cognac.

The public phone booth with the accordion door was in the hall at the back of the lodge, past the guest bedrooms. I picked up the receiver lying on its side.

"Lisa?"

"Darling! Hello! How is the fishing?"

"Fantastic. I've caught thirty-eight salmon in two days. None less than four kilos."

"That's wonderful. And the boys?"

"They're all good. They're on the river now. We just had lunch. I took a brief siesta afterward, and the boys went directly down to the river to fish. They don't want me to pull too far ahead. They've caught twenty-seven fish—altogether."

"I'm so pleased. I hope Rob has caught a salmon on the fly rod. He was so determined it would happen this time."

"Not yet. But it will happen. The fishing is good."

We talked some more, about the house in Ägeri; about how many kilos of cherries we harvested this year; how the farmer who was leasing the outer fields was now cutting the tall grass to make winter hay. We told each other we loved each other, in that perfunctory way long-married couples do, and then hung up.

I stared at the phone, back in its cradle, deciding what I should do next. I knew it was a mistake, but I couldn't help myself. I fished inside my pocket for my little black address book. I picked up the phone, called Switzerland again.

"*Hola, Miguel.*"

"*Papi*! What are you doing calling? I thought you were in Iceland."

"I am. I had to hear your voice."

I could hear, in the background, the sound of music, a deep voice.

"That's so sweet of you. How's the fishing?"

"Fine. What's going on there? Sounds like you're having a party."

"No. No . . . it's a client. He just arrived. So I can't talk now. I've got to get off the phone. See you soon, *Papi*. I can't wait until you come back."

As he went to put down the phone on his end, I distinctly heard a voice, speaking Swiss German, calling out from somewhere in the apartment. I knew instantly it was Miguel's friend, the bouncer from the nightclub.

"Did you get rid of that boring old fart? Now come here, handsome."

I put down the phone. I wanted to gaff the bouncer's face.

I banged hard on Sigi's door in the staff quarters and some seconds later the young ghillie peered myopically out from his room. He was tousle-haired and smelled of Brennivin, the local firewater. He was the ghillie assigned to guide the Álvarez family, shuttling us back and forth from the river. The head ghillie and another assistant were working the lower beats of the river with a larger group of wealthy French and Italian clients, who were also staying at the lodge and somehow connected to each other through the car industry.

"Sigi, I've paid a hell of a lot of money to fish here. I don't think it is unreasonable to expect someone to take me to the river."

"No, sir. You can get into the Russian jeep. The Lada. I'll be right there."

I stomped back to the mustard-colored jeep that looked like a squat bug, climbed into its passenger seat, and slammed shut the rattling door. I had already attached my rods to the hood. I lit a cigarette, leaned over, and blasted the car horn several times. Sigi came tearing out from the back of the lodge, buckling his pants, as if he had just taken a piss.

The young Icelander climbed in behind the wheel, fired up the Lada, released the hand brake, and rolled us forward—all in one seamless motion.

"Sorry. I fell asleep."

"Listen, Sigi, I'm not paying twenty-five hundred dollars a day per rod so you can drink Brennivin and fuck the cook's help. I've lost twenty minutes of fishing looking for you. Do you need me to do the math as to how much that cost me?"

"No, sir. I understand. You are right. I'm sorry."

"The boys are still fishing the Pools of the Lost. They'll be there for a while. Take me to Red

Rock. Let's get ahead of the boys and fish the rested pools. I think the large run of fish we saw last night has already moved farther upriver."

Sigi sucked in his breath, the look on his face making it clear his sense of river etiquette had been violated. "Your sons told me they were going to fish upriver this afternoon, into Red Rock, and that you were going to fish the pools below Devil's Gate. This is what was agreed."

"Yes. That is what we agreed at breakfast this morning, but now river conditions have changed, and so I have changed the plan. Do you have a problem with this?"

"No, sir."

"Well, then. Do as I say. Let's go."

We came to where the dirt road finally met the valley's hard and flat lava bed, the lacing branches of river stretched out before us. For a moment, a back tire was suspended high as it rolled over a large boulder, while the front wheels were already on the flat plain below. When the back wheel rolled completely off the high rock, we hit the lava bed with a hard thud and I was thrown against the dashboard, banging my head.

I exploded in Spanish curses.

"Sorry, sir."

"*Cabrón.* You're always apologizing. It's annoying."

"I'm sorry . . ."

Lurid images of Miguel and the bouncer, rolling

around in bed, filled my head. I was furious he had lied to me. Thought I might get sick.

"Do me a favor, Sigi. Just don't talk."

Sigi switched into four-wheel drive and carefully crossed the bottom end of a pool, the water rising to the top of our wheels. We continued in silence like this, me fogging up the door window with my hot breath, Sigi concentrating as he maneuvered the swaying vehicle over the submerged rocks.

On the far side, he pulled out of the pool, water pouring from the underbelly of the jeep. Back on dry land, he leaned over, switched out of four-wheel drive and back into higher gears, and we were soon racing across the plain.

"Your youngest son has a fish on."

Rob, fishing the middle branch of the river, came into view, just as we plowed over a small and shrubby island and plunged back into the river. He was some three hundred meters ahead, his fly rod bent in two as he played a nice-sized fish in a small pool.

Rob slowly backed away from the water and the fish jumped, always a dangerous moment. But my son, just seventeen, expertly lowered his rod, to avoid pulling the fly out of its mouth when it was airborne, and then just as quickly raised his rod again and tightened the line when the salmon fell back into the water—just as I had taught him.

"Nice fish," said Sigi. "About eight kilos. It's well hooked. You can tell."

A flash of light caught the corner of my eye and I turned in its direction. It was the sun, glinting off the nylon of Rob's worm rod that was leaning against a shrub. I remembered, then.

This is the first salmon your youngest son has ever caught on a fly rod.

Sigi had been cheering Rob on these last few days, giving him his best advice, and I could see, in his expression, how pleased he was that my son finally had hooked a decent fish and was well on his way to bringing it ashore. The young ghillie applied the brake and began to slow the jeep down, so I could jump out and assist Rob and share with him this father-son moment.

As he did so, however, we spotted Sam. He was striding hard across the tundra and gravel, heading back to help his younger brother land the fish and celebrate this rite of passage. He was only two hundred meters or so away.

I smacked the dashboard of the Lada. "Keep going. Sam has this. I want to start fishing. Keep going. Go on. Go."

Sigi opened his mouth, as if he was going to speak, but I must have bristled a warning not to meddle in my family affairs, because he closed shut his mouth with a chop, and moved into higher gear, picking up speed again.

Rob was too busy concentrating on playing the

fish to worry about what we were doing behind his back, but on our way upriver we passed Sam, coming up on our eastern flank. I remember that initial look of surprise on his face, as he came over the gravel bar and saw the Lada roar past him, its tires spitting stones, my face pressed up against its fogged glass.

Sam's shock quickly morphed into disappointment, then anger, all of which I saw in that brief moment when he and I locked eyes, just before the Lada sped away, taking him out of my sight.

Now that time has passed and the memory is before me, I am filled with shame and regret. But I did what I did, there is no denying it, blinded at the time by my rage and hurt over Miguel. I cannot change that. It crowded out all the other feelings I was having or should have been having about my boy, and at the time all I could do was fish—the only balm that has ever soothed the wounds inside me.

The Nordic sun was still orange and hovering at the horizon when they picked me up at Red Rock. It was 9:00 p.m. and I was sitting by the river, tiredly smoking a cigarette. A bloody line of seventeen salmon was laid out behind me on the riverbank.

Sigi jumped out of the jeep with a roll of plastic under his arm. "José!" he exclaimed. "That's a river record! You caught twenty-four salmon in one day. Congratulations!"

He bagged the fish I had already bled with a cut into the gills. Sigi was visibly excited. "Incredible! The Professor has struck again. I have to say, you are the best fisherman who has ever fished this river. It's amazing what you can do with the fly."

I flicked away my cigarette. "Thank you. I once caught more, long ago. On the Ribadesella in Northern Spain."

My three sons slowly climbed from the jeep. They were standing in a tight line on an elevated grassy knoll, silently staring down at me and my fish slaughtered on the riverbank. When I looked up at their blank faces, dead of expression, I was reminded of the way the peasants stared stonily down at Franco from Omedina's town bridge.

It was my youngest son who broke the silence.

"Congratulations, Dad."

He spoke, I recall, in a small voice.

That night we celebrated Rob's salmon in the most appropriate way—we ate it for dinner. The Frenchmen and Italians who were fishing the lower beats joined us in the lounge for the customary predinner drink, and among them was a white-haired Italian who owned three Ferrari dealerships, accompanied by his charming and fleshy mistress. The lodge filled with our chatter and laughter, in several languages, as we merrily drank vodkas and scotches, while entering our day's catch into the log and boasting of our river conquests. The dinner bell rang. Inge brought out the steaming platter of fish, and we all, starving after a day of hard fishing, scampered to our positions around the table.

My sons did not sit next to me, as they normally did, but strategically placed themselves in between the lodge's other fishermen. I didn't say a word. Whether they did so to make the other guests feel included and festive in our celebration of Rob's fish, or to keep their distance from me, I wasn't sure.

The Ferrari dealer in the pale yellow Armani sweater lifted his glass of white wine in Rob's direction, and sonorously said, in his Milanese accent, "To you, young man, for so fantastically losing your virginity."

Rob blushed and we all roared with laughter, but for the Italian's mistress, who smacked her white-haired lover on the arm in a mock-angry way and told my youngest son, "Ignore these crude old men. They're just jealous."

Shortly thereafter the head ghillie came out of the kitchen, to congratulate Rob and hand him a wooden plaque, engraved with his name, the date, and the Icelandic name of the pool where he had caught his fish.

"That's so cool. Thank you." Rob was beaming.

A short and stocky Icelander was standing by the head ghillie's side, a craggy-faced fellow with spiked hair and an impish smile. "For those of you who don't know, this is Orri," the head ghillie said. "Orri Vigfusson. You might have heard of him."

The effect was electric. A Frenchman at the table leapt out of his chair, bounded across the room, and energetically shook Vigfusson's hand. "Such an honor to meet you, Orri! Such an honor! Please. Come join us at the table." He turned back to us and said, "Orri is the man who is single-handedly saving the salmon from extinction."

Sam, in his second year at Bowdoin College, leaned across the table and whispered at me, "We've been studying what Vigfusson has done in our Economics and the Environment class. He's a rock star in the environmental movement right now. Because of him, many environmentalists are waking up to the fact the private sector has an important role to play in saving the planet."

I was not, I confess, that familiar with Vigfusson's work, so I eavesdropped, as the Italian's mistress demanded to know what the fuss was about from her lover and the enthusiastic Frenchman to her right.

"Look, *cara*," said the Ferrari dealer. "The young salmon leave the river after two years and enter the sea, to fatten up on arctic squid and shrimp, before they come back to the river, big and strong, to spawn. It was always a mystery about where the salmon went to feed in the vast oceans. *Mah*, a few years ago, fishing vessels with the latest sonar technology pinpointed the salmon's feedings grounds off the Faroe Islands and in the deep waters off Greenland. The mystery was solved."

"But that's a good thing. No?"

"*Non, non, madame*," said her neighbor. "The commercial fishermen everywhere immediately rushed to where the salmon were congregating to feed, and strip-mined the sea with their drift nets, scooping up hundreds of thousands of tons of wild salmon and whatever else got caught in their nets."

"Oh no. The poor fishes!"

"You can imagine. The Atlantic salmon's population was cut in half in just four years. At the current rate, the salmon will be extinct in a few more years."

"But this is terrible! The governments must do something."

The Italian waved his hands dismissively. "The World Health Organization and national governments, their fisheries and maritime authorities, are all sucking their thumbs. They want to 'study the issue' further and commission more reports from marine biologists."

Vigfusson, who had been listening in on this

account from the other side of the table, couldn't help himself and roared, "But we know what the issue is! We are overfishing! Catching too many fish at sea. It's pure human avarice!"

I looked over at Sam and was shocked to discover he was looking up at the Icelander with an expression I had never seen in him before. It was sheer adulation.

I turned back, as the Italian woman turned her rapid-fire questions directly on Vigfusson. The Icelander was, we learned, part owner in three salmon rivers on the eastern coast of Iceland, which is possible in that country. Vigfusson's livelihood was of course threatened by the overfishing, and, disgusted by the inertia of the multilateral organizations, he created a philanthropic foundation called the North Atlantic Salmon Fund and raised capital with wealthy families and passionate sport fishermen from around the world. He then used the fund's war chest to pay a premium for the commercial fishermen's nets and salmon quotas at sea. Within six months, he had removed 72 percent of the commercial nets in the North Atlantic.

Salmon stocks rebounded rapidly. "There's a simple arbitrage behind the net buyout," Sam whispered across the table. "A sport fisherman will pay one hundred times more per pound of Atlantic salmon, to catch them on a fly in the river, than a housewife is prepared to pay for ocean-netted salmon bound for the family dinner table. That's why it made economic sense for river entrepreneurs like Orri to buy out the commercial nets at sea."

We were all suitably impressed and grateful for the Icelander's understanding of free-market economics and his efforts to save the salmon, of course, but eventually all this adulation began to bore me. Happily, we all returned to smaller chats with our immediate neighbors when two massive bowls of sherry trifle, one of my favorite desserts from childhood, were plopped down at either end of the long table.

I used the opportunity to tell the Italian woman how I had caught my biggest fish of the day, and, as she politely listened to my account, I dipped the big spoon into the trifle, smacked three dollops on my plate, and then pushed the pudding bowl across the table, toward my oldest son.

Sam, who moments earlier had been looking at Vigfusson with nothing but awe, looked at me with undisguised disgust. He paused a second, deciding what to do, and then leaned over and said, "Dad, that's the third time tonight you took more than your fair share of the food. There are other people at the table here, you know."

"Don't talk to me like that."

"Don't be so selfish and greedy and I won't."

I pushed my plate away. I had no more appetite.

• • •

Bad news awaited us when we got back to Switzerland. Lisa's father had inoperable pancreatic cancer, and her mother was both hysterical and insisting on caring for him herself. She refused to hire outside nursing help. "I don't know what to do," Lisa said.

The look on Lisa's face that night, when we climbed into bed, broke my heart. She was back—that person who had been terrorized by the alcoholic father and enabling mother, who had stood helplessly by and watched her brothers get beaten into the floor by their father for the simple act of trying to protect her.

But, in the middle-aged face getting slathered with moisturizer that night, there were also traces of memories that recalled her sober father patiently and lovingly repairing her dollhouse, those giddy childhood moments when her mother dressed up as a fairy and took her and her friends trick-or-treating on Halloween. Those flashes of memory existed, too, between the scenes of carnage, and they all seemed that evening to bang violently up against her own strong, internal sense of loyalty and family duty.

"Ohhhh," she sighed, before turning off the light.

We lay there in the dark, both in our own confusing space and staring at the ceiling. The silence built until I couldn't stand it any longer.

I rolled over. Hugged her tight.

• • •

The next morning, at the kitchen counter, Lisa sat pale and deflated in front of a half-eaten bowl of Greek yogurt and blueberries, toying at her breakfast with a spoon. "I hardly slept," she said. "This is such a mess. My brothers won't help. Paul says he's in the middle of closing a deal out in San Francisco, and Charlie has his own health problems. Of course, it's also very convenient. They're washing their hands of Dad because of what he did to them when they were growing up. I can't blame them."

"In the end, he is your father. You should go see him. Before it is too late."

"Don't tell me what to do. You didn't even go to your father's funeral."

"*Qué pasa aquí*? You said you didn't know what to do—so I gave you my opinion. Why are you jumping down my throat?"

"Your judgment is not valued or respected anymore."

I slowly turned in her direction, my heart thumping wildly.

"What makes you say that?"

"The boys told me you didn't stop to help Rob catch his first salmon. Shame on you, José."

I poured some milk into the coffee.

"You're even competitive with your own sons. What's happening to you? I almost don't recognize you anymore."

When I brought the espresso back to the counter, I spilled half of it. I swore, went back to the machine, and started again. "It was not my finest hour," I finally said, banging the old coffee grounds out of the portafilter. "I should have stopped, to be with him. But I was upset—had some bad news from the office—and wanted to fish. I needed to fish. You know how I am."

She pushed her half-finished bowl of yogurt away from her. "There is no excuse, José. It was Rob's first fish. You always go on and on about how it was an Álvarez ritual to make a fuss over the first salmon on the fly. My God, how many times have you bored me repeating that story about the day your brother caught his first salmon? And how you of course caught more fish than anyone else."

"OK. I get it. I behaved badly. I let my son down. *Coño*. Now stop it. We were talking about you and your parents. What are you going to do?"

"I don't really have a choice. I have to go."

Right then we heard the sound of Sam above us, clearing his throat and pounding his way down the hall to the bathroom.

"Do you have your passport?"

"Honestly, José. What has gotten into you? I am a forty-six-year-old woman. I have traveled before, you know."

"Yes. Of course. I'm sorry."

Her bags were packed and she was sitting at her vanity table, sorting through her purse. "Why are you so nervous? I'll be fine. And the boys are teenagers. You'll hardly see them. They'll be off with their friends."

"That's what I am worried about."

Lisa smiled wanly at me in the mirror. I don't think she had ever looked so beautiful—the worry about her father and mother had softened her, and, in that moment, I just wanted to put my arms around her and tell her I loved her more than anything in the world. But I did not move. Whether it was guilt or shame, I do not know, but I did not close the space between us.

"Boys!" I yelled. "Come say goodbye to your mother."

There was the sound of sullen teenagers on the move. Frye boots came thudding down the old wooden staircase with such force they made the old farmhouse shudder.

"*Dios mío*. They sound like a herd of elephants."

Lisa was dropping a lipstick into her purse when John came in. He bent down and tenderly kissed her forehead. "Have fun, Mom . . . Oh, shit, that's probably not the right thing to say. Sorry, but you get it. Give my love to Gramps and Grandma."

"You could call them directly or write a letter."

He looked vaguely out the window, scratched his chin. "Yeah, sure, I'll do that . . ."

Rob squeezed my shoulder, a morning greeting as he passed, and then threw his arms around his mother and kissed her.

"You rock, Mom. Don't let Gramps be an asshole and bully you."

As he hugged her, Lisa lifted up an arm and gratefully touched the back of Rob's head. After a few seconds breathing in his warmth, she opened her eyes and patted his forearm in appreciation.

"No, Rob. I won't. Thank you."

"How long will you be gone for?"

"I'm not sure. Three weeks at minimum. Maybe more. Depends how things go and what stage he is in and whether Mother will listen to reason."

Lisa turned on the stool as Sam entered. Tall and gym-fit, Sam was already exuding a natural authority. He, too, bent over and wrapped his mother up in a bear hug. "Mom, don't forget to treat yourself to something fun every now and then, so the whole trip isn't just about caring for your psycho parents. And, remember, your mom can be a needy bitch, too, almost an equal match . . ." He was probably going to say "to Gramps," but I had a sense he was also thinking of me.

"Thank you. Good advice." Lisa was teary with gratitude. She stood and grabbed her coat. "All right. I am ready for this. You are so darling. You boys are the greatest thing I have done with my life."

John and Rob carried her bags downstairs and loaded them into the back of the Mercedes, as Sam held open the passenger door for her. I took out my keys, was just about to get in behind the wheel, when Sam spoke over the roof of the car.

"None of us will be here when you get back from the airport. We all have plans with our friends. So you're better off just doing your thing."

I responded, with as much composure as I could muster. "I didn't expect anything else, Sam. I was young, too, once. Have fun."

But I slammed shut the car door with perhaps more force than I intended.

I went directly to the apartment at Hechtplatz, after dropping Lisa off at the airport, and called Miguel. He said I could come over to his apartment at 9:00 p.m. Miguel was now earning enough money, from regulars like the Sweet Freak and me, to afford his own apartment above the Wellenberg Cinema in the Niederdorf. He needed to be closer to his "office," he told me, which was a rather amusing line, I thought.

But he was gradually becoming someone different than the young immigrant I had first met. He took out escort ads on the back pages of local weeklies, wore Ferragamo and Jean-Paul Gaultier, and his natural and rugged Catalan looks were becoming more feline. He had started dying his hair a brassy blond, which I did not like, but not enough to stop seeing him.

That night I stretched out on his bed, the sheets rumpled beneath me, my ankles crossed. He was in the bathroom at the sink, washing himself with a washcloth. He suddenly looked up from what he was doing and stared at himself in the mirror. He moved his head, this way and that, like he was studying every angle of his face, trying to decide who he was.

"Do you think I should go back to my natural hair color? I think it's so mousy."

Lisa called from her parents' home on Philadelphia's Mainline, crying, barely able to speak. I am not sure what I mumbled, just sympathetic-sounding noise. She got ahold of herself, blew her nose, and said, "Thank you, darling, for the sweet words."

She then distracted herself by asking about the boys, what they were up to, what we were doing for meals. I talked, filled the void, until I had nothing more to say, other than the silent truth that hung between our words. Lisa must have heard that silence, too, because she said, out of nowhere, "José, there are days when I don't know why we ever married, and why I am sitting in that goddamn cow pasture in Ägeri. Some days I think I will go mad there, I am so alone. And you sure haven't made it easy for me these last few years. But coming back here, I remember. You took me away from all this. And it suddenly all makes sense, the strange direction my life took. You rescued me from all this and we built a good life together and raised fine sons. I love you for that fact. Remember that—whatever you are up to."

Before I could speak—express my love for her, tell her about my ache and confusion and this compulsive hunt for fulfillment—we were interrupted by the background sound of pans clattering to the floor.

"Here we go again. Mom is having another meltdown. Got to go. Give the boys my love. I'll talk with them another time." And then she hung up.

Summer transformed our coldly Protestant city, and everyone was in a better mood. The Lake of Zürich filled with sailing boats; the beaches with bathers lathering up in coconut oil; the cafés and bars with couples and packs of friends, sipping Fendant and enjoying a night on the town. I packed Rob off to summer school in Gstaad, so he could make up for his poor grades the previous year. Normally such a good boy, Rob was suddenly giving us concern and acting out. He wouldn't do his homework and seemed only interested in making home movies with the Toshiba TA-11 video camera I had given him for Christmas.

The other two, thankfully, were just fine. It was Sam's second summer at Privatbank Álvarez, and he was in our accounts department, just as my father and I had both started back at the family's retail bank in San Sebastián. He had a natural aptitude for numbers and a good analytic mind, and his grooming—to eventually take over the bank—was going well.

John, meanwhile, still had some maturing to do, and so I made him our office boy that summer. But he, too, turned out to be a huge addition to the bank, running energetically through the office halls, making the secretaries laugh. It was fun to watch him flirt and make jokes, and, I realized, of all of them, John was in some ways most like my father, outgoing and never really caring what other people thought of him.

But, outside of the bank, I didn't see much of either Sam or John. They were never around, the summer Lisa was away, neither at the Hechtplatz apartment nor at the house in Ägeri. Sam had use of Lisa's BMW and he made sure, when he wasn't working, that he and John were always out with their own friends, as they should be at that age.

Miguel and I headed back to his apartment. It was a balmy Friday night. "Do you want to eat in or out tonight?" he asked. "Maybe we should book a table at the Saffronstube. It will be busy and I want to sit outside. I better call."

We had just turned off the Niederdorfstrasse, and were climbing the stone stairs that threaded up through the hills of the old city, to the side entrance of his apartment building. Miguel had his back to me, and was fishing in his pants for his keys. I was again struck by his good looks, and, unable to contain myself, I leaned forward and pressed my face into the swan's curve of his neck, just as the sound of animated voices drifted down to us from up above, the clatter of feet clumping down the steps we had just climbed.

Miguel had his key in the front door, and yet still managed to gracefully lift his other hand around to the back of my head, gently pressing my face deeper into his neck. I moved one of my hands down the front of his pants.

There was a sudden and cold silence on the stairs behind us, almost physical in its manifestation. Miguel sensed it, too, and we both turned to look at what was going on. Teenagers, in the sulfuric glow of the street lamp, were standing stock-still up on the raked hill, staring down at us.

My eyes stopped on the boy in the rear. John, averting his eyes, was red-faced and too humiliated to know where to look. His best friend, Marco, was staring at me with a crude smirk. One of the boys in the front of the group clutched his hands, like he was trying to contain himself, and my focus shot forward, feral-like, sensing danger.

Sam stared at me, his eyes wide with disbelief. The roar in my ears, the nausea, the vertigo of my spiraling descent, it all made me return to my other life and step away from Miguel. I turned and looked anew at him, as if he were a monster from the deep, as if I had been enchanted by a warlock and the spell was in that moment broken, revealing the evil figure of my undoing.

Miguel saw the revulsion I suddenly felt for him, and turned to finish unlocking the door. The hurt and pain in his eyes was exactly what I had seen in his face at that temple in India—and no less real than the looks of pain and suffering that were in my own sons' eyes at that same moment.

You are responsible for all of it—all this immense suffering.

But my sons came first.

I turned around, to face them, as Miguel slipped inside the building, leaving the door slightly ajar, suggesting I could still come to him for comfort.

"Boys. This is not . . ."

The sound of my bravado, my attempt to bluff, was too much even for my own ears to hear, and I let the sentence trail off, unfinished. A voice chanted inside—

If ever there was a time you needed to be a man and stand up, this is it. This is it.

So, I gathered all my strength and started again. "If you want me to, I will explain . . ."

Sam winced, had to look away. He shifted his weight onto his left foot and turned toward his brother and friends. "Let's get out of here," he said.

His friend, a young man I had known since he was an infant, put a hand on Sam's shoulder. "Sure, buddy, whatever you want."

Before I could fully register what was going on, they had turned their backs on me and were clattering down the stone stairs that fed directly into the Niederdorfstrasse. I knew then that they were pulling away from me, forever, and nothing would ever be the same between us. We were broken. And still, as they passed me on the building's half landing, I could only think of myself. I held up a hand and cried out, "John! Sam! Please don't tell your mother."

John was still too shocked to speak, after catching a glimpse of the man living behind his father's façade, and he kept his head down as he walked by. But Sam glanced up at me as he passed, and from a cold distance said, "Trust me, you have nothing to worry about on that front. We won't tell Mom. She deserves much better than this."

The street-lamp overhead was buzzing and crackling as the fluttering moths banged against its curved glass case. I don't know how long I stood on those steps, in the halo of that lamp, my face red and hot and throbbing. Eventually, I turned around to the front door of Miguel's apartment building, which was still ajar, as he had left it. Crossing the border, to enter his world full time, was still an option.

I grasped the door handle. For a while I was unable to move forward or back, but stood teetering on the border of two worlds. In that moment, however, I could only think of Lisa— not of my sons, not of Miguel, not of my father or mother or my brother, not even of myself. Just Lisa. And I wasn't thinking about her in any sentimental way, but more like seeing visions, postcards from our long life together, as she drove our sons to school, brought me tea, sat quietly in the chalet's courtyard with her sketch pad.

And so, with time, I did the only thing I thought I could do. I leaned forward and gently pulled shut Miguel's front door. But the price I paid, I am not sure if I would do it that way again, for I returned, after a brief vacation, to the country I had occupied since my brother's death—the land of the walking dead.

I looked up one last time, in Miguel's direction, before I walked back to the family penthouse. He was standing at his window, one hand clutching the curtain, looking down at me in the street, watching which way I would go. His face was stony, impenetrable. But an internal switch must have been thrown, because his eyelids began rapidly falling and rising, tears came, and I finally got a good look at the hurt and lonely child lurking just behind the man's hard-edged brassy hair and gym workouts. But still I turned my back and abandoned Miguel—and my empty prayer to save him.

Part VII

2019

ÄGERI, SWITZERLAND

FIFTEEN

"I always forget how much I love this old farm-house. It's so special."

Rob stands in the study's doorway, holding a plate of toast.

"How so?"

"Not sure. Maybe it's because I have to travel so much with my job. I appreciate the solidness of this old house. It's so grounded. Just has a good vibe."

"That's nice to hear, *hijo*."

"Why don't you come upstairs? Have breakfast with us."

"It's too much. Getting up the stairs." I gesture at the half-eaten and congealed bowl of porridge on the side table. "Besides, I ate earlier."

Big Bertha has already paid me her stool-softener visit, still without success, and the mere mention of food is making my stomach cramp up some more. Rob has no idea, of course, and strides into the room, sits down in the armchair opposite the bed, and licks a smear of jam off his forefinger.

"So, tell me, what kind of drugs are you on?"

"Opiates."

"Fun. I'll take some."

"Oh, God. Don't tell me you still take drugs."

"Just kidding, Dad. Relax. I'm a boring father in his fifties."

"And a *cabrón* bass fisherman. I brought you up to be a fisher of salmon. Not some farmer with a ball of bread at the end of his hook."

Rob freezes.

"Is a joke. I make a bad joke."

"Yeah, well, I make thirteen million dollars a year with the cable show and I spend my days fishing. Some people would think I have a pretty good gig."

"*Joder.* You make that much money?"

"Dad," he says with weary resignation. "I have eleven million viewers around the world." He won't look directly at me, but I can see, in his narrow and flashing eyes, he is angry that I know so little about him and his life. I shift uncomfortably. But then he takes another bite of the toast, and when he does, the heat in his face disappears, as his mind again becomes preoccupied with work.

"We're in intense negotiations with ESPN right now. Hope to have a richer deal soon." Rob's leg is jiggling, just like my brother's. "My agent is demanding I get more equity in the cable series, or else, he says, we're going to walk away and create our own streaming series. The new technology means we don't actually need cable stations anymore, but I don't know. I still want to stay with ESPN, if I can. We've done well together."

"I thought I heard a party."

John stands tall and bald in the doorframe, his blue eyes and diamond earring catching the light as he bends his head slightly forward to sip his espresso from a demitasse cup. He has a uniform these days. For some reason John now only wears long-sleeve turtlenecks.

I wave him forward. "Come in. Sit."

Rob, always the family diplomat, jumps up and wheels the desk chair around so his brother can sit on the other side of the bed. John sits back in the chair, legs crossed, sipping his coffee, eyeing the world as if everything is just fine by him.

"Did you get your bath?" I ask.

"I did. So miss that old bathtub. It's the perfect fit for my body. I just sink up to my chin. Honestly, I wish I could rip it out and move the entire thing to our Chelsea apartment. Joanne would love it. Americans just don't get baths. They make these shitty little shower tubs with the drains two inches off the bottom. Half your body is out of the water. What's with that? It's not exactly rocket science, making a bathtub that people can fit into."

"I miss taking baths, too." I gesture at the study's bathroom, behind the wall of books. "Your mother and Sister Bertha bathe me, sitting on a chair in the shower. So humiliating."

John is horrified by the idea. "That's awful. I am going to arrange for you to have a proper bath while I am here. You must."

"What's that?" Sam is leaning against the doorframe.

My three boys are with me. I am in heaven.

"We have to give Dad a bath."

The stomach cramps make me groan inside a little, and I shift my weight, to ease the pressure. Much to my relief, they don't notice my discomfort.

Rob turns toward Sam. "What's on the agenda for today?"

"I've got an idea," Sam says. "Dad, it's a glorious day outside. A really beautiful, sunny fall day, like you can only get in Central Switzerland. What do you think of lunch on the terrace of the Hotel Seefeld?"

John snaps his head up and says, "How cool. I remember how Dad used to take us down to the Seefeld, when we were kids, for those ice cream sundaes." He looks over at me. "It's also where you taught us how to play hearts . . ."

"While you were getting totally ripped on shots of Williamine," Rob adds.

"I was not," I say, but we all laugh, because everyone knows I enjoy my eau-de-vie.

"You were so checked out as a parent," John says. "Our wives would skin us alive if we did half the shit with our kids that you did with us. I remember, by midnight, the three of us were bouncing off the Seefeld's walls on a sugar rush and because we weren't put to bed at a normal hour. We'd wind up running and hollering through the restaurant, and you'd, like, wave your hand: Doesn't matter. '*No importa.*' "

They fill my little room with laughter.

"The bell captain," John continues. "That nice Spanish guy with the green apron. What was his name?"

"Señor Gomez!" Rob and Sam shout at the same moment.

"Poor Gomez. He was so homesick. He loved talking to Dad in Spanish and he would come sit at our table for hours, late into the night. He'd join Dad for the shots of Williamine, as they rat-tat-tatted away, and he loved it how we kids were so lively and shattered the silence of Switzerland. And then, when he was all buzzed, he'd get all emotional remembering his own kids, back in Spain, with their mother . . ."

"And, by the end of the evening," Rob adds, "Dad and Gomez were so fucked up, we'd have to leave the car. Dad would sheepishly call Mom, for her to come pick us up."

Their laughter swells in the room, so powerful a force I see the walls of my study pushing out, making room for their presence. Alfredo gets up and goes from one to the other, nuzzling their legs, wanting to be included in their fun. I am made dumb by the unexpected joy welling up inside me, and I see a series of scenes from those long-ago nights at the Hotel Seefeld, like a slideshow.

"Well, Dad. What about it? Lunch at the Seefeld for old times' sake?"

My stomach lurches. The idea of getting out of bed, getting dressed, packed into the car, dragging my drip through the restaurant, every Swiss turning his head to gawk, eating a full meal in public—the very idea makes me sick to my stomach.

But my boys' faces, so expectant, so flushed with the memories of their youth, I cannot bear to let them down.

"*Por qué no?*"

The morning fills with the logistics of our family outing. It is decided—by Sam—that we should take two cars. I am laid out flat in the folded-down posterior of the Volvo station wagon. I cradle my drip by my side, Alfredo on the flatbed beside me, his ginger-fringed head resting between his great paws. John and Rob, after packing me into the car, look anxiously down at me.

"Are you OK, Dad?"

"*Sí, hijos.* So is Alfredo. We are ready."

John and Rob climb into the front seats and we pull out of the driveway. Sam follows in the BMW with Lisa and Sister Bertha. Our caravan sets off, around the lake, until I finally sense we are pulling into the village of Morgarten, with its boat pier and restored fifteenth-century church tower.

Sam has called ahead and the Hotel Seefeld's new manager, a young man from Canton Vaud, is waiting for us as we pull into the crescent driveway at the family-owned inn. I notice, with sadness, the cream-and-white Jugendstil villa with twenty-five rooms has, since my last visit, had an ugly modernist glass-and-steel extension attached to its face, like an ugly wart.

"*Bienvenue, Monsieur Álvarez,*" the manager says.

He is smiling and bobbing his head like a car ornament. John and Rob come around and help lift me from the back of the car. I emerge from the Volvo with trembling effort. But I am here.

"*Merci, Monsieur le Directeur,*" I pant. "*Vous êtes très gentil.*"

The young man kisses Lisa's hand—a European affectation that has always made her skin crawl—and then invites us to enter the hotel. Behind us, Sam and Rob are chatting about their families back home, while John, stretching out his long torso and hamstrings, is leaning against the hood of the car.

The manager makes a discreet gesture and the Seefeld's bellman—a Tunisian, by the look of him—emerges from the shadows, pushing a wheelchair. He bends forward, helps me get settled in the chair, and then turns me around and wheels me up the ramp laid down for my arrival.

The family follows and together we move

through the sliding glass doors and across the hotel's lobby, like a close-knit military recon-naissance mission, Alfredo's toenails clicking on the marble floor. I lead the family; Sam is next; Rob, off to the side, holds the dog's leash tight. Lisa picks up her pace, so she can walk by my side, while Big Bertha and John bring up the rear, dragging along my drip.

On the far side of the lobby, the hotel manager flings open the doors of the Alpenrose restaurant, with an excess of theatrics, and we start our walk through the dining room, past the beautifully set tables, the cheese trolley, and the centerpiece vase filled with thorny berry branches. The dining room falls silent. Elderly Swiss couples and two-children families, sitting before roast chickens and veal medallions in a wild-mushroom sauce, lift their heads and stare at us. They look like cud-chewing cows, peering astonished at hikers crossing an Alpine meadow. But we are used to such things, after so many decades in Switzerland, and we sail through the dining room, like only our family exists in this world.

The open French doors on the far side of the dining room reveal a gray-slate terrace facing the glassy Lake of Ägeri, its water so clean and clear and pure, I have to catch my breath.

"What a wonderful idea, Sammy," Lisa says, pulling off her silk scarf. "Thank you. We so needed to get out of the house and get a change of scenery."

She gently touches my shoulder. "Isn't that so, José María?"

I pat her hand. "*Claro, sí*. It's perfect. Very nice."

Sam moves on ahead through the French doors, to make sure the terrace table he requested is ready, and I am wheeled out after him. The maître d' is waiting for us. He pulls out the head chair facing the mountains and lake, and, with a courteous dip of his head, signals for me to take the place of honor.

A white-jacketed waiter, who has been at the restaurant since the boys were little, warmly greets the family in Swiss German, and pulls out a chair for Lisa. She sits down immediately to my right. Sister Bertha, knowing her place, whispers to Lisa she will eat at the café down the street, but my wife says, "You will dine with the family, Sister Bertha. You have been so good to us, and seen us all at our very worst. Whether you like it or not, that makes you part of the family. Please, I insist you join us." And so the nun blushes and moves to a spot at the end of the table.

I stick to sparkling water, while they all drink the wine, including Lisa, who is visibly relieved to have a few carefree hours. They talk about this and that, about the mountain in front of us at the end of the lake, and about the time the boys went skiing on its northern slope, with the American

International School of Zürich. Lisa went on the school trip, too, as one of the parental chaperones; she recalls, with humor now, how the boys were caught by the school's history teacher, trying to sneak out of the hostel's bathroom window, for a nighttime rendezvous with the girls in the far dorms.

I half listen. I am mesmerized by the view before us: the gray and jagged peak, its flanks looming mauve and purple over the blue-green lake, the villages dotting the shoreline like decorative trim around a cake. There is a cluster of boats—I recognize Iten's red-and-white hull—hovering before the Morgarten Strandbad, the public swimming beach, above a hole in the lake known to be a favorite feeding ground for the *Felchen*.

But my tranquil reverie is interrupted by sudden gun blasts in the forests up and off to the left of the hotel. Half a minute later we all hear thundering hooves, as a magnificent six-point stag plunges through the garden hedges to the right of the hotel. Alfredo jumps up, barks with deep excitement, and pulls hard at his lead that is, fortunately, secured tightly to the leg of Rob's chair.

As it shoots past us, I get a strangely clear and close look at the stag: at the branch bones of furred antlers; at great jets of steam and snot shooting from his flared nostrils; at the adrenaline-filled muscles, rippling under the red hide, moving like waves washing over slabs of slate.

But then he is past the hotel and thundering down the lawn, sending up clods of turf. He heads straight for the lake, and for a moment, we don't know what he is going to do, perhaps veer off at the last moment. But the mighty beast never hesitates, and at full gallop, jumps off the hotel's pier. There is a great splash as the magnificent animal disappears underwater. We all sit a little straighter with anxiety, wondering if he will come back up, and then erupt in cheers when he surfaces, head and antlers held high, eyes wide with terror—heading straight across the lake.

"Go," I whisper. "Go."

A third of the way across, the deer starts to tire and I begin to think he will not make it. But there is a peninsula jutting into the lake, just past the town of Egg, and, perhaps seeing this spit, outstretched like a helping hand, the deer changes course and heads in its direction. I hold my breath until it finally, wearily, wades into the shallows and stands panting hard on the far shore.

Steam rises from its hot and wet flanks. It regally turns its head back in our direction, snorts a few times, and, then, his head still held high, he is up into the forest—and gone.

"My God. That was amazing," says Rob. "I wish I had my film crew here."

I turn and see that everyone at the table is flushed and peering at the wooded peninsula where the stag has just disappeared.

The old waiter comes out with glass bowls filled with salad and chives, and wicker baskets filled with crusty brown bread. He has seen it all, too. He places a salad bowl before Rob and me.

"A pity. That was my son, hunting above. Would have been a nice set of antlers to go above the garage door."

"After a hunt like that, isn't the deer's meat gamey and filled with toxins?" John asks. "I remember once, in upstate New York, trying to cook deer that had been running for its life like that, before it was finally felled by a hunter. We couldn't eat the meat. Had to throw it away. It was awful. The muscles were so filled with adrenaline you could taste the animal's fear in the meat. I stewed the venison for hours, with vinegar and mustard, to get rid of the bitter taste, but even that didn't help."

"That's true," says the old waiter. "It is not a good taste. But the antlers—a trophy."

"Well, thank heavens it got away," Lisa says. "I would have gone off my food if they had shot it in front of us. Such a magnificent beast."

But I have lost the trail of their chatter, for my watery eyes are peering at what is happening at the bottom of the hotel's field. A park bench and stone birdbath stand next to a stream emptying into the lake, a brook that marks the property's boundary. My brother, Juan, is sitting on the bench, jiggling his leg and smoking a cigarette. I can see, even from this distance, he is talking with a great deal of passion, his hands flapping, Spanish style, this way and that.

His discussion partner is quite the opposite in temperament. The Frog Queen sits coolly and regally next to him in the wet grass, gulping, her eyes wide with intelligent curiosity. She is again somehow communicating telepathically, because there are moments when Juan turns his head in her direction, clearly listening to her counsel, before returning to his anxious cigarette puffs and the hand gestures and the rat-tat of Northern Spain.

I know in my bones that I am the subject of their discussion, and that they are quietly joining forces, plotting their next steps on precisely how they will get me to do their bidding.

"Darling," Lisa says, putting her hand on mine. "Are you all right? You look pale and far away."

"The hunters. They are hunting."

"Yes, José. They are. It's that time of season. Fall."

I must have nodded off at the table for a while, and again in the car, because when I wake up, we are back in the chalet's courtyard. It must be late afternoon. The sun has dropped behind the barn when my sons pull me from the back of the Volvo. Sister Bertha leans forward, wipes some drool off my chin.

"Not so rough," I whimper.

My bloated innards hurt to the touch.

"Sorry. Here you go, Dad."

"Is time to wash," says Sister Bertha. "Before dinner."

I make a face. "I'll get him washed today," John says. "Not to worry, Sister. I'll give him his bath."

Sister Bertha looks unsure, isn't happy with this break in protocol. "He must be properly cleaned and scrubbed. Carefully—also his private parts."

This time both John and I make a face, not over the task at hand, but that this nurse has absolutely no sense of decorum or concern about my dignity.

"Don't worry," John says. "We can manage . . . Hey, Rob, Sam. I'll need your help getting Dad upstairs. We're going to give him a bath."

"What a great idea," Lisa says. "Isn't it, José?"

They get me upstairs, to the bathroom off the master bedroom, where Lisa and I slept for nearly fifty years. I have not been in our room since I moved downstairs into the study, and I feel a pang, when I see Lisa's lonely nightgown draped across her armchair, her book and glasses on the bedside table. My side of the bed is cold and barren.

I don't know what to say and then we are in the

wood-paneled bathroom, off the other side of the bedroom, with its familiar leaded window with the crank handle.

Lisa begins to fuss over me, and starts lecturing the boys about the dangers of this and that and falling in the tub. "OK, Mom," John says sharply. "Leave now. We've got this." She takes a deep breath, grateful that her sons are home and taking control, and surrenders to John's authoritative voice.

She kisses my forehead. "Enjoy your bath, José."

She is gone. For a little while, as my sons run the bath, I stand shakily, gripping the back of a stiff-backed chair that John has dragged into the bathroom. As he fiddles with the taps, tests the temperature, Roberto and Samuel help me out of my fleece, the jogging suit, the Velcro sneakers on my feet.

There is an awkward moment, when I try to pull down my underwear, but can't. They help me get it below my knees, Sam kneeling at my feet as he tenderly helps me step out of its tangle.

Rob and Sam each grab one of my elbows and slowly, carefully walk me up to the rim of the bathtub. The water filling the tub is blue-green and steaming. They help me lift one leg, and then the other, over the porcelain rim.

I am finally standing in the tub. The hot water comes to just below my knees.

"There you go. Lower yourself now. Easy does it."

"Sam, grab some of the bath salts from the shelf over there. Should help soothe some of his aches."

"Which one?"

"I don't know. Try the big green bottle. The one with fir-tree oil."

With a son holding on to each of my arms, I slowly drop into the water. The heat is bliss. John stands at the head of the bath, shaking salts into the funnel of hot water pouring from the tap, and the room fills with the delicious smell of pine trees, the air of Spain in the summer.

I close my eyes, sink lower into the water with a sigh. I slip into an amphibious state, half my body undulating sleepily underwater, the other half sticking into the air.

"How is it?"

For the first time, in weeks it seems, I am no longer cold.

It takes some effort, but I find my voice, and release a heartfelt *"Gracias, hijos.* Thank you. All of you. It feels wonderful."

My sons are all smiling.

"You sure look blissed out."

"Claro. I am very content."

"OK, guys. I can take it from here," John says. He pulls the chair forward, so it is flush against the bathtub, and sits down. The room is filled with steam and I wonder how he can tolerate the heat in his long-sleeve turtleneck.

John dunks a sponge into the warm water, smiles sweetly, like when he was a boy. "Dad, before you drift off, we've got to wash you. Don't want Big Bertha giving me hell."

Sam and Rob leave the bathroom as John slowly soaps my arms, my armpits, around my neck. I surrender happily, close my eyes. He sponges me calmly and soothingly for several minutes, gently washing off the soap, like a mother might wash her baby in a plastic tub.

"Are you in pain?"

"*No, hijo.* No pain."

The bathtub is milky white, and soap scum is starting to cling to the sides at the watermark.

"OK. That's over. Relax now. Dream a while."

"A little more hot water, please."

John empties the tub a little, fills it again with hot water and some more bath salts. I am again awash in that summer smell of Spain. John leans back in the chair, crosses his long limbs, and pulls out his iPhone. Beads of sweat pop up on my forehead. For a while we both sit there, calmly, each happily adrift in our own world. John absentmindedly lifts a hand to the back of his head. I drift off to another place.

I open my eyes.

John is no longer sitting in the chair next to me.

But Juan is, a little older and grayer than the last time I saw him, and looking very sad. His hands are folded in a steeple. He leans forward in the chair.

"José María," he says softly. "*Hermano*. It's time. You have to come home."

"What are you talking about? I am home."

He is filled with sadness. He looks down at the floor and shakes his head.

"Stop being so ridiculous," I snap. "I have lived here with my family for nearly fifty years. This is the home I made. The home I chose. Why do you keep telling me I have to come home?"

He looks around the room, like he is seeing it for the first time. "This isn't your home. It never will be."

"Get out of here! I am trying to have a relaxing bath!"

Juan's sigh is so heartbreaking it fills the entire bathroom, pressing so hard against the walls I hear them crack under the strain. He gives his head a final shake and then swivels his torso to look back at the corner of the bathroom.

"I have tried," he says, wearily. "He won't listen to me. It's your turn."

I crane my neck and for the first time see the Frog Queen, sitting bloated in the corner, crouched in the shadows of the hamper. She doesn't move, just blinks, and on occasion opens and closes her rubbery lips.

This is nonsense, expecting a frog to understand the spoken word.

But I am promptly visited by a powerful sense the Frog Queen has understood my every thought, including my contempt, and it must be so, because with one massive thump of her meaty back legs, she is flying at me, from across the room.

"Ohh," I cry.

She lands with a splash in the bathtub and the room fills with a clap of thunder and lightning, as happened when I saw her for the first time. I am not as frightened this time, more surprised, and I am once again overtaken by this warm and not unpleasant feeling of being half in the water, half out, suspended in some strange in-between state.

I look down at the bath. There is no sign of the Frog Queen. She has disappeared. But my legs, stretched down the length of the bath, are green and speckled and end in webbed feet, my flippers gently undulating in the water and pointing in opposite directions. My arms, lightly resting on the rim of the bathtub, are also green, dark and stringy. My white stomach is half in and half out of the bath, large and rumbling and loaded.

I smack my lips and with a sigh, tip back my head.

Something opens between my legs, and I begin to release tens of thousands upon thousands of eggs. Out they slide, speckled sacks of genesis, popping up to the surface of the water. But they won't stop, keep shooting out of me, and soon the entire tub is dense with the egg sacks, an abundance of clumps and clusters, gelatinous life bobbing against the tub's rim.

There is pain. On my arm.

John is gripping my forearm hard. His mouth is open, but no sounds are coming out. Not at first. But then I seem to come back to this world, find the right frequency, and I can suddenly hear his cries of anguish.

"Oh, God! Oh, God!"

John jumps up and runs to the bathroom door, throws it open and yells at the top of his voice, "Mom! Sam! Come quick. Something's happened!"

There is something in the air. The lovely pine smell is gone and the bathroom now has a barnyard odor. I look down. My arms along the rim of the bath are mine again, which is a relief, but the bathwater is in an alarming state, dark brown and lumpy. It takes me a moment to understand that I am not sitting in frogs' eggs, but my own shit. And there is blood, too.

This is perhaps what Juan and the Frog Queen have wanted all along, and I finally let the reality in. I am sitting in my own *mierda*. It helps me find the voice I have for too long been avoiding.

God forgive me. Forgive me my sins.

Lisa and the boys and Sister Bertha come rescue me, like angels from heaven. They come running up the stairs, summoned by John's cries of anguish, and I don't exactly know what happens next, but I am standing, hauled up by multiple hands, all clutching tight my flesh and bones.

Sam rolls up his sleeve, turns his face to the ceiling, and sticks his hand into the bath, trying not to gag. He pulls the plug. The room fills with the sound of water and shit getting sucked down the drain.

"Get a bucket."

"José. Can you understand what I am saying?"

I nod.

"Then lift your right foot."

Bertha and John are hosing me down with the bathtub's showerhead, while down below, Lisa and my other sons are scooping brown slop into a bucket.

"*Perdóname, perdóname, perdóname,*" I whimper.

They get me out of the bathtub and move me to the glassed-in shower on the other side of the bathroom, where they wash me again, everywhere, even shampooing my head.

I am wrapped in a hot towel and shuffled out of the bathroom.

I am shivering.

"He is not going downstairs," Lisa says in

a steely voice. "I am putting an end to this nonsense. Put him in our bed. Where he belongs."

Lisa pulls down the top cover and I slide, with effort, into that familiar depression of the mattress. It perfectly envelops my body and I begin to cry. It feels so good to be back in the old dip of the mattress, to smell my wife again.

What was I thinking?

Lisa lies down next to me, wraps me in her arms, and whispers, "It's OK, José. We love you. We're here. Your family is here."

"Forgive me, please. Such a bad husband and father and brother."

There are protestations, they say the right things, but I know the truth. I feel Lisa's breath, her little kisses, her hand stroking my cheek. Sister Bertha has drifted to the back of the room, to give us privacy, while my sons stand at the end of the bed.

Rob is wiping away tears. Sam looks grim, gripping his arms across his stomach, and John has a wry smile on his face, the sign, ever since he was a boy, that he is completely overwhelmed. I have trouble speaking, because I am trembling so much, but I get the words out.

"Boys, please, a favor . . ."

"Anything, Dad."

"Take me home."

Lisa sits up. "Home?"

"Yes. Home. To Spain."

"The house in San Sebastián? It was sold long ago."

"No. To Ribadesella. Please. I beg you. I need to see the Sella River again. In the time I have remaining. I need to go home."

SIXTEEN

Strange, bearded men are in my room.

Before I understand what is going on, they are hoisting me off my bed and onto the stretcher, strapping me in and taking my vitals. "Who are you?" I ask.

"We are your medical escort. I am Dr. Habib."

Sister Bertha looms over me. "Now, I leave you, Herr Álvarez. You are going on and I must go help another family." Sister Bertha tugs at my tracksuit, straightens me up, and speaks gently. "I will pray for you on your final journey." She shakes my hand. "Goodbye, Herr Álvarez. *Schöne Reise.* I wish you a good trip."

She leaves the room and I stare dumbfounded after her.

"But where am I going?"

I am suddenly boiling angry and yell. "*Coño*! No one ever tells me anything!"

Everyone in the room tenses. I feel it.

"Remember, José?" Lisa says, standing next to me. She has materialized out of nothing. "We are taking you back to Spain. Like you wanted."

"Oh. That's all right, then. Will be nice. Mamá and Papá haven't seen me in a long time. They will be relieved to see me."

I am not sure why, but the news we are going

to Spain makes me talkative, and I tell the doctor and the male nurse about our summerhouse, Miramar, in Ribadesella; about Felipe del Toro, my friend and ghillie, grandson of the Sella's famous head ghillie, Ignacio del Toro; and about how Felipe's father used to beat him when drunk. But I am not sure if I am actually saying what I am saying, or just imagining I am speaking, because the doctor and nurse are looking blankly at me.

"What is it you want?" the nurse asks. "Water?"

We are on the private-jet tarmac of Zürich's Kloten airport. The captain and a steward stand below the Dassault Falcon's nose and solemnly shake Lisa's hand and take our luggage. The EMT team expertly hauls me from the helicopter and up the short set of stairs into the back of the jet. We pivot into the cabin. Rob and John are sitting upright, with forced smiles, in tan leather executive seats.

"Hey, Dad. We'll be on our way soon. Hang in there."

My beloved Alfredo is at their feet and instantly stands, whines, and licks my hand dangling from the passing stretcher. I am so moved by this. I try to speak, pet him, but the stretcher won't stop and continues to roll toward the front of the plane.

In the jet's forward compartment, behind the bulkhead, the stretcher is snapped into place and secured via floor clips. Lisa collapses next to me, in one of the executive seats under the windows, complaining how stiff she is after the cramped helicopter ride. The EMT team makes sure the stretcher and drip are secure, and checks the wires and metal box monitoring my vitals. The doctor is about to inject something into the bag.

"What is that?" I say.

"Morphine."

"No. I need to talk to my family. I cannot on morphine."

"I don't recommend that. The pain could come on very strong and very quickly. You must, at the first sign of pain, tell me—please."

"All right."

Sam strides through the cabin and sticks his head into the cockpit. "We're ready to go."

I hear the captain's voice. He is behind and to the left of the cockpit door. But I catch a glimpse of the copilot, her sinewy green arm reaching up to fiddle with a dial. She turns and winks at me, smacks her lips.

The Frog Queen.

I point and make alarmed squeaks. Our fate is in her hands.

Lisa jumps out of her chair.

"What is it, honey? What's bothering you? Do you need to pee?"

I keep on pointing at the copilot. But no words come out.

• • •

I wake up. Engine roars fill my ears. I am in darkness. All the blinds are down, the cabin lights dimmed. I smack my parched lips, try to wet them with my tongue.

"He's awake," says the nurse.

Lisa comes over with a bottle of Evian and pours me a cup. She carefully lets me sip from it, like I am a wild animal lapping up water on the shores of a river.

I look at her, pleadingly. She bends over.

"There is little time left. I need to talk to you. Send them away."

Lisa pulls back, looks at me for a second.

"Dr. Habib, Sam, young man—all of you. Please leave. I want to talk to my husband. Alone." I gesture that I want them to pull up the porthole shades, before they leave. They do so, one after another. Shafts of white light pour into the cabin.

Lisa follows them out past the bulkhead and returns with a cold towel.

"You're clammy and a little feverish." She gently wipes my brow. "Now, what is it you want to tell me?"

"I have sinned."

"We have all sinned, José. You're not that special."

"You don't understand."

All the secrets I have held in silence for so long

come tumbling out of me: I tell her about how my sex-obsessed father introduced me to prostitutes when I was a boy and how he humiliated my mother. I tell her I have other secrets, terrible secrets, about my mother and uncle, but that I promised Juan I would never reveal them, so I cannot, even now. But she should at least know the most terrible secret of all—that I killed my beloved brother with a push into the road.

Lisa backs away, almost like it is too much, and drops herself into the padded chair. She listens from across the aisle, grave, her face half in shadow. I can see she is bewildered by my confession, almost like she doesn't fully understand it, like it is too much for her to take in. But my need to confess, my need to unburden myself of all my secrets, it's overwhelming, and I proceed to tell her about Miguel, every sordid detail.

When I am finished, finally emptied of all, a searing pain shoots up from my stomach, my legs scrabble, and I double over. Lisa's defensive stance, her body language, instantly changes. She is up, out of her seat.

She soothingly strokes my forehead, whispers in my ear. "Try and be calm, honey. Know that I have always loved you. Know that. We stayed together, through our bad years, and made it through to the end. I love you. Now, hold on. I am going to get the boys." And she is true to her word, because soon after my sons are huddled around me, like they are at a séance for the dead. She is right. They must hear my confession, too. "I need to tell you something, *hijos*. I am just like my father. Selfish. Please forgive me . . ."

We hit turbulence and they hold on to the stretcher's metal rails, raise hands, and press them against the cabin walls for support. I bring my secrets into the light, how I catastrophically and fatally failed my brother, the person I loved most on this earth. They are blinking, visibly shocked, for all their life they have heard only glowing accounts about my brother and me and our relationship. And then I say I am sorry beyond words that they saw me with that young man, Miguel, but that they must know, I have no regrets. Miguel gave me something I needed at that time. I cannot explain fully what happened then. I am not sure I know myself. But I am sorry, so sorry, for all of my failings as a father and a man.

I grasp the closest hand I can find, John's, and say, "Don't live in the shadows like I did. Be better than me. Be brave. Secrets waste a life."

John's eyes reveal, I am sure of it, he knows exactly what I am talking about, but before he can respond, the captain announces we are approaching Bilbao International Airport and everyone must be seated. So they bend down, each in turn, and kiss me on the lips—even

Sam—before returning to their seats. I notice then, for the first time, that Sam is clutching a rosary, its mahogany beads dangling from the sweater pocket where his fist is clenched and buried, a tense clutching of beads that I remember my mother similarly kept up for hours. I did not know Sam had found the Church. But this is a painful truth, too—there is a lot I never bothered to learn about my boys.

The doctor is next to me. I point at the center of my chest. "The pain. It is here." He nods and pumps me full of morphine. I sigh as the rush comes in. But just before I go under, and my wife and sons step behind the bulkhead, Sam's voice reaches me through the ether of the cabin.

"Mom, can you tell me what the hell that was about?"

"No idea. But he has done that before. That was Basque he was speaking."

The smell of Spain is in the air. They haul the stretcher down the jet's steps. I feel featherlight. Spain fills my lungs and makes me whole again—the smell of rosemary and diesel fuel and hot tar and fried olive oil and of sage baking in the sun. The sky is so blue, bluer than anywhere else in the world. It is a Spanish-tile blue, dotted by rolling clouds that look like meringue. I am in morphine heaven.

"*La patria.*"

"*Sí, Papá*," says John. "*La patria*."

I am my father. Back in my homeland.

Lisa and John are on either side of me, each holding a hand. Rob is off to the left of the stretcher, red-eyed but smiling and holding Alfredo's leash tight. Sam is slightly behind us, watching closely as the captain and steward pull our luggage from the hold and pile our bags into the trailer attached to a BMW SUV.

Dr. Habib hands me over to the local EMT team. It is too much, this constant relay.

"When will this journey end?" I say. "I am so tired." But I must be talking too low for anyone to hear, because no one responds.

Lisa bends down and kisses me on the lips. "We'll see you at the house, darling."

There is a throbbing sound. It's the ambulance engine.

I am heading home.

As we drive off, I recall a memory from long ago. Papá was reading *El País* around the table bedecked with coffee urn, toast, and a silver pot of quince jam. We were having breakfast on the first-floor terrace of the San Sebastián house. Mamá was looking dreamily out across the garden, dressed for church. She was sitting next to Juan, asleep in a pram, rocking him slightly with one hand as she traveled elsewhere in her imagination.

I stood on my four-year-old legs and made my

way to the powder-blue bassinet resting atop the pram's heavy steel chassis. Mother turned her head, smiled, as I looked down at my brother. "Don't wake him," she whispered.

Juan's long eyelashes.

They were closed tight against the pain of this world.

I return, am full of ache. I look up to see pine trees, telephone poles, mountains going by the window. The doctor has his arms crossed and is dozing on a clap-up bench at the bottom end of the stretcher. John is sitting up front next to the driver, his head cocked to the side, listening to Rob, who is sitting behind him on another clap-up bench.

"Did you hear yet whether ESPN took the deal?"

"Not yet. They said they needed more time to respond to our proposal. Should hear by the middle of next week."

"Ugh. I hate the waiting. It sucks."

"Yup. So, how's the restaurant?"

"Honestly? I'm struggling. Remember how shitty the neighborhood was when we first moved in ten years ago?"

"Never saw so many happy-ending massage parlors in one place."

"That's all changed. The *New York Times* recently published an article about how our block has become a dining mecca, and they credited me as the pioneer that made it all happen."

"That's so cool. Congratulations."

"Yeah, well, no good deed goes unpunished. The original lease on the restaurant is now up, and my landlord is raising my rent a hundred and sixteen percent. Can you fucking believe it? There's no way I can make money paying that sort of rent."

"Ouch. That's rough."

"I'm the only Álvarez who's a failure."

John says this lightly, with a self-mocking laugh, and Rob airily waves the remark away. "I bet you'll find a much better place," he says.

John looks out the ambulance window and then quietly says, "Securing and refurbishing a new location will mean another five to seven million dollars down the hole. I'm so ready to give up on New York. It's become impossible."

"*Nooooo*—I *love* visiting you there!"

"Ha. Yeah, we have fun."

I am distracted by something in the air.

It is the smell of sea and salt and fish.

"Help me sit up," I croak.

There is a flurry of arms, grunting, as Rob and the doctor prop me up with pillows. I stare out the back window.

Ribadesella, the Roman town on the river bend, comes into view. I can see the old stone wall, the steel bridge, the Picos des Europa standing jagged in the background. There is a familiar noise, the sound of the ambulance's Pirelli tires rolling over ancient cobblestone streets, and I remember that sound from the Hispano-Suiza.

I know then I am not in a drug-addled dream. I am truly back in Ribadesella.

The air gains a phosphorous luminescence, like we are in some portal to heaven, and it is beckoning me to step through that frail curtain, separating the two worlds. In that moment, I know that I have very little time left, and that I am disappearing beyond the borders of consciousness ever more frequently and deeply.

I pray, from a deep place, that I might fight the best fight I can to stay lucid a little while longer, that I might savor and cherish and use wisely the last moments of consciousness I still have in me.

Please, God. Please.

I turn back to the view, breathing in the town: the indigo-blue houses and the low-rises with glassed-in staircases. I marvel that the orange awnings still exist, dropped and giving shade to the green tables of the fish restaurants, while down in the river, the gray-green Marisqueria fishing boat is tied to the old wall, unloading white plastic tubs of flounder and hake, just as I remember it.

We cross the bridge, drive for some time up the river, and then turn onto a narrow farm lane, through a pasture full of yellow dandelion and purple thistle. Border hedges cinch our way, scrape the side of the ambulance, and the sound is magnified in my diseased head. We turn sharply, again, this time onto an earthen drive. The ambulance rolls to a stop.

Sheep's Corral.

My heart surges. It is smaller than in my imagination, but otherwise the same—the white-washed walls, the green shutters, the lichen-covered terra-cotta roof tiles. There is the old bench we used to sit on when taking off our fishing boots. The only new detail is the swoop of small pink and white carnations exploding from a mossy basket hanging under the front-door eaves, and a large outdoor metal rack that appears to be a place to stack kayaks.

I look up. Smoke is pouring from the chimney, just as in the days when Conchata ruled the kitchen, and, as if on cue, a housekeeper comes out of the front door, drying her hands on her apron, smiling and ready to greet us.

"Is this where we are staying?"

"Yes, Pops."

"*Oh Dios mío. Gracias.* I am home."

The back door of the ambulance opens. The blue BMW is already there, and Sam is waiting for me, making sure I am properly carried out and everything is in order. He looks at me with concern, trying to read my state, as they pull me from the back of the ambulance.

I touch his hand. "Don't hate me, Sam."

He can't help himself. He recoils at my touch. "Jesus, Dad. Give it a rest." But he catches himself and I can see in his stance the struggle that is raging inside of him. His face suddenly softens. He puts his hand on my forearm.

"Dad, I want you to be at peace. I love you."

I grip his hand, fiercely. "I am so ashamed you saw me with Miguel."

This time I know I am not speaking Basque. Sam looks out across the field for a while and then quietly says, "It's OK, Dad. It was what it was. Maybe seeing you that day gave me the courage to finally take you on about the bank and strike out on my own. Everything happens for a reason." He strokes my face, kisses my forehead. "Now be at peace, Dad. Rest. I love you."

I am about to respond, but the Spanish medical team wants to take me inside, to my deathbed where the lambs were once born.

"*Por favor.*"

I point to the oak trees where we used to tether the horses and where you can still see across the field of wildflowers to the river. "Let me rest there a while."

They turn and wheel the stretcher out under the trees, Sam watching them like a hawk from the gravel drive. The doctor starts fiddling with the drip, which he hangs from a tree branch. The nurse sits on the stump next to me, reading a novel on his electronic tablet, periodically looking up to see how I am doing.

An eagle soars overhead, looking for rabbits. There is a breeze.

Lisa is inside Sheep's Corral with the housekeeper, preparing dinner, and the boys are now off together somewhere, perhaps grabbing a drink at a local bar.

"*Yo estoy en casa.*"

I stare slack-jawed up at the sun-filtering leaves and tree branches overhead—and the sound of the river takes me.

I am on the bank of Dead Priest's Pool, the long and deep water where once I swam with Juan and Felipe. I stand there, alone. There is movement and light under the water's surface, which I think is moving fish.

It is not. A bloated, moonlike face emerges from the river, followed by black robes. It is the dead priest who drowned, two hundred and fifty years earlier, when he came back drunk from his mistress and slipped from the path.

He is bald. He points at me.

"You have not yet properly atoned for your sins."

"*Cabrón*! I am trying! I am doing the best I can. I have confessed to my family."

"You must repent all your sins. All your sins."

"I am. I am trying."

"Try harder. You must peel through to the deepest layers of sin, just like you peel an onion."

"*Coño*! What bullshit is this? What does that even mean?"

"Are you so shallow and selfish you cannot see how you hurt much more than just your own family?"

"Why should I listen to anything you say? You are just a depraved priest. A drunk who kept a mistress."

"Aah, the Álvarez arrogance. Be careful. That familiar friend of yours will lead you to hell."

I crawl back across the border on all fours.

I pull myself together. I focus, gather my senses, try to sit up a little. I recite the same phrases again and again.

Stay conscious. Be conscious.

There is noise behind me, the sound of a car rolling over gravel. I turn my head. Lisa and Sam are enthusiastically greeting an old man. They turn and march him across the grass. He is white-haired, his hands gnarled with arthritis, but he is also thin and fit for his age. He stands erect, putting one foot solidly before the other.

He smiles across the grass. His black eyes look familiar but I can't place them. There is something dead in my brain. It will never come back.

The old man steps forward and shakes my hand.

"*Buenas tardes, Don José.* It's been a long time."

He has a gravelly voice, like he has enjoyed his cigarettes and brandy. "We had given up hope you were going to visit us again."

"Thank you. Forgive me, but who are you?"

"I am the mayor of Ribadesella. Or was. I am retired now."

"I am honored. That you should visit a dying old man."

"But of course. We are old friends."

"Are we? I am sorry . . ."

"I am Felipe. I was your guide on the river."

"*Oh Dios mío* . . . Felipe, Felipe, old friend . . ."

I clutch his hand, he bends down, and we hug. Both of us have tears in our eyes. Sam's voice rises, from somewhere behind us. "Dad, when Felipe heard you wanted to come back, he offered us Sheep's Corral. He arranged everything for us."

"I am so grateful."

"It was nothing. It is still in the family—thank God."

I point to the Rock Pool we could just see through the trees at the far side of the field. "Do you remember? Papá loved to fish that pool during high water. He loved how the fish would take, just above the gray rock."

"Your father was a great man."

"He had his moments. But he could also be a selfish shit."

"Yes. Fathers can be that way."

"*Coño*. The mayor! Congratulations!"

"Ex-mayor. Retired. But I held the office for twenty years."

"That long?"

"I became political when the salmon disappeared from the Ribadesella. I wanted to stop the overfishing outside in the bay, and to get the EU to subsidize a salmon hatchery on the river, up near Omedina, so we could build back the fish stocks."

"We ate what we caught. There was such abundance. We didn't know then how fragile it all was."

He shakes his head. "We did much more than just hunt for our dinner. Let us at least be honest about that. We slaughtered fish because we could, to inflate our importance, to satisfy our greed, to score points, to show off how we could throw a fly. We slaughtered the fish for many vain reasons."

I am uncomfortable. Shift my weight.

"We forgot that old proverb from these parts. Do you remember it? 'Take what you want,' God said. 'Take it—and pay for it.' "

We sit silently with our grief for a time. "It makes me so sad," I say. "It's almost unbearable. Are there any fish at all coming up the Sella?"

"They count a few each year. I am not sure how they hang on, but the salmon are like men—some roll over instantly and others are tough and refuse to die. But all our days here are numbered. It's a different river than the one we knew."

"It still looks beautiful."

"It is one of Europe's 'five-star' kayaking destinations. The tourist industry, those bastards, they are the new mafia. Everything in our culture, everything that is good and authentic, must now bow down to hordes of tourists. All year round, the Sella is noisy with Scandinavian and German tourists in their damn kayaks."

Right then, in the stretch of white river we can glimpse between some birch trees, three kayaks shoot down the rapids. An overweight woman in the back of one kayak is squealing with fright.

The sun is setting. I am cold and shivering. There is no time left.

"I remember a story you used to tell us about Dead Priest's Pool."

"That was so long ago. I am impressed you remember. The old women of the village used to say that the penitent priest, trying to get out of purgatory, visits the near dead, urging them to fully repent. They say he is God's messenger, protector of the land and sea and river and mountains in these parts. I am not sure, in these times of iCloud and cell phones, if it is true anymore."

"Funny how things turn out. In those days, you believed the story—I did not. These days, you no longer believe—and I do."

"We all become what we deny."

Lisa comes to us under the trees and gently puts her hand on my shoulder. "Dinner will be ready soon. Do you think you can eat something?"

"No. But I will watch you eat. It's time to go inside."

"You will stay for dinner, Señor del Toro."

"No, Doña Lisa, but thank you. I must visit my granddaughters. They are expecting me for dinner tonight." He squeezes my shoulder. "*Bueno*, old friend. I will visit you again tomorrow."

I pat his hand. "Bless you, Felipe. You are a good man. Papá always said you were like your grandfather. A natural gentleman."

Even in the fading light, I can see he is blinking back tears, as he looks across the field. "Thank you for saying that. I worked hard. Not to be my father. There was nothing good about him. Nothing at all."

"Yes, there was. He gave the world—you."

"Any fucking goat can do that."

We laugh.

"Goodbye, Mister Mayor."

"Good night, Don José. *Ve con Dios.*"

It is night and the witching hour approaches. I am in the front parlor of the narrow lodge, filled with anxiety. I know there are things I must still do, but I don't know what they are. My foot jiggles, like it has a power of its own. I toss and moan. I am racked with pain.

The coffee table is pushed against a wall, and my stretcher is parked before the cottage's stucco chimney. That, at least, is little changed. The kindling and logs inside are ready for a match, just as they always were in my day.

The drip hangs overhead, feeds me its opioid honey. There is clatter and chatter, much travel between kitchen and dining room, as the clucking Spanish housekeeper caters to her foreign houseguests. The boys scrape chairs across the dining alcove's wood floor, take their seats around the table, talk quietly in deference to my enfeebled state at the other side of the room.

Lisa comes to look in on me. I close my eyes, pretending I am asleep, so she won't make a fuss. I hear her return to the kitchen and I open my eyes again. The housekeeper comes out with a porcelain urn undulating the yellow vapors of a potato-and-leek soup. She ladles out the soup, bowls are passed down the table, and I drift in and out, to the music of my family together again.

"The last opera I saw, before your father got sick, was *La Traviata*—at La Scala. I was so disappointed. The soprano kept missing the top notes."

A knife scrapes a plate.

"We just found a terrific river on the west coast of Greenland. It's about twelve miles long and feeds into a beautiful bay. It was too cold to sustain salmon, just a decade ago, but now it's at the perfect temperature for breeding salmon . . ."

"Pass the butter, please."

A cell phone rings.

"Honey, we're just eating. Can I call you back in an hour?"

My eyelids are heavy. I smell blood.

I am standing on a hillock. Dead salmon of all sizes, bloodied and gaffed, are laid out nose to tail, without end, over hill and dale and continuing to the horizon. Silver corpses are everywhere, stretched to the borders wherever I look. Some nerves twitch, a tail or two flaps. The salmon still ooze from their mortal wounds, and the metallic smell of their blood is heavy in the air.

These are my killing fields, and the endless dead command such respect that even the wind refuses to make a sound. The world is filled with their silence.

The Frog Queen sits atop a mountain on the far horizon. She beckons me with her stringy arm. She wants to show me yet more fields—filled with dead frogs.

That poisonous phrase comes, then, from behind me.

"All quiet in the Alcázar, my General."

I scream and sit bolt upright on the stretcher.

The family jumps frightened from their chairs.

"Sam! Sam! Get Hans-Peter Grieder down here. Now! Get him here and tell him to bring the bank's trust lawyer!"

"Darling! What is it?"

"Sam! Did you hear me? Promise you will get Hans-Peter down here . . ."

"Yes, Dad, I promise. Jesus."

He sees how anguished I am and he pulls out his phone. He's dialing as he crosses the room. "See. See. I'm calling him right now. It's OK, Dad. I got this. Relax."

SEVENTEEN

A car rolls into the lane; metal doors open and slam shut.

The front door of the lodge slaps open and a round of greetings are exchanged. My drip, dappled in leafy light, hangs from the branches overhead, like a goat's udder hung out to dry. I turn my head creakily away from my beloved Sella, and see my sons and Lisa standing anxiously around a man sporting black-rimmed eyeglasses and a severe haircut.

Hans-Peter Grieder has arrived. My muscles unclench, and I sink into the stretcher, letting out an involuntary sigh of relief and exhaustion.

But I don't let myself go all the way.

Hold on a little longer. You are almost there.

Across the lot, I see my old partner quietly reassure Lisa and the boys that he will take care of everything. Hans-Peter is wearing his Swiss-banker uniform, a dark box suit, and he takes out the white handkerchief from its pocket and absentmindedly cleans his black-rimmed eyeglasses, as he talks earnestly to the family. I know what he is saying. I have given countless such speeches in the past.

If any changes I make to the will are outlandish and likely the byproduct of the brain tumors, he's probably saying, Lisa and the boys will be able to challenge my last will and testament in the courts. The process will be costly and unpredictable and there is no guarantee of outcome. But he has known me a long time, he says. He will be able to make an assessment as to my mental state, and can advise them better, after I have stated my intent and rewritten the will. But, he insists, he cannot disclose its details. They must understand the limits of what he can convey back to them.

The talk with the family is over. Hans-Peter turns and strides purposefully across the grass with Lisa. The bank's trust lawyer, a blond-haired woman whose name I forget, is carrying two black leather briefcases, and follows Hans-Peter and my wife. I remember she graduated with highest honors from the University of St. Gallen, but nothing else about her. I dealt with her almost daily. Now she is mostly a blank page to me.

I feel something cold on my forehead. I look up. The Frog Queen is leaning over me from the top of the stretcher, brushing my hair with her webbed hand. Her long gray tongue licks my forehead.

"Get away, you foul beast."

She smacks her lips. She doesn't say anything, but I can read her mind. "You have always underestimated and misunderstood me. I have always been on your side." But then she smiles, maliciously. "Well, sort of."

Lisa touches my shoulder. "Darling. Look who's here."

"José María," says my old partner, clasping my gnarled and spotted hand. "It's good to see you. We came at once. As soon as we got Sam's call."

"Thank heavens you are here. I want to change my will."

Lisa exchanges a worried glance with my former protégé, who gives her another one of his reassuring private-banker looks before turning back in my direction. "Yes, of course, José," he says soothingly. "Let us get right to it. Should we go inside?"

"No. We will do it right here." I gesture at Lisa and point at the house. "Please get them chairs."

She smiles, leans over and softly kisses my forehead, then walks back toward the lodge.

"You, St. Gallen! What is your name again?"

"Gisella Ohrbach."

"Did you bring a tape recorder?"

"I did."

"Turn it on now."

She undoes the clasp of the leather briefcase, rummages around inside, and then retrieves a digital recorder. She turns it on, states the time and date and place, who she is, who is there, and why we are there. Then she places the recorder on the stretcher, next to my head.

"This is the last will and testament of José María Álvarez de Oviedo. I am dying of a brain tumor. But I am, at this moment, fully compos mentis. I am alert and conscious and, after reflection, have decided to make changes to my last will and testament. Both Hans-Peter Grieder and . . . and . . ."

"Gisella Ohrbach . . ."

". . . and Frau Ohrbach are witnesses to my state of being and can attest I am fully in control of my mental faculties at this moment. And so, now we start."

John and Rob bring two dining-room chairs from the cottage, which they position under the oak trees. "Do you need anything else?" Rob asks.

"I am fine. Now go. Go. I need to be alone with my banker and lawyer."

"Relax," John snaps back. "Seriously."

Don't get upset. He doesn't understand how important this is.

Hans-Peter and the lawyer smile apologetically at the boys, who withdraw. They take out notepads and pens and sit in the chairs under the trees.

I gather my last reserves of energy and look across the field. The Drowned Priest and the Frog Queen are deep in conversation, walking back and forth along the river. I know they are discussing me.

"God wants me to pay for what I took from this world," I say.

"We are listening," Hans-Peter says carefully.

The Frog Queen and the Drowned Priest have stopped in their tracks, and are silently looking at me with beady, glittering eyes from across the field. They are like vultures, waiting for me to die, and the bile of panic starts to rise inside of me. I have not seen my brother in a long time.

Juan—where are you? Don't desert me now.

But he is nowhere to be seen. I am alone.

I hear Papá's deep voice, urging me to forge ahead. This is the place where we all are in the end—completely alone. So I muster all my strength, all my powers of concentration, and turn my attention back to Hans-Peter and the lawyer.

"I want you to sell Privatbank Álvarez to Zürich Union Bank, to Swiss Federal Credit Bank, to whatever firm is going to pay us the best possible price."

Hans-Peter and the lawyer glance at each other, with real alarm, but they hear me out and take extensive notes. At the end of it, Hans-Peter snaps shut his notebook, looks me solidly in the eyes, and says, "I will execute your wishes, José. I promise."

"You won't help them contest this will?"

"I will tell them it is my professional opinion these are all reasonable changes to the will. They are."

"*Bueno. Gracias.*"

I slump back against the pillow. There is a strange popping noise coming from my chest. "I am finished. I have nothing more to give."

"We'll let you rest, then."

When I wake up, my old friend and guide, Felipe, is sitting on the stump where the male nurse was formerly sleeping off the previous night's bender.

"*Hola, Don José.*"

"*Hola, Felipe.* Have you been here long?"

"About an hour."

"Why didn't you wake me? . . . *Cabrón.* Tell them I need more painkiller!"

But before Felipe can stand, the nurse, discreetly hovering in the leafy shadows, steps forward and injects more opiates into the drip.

I feel the rush.

"For what reason should I wake you?" Felipe says. "You were sleeping so soundly and I was having such pleasant memories. It is no hardship to sit under the trees by the Sella River and think of the days when I fished it with my grandfather and served as your family's guide."

Lisa and the boys come out of the lodge, laughing.

"Darling, there's a farmers market today in Ribadesella," Lisa says. "The boys and I have decided to run into town and take a look. See what's fresh in from the sea. We're all in the mood for fish tonight."

"A wonderful idea."

I try not to show how much pain is coming at me. "Kiss me, my lovely wife."

Lisa kisses me full on the lips and says, "Goodbye, you old grump. I love you."

"I love you, too, good woman. Now go have fun with the boys."

"Love you, Papá," says Rob. "Anything you want?"

"Just a full report on what the fishing boats brought in. My brother and I used to love watching the fishermen unload their catch."

"Will do."

John gently brushes my hair. "Try and sleep, Dad. So we can all enjoy dinner together. I'm going to cook us a fish feast tonight."

"*Bueno*. I will do my best. If you get a chance, get the almond-and-hazelnut biscuits at the corner bakery, just off the river. They're fantastic, with a coffee and Fanjul, the local cider brandy. You'll see the cookies in the bakery's window."

"Sounds great. Later."

Sam kisses my forehead and quietly says, "Get some rest, Dad."

I grab his hand and say, "Please, do that again." He furrows his brow but leans forward. I grab him around the neck and pull him tight to me. "You make me so proud," I whisper. "My great regret is that my brother and father never got to meet you."

Sam pulls back and stiffly says, "Yeah, thanks. Me too."

He turns and joins the others, who are across the grass and opening up the doors of the BMW. Rob jumps behind the wheel this time, as John solicitously helps his mother get into the front passenger seat. Before she swings her second leg up into the high SUV, she twists and turns in my direction and waves at me.

I lift my hand. "Goodbye."

Sam is arguing that Rob should be in the back and he should drive. John waves one last time, the light of Asturias briefly catching his earring. He hops into the back seat. They all yell at Sam to shut up and just get in, and he, too, slides into the back seat. Sam never looks back in my direction, but then, I don't expect him to. We cannot expect miracles.

The BMW's white reverse lights go on. The car rolls back, stops, and rolls slowly forward toward the parting in the hedge. Rob honks the horn twice, his hand shooting out the window in a final wave goodbye, and then the car turns right onto the country lane.

They are swallowed by the trees.

The afternoon light comes in slanted over the oak trees.

"Felipe. Will you be my guide?"

"Of course, Don José."

"I want to fish with my brother. I miss him."

"Then let's go fish with Juan. The pool over there, the one your father loved, is filled with salmon."

"No. No. I want the pool where we swam that time Juan was stung by the bee."

"Aah. The Dead Priest's Pool. Good choice. It's special."

"Let's go."

We walk, two old men, down to the river.

Felipe carries my fly rod, as ghillies do, careful not to get it entangled in the low-hanging branches. We talk about the old days, as we follow the goat track along the riverbank. Felipe is in a talkative mood and recalls stories about his grandfather, Ignacio, the man who reared him. How, when they fished together, his grandfather insisted they take a break every few hours, in order, he said, to give the fish a chance to swim upriver without being harassed and caught.

"God demands we give the fish a fighting chance," he used to tell Felipe.

In such time, during the forced pauses in their fishing, Ignacio would cut thin pieces of chorizo, place them on a dip in a slab of riverside granite, and then douse the chorizo and stone in *aguardiente*. He'd set it all alight with his battered brass lighter, until the alcohol was burned off and the oily sausage slices were crispy and sizzling in the dips of the rock.

After lunch, his grandfather would yawn, lie down on the riverbank, his hat over his eyes, and sleep for exactly twenty minutes. You could set your watch by it, and after the allotted time, Ignacio would unhurriedly rise, scratch, drink some water, and piss in the bushes—before they took up their rods and started fishing again.

Felipe has me mesmerized by the story, about him and his grandfather and the slow way things used to be done, but, as we walk up along the gurgling river, I am also noticing what is around us. There is constant movement in the corner of my eye. To the left, in the tangle of brambles, I see the eyes of rabbits staring out of warren holes; to the right, the snout of a badger pokes from under a hedge. A sleek silver vixen crosses the goat's path ahead of us, two cubs in her mouth. She pauses, one foot up like a dog, and stares curiously back at us, before unhurriedly continuing her journey with her offspring. The land is teeming with life. Butterflies flutter, the bees hum and buzz, the spiders spin their platinum webs between the branches. Hawks cry overhead, squirrels dash up a tree, wild boars rummage for acorns in the copse across the field.

Suddenly, in a run along the riverbank, there are repeated flashes, deep in the pool. I am too moved and teary to speak. All I can do is point at the river, so Felipe can see them as well.

Fish.

Everywhere I look, the waters are filled with fish. A massive salmon—twenty kilos and of the purest silver—takes a roaring jump in the deepest part of the shimmering pool, hitting the water with such force there is a thunderous splash.

"*Oh Dios mío.*"

"*Claro.* You can walk across their backs. You picked the perfect day to fish with Juanito."

We come up to a bend in the river. Felipe sees I am struggling a bit and grabs my hand, helping me over a difficult bit of rock. I am panting.

"It's hard for me now."

"*Hombre.* It's hard for all of us."

At the top of the rock, I must catch my breath. I glance upriver and see where we are heading—Dead Priest's Pool. I think of how this pool has repeatedly visited me in my dreams, over the decades I wandered the globe. It's engraved in my soul, in my imagination, like no other patch of earth.

Now, here it is, for real.

My heart pumps with life. I feel vital again.

The pool is still bottle green and deep, as I remember, the far side of the river sharply defined by that sheer wall of black rock dotted with saplings. I look over and up, at the top ledge of forest above the pool. I am reassured. It is all as I have imagined it over the years. High up on the rock stands the tiny chapel with the naïve painting of the friar. The chapel is still catching the day's light, while recently lit candles flicker. I am so excited to be here. I feel youthful again.

"Push ahead, old man," I say. "We're almost there."

Felipe laughs and turns toward the river. I follow my guide, down the other side of the rock, through a side stream choked with crayfish, and then up along the Sella's baked riverbank and the path sprinkled with goat droppings.

Felipe takes off his fedora and wipes its brim. We are standing at the bottom of Dead Priest's Pool, where we used to tie up the horses.

"All right. Here we are. I can go no farther."

"What do you mean?"

He squints up at the blue sky. "The wind is coming from the west. You need to fish the sandbar on the far side of the river, up near the falls, so the wind is at your back. See, up there? There's a big line of resting fish, just off that sandbar."

I follow his pointing finger. Near the top of the pool, there is a natural cove hollowed out in the rock face; in it stands a tangle of very old and leafy trees. There is a fairly shallow bit of green-blue water off this bank; and then, ten meters from the shore, a long sandbar of gray, chestnut-size pebbles sits in the stream. I see what he means. You can easily fish a fine stretch of fly water, starting just below the falls, if you stand on the sandbar. That's where the resting fish will be lined up.

"I'm staying on this side, Don José. But it's perfectly all right for you to cross to the other side. Go on. You don't need me to guide you any farther."

"Are you sure?"

He points at the shallow end of the pool, just before the water starts heading down a rapid. "See that white stone in the middle? When you cross, stay above the white stone, and you'll be fine. Perfectly safe. But mind your step—below the stone there is a ledge that drops off. The water there is strong and deep."

"Come with me."

"No, sorry, old friend."

He hands me the rod. "My granddaughters are expecting me for dinner. Not this time. But look—Juan is there. He's waiting for you on the other bank."

My brother comes out of the trees on the far side. A cigarette dangles from his mouth, trailing smoke. He walks down to the water with his fly rod. He is wearing green waders and our father's canvas fishing coat. He pisses in the water and spits on his fly, as we used to do, and then expertly gets out his line and starts casting long across the river. Juan throws the red-and-black fly with grace and elegance, like he once flicked his cigarettes. The waxed-canvas line unfolds across the river, languidly and powerfully, full of elegant thrusts and curls, and then just as sweetly, he retrieves it, and casts again. He makes it all look so effortless. And then it occurs to me that Juan is no longer the long-haired man I have been seeing these last months, but at that beautiful and youthful age just before he died.

I am filled with my unbearable ache. I remember Juan pleading to go sea-trout fishing with Manuel and me, so he wouldn't get stuck alone with our parents—and how I prevented him.

But it's as if Juan and I are one, like he can read my mind, because he suddenly looks up from his focused fishing—and smiles at me.

"What are you waiting for? Come fish with me."

"Is that really you, Juanito? How do I know my mind isn't playing tricks again?"

He rolls his eyes, just like he used to. "*Cabrón*! Just cross the fucking river and fish with me. Don't be such a pussy."

"I'm not sure."

"You're going to let me catch all the fish? What happened to you? Where are your balls? You're missing all the fun."

A massive fish rises and takes Juan's fly, almost in slow motion. He leans back and sinks the hook. His rod bends in two and the air fills with the sound of the screaming reel, as the mighty salmon makes a run.

Seeing what he has hooked, the desire to fish

with Juan turns overwhelming, an ache so deep and burning it's like molten lava bubbling in my veins. But I am still torn, vaguely anxious, and wondering if I should go back and wait for Lisa and the boys to return from town. But the hunger and ache won't go away. I want to stand shoulder to shoulder with Juan, to work the pools, to again cast our long lines out into the blue reaches of the river, like we once used to, so many years ago.

"*Bueno.* I am ready. Here goes."

I take a step into the river, but then remember my guide and turn to say a final thanks and goodbye. Felipe has already moved away from me. He is standing on the rock where I had to catch my breath, lighting a cigarette and looking calmly in my direction.

I wave at him. He snaps shut his lighter and waves back.

There is another massive splash and I turn to face the river. Juan is impatient and too soon trying to beach the fish, which is not nearly ready to come in. He's just about to lose the fish, I can tell. He needs my help.

"*Relájate, Juanito*! Stay calm! I'm coming."

"Hurry!"

I move deeper into the current. The water is cool and surprisingly gentle and comes just to my knees—as I cross the river to be with my brother.

EPILOGUE

Hans-Peter Grieder is waiting for us when the elevator doors ping open in the bank's reception. He kisses Mom on both cheeks, shakes my hand. "My deepest condolences, John," he says. I murmur something back. Several of Dad's employees come out of their offices to express their sorrow as well.

"Thank you," Mom and I say. "How kind."

Hans-Peter ushers us into the conference room. Gisella Ohrbach, the bank's trust lawyer, is seated at the table with legal documents spread in front of her. She rises and greets us politely, as does the large woman next to her, who extends a beefy hand.

"Sister Bertha," Mom says. "What are you doing here?"

"*Ja, Frau Álvarez.* It's a mystery. I don't know. I was summoned by Herr Grieder."

Hans-Peter talks quietly to a secretary, who leans over and fiddles with the speaker at the center of the table. Sam and Rob have dialed into the room by conference call.

"Hi, Mom," says Sam.

"Hi there," Rob adds. "Thanks for being there with Mom, John. I would be too if I wasn't closing the deal with ESPN."

"It's OK. We're good. Aren't we, Mom?"

"Yes. We're fine."

There isn't much conviction in her voice.

"We are all here," says Hans-Peter, standing at the front of the conference room. "Thank you for coming. Let us start first with an announcement that concerns all of you. This morning, as per José María's instructions, Privatbank Álvarez GmbH was sold to Zürich Union Bank for two point two billion Swiss francs."

Mom takes the news rather coolly, like she kind of expected it, but my brothers and I freak out. We all start talking at once. That was the last thing we expected. It never entered my mind that Dad might sell the bank he loved so much. Sam is actually pissed. "He was busting my balls about taking over the bank just days before he died," he fumes through the phone.

We finally settle down and let Hans-Peter continue. "We are here now to distribute the proceeds of the sale and to carry out José María's last wishes, as laid out in his final will and testament."

He turns in Mom's direction. " 'To my beloved wife, Lisa, I bequeath the Hechtplatz penthouse and the Sutton Place apartment in New York City.' "

Hans-Peter peers at her over his eyeglasses. "José has also left you all the cash in the money-market accounts, currently worth forty-six million

Swiss francs, and all private equity proceeds, as they get paid out over the coming years. Knowing that you intend to move back to New York, José María also instructed me to set up an endowment that will give an annual fifteen-million-dollar gift to the Metropolitan Opera, in your name, which is, as we speak, getting chiseled into the marble wall of the opera house's lobby. I spoke with the chairman of the Metropolitan Opera, and he will shortly be inviting you to join the opera's board."

Mom has a strange look on her face. I can't tell if she is happy or enraged or both.

"Why did José do that?" she says in a strangled voice.

Hans-Peter pulls off his thick-rimmed glasses, drops his officious Swiss-banker's tone, and talks to her more as a family friend. "José was deeply concerned that you would have few friends in New York, after living so many years overseas. He reasoned that the gift would plug you into New York's social scene and provide a springboard to quickly make friends around your great passion."

"I specifically asked him *not* to micromanage my affairs after he was gone."

It's all too much for her, the mixed emotions she's feeling, and Mom again starts crying. She's been like that since he died. One minute she is depressed and flat; the next minute recalling sweet memories of Dad, and laughing about some of his weirder habits, like his love of sheep's cheese covered in honey; and then blink again and she is angry and crying and scared for her future. She's all over the place.

I do the only thing I can do—I reach out and rub her arm. She pats my hand, to signal she is OK, and then blows her nose in a tissue.

Hans-Peter moves on to his next item.

" 'All my sons—Sam, John, and Rob—are to receive ten million dollars each, enough to enjoy life but not enough to kill off their professional ambitions.' "

Ouch. That's virtually like cutting us out of his will.

I do not say a word, neither do my brothers, but I suspect our silence speaks volumes. I fight the impulse to get up, leave the room, and punch a wall. I could really use some serious money to get me out of my hole. Moving my restaurant, getting it reestablished in a new location, will easily burn through the ten million in a few months. Mom, bless her, she's red-faced angry and has no problem voicing what we're all thinking.

"That's disgraceful. I can't believe your father would do such a cruel thing."

"Please, be patient," Hans-Peter says. "We are not finished. 'To my youngest son, Roberto, I additionally bequeath the farmhouse and boathouse in Ägeri, which he, more than anyone

412

else, loved and appreciated. However, the top-floor bathtub of the chalet is to be ripped out as is, and delivered and installed intact at John's New York apartment.' "

We all laugh. We can't help it.

"Nice one, Dad," Rob says.

Mom's lioness hackles have settled down a bit. She whispers to me, "I'm so happy I don't have to deal with Ägeri anymore but that it's still in the family."

Hans-Peter has not finished with me, apparently, because he is staring intently in my direction and waiting for my undivided attention.

"John, your father has instructed me to use estate proceeds to buy the building where your restaurant, Upstream, is located."

I can't speak.

"I am currently in negotiations with your landlord to buy the building, a deal that I hope to conclude by the end of the month. Your father wanted you to own the property, so you can generate additional income as a landlord and never again have to worry about being evicted or gouged."

"What if the landlord won't sell?"

"He will. Your father's instructions were very clear—I should buy the building 'at any price' and give it to you, free and clear."

I am so moved I don't know what to say. It takes me a moment before I can manage a lame "OK."

But a thousand thoughts are going through my head. I am first and foremost elated that I can climb out of my financial hole and save my restaurant. I can't wait to tell my wife. But then I am ashamed that I ever doubted Dad and his generosity, and also amazed that he registered what I told Rob about the restaurant's lease. He seemed so out of it at the time.

"We now turn to two charitable gifts . . ."

"Wait a minute," Mom snaps. "What about Sam? What else did he leave Sam?"

"Please, Frau Álvarez, patience. There is a certain order to the proceedings here . . . Ten million Swiss francs has been left in trust to Médecins Sans Frontières, a charity José María supported during his lifetime, while an additional fifty million Swiss francs has been set aside to create a new charitable organization."

Hans-Peter peers down the table at Sister Bertha.

"I recently learned from Herr Álvarez, for the first time, that he once had a male friend called Miguel. This young man died at an early age, and you cared for him during his final days."

"They knew each other!" says the startled nun. "I had no idea. He never said a word."

"Herr Álvarez was touched by your stories and instructed me to set up a fifty-million Swiss franc foundation in Miguel's name, and to put you in charge. The sole purpose of the foundation is to serve the practical needs—food, housing, health care—of young men in the sex industry who are living off their wits in the street."

I look over at Mom. She is clutching a tissue to her mouth and looking away, out the conference-room windows. You can tell she is too upset to even listen to what Hans-Peter is telling Sister Bertha about the foundation.

I remember that time, when I was a teenager, coming into her bedroom in Ägeri and finding her on the floor, crying hysterically, cutting into a photo of Dad with his hustler fuck. I think they had been in India somewhere. None of my brothers had told her about the guy, but somehow she had found out.

I was so upset to see her like that and said, "Mom, why don't you divorce him? He's an asshole. He doesn't deserve you."

I'll always remember her response.

"Stay out of things you don't understand. We are meant for each other."

She was right. I didn't understand their relationship. They had some twisted thing going on that never made sense to me. But, if I am honest, my relationship with my own wife is pretty complicated. I can't judge.

Rob, over the conference phone, says, "Mom, are you OK?"

"Yes. Let's move on."

The trust lawyer hands Sister Bertha a glass of

water. Hans-Peter swivels his attention back to the center of the room. He is again addressing the entire family, and his body language signals he is getting down to the main event.

"When Frau Ohrbach and I visited José in Spain, he said to us, 'For too long I had the mistaken belief the bank was my legacy. In actual fact, my sons are my legacy.' Then he pointed at the Sella River, which was, at the time, running just near us. 'This river empty of fish—that, too, is my legacy.' "

"A moment of reflection," Sam says dryly over the phone. "How unlike him."

"Now we come to the bulk of the estate, which after the sale has been approved by bank regulators, should amount to one point nine billion Swiss francs held in trust," says Hans-Peter.

Mom and I lean forward in our chairs.

"José asked me to set up a family charity called The Three Brothers Foundation. It is Sam's to run as he sees fit. He will be CEO and chairman. His two brothers are to have seats on the foundation's board as well, which explains the 'three brothers' name. But Sam will have majority voting rights."

"What will the foundation do?" my older brother asks warily.

"The foundation's sole purpose is to rebuild the Atlantic salmon's river habitats. I quote: 'If anyone can figure out how to secure the salmon's future by rebuilding rivers—it is Sam. I leave him the family fortune to accomplish this vital task. It's a tall order, I know, but he can do it.' "

"Jesus," Sam says.

"And although José left no specific instruction on how to go about saving the Atlantic salmon, he did have one final request. 'Ask Sam to start with the Sella. I took from that river, and God wants me now to pay for what I took from this world.' "

"We'll do that. We'll do that," Sam says.

He is choked up. I can hear it in his voice.

Hans-Peter looks up from his papers.

"That is it. This was José's final request."

We're all reeling from the reading of the will, filled with a slew of emotions we can't yet process, and both Mom and I can't get out of that conference room fast enough, so we can talk this out. We say goodbye to my brothers on the phone, say we'll catch up later, and thank Hans-Peter and Gisella for their help.

We're downstairs on the Bahnhofstrasse.

"Well, that was intense," I say.

"Yes, it was. Just like your father."

"What do you want to do now?"

She points across the street. "I want a Coupe Dänemark."

"Let's do it."

I gently take her arm and steer her across the

tram tracks, to Café Sprüngli on the corner of Paradeplatz, but as we cross from one side of the street to the other, a remarkably vivid vision of Dad pops into my head.

I am thirteen, sitting cross-legged on a lip of lava overgrown by tundra grasses, watching Dad fish the pool below. His back is to me and he is standing in the current, calm and serene, throwing his line perfectly straight, his left hand holding the slack part of the fly line, ready to react when a fish comes on.

I am in awe of the way he appears to use so little effort when casting, but still can, in any kind of blowing weather, punch his fly through the gusts and gales and have it land perfectly wherever he wants it in the pool. At such times, when he is fishing, Dad isn't really Dad, I don't think, but something greater—some kind of divine excellence so far beyond me and the small person I am that it doesn't feel like we are even in the same plane of time together.

Right then a fish takes his fly and they begin to dance at the bottom of the pool. I get off my butt and carefully make my way down the canyon to help him land the fish. The fight is coming to an end when I reach out and grab the salmon by its tail, and, just like Dad taught me, both twist my wrist up and lift, so the fish's spine is stretched, momentarily rendering it immobile.

I carry the salmon onto the rocks behind us.

Dad kisses the top of my head and then bends down over his fish. "Look at that," he says, pointing at a wound gouged into the salmon's underbelly. It's a silver-dollar-sized hole that is raw and red and crisscrossed with white scar tissue.

"Must have been attacked from below by a seal. Took a bite out of him."

Not sure why, but the raw-looking sore makes me sad. "Poor fish," I say.

Dad looks up, studies me a while, and then says, "But he survived and lived another day, Juanito. That's a good thing. My father used to say to me, 'Never forget that scars *are* life. They tell us that our wounds have healed.' "

He smiles at me, turns—and clubs the fish to death.

ACKNOWLEDGMENTS

I am extremely grateful to Jeff Belle and his talented team of professionals running Amazon Publishing, for buying this novel and for their steadfast support. Special shout-out in particular to Carmen Johnson, Little A's editorial director, who edited this novel with great sensitivity and encouraged me to improve the work. Lovers of literature and innovation still exist—and I am blessed to have found them at Little A, the literary imprint of Amazon Publishing.

As always, my deepest thanks also go to my team at InkWell Management, from superagent Richard Pine to his excellent support staff Jenny Witherell, William Callahan, Alexis Hurley, and Eliza Rothstein, among many others.

ABOUT THE AUTHOR

Richard C. Morais is an award-winning American novelist and journalist and the author of the *New York Times* and international bestseller *The Hundred-Foot Journey*, which was adapted into a 2014 film starring Helen Mirren. He is also the author of the novel *Buddhaland Brooklyn* and the critically acclaimed biography *Pierre Cardin: The Man Who Became a Label*.

Morais was both the editor of *Barron's Penta* and the European bureau chief for *Forbes*, and he has won three awards and six nominations at the Business Journalist of the Year Awards. His literary works were semifinalists in the William Faulkner–William Wisdom Creative Writing Competition and short-listed for Britain's Ian St. James Award. In 2015, Morais was named Citizen Diplomat of the Year—the highest honor granted by Global Ties U.S., a private-public partnership sponsored by the US State Department—"for promoting cross-cultural understanding in all of his literary work." Learn more about the author at www.richardcmorais.com.

Books are produced in the United States using U.S.-based materials

Books are printed using a revolutionary new process called THINKtech™ that lowers energy usage by 70% and increases overall quality

Books are durable and flexible because of Smyth-sewing

Paper is sourced using environmentally responsible foresting methods and the paper is acid-free

Center Point Large Print

600 Brooks Road / PO Box 1
Thorndike, ME 04986-0001 USA

(207) 568-3717

US & Canada:
1 800 929-9108
www.centerpointlargeprint.com